Katy's Ghost

TRISH EVANS

Katy's Ghost

StoneArch Bridge Books

Westlake Village, California

Katy's Ghost: A Novel

Published by
StoneArch Bridge Books

For more information visit
trishevansbooks.com

Publisher's Cataloging-in-Publication Data
Names: Evans, Trish.
Title: Katy's ghost / Trish Evans.
Description: Westlake Village, CA : StoneArch Bridge Books, 2019. | Summary:
    Now in her mid-30s, Katy has been cancer-free for three years and wants
    to start a family with her husband. That's when her late grandmother Nellie
    arrives and leads Katy on a painful but sometimes humorous journey into her past.
Identifiers: LCCN 2019908265 | ISBN 9781733234900 (pbk.) | ISBN
    9781733234917 (EPUB) | 9781733234924 (MOBI)`
Subjects: LCSH: Cancer – Patients – Fiction. | Families – Fiction. | Ghost stories.
    | Pregnancy -- Fiction.. | Pasadena (Calif.) – Fiction. | BISAC: FICTION /
    Family Life/ General. | FICTION / Ghost. | FICTION/ Women.
Classification: LCC PS3623.A43 K38 2019 (print) | PS3623.A43 (ebook) | DDC 823
    W35--dc22
LC record available at https://lccn.loc.gov/2019908265

DEDICATION

To Bruce and Michael, proof that miracles do happen.

KATY'S GHOST: A NOVEL

*Come to the edge, he said. We can't. We are afraid. Come to the edge.
We can't. We will fall. Come to the edge. They came.
He pushed them. They flew.*

~Guillaume Apollinaire

CHAPTER

ONE

I was sitting alone at our dining room table when Gram appeared. Maybe I should have been startled as I looked up and saw her sitting in the chair across from me, but I wasn't. It was as if she'd been there all morning, just visiting. Nothing unusual about that. Unless, of course, you considered the fact that Gram had been dead for eleven years, almost to the day.

I said nothing at first. I simply watched as she rubbed her hands over the uneven wood surface of my dining room table. How odd it seemed that Gram paid no attention to me as she softly hummed a melody, a vaguely familiar hymn. Instead, her eyes were intent upon following the strokes of her hands, and her hands were intent upon swaying to the cadence of her humming. I listened a moment longer, and with no forethought, without knowing what I was doing, I began to sing, "And He walks with me and He talks with me and –"

"You didn't keep it," she said and looked up straight into my eyes.

Hot, prickly needles pressed against the back of my neck and along my arms, for I knew very well that Gram was referring to her own beloved dining room table. To most people, Gram's table was just one piece of a dramatic and elegant ensemble of dining room furniture, but to Gram, it had been much, much more. To Gram, her table and the eight chairs cushioned with a velvety green-and-gold striped fabric had personified nourishment and healing for her fragmented and wounded family. Accompanying the table and chairs at either end of the dining room were an imposing buffet table and a handsome but somewhat superfluous liquor cabinet.

Gram had loved to tell me how the wood for her table set had been carefully selected from the finest black walnut trees in North America and had been designed and built by acclaimed nineteenth century furniture makers. "True artisans!" she would effuse, and then she'd laud the craftsmen who had sanded the wood to perfection, allowing just enough of a rich, red hue to blush through the dark walnut surface.

With the same impact of a grand finale, Gram would tell how the artisans had painted soft, wispy strokes of gold and green vines with sheer gold and green leaves along the edges of the table. "Katy, I truly believe Spanish royalty dined at this very table centuries ago," Gram would proclaim. And because I had loved Gram so much, I had believed it right along with her.

Over the years, I had grown to appreciate the uniqueness of Gram's dining room set almost as much as she had, and I told her this many times as the two of us sat at her table eating ice cream or playing a game of 500 rummy. I supposed this was why Gram would tell me every so often that I was to inherit her table after she died. I hadn't liked thinking that Gram would ever die, and I thought that even if she did, she couldn't have been serious about giving such a colossal gift to a child. "Where would I put it?" I'd ask.

Gram would giggle, kiss the top of my head, and then explain that I appreciated the value of such splendid furniture more than anyone else in our family, and she had no doubt that I would cherish it as much as she did.

Now I was rubbing a hand on the surface of Tom's and my humble table. "We sold it." I barely let the words out, trying to avoid looking at my grandmother.

"Excuse me?"

"Tom and I sold the whole set." I felt my face burning red with shame.

Gram had probably never dreamt that I would sell her furniture, but then, neither had I. It's just that when she died, Tom and I lived in a tiny apartment with no garage, just a carport. We could barely afford rent, let alone one of those temporary storage places. So, we had sold the table and the buffet and liquor cabinet. At the time, it had seemed like the best thing to do. Besides, Tom was not in love with such dark and dramatic furniture, and, well, as he had gently pointed out, Gram was dead. She would never know.

"Well, I hope you've been feeling guilty," Gram said as if reading my mind, a talent that I supposed came quite naturally to a...?

"I sold a part of you. I'm so sorry, Gram," I whispered with a voice truly burdened by the very kind of guilt to which Gram had just referred.

It almost felt cathartic to be able to tell Gram what Tom and I had done. I should have apologized sooner, but how could I have when she was deceased? But right then, right there at my own table was...was Gram no longer departed? I had to ask!

"Oh, Katherine, it would be impossible to sell a part of me," Gram lightly chided.

Katherine? Gram knew I disliked being called Katherine as much as she had disliked being called Grandmother. As a young child, I had been exceedingly bothered that all my friends had Grandmothers or Grandmas. Even Nanas. Not one of them had a Gram. Gram just didn't sound as cuddly or grandmotherly to me. But long before I was born, my grandmother had decided she was to be called "Gram" by all her grandchildren. She felt it was a more youthful sounding name compared to her other choices.

I was nearly six years old the day I innocently asked Gram if I could call her "Grandmother." Two friends of mine were scheduled to come to my house the next day when Gram would be babysitting, and I had been anxious about introducing my grandmother to them as Gram. It just wasn't right.

Gram had looked a little surprised by my question, but then in a rather formal tone of voice she said, "Well, my dear granddaughter, that would be fine as long as I can call you Katherine from now on instead of Katy."

I was taken aback by her reply but thought about it for a second, maybe two. Then I straightened my neck and shoulders and replied with the same formal, emotionless voice that Gram had used, "Well, Grandmother, I'd prefer Katy, thank you very much."

"And I'd prefer Gram," she said.

My childlike pride understood her point, sort of, but I hadn't been truly overjoyed with it, which is why over the years when I felt like teasing Gram, I would sigh with feigned prim and proper exasperation, "Oh, Grandmother." That was all I needed to say to make my sweet and silly Gram burst with surprised laughter that quickly dissolved into a warbled giggle, finished – or as Gram would say, "finaleeeed" – with her own artificial sigh of annoyance, "Oh, Katherine."

I calmly smiled at what seemed to be the very likeness of my grandmother sitting across the table, now rubbing her hand along its edge.

"I've missed you," I said.

"I know, dear. But –" She paused. "I have always been very near." She smiled as if proud of the quick rhyming of words she'd just spoken.

"When have you been nearby?" I asked.

"Don't you remember?" Gram coaxed.

Gram had stopped rubbing the table's surface, but now she appeared to be examining the straight lines of the legs of our dining room table with just as much interest, as if to be sure there were four legs, not ten. For some reason, I felt uneasy as I watched Gram completely disappear under the table.

A knock-knock sound vibrated from below, and I jumped.

Gram's head came up, as if for air. "Katy, this is not a table! It's a door!" Gram said, aghast.

"No, it's not. Well, it once was a door," I replied.

"You eat your meals off of a door?" Gram asked with utter amazement.

"It's not really a door anymore," I said defensively.

"Well, yes, it is! All it's missing is a door knob," Gram argued. Now,

5

both her head and shoulders had surfaced from below.

"Gram, I promise you, this is a dining table."

Why was I defending Tom's and my door, our table? It was obvious that my grandmother didn't appreciate how "fashionable and in" pine-doors-turned-into-tables had become, especially if they'd been imported from Mexico like ours had been.

"And it's all marked up! What do you and your guests do, throw the dishes on the table when you're finished eating?"

I didn't think it would go over well with Gram if I'd told her that Tom and I had paid extra, a lot extra, to have the distressed marks added to the table's surface. So, I remained quiet.

Not satisfied with my nonverbal response, Gram huffed slightly and then lowered her head and shoulders back under the table. "And it looks nude to me."

"What?" Certain that I had misheard her, I tilted my head downward and met her eye to eye upside down.

"Nude! You have nude furniture," she said, shooting a convicting glance my way.

I sat fully upright in my chair. I was not going to hold an upside-down conversation with...what? I had to ask! "Gram, are you –"

"Where's the buffet table?"

"We don't have one."

"No liquor cabinet? No hutch?"

"No. And no."

"Nude and lonely." Gram's voice echoed from under the table.

I didn't have to be a genius to understand that "lonely" by way of my grandmother's thinking meant that my poor little table had no dining room furniture to keep it company, no people of its own. And it was quite obvious that Gram's "nude" suggested that this sad and neglected table of mine was not properly coiffed and adorned with decorative, hand-painted inlays of gold and green vines like hers had been.

"So," Gram said, rising once again from below. She carefully, and very ladylike, slid into her chair as if she'd just returned from the ladies' room. "I want to hear about this. Tell me when you have known I was nearby."

I sighed with gratitude, because she wanted to talk about something other than my nude furniture.

"Well –" I paused, remembering some of those moments. "This will probably sound silly, but I can be at a restaurant, and if there's a gardenia floating in a vase at the table, with its glorious scent drifting in the air, I swear, Gram, I can almost feel you standing right beside me, telling me – I altered my voice to a high-pitched warble like hers – "Oh, Katy, gardenias are the most beautiful flowers in the world."

"And they are!" Gram slapped her right hand on the table for emphasis, which abruptly caused her to begin knocking on the tabletop, knocking all the way to the edge, only to continue her knocking underneath once more. It was a sight to see how effortlessly her entire body slid under the table once more. Knock-knock-knock. Why she was knock-knock-knocking, I didn't want to know.

"But there are more times when I have felt you are very far away." I emphasized the "far away," hoping she might take a hint at my sarcasm.

"When's that?" Her voice grew less distant and hollow, a tip-off that she was about to re-emerge.

"Um, well, I never remember to buy lemons at the grocery store, which is weird, because I am always needing one or two to add to a fish recipe or to enhance a glass of water. That's when I think of you and how you'd bring over bags filled with lemons you'd picked from your backyard tree – more lemons than I could use up in a year or before fuzzy green and white mold spots appeared on their skin."

"Well, now you know," Gram said, breaking the spell of that long-ago memory.

I noticed that Gram had returned to a normal sitting position and was not knocking away or rubbing her hands all over my table

"Now I know?"

"That I'm really here with you."

"Yes, I guess you are." I examined my grandmother. She had no wings at her sides. No halo over her head. She wasn't even holding a trumpet or a tablet or whatever most angels hold in their hands.

"But why?" I asked.

Gram paused and looked at me with an octogenarian's version of a cherubic smile, almost as if she were teasing a small child. "To help you remember," she said kindly.

"Remember what?"

"What you've forgotten, of course."

I had no idea what Gram was talking about, so I simply tilted my head and waited for her to explain. She didn't though, because she wasn't there anymore. I looked under the table. Nope. I looked back at her chair. Still gone. She didn't even say goodbye.

But then, she never said goodbye when she was alive either. Long before I was born, Gram had read about one of her favorite soap opera actresses who never said goodbye because it was too permanent sounding, as if one might never return once those two words were spoken. To Gram, this was quite a profound concept, and it made perfect sense. So, she adopted the same stance regarding farewells and never again said goodbye to anyone. Instead, she would depart from one's company with the words, "See you soo-oon." Her cheerful, jingly "soo-oon" always seemed to linger in the air and then slowly drift away.

Suddenly, the house felt terribly hot and stuffy, so I stood up and left my nude and lonely dining table. I strolled into our small living room and over to the French doors that led to our backyard. Pausing just long enough to keep the screen door from slamming shut, I stepped down onto our spacious used-brick patio. I passed by the outdoor table with its dark green umbrella and walked over to the steps leading to the shallow end of our swimming pool.

At that moment, I realized how removed I felt from the world around me. I hadn't been distracted by the usual commotion of the birds and squirrels as they jumped from tree to tree. The leaves of the trees seemed silent and still. And even though it was one of those blazingly hot, Southern California days one expects in mid-September, there was not a single drop of sweat on me.

I carefully knelt down beside the pool to splash my hand in the water and was at once grateful to feel the icy, cold wetness of the chlorinated water - confirmation that I hadn't been dreaming moments before. But my relief was fleeting, for I immediately began to wrestle

9

with the realization that Gram was the first deceased relative to pay me a social call.

I looked back at the house and wondered how I could possibly explain Gram's visit to Tom. If only Tom had come home while Gram had been here, he would have seen her. Or would he have? No, of course not. It would be just like those old, old comedy movies. Tom would walk into the dining room and ask whom I was talking to. "Look who's here for a visit," I would say, thinking he would recognize Gram. After all, she looked just like she did before she died. Then Gram would say something to me, and I'd answer, thinking Tom could also hear her.

"Very funny," he'd say, and I would act surprised and maybe a little angry that he didn't see or hear what was clearly there. Clearly to me and all the other paranoid schizophrenics in the world, not to mention the ones in my own family.

If I tried to convince Tom that Gram really had spoken to me, had really sat at our table, I knew what he would do. He would act calm and understanding, probably thinking this odd behavior of mine was a stressful reaction to what Dr. Chang had told us three days earlier.

"Do not try to get pregnant," Dr. Chang had told Tom and me as we sat in his Westwood office. "You risk having your cancer come back if you do."

"But three years ago, you said if we waited this long and my cancer didn't come back, we could think about starting our family," I protested. "And now –"

"I said we could think about it," Dr. Chang interrupted. "And I've thought long and hard. In my professional opinion, you should not attempt a pregnancy."

"But other women who have had breast cancer have gotten pregnant and not had their cancer return," I said in desperation.

"You're not other women. Every cancer patient is different, and you have several high-risk factors that point to your cancer returning. A pregnancy will greatly increase the possibility. Obviously, it's up to you, but I strongly recommend that you not become pregnant." Dr. Chang spoke with a hint of irritation in his voice. Then he stood up from his desk to let us know it was time for us to leave.

I silently screamed, "Wait a minute! Wait a minute!"

But that was it. End of discussion. For Dr. Chang anyway. He walked to his door, opened it wide, and waited for us to gather our coats and leave.

Tom and I had been stunned. We were so certain after bilateral mastectomies and three years of being cancer free that finally, finally, it would be safe for us to start our family. I was thirty-eight years old. We knew it was now or never. Never. Never to have children of our own. Never?

Tom and I didn't talk on our way home from the doctor's office. Tom held my hand as he drove. There weren't any words to ease our pain. We needed time to let Dr. Chang's advice settle. As if it ever could. And on top of all this, Tom was under a lot of pressure with his current film. He was up by four most mornings and not home until midnight.

No, I couldn't tell Tom about Gram's visit. He didn't need to worry about my mental health, too. Besides, Gram didn't say she'd be back. She just said she had come to help me remember something. But remember what? She never told me.

11

I paced the patio, looking at the bottlebrush trees with their strange, sticky red flowers, then stopped to dangle my feet into the pool water. Maybe Gram thought I'd begun to forget about her. Well, that was impossible. Everything about Gram was engraved in my memory forever. Everything.

Cornelia Carlton Colburn. It was Gram's maiden name, and she had hated it. I hadn't. I thought Cornelia Carlton Colburn was the most beautiful, most romantic name in the world, but every time I told this to Gram, she grimaced.

"C.C.C.," she'd say referring to her initials. "And then I married Carlyle, and I became C.C.W."

The "W" stood for Welborn. That name she liked. It was the Cornelia and the Carlton and the Colburn to which Gram objected. "Of course, no one ever dared call me Cornelia," she would tell me. "All my friends know me as Nellie, which I've never cared for either, but it's a mite better than Cornelia."

Nellie. It was the perfect name for my grandmother. She wasn't a Dorothy or a Margaret. She was a Nellie, full of love and laughter. I liked the name Nellie so much I once confided in Gram that I intended to name my daughter after her. I was only six years old at the time.

"Cornelia Carlton Colburn?" Gram was aghast.

"No. Nellie," I told her.

Gram giggled. "I don't think your daughter will thank you for it," she said. "Now, if you really wanted to name your daughter after me you could call her Abigail."

"But that's not your name," I protested.

"No, but it's the name I wish I'd been given. Abigail is from the Bible, you know. King David could see what a good and intelligent woman she was."

"But Gram," I protested.

"Abigail wasn't just beautiful, she was a counselor, someone who could see beyond herself," Gram continued. "Don't you think Abigail has a pretty ring to it? You could call your little girl Abby for short."

I agreed that Abby had a nice ring to it, but I liked Nellie better. Besides, my mind was made up. If I ever had a daughter, Nellie was going to be her name.

If I had a daughter ... Those little-girl thoughts were from a long time ago, back when I had assumed I'd have a child of my own like everyone else in the world.

Well, at any rate, I was pretty sure Gram hadn't come to see me eleven years after she died just to be sure I hadn't forgotten her maiden name.

So, what was it she wanted me to remember? I wondered as I sat down at the edge of the pool. I slowly lowered my legs into the cold water, and a refreshing chill ran up my spine. Then with my eyes closed, I looked upward and allowed the sun to spill over my face as thoughts of Gram flooded my mind. So many things about my grandmother had seemed magical to me when I was little, which was the reason I had always wanted to be just like her.

A bead of sweat dripped down my temple. With my eyes still closed, I recalled how much Gram had hated hot summer days like this one and how often she would reach for her handkerchief and, with exaggerated frustration, wipe the drops of moisture from her forehead and arms.

13

Straight away, I would reach for a tissue too and, with panache and just the right amount of drama, sweep it across my own dry forehead and arms.

"Katy, are you making fun of your Gram?" she would ask as if she was hurt.

"No, Gram. Honest! I just like to do the things you do," I'd say with complete sincerity.

One time she laughed at my answer and asked, "Why in the world would you want to sweat like me?"

"I don't know. I just like the way you do everything." I remember pausing in thought while continuing to pat away the imaginary moisture from my forehead and arms, and then I added, "I want to be just like you...and I want to be pretty like you too."

"Oh, Katy, that's such a silly thing, wanting to be like your little, old grandmother. Do you know when I was your age, I dreamed of being as pretty as you?"

"But you didn't even know me!" I yelped.

We both giggled at the thought of knowing each other when she was young.

"We would have been best friends," I said with such sincerity that Gram laughed.

"Oh my, yes. But you probably would have made fun of how short I was, like all my friends did. I didn't like being so short, and all I wanted was to be tall like you." Gram breathed a long sigh and then added, "God decided I was to be short. That's all there is to it."

Gram knew I didn't like being tall. By the sixth grade, I'd reached my adult height of five feet seven inches. I was always taller than my girlfriends, and I hated it. To me at that age, Gram was the perfect height at five feet two inches. Nobody could make fun of her for being too tall.

"And when I was your age, I prayed every night I would wake up the next day and find I had long blond hair as pretty as yours. Do you know how lucky you are, Katy?" Gram would ask.

I greatly suspected that Gram had never really wanted blond hair like mine, for each time I had told her that I wished I'd been born with hair the color of hers, she had responded with great pride, "It's dyed to my natural color, you know. Sun Sprinkled Auburn." Then for effect, she'd gently pat one side of her bright, orangey-red, stylishly coifed hair.

I opened my eyes for a moment and looked down at the little waves of water rippling along the length of the pool. Maybe it hadn't been the color as much as the style of Gram's hair I had envied. For as long as I could remember, she'd worn it in the same perky pageboy, cut short, slightly below the earlobes, with a single row of tightly curled bangs. It was a much more attractive style than the two droopy pigtails my mother made me wear until I reached junior high school.

"Why can't I wear my hair like you?" I asked Gram over and over again.

"When you're grown up, you can wear it any way you want," she would tell me.

"Well, when I am grown up, I'm going to wear my hair like yours," I sincerely vowed. But by the time I reached high school, hippies and the Beatles dominated the way teenagers looked. I had been proud of my long blond hair and forgot all about cutting it into a pageboy.

Slowly I lifted my hand from the cool water to rub the back of my neck, and then with a smile, I realized that I had kept my vow - my hair was cut short like Gram's, but the bangs I wore were not tightly curled against my forehead; mine were long and thick, cut just below the eyebrows.

It wasn't just the genes for height or hair color that I didn't inherit from Gram. Where were the freckles that clustered around Gram's nose and cheeks? And why were my eyes so blue when hers were so brown? And most of all, what was it within Gram's spirit that allowed her to break into fits of joyous laughter until her sides hurt? Why couldn't I feel as lighthearted as she?

"Katy, dear, when did you become so serious about life?" she lovingly asked me through the years.

Gram hadn't understood. I hadn't been serious about life but afraid of it.

Feeling a little too warm, I leaned forward and lightly splashed both hands in the pool. They looked large and grotesque as the water spilled over them. And then I remembered. Why was the one feature I did inherit from Gram the very thing she was least proud of? I stared at my short, stubby fingers and less-than-dainty hands for a moment as they rested just beneath the surface of the water.

Gram's hands had been large like mine, but over the years the joints around her fingers had become unusually thick, gnarled with arthritis, and I knew their slightly misshapen appearance upset her much more than the pain they must have caused her.

Quickly I splashed my face with water, hoping to stop the memory of Gram reaching for my hands, studying them carefully and then sighing, "I'm afraid you and your uncle inherited these from me."

Why did she have to say that, putting Uncle Rollie and me in the same sentence? Gram knew I didn't like to hear about him. I didn't like to talk about him, I didn't like being near him, and I certainly didn't like anyone suggesting that anything about me remotely resembled anything about Rollie, not even my hands. Gram knew better than anyone that I spent most of my childhood and all of my adult life avoiding the mere thought of my uncle. It didn't matter that he was Gram's son, my father's younger brother. As far as I was concerned, Uncle Rollie did not exist and had nothing to do with me, my life, or my hands!

Anxious and upset, I pulled my hands and feet from the blue-green water and stood up. The yard was quiet as I looked around in hopes of finding a distraction, anything to help block the memory of Uncle Rollie. A dancing tree branch swayed overhead and I gratefully remembered the times Gram and I had danced together in her living room. Gram could lift my spirit just by moving a chair or two. Then with her record player running, we'd dance the Charleston and the waltz, the mashed potato and the twist.

A squirrel scampered across the bobbing tree branch, almost losing its balance, and I smiled at the memory of my grandmother twisting her arms from side to side as she sang, "Let's do the twist," with Chubby Checkers and me. "Katy, you're such a good dancer," she'd shout above the music. And I'd move around the room with unrestrained merriment – unless she added, "Just like your Uncle Rollie."

That day by the swimming pool, I sadly realized for the first time that it would be impossible to remember Gram, the things she had liked, the way she had laughed, the happy times we had shared together, without also remembering my Uncle Rollie.

"That couldn't be the reason Gram appeared at the dining room table - to make me remember someone, something so painful," I whispered to myself. "Please, God, please, no more memories of Uncle Rollie."

I turned my back on the pool and walked to the house, determined to dismiss the past that I'd locked away so long ago.

CHAPTER

TWO

Our house sat on a quiet cul-de-sac on a weary and almost forgotten street of Westwood. Most of the homes in our neighborhood were built during California's post World War II housing explosion, and our imitation ranchette with shake roof and white shutters was no exception. From the street, our house looked like a basic, single story, rectangular dwelling. But looks were deceiving, for both sides of our house extended along the backyard in horseshoe fashion and offered the bedrooms a quiet view of the swimming pool and the patio that we finished in used brick and adorned with bursts of impatiens. The tree-lined backyard and a large living room with wood-beamed ceiling and wall-to-wall bookshelves were the main attractions when Tom and I had first seen our house. We had finally found a home that felt like us and, miracle of miracles, a house we could afford to buy – just barely.

I would never forget the day we first saw it. It was a warm Sunday afternoon when our realtor called to say she'd found the perfect house for us, but it would be sold before the end of the day. She'd had that familiar agent's sense of urgency in her voice, which did not convince Tom that we should stop everything we were doing to go see this house.

Tom had already calculated that we'd looked at over 150 "perfect homes" that had ended up not being so perfect after all, and he really, really did not feel like missing "a very big deal NFL Playoff game just to see the one hundred and fifty-first perfect house." But Tom relented, and by nightfall, we'd placed an offer on our absolutely one hundred percent perfect home.

Ever since that time, my dear, sweet husband had often found the ideal moment to publicly lament his sacrifice of missing what he called "the all-time most famous last-minute Viking comeback against the Packers, all because of house hunting." I always knew Tom was only teasing me when he said it was a huge sacrifice, because he'd always be quick to add, "But the sacrifice was worth it."

Tom's sacrifice...how I wished that had been the only sacrifice I'd forced him to bear. This thought lingered in my mind as I sat in one of the bedrooms of our house, the little one with the sloping ceiling. I don't know how long I had been staring out the window before Gram's voice woke me from my trance, but there she was, a few days after her first visit. Without panic or surprise, I looked across the dimly lighted room and listened as she softly hummed my favorite hymn. The lyrics rushed into my head.

"Amazing grace, how sweet the sound," I quietly sang without interrupting the back and forth motion of the white wicker rocker in which I was seated.

"That saved a wretch like me." Gram sang soprano to my alto, seated on the trundle bed, eyes closed, right hand lightly swaying to the rhythm.

"I once was lost, but now am found," I soloed, and then we finished the stanza together as we had so many times before, when she was alive. "Was blind, but now I see."

Gram interrupted with a sigh. "You haven't forgotten!"

"How could I?"

Gram and I quietly smiled at each other as the lyrics of the hymn lingered in the air. Still rocking back and forth, I was struck with a bizarre thought: I had been singing a duet with...an...?

"Gram?" I was about to ask about her, umm, status, when she said, "You've changed your hair style." Absentmindedly, I felt the back of my neck with my right hand and pulled at the short strands of hair.

"It reminds me of Mary Martin in Peter Pan," she said and tilted her head to one side to analyze the haircut some more.

"It's a little longer than that," I said.

"Well, I think it's very attractive on you," Gram said kindly. "I didn't like it on Mary Martin, though. It made her look like a boy."

"I think it was supposed to, Gram."

"What?" she asked.

"Make her look like a boy. Like Peter Pan," I added with playful annoyance.

"Well, of course. I know that." Gram giggled and then asked, "How long have you worn your hair so short?"

"About three years," I said as I recalled why I'd decided to cut my long hair.

After my first mastectomy, and then my second, I had found it too painful to lift my arms to wash and brush the long, heavy tresses I'd

21

worn for most of my life. The nerves and muscles of the upper arms were numb when touched but oddly sensitive to motion of any kind. If a slight breeze blew by and touched my skin, the same numbed nerves sent waves of pain screaming through my arm muscles and tendons. The muscles and tendons seemed to hold onto each other for dear life with no reprieve. It made lifting and reaching while doing the simplest of activities, like holding a blow dryer and roller brush to smooth out my hair, much too painful. My doctor had recommended physical therapy. I tried it, but it didn't seem to help.

So, I had cut my hair short. Tom had understood and affectionately told me he liked my new tomboy look. But I knew he didn't and that he still hoped someday I would let my hair grow out again. I didn't think I would, though. My face was much thinner since my cancer, and long blond hair would only make it look more so.

"I see you're still wearing jeans and T-shirts."

I looked down and noted the faded denim jeans, white T-shirt, and black vest. When I was younger, Gram had often begged me to trade in my tomboy attire for a pretty dress.

"And you're not eating enough. You're much too thin for your height," she added without sounding critical.

"You always thought I was too thin," I reminded Gram. "I've never been overweight, but after my cancer, I lost ten pounds and never seemed to gain it back. Still, I don't look too thin. Just right, I think."

Gram stopped paying attention to my appearance and began looking at the four walls surrounding us. "This is a sweet little room," she said.

We were in "the kids' room." That's what Tom and I called it anyway. I knew we shouldn't have named it the kids' room two years ago, but then we shouldn't have filled the room with some of my old teaching things, either, like stuffed animals and storybooks. We should have kept them packed along with all our dreams of having children. It wasn't as if we'd forgotten my doctor's warning to postpone getting pregnant for three years; it's just that Tom and I had held so much hope. I'd been cancer free for twelve months already, and there we were in our new home with this darling little room with the sloped ceiling and the pretty picture window. It would be the perfect nursery for our baby, the one we hoped we would conceive.

That was the reason Tom originally wanted to call this room the baby's room. He had said that we needed to distinguish it from the other bedrooms. Besides, he said it was too much trouble to keep calling it "the room with the sloping ceiling."

But then I warned Tom how calling it the baby's room could only bring us bad luck. After all, hadn't I seen it happen to those two girls at Northwestern University, my sorority sisters who had been so obsessed about marriage that it seemed to be their only reason for living – the same two girls who had moved into our sorority house dragging imposing hope chests filled with dishes and linens? Yes, I had, and I knew the exact moment that their luck had gone bad: at the party hosted by the towel and linen manufacturer from Chicago.

To me, it had seemed a ridiculous kind of party to hold for coeds in only their second year of college, but I had obviously been wrong, because that Chicago salesman smooth-talked those two sorority sisters,

23

the ones with the hope chests, into ordering hundreds of dollars' worth of monogrammed bath towels and hand towels and monogrammed sheets in silk and in one hundred per cent cotton with thread counts up to a zillion. They weren't even engaged, for Pete's sake, but there they were, all giddy and excited with their new purchases and acting as if they were marching down the aisle the very next day.

No doubt about it, those girls had been jinxed the minute they placed their orders, and nothing could have made me think otherwise, for not too many months later, their boyfriends had broken up with them, the same boys whose initials were to be embroidered on their pillowcases. Had it been a coincidence that neither one of those sorority sisters ever married? I didn't think so.

So, when I had told Tom why we couldn't call this room with the sloping ceiling and picture window "the baby's room," Tom, who had never been superstitious about anything, had agreed that it might be too risky. "So, let's call it the kids' room," he said, "in reference to our nieces and nephews who stay overnight."

The kids' room. It sounded safe enough, but only as long as Tom and I promised we wouldn't think of the kids as the children we hoped to have, and as long as we didn't fill the kids' room with a crib and lots of baby stuff – not until I was pregnant anyway.

We had been careful to decorate the kids' room very simply, adding only the trundle bed with the quilted comforter and pillows and the pretty white dresser. I had never thought that adding the border of pink and blue wallpaper with the baby lambs could jinx us, since two of our nieces who visited had still been in diapers. And I certainly hadn't added the white wicker rocker with the quilted cushion in hopes of rocking our own baby in it. I just thought it went with the bed and dresser, and besides, every room needed a comfortable chair to sit in.

"Tom is working late," Gram said matter-of-factly.

"Yes," I answered.

"Carlyle did too." Gram sighed as she tried to prop her back against one of the quilted pillows on the trundle bed.

"Hmm?" I squinted in Gram's direction. The little light on the dresser cast a warm glow on her face.

"He worked late most nights."

"Oh." I nodded.

Gram's husband, my grandfather, had played first cello for the Los Angeles Philharmonic Orchestra and had worked nights, because most concerts took place in the evening.

"Did you mind his working late?" I asked.

"Oh, no," Gram said. "Carlyle loved his job, and I was very proud of him, so I didn't mind."

"I feel the same way about Tom's long hours," I said, which was true. "He's a good producer, and he loves it."

"And I never worried about other women," Gram continued as if she hadn't heard me.

"Mmmm." I nodded my head again and wondered if she thought I worried about other women. I didn't, and I never had. I knew Tom loved me and couldn't love anyone else, and it wasn't just because he was always telling me he couldn't live without me, that he and I had come into the world to be with each other. It was just because I knew.

25

"Of course, I was too busy to sit around and wait for Carlyle to come home." Gram looked away as she said this.

"Gram, I'm not worried about other women, and I'm not sitting here waiting for Tom to come home."

I knew I sounded slightly defensive, but I was embarrassed that she had found me once again sitting around doing nothing. Most nights when Tom worked late I usually painted at my easel or read a book or had dinner with a friend. But I'd had such little energy since the meeting with Dr. Chang. How many times had I started to go to my easel and instead ended up in the kids' room seated in the rocker just rocking back and forth and thinking.

"Do you still call it your Thinking Chair?" Gram asked. Her short legs dangled halfway to the floor, and her upper torso leaned awkwardly against the trundle bed's back pillow.

"Of course." I smiled.

Gram was referring to the rocker in which I was sitting, the one she gave me on my tenth birthday, the one in which as a child I sat for hours on end, pondering the events of my life. It was the same rocker whose back-and-forth cadence hushed the foreboding feelings growing ever stronger within me, the same rocker that had become my comforter and my solace.

How many times had Gram peeked through the doorway of my bedroom and found me rocking back and forth, back and forth? "What are you doing?" she had always asked.

"Just thinking in my Thinking Chair," I would answer each time. Then she would tiptoe to my bed and sit down to think with me.

We had done that a lot, rocking and thinking together. I believed Gram had known how worrisome my world had become. Often in the midst of our thinking together, Gram would pray a short prayer, something simple like, "Dear Lord, help this sweet grandchild to know you are here watching over her. Amen." She had never asked me to join her in prayer, had never expected me to bow my head and clasp my hands. But her earnest requests to God on my behalf had made me feel safer, protected – at least for a short while.

"You know...?" Gram paused for a moment as she looked up at the pink and blue lambs on the wall. "Truth be told, there really isn't any such thing as good luck and bad luck."

The Thinking Chair made soft crinkly noises the way wicker does when it moves.

Gram eased herself off the trundle bed and walked to the wall where I'd hung various pictures of each of our eleven nieces and nephews.

"This little one looks a bit like Rollie when he was a boy."

I looked at nine-year-old Patrick's picture and was horrified to see the resemblance. I'd never noticed it before, but the look on Patrick's face, his furrowed brow and half smile, was vaguely reminiscent of photos taken of Uncle Rollie when he was a boy. Rollie was always scowling at the camera with angry, brown eyes. But then, smiling was not in my uncle's repertoire of behaviors. It was in Patrick's, though. He smiled all the time, and I shuddered to think Patrick had even the slightest resemblance to Rollie.

"Patrick looks nothing like Uncle Rollie," I said, thinking I needed to find a different picture of my nephew to hang on the wall.

"Patrick's from Tom's side of the family so he couldn't possibly look like Rollie, and besides, he doesn't have a million freckles on his face like Rollie did. And look a little closer. Patrick's hair is dark blond, not red like Uncle Rollie's." I knew I sounded a little too desperate in arguing my point.

Gram seemed to ignore it, though, as she removed Patrick's picture from the wall to get a closer look. "You know, life has a terrible hold on a person when he starts to believe in hocus-pocus, mumbo jumbo." Gram sighed, not responding to what I had said about Patrick.

"I don't believe in hocus-pocus," I blurted.

I felt confused by Gram's sudden change of subject. First it was something about good luck and bad luck, then Rollie and Patrick, and then on to hocus-pocus. Was there a point to all this? Was I supposed to connect the dots?

"Putting up pink and blue wallpaper and adding a rocking chair can't cause bad luck," Gram said, looking around the room.

I didn't say anything. I just kept rocking.

"It can't cause cancer to come back," she continued.

I remained silent, but I felt my heart beating rapidly against my chest.

"And it can't jinx a nice young couple who want to have children."

"I know, Gram," I said stiffly, hoping she would not continue. I stopped rocking and became conscious of how quiet the room was without the crinkly noise of the wicker.

"Do you?" she asked gently.

"Yes." I quietly drew in a deep breath, then slowly exhaled. "But sometimes it seems as if there's a cause and effect. We put up the wallpaper with the lambs and –"

"And abracadabra the doctors tell you not to have children," Gram finished my thought for me.

"Yes." I began to rock again.

"Well, let me tell you, I've seen people behave very strangely when they start to think like you." Gram said this with a slight twinkle in her eye like she was egging me on.

"Oh, really?" There was more than a hint of playful sarcasm in my voice. "You mean like simultaneously wrinkling their noses, winking their eyes and sticking out their tongues for good luck?"

I was referring to the ritual Gram had always made us perform before she opened her oven door to remove the cakes and cookies we had prepared together. She had said it was for good luck so the cakes wouldn't fall and the cookies wouldn't burn. And unless we completed the sequence of wrinkling our noses, alternately winking our eyes, and sticking out our tongues three times in a row and without laughing, Gram would make us start all over again. It was a wonder that we never ended up burning any of our concocted delights.

"Precisely," Gram said as she wrinkled her nose three times and winked her eyes twice.

"I knew you didn't really believe in that," I said. Then I wondered out loud, "Did you?"

"Certainly not," Gram said as she returned Patrick's picture to the wall and began studying the rest of the photos. "You and Tom make such a nice couple."

Gram was looking at the family picture with all the relatives on Tom's side of the family. Tom and I were the only adults in the photograph without our own children. I sometimes wondered when I looked at it if we hadn't stuck out and looked incomplete, because there were no babies resting in our arms, no small children clinging to our sides. But it didn't matter. I loved the picture anyway. Everyone looked so happy.

Especially Tom. He was standing behind me with both arms gently draped around my neck, and you could tell that he was laughing as my head rested against his chest. It was funny how our blond hair, blue eyes, and fair complexions made us look younger than our late thirty-something years, as if we still had plenty of time to plan for a family.

"Did you know I had Rollie when I was forty-one?" Gram asked. "About your age," she added as she glanced my way.

"I'm thirty-eight!" I gasped, more than a little indignant. In my mind, there was a big difference between forty-one and thirty-eight.

"I suppose lots of people thought your uncle was an accident since I was so old," Gram continued.

"Was he?"

"Oh, noooo." Gram shook her head emphatically. "Your grandfather and I wanted another child very much. Oh, I prayed and prayed for a baby. After all, your own father was already twelve and, well, I realized that I'd taken my singing career as far as I could." Gram paused for a moment and seemed lost in thought; I detected a quiet sadness to her words.

"Of course, Bertie didn't approve," she quietly added.

Bertie was my great-grandmother, Gram's mother, and even though I had been quite young when Bertie died, I vividly remembered her presence at family gatherings. To me, she seemed to be the oldest person in the entire world, heavy-set, with a dense and wrinkly goiter that hung loosely from her chin. She never smiled or laughed, and her ever present, green tinted glasses didn't allow me to see what color her eyes were, let alone whether there was any warmth or emotion in them. She wore heavy, dreary dresses that ended just below her knees. From where her dresses ended, emerged two legs so swollen that her knees, ankles, and feet simply vanished into her wide black orthopedic-looking shoes.

I remember how Gram had anxiously doted on Bertie, fetching anything Bertie requested, and how this great-grandmother of mine had not appeared to be impressed by Gram's overly solicitous attention. Bertie would hold her head high, never making eye contact but, looking in the general direction of my hovering grandmother, she'd make a quiet, inaudible request. Whatever the request, it immediately caused two things to happen: Bertie's goiter lightly vibrated and swayed, and Gram nervously darted and dashed around to bring to Bertie whatever she had requested.

As I observed these things, I imagined that my great-grandmother, with cane in hand, looked very much like an antediluvian monarch, a retired queen, holding court in my grandmother's humble living room.

"You see, Bertie thought I had a great singing career ahead of me until I married Carlyle," said Gram. "Then when I became pregnant with your father, well, she just about disowned me."

"Why?" I asked.

"Oh, poor Bertie wanted to pursue a singing career when she was a young girl but found she couldn't after she married and had me. From the day I was born, all her hopes and dreams of fame were transferred onto me. And then I went and did the same thing she'd done. I fell in love and had a baby."

"But you kept singing," I said.

"Yes, but you see, I couldn't travel with an orchestra since I had a child at home, and I couldn't very well become famous just by singing locally. Not by Bertie's standards anyway."

I knew that Bertie had arranged all of Gram's singing engagements, the ones on the 1940s radio programs and her appearances with the philharmonic, but Gram had never told me that Bertie had wanted her to go on the road.

"I always thought you were proud of having a singing career," I said. I assumed this because of the many stories Gram had told about the concerts where she performed as the first soprano. How many times had Gram described the beautiful gowns she'd worn and the many ovations she'd received? And why else had she shown me the faded newspaper articles praising her singing style and poise?

"I was proud of my success." She sighed. "I just didn't love it or need it as much as Bertie."

"So why did you continue with your singing?"

"Guilt," Gram said.

I tilted my head, needing more of an explanation.

"I didn't want to disappoint your great-grandmother. She invested so much of her life into my career, you know." Gram paused in thought as she turned her back on the family portrait and moved to the picture window.

"But when I had your Uncle Rollie, I told Bertie I was too tired and too old to raise a young boy and continue with my singing. Bertie was so despondent that she went through severe depression."

"Really?" I was aghast.

"Oh, yes. I felt dreadfully responsible, because I just knew it was my fault." Gram clicked her tongue twice as she shook her head. "Such a worthless reaction."

"Bertie's depression?" I wasn't certain what Gram meant by "worthless reaction."

"Well, that, too." She smiled and then turned to look out the window. "But I was thinking more of my feeling guilty."

I knew a lot about feeling guilty. How many times had I convinced myself that something I'd done or not done had caused my sister to become so troubled? I was to blame, and I knew it with every drop of my Welborn blood. I hadn't included her when my friends came over. I wouldn't let her borrow a sweater or a dress. When she had yelled and screamed at my parents, I had shunned her. I wasn't a good big sister to Wendy.

"Maybe there are good reasons why one should feel guilty," I said.

"Maybe so, but by and large, a guilty mind-set makes a person do things he probably shouldn't." Gram paused. "If I hadn't felt so blameworthy about Bertie's unhappiness, maybe I wouldn't have allowed her so much say and control in the managing of Carlyle's and my home – and in the raising of Rollie."

The moon cast broken shafts of light through the shuttered window and onto Gram's silhouette. I was slightly distracted by the thought

33

that Gram's presence was able to make a silhouette. Did angels cast shadows, and if they did –

"Bertie was a very strong-willed woman. You knew she lived with us after Rollie was born." Gram turned to look at me.

I knew that Bertie had moved into Gram and Grandpa's house during the Depression and had lived there for many years after. I also knew that she had not been an easy person to have around.

"Of course, she pampered Rollie, spoiled him so much he really only listened to her. Oh my, so many times I felt the weight of Rollie's problem. Maybe if I hadn't felt so guilty... Of course, that isn't the reason your uncle..."

The rocker quietly finished Gram's thought. "He was such a sweet little boy," Gram whispered as if to someone other than me.

"Uncle Rollie?" I shouldn't have said this with such incredulity, but it slipped quite naturally from my lips.

"Oh, I know it's hard for you to imagine. You didn't know him when he was young and innocent. By the time you were born, your uncle was sixteen and showing signs of his illness."

I may have been just a newborn when Uncle Rollie was a teenager, but I felt certain that even then I instinctively sensed that he was very different from the other members of my family, and not a good kind of different.

I had often wondered why I felt fearfully anxious around my uncle. Maybe it was the way Uncle Rollie rolled packs of cigarettes in the sleeves of his T-shirts all the way to the top of his shoulders. Maybe it was the black jeans he wore with the black, pointy boots, or the way he chewed gum on one side of his mouth and squinted both eyes as if he was keeping something dark and ominous from seeping out from behind their lids. Or it could have been the way he greased his fiery red hair tightly against the sides of his head. Everything about my uncle seemed icy, cold, and threatening, and I had silently understood that my uncle didn't want little children like me hanging around him.

My suspicions had been confirmed at a family gathering when I was only four years old. I was sitting on the couch in my parents' living room with my aunt beside me as she held my year-old sister. The doorbell rang, and both my parents went to the door in the large foyer to greet Gram and Uncle Rollie.

As my grandmother and uncle stepped inside, greeting everyone and handing their coats to my mother, my aunt had leaned her head against mine and whispered in a menacing tone, "You stay away from your Uncle Rollie. He's not like other people. He's not a well man."

Those ominous words, "He's not a well man," only substantiated what I'd secretly felt in my gut for as long as I could remember. But upon hearing my aunt's warning, I became even more cautious and wary of my uncle. I studied his every move the same way a baby studies an older child. I studied his facial expressions and noted how his eyes focused on one object and would stay there far too long. I listened to his conversations with my other relatives and noted how intelligent his words seemed but how his sentences rambled on into disconnected thoughts. And I became aware of the many mood swings my uncle exhibited in the course of one evening. How he could be remarkably calm one minute and suddenly jittery and tense the next.

As I grew older, my fear of Uncle Rollie did not wane. Instead, by the time I began fourth grade, I was certain that Rollie's illness was as contagious as the disease the lepers had in Ben Hur. I decided this on my mother's birthday when my father treated us to the premiere of Ben Hur in downtown Los Angeles.

It was such an extravagance for us to go to a premiere, and I was excited and happy on our way. Movies had always left me with feelings of delight and wonder. But not this movie called Ben Hur. I left the theater feeling anxious and disturbed, not just because of the violence or the terrifying chariot races but because of the startling appearance of the horribly disfigured people who carried a terrifying disease, a disease with an ugly, foreboding name. They had leprosy.

"Why did those people with leprosy have to live alone inside caves?" I asked my parents on the drive home from the movie.

"The disease was very contagious," my father answered. "Just touching lepers or their belongings, even drinking from the same water goblet could spread the disease. They were forced to live far away from the rest of the population so no one else would get leprosy."

Instantly, my aunt's words, cautioning me to stay away from Uncle Rollie because he wasn't well, came to mind. Was my uncle's illness contagious like leprosy? That's when leprosy and my uncle's illness became one and the same, indistinguishable and equally horrifying, which, in turn, triggered an even greater fear regarding my uncle's presence at family gatherings.

Could the germs of Uncle Rollie's disease jump onto my parents or Gram or my uncles and aunts? What about Wendy and Sam? What was to stop Rollie's dreaded illness, one for which I did not yet have a name, from spreading to them, too? Why wasn't Uncle Rollie treated like the lepers in Ben Hur and sent far away forever to a place where no one could get his illness? I didn't want Uncle Rollie to have to live in a cave like the lepers in Ben Hur; I just wanted him to live far, far away with people like him, people with his disease. Sadly, I never asked these questions out loud; something always stopped me. Maybe I had thought that the answers would be more frightening.

Instead, I had become neurotically watchful of everyone at our family gatherings, looking for any sign of infection – nervous twitching of the hands, or squinting of the eyes, even unusual strands of fiery-red hair – always hoping my adult relatives knew how to protect themselves.

But the more I watched over my family, the more I realized that no one seemed to be cautious or careful when standing close to Uncle Rollie. In fact, just the opposite seemed to occur. Everyone greeted Rollie with a pat on his back or a firm handshake; some even hugged him when he arrived and again when he left.

Observing all this caused me to wonder if adults were immune to Rollie's disease like they were immune to the mumps or chicken pox. Could it be that only children, especially younger children like Wendy, needed protection? With this reasoning, I began to notice how my sweet little sister seemed to gravitate to Uncle Rollie, begging him to lift her into his arms and swing her around and around. She seemed determined to find Uncle Rollie, holding his hand while escorting him to the dinner table. I instinctively knew then that it was my responsibility to keep Wendy safe from infection. This is why I had done everything

I could at family gatherings to engage and distract Wendy, to distance her from my uncle.

Rather than enjoying my sisterly attention, Wendy seemed determined to seek out Uncle Rollie no matter how hard I tried. My stomach, my soul, my whole being felt sickened and troubled. I worried that Uncle Rollie had already contaminated Wendy the same way the lepers in Ben Hur had contaminated each other. I felt desperately alone and fearfully certain that there was no one I could share this knowledge with except, maybe, God.

So, I had prayed every night and every day that God would stop Wendy from seeking Uncle Rollie's attention. I had begged and pleaded with God that He would keep Wendy from becoming infected with Rollie's disease.

Why I hadn't broken down from such suffocating fear and hadn't confided in my parents, I may never know. However, I did remember one night when I had come close to revealing my dark, lonely secret to my father.

I had been five years old, so it was long before I knew anything about leprosy and the concept of contamination. I remember well that it was the week my mother stayed at the hospital where my sister was being treated for severe pneumonia. My father needed to leave Sam and me with Gram for a few days so he could go to work during the day and then visit my mother and sister at night. Before I had a chance to worry about Uncle Rollie's presence, my father told us that Uncle Rollie was on a trip and wouldn't be at Gram's while Sam and I stayed there.

I was certain my father was using a secret code when he said the words, "Rollie is on a trip." He was letting us know that we were safe to stay at my grandmother's without having to say it out loud. By age five, I didn't need anyone to tell me that my uncle wasn't vacationing on an exotic island or on a Caribbean cruise. He was more than likely staying in one of "those sanatoriums" I'd heard my aunt discussing with my mother.

I had felt joyous relief knowing that Uncle Rollie would not be at Gram's while Sam and I visited. But the feeling didn't last long, because the first night at Gram's house, I discovered that my father had forgotten to pack my pajamas. Normally this wouldn't have been such a terrible thing, but Gram decided I should wear one of Uncle Rollie's T-shirts to bed.

"All you have to do is roll up the sleeves the way your uncle does and voila! It's like a long nightgown," she said.

Gram might as well have told me to put on the boogeyman's T-shirt. Boogeymen and Uncle Rollie had become synonymous during my childhood, and I was forever on the lookout for both of them whenever the lights were turned off. Which is why I told Gram I wouldn't wear Rollie's shirt.

It was only after I refused every bribe Gram offered in exchange for wearing the substitute nightgown that she lunged towards me with the neck of the T-shirt open wide, ready to drop over my head. But I was quicker than Gram and ran for protection behind the dining room table. I didn't count how many times she chased me around it, but I would have gone around and around all night if Gram hadn't suddenly stopped her pursuit of me and gone into the next room.

I heard her dialing the phone and wondered why she had decided to make a call all of a sudden. Suspicious, I waited behind one of the dining room chairs. I was ready for another run around the table in case Gram charged back into the room. But she didn't. Instead, she called from the living room. "Katy, your father wants to talk to you."

I was not convinced that Gram had actually called my father, for in my mind, there was the possibility she was setting a trap to lure me from the safety of the dining room table. But then again, if my father was on the phone, he would tell Gram that I did not have to wear Rollie's T-shirt. Wouldn't he?

Cautiously, I stepped away from the security of the table and the high-backed chair and slowly moved into the entry of the living room. Gram stood by the rose-colored couch and held out the telephone receiver for me. She was sweating and did not look happy.

I stepped close enough to grab the telephone and whisper into the receiver. "Daddy?"

My father was gentle enough as he apologized for not packing my pajamas. He even said he'd bring them by the next day if I'd wear Uncle Rollie's T-shirt this one time.

"I can't," I told him.

"Why? Can you me tell why?" he begged gently.

I wanted to tell him and would have, but Gram was standing right in front of me, and I knew it would hurt her feelings if she heard me tell my father how everything about my uncle, her son, scared me to death, even his T-shirts with his germs on them.

So, I cupped my hand around my lips and whispered into the phone. "I can't, Daddy."

40

This didn't get me very far, because my father quickly took a firmer stance and ordered me to apologize to Gram, put on the T-shirt, and go to bed.

I was defeated, and I knew it. So, I did as my father told me, because I didn't dare disobey him. But I didn't sleep that night. Alone in the dark, lying on the living room couch, I desperately tried not to feel Rollie's T-shirt wrapped around my body. I tried to pray. My hands and fingers remained tightly clasped together at my chin, but I knew my endless and desperate prayers were so frozen in fear that they didn't have the strength to reach God. How could they when the weight of my uncle's T-shirt pressed heavily against my chest, making me worry that each strangled breath would be my last.

"Katy?"

It wasn't Gram's voice lifting me from the memory of Uncle Rollie's T-shirt and causing me to gasp in a quick breath of air. It was Tom's. I looked at the doorway of the kids' room and saw him standing there with his coat slung over his shoulder. He appeared tired and a little worried.

"Hi, you," I softly said as if I'd just awakened from a deep sleep. I had no idea what time it was or how long I'd been sitting in the rocker.

"Katy, it's one-thirty in the morning," Tom said with concern.

"Really?" How did it get so late? Gram. Where was she? My eyes quickly scanned the room, but she wasn't there.

"Yes, really. Why aren't you in bed?" Tom walked over to me and reached out with both his hands.

I took them into mine, and he pulled me from the rocker into his arms. "I don't know," I said. "I wasn't able to sleep, so I came in here to think for a while." I rested my head against Tom's chest as he tucked me under his arm and guided us to the dresser, where he turned off the light.

"Let's go to bed," he whispered and then eased us out of the kids' room and down the hallway.

I looked around Tom's shoulder, thinking I might see Gram following behind us. Instead, I caught a glimpse of the wallpaper with the pink and blue lambs.

"Tom," I whispered.

"Hmm?"

"Do you ever wonder if I jinxed us by putting up the wallpaper in the kids' room?" We entered our own bedroom with the four-poster bed and the red and blue plaid sheets.

"Geez, Katy, what a ridiculous thing to say." Tom sounded mildly upset as he moved his arm from my shoulder to switch on the light by the bed.

"I know. I just thought I'd ask." I sighed.

"It isn't the wallpaper that's to blame. It's me," Tom said. He sat on the bed as he unbuttoned his shirt.

"Tom..." I tried to stop him from saying what I'd heard many times before.

"No," he said. "It's my fault for not insisting that we start our family sooner. You wouldn't have had the cancer if you'd gotten pregnant before you were thirty."

Tom had read the theory somewhere that women who postpone their first pregnancy into their thirties increase their chances of getting breast cancer. It has to do with all those hormones bouncing around with nothing to do. I didn't know why he kept blaming himself. It had been my decision to wait. But in Tom's mind, someone had to be at fault for my cancer, and it couldn't possibly be me, because he loved me too much. So, he'd decided it was his fault, and he'd felt terrible guilt ever since.

Hadn't Gram mentioned something about feeling guilty and making wrong decisions? I felt weary and too tired to remember exactly. I'd think of it later. "Tom, you know there was no way I could be talked into having children back then." My words were just an echo of the words I'd said to Tom many times before.

But it was true. When we first met at Northwestern and fell in love, I'd told him I would never have children. Not his, not anyone's. Tom had been surprised by my proclamation, since he had never considered not having children of his own, but at the time, he had been intrigued by what he thought was an avant-garde stance. The girls he had dated before me all dreamt of having children. Tom didn't think I meant what I'd said, and even if I had, he felt certain I'd change my mind.

Every once in a while during our engagement, Tom brought up the subject of children just for the purpose of discussion. It usually led to the same argument, though. I'd tell him that children were a lot of work, and Tom would tell me that children were a lot of fun. I'd say children ruined the romance in a marriage and Tom would say, "not in ours, because we'll go out every Friday and Saturday night without the kids." And then, when I finally tired of our senseless banter, I would tell Tom that there was the potential of children bringing pain into people's lives. "Not if the children have loving parents," Tom would argue.

I didn't tell him that Gram had been a loving parent and had ended up with a son who brought her a lifetime of pain. And I didn't mention how my own mother and father – good, loving parents – continued to be tormented by the paths my sister took. Those things I kept to myself. Tom hadn't grown up in my home, so he wouldn't have understood.

During the spring semester of my senior year, it was obvious that Tom intended to have children someday, and I knew he would eventually force the issue. Tom even told me that he prayed for me to change my mind. The idea of his praying that I would someday want to have a child terrified me. So, I told him that nothing would change my mind, not even his prayers. That's when I told Tom that I wouldn't marry him, and I meant it. Our breakup lasted eight months before we were engaged again but only after Tom agreed that we would never discuss having children unless I brought it up.

And I didn't bring it up. Not during our first years together anyway. Even if I'd wanted to think about having children, Tom and I managed to stay too poor and too busy to consider it. Tom was making documentaries few people ever saw and winning awards no one ever heard of. I was a poorly paid teacher going to graduate school. Between the two of us, we were lucky to pay the rent.

But during the seventh year of our marriage, when Tom began receiving broader recognition for his films and I was nearing the completion of my Master's degree, I caught myself doing things I'd never done before. I began staring at babies in strollers and stopping in front of store windows displaying cribs and baby clothes. Once while standing in line at a grocery store, I smiled at a small child whose blue eyes peeked over her mother's shoulder. The baby returned my smile with a big, toothless grin and then laughed as if we had just shared a joke. Why had tears rushed to my eyes, and why had I suddenly felt so empty inside?

That same year, when I was thirty-two and Tom thirty-three, I continued to believe I did not want children, but the subject came up a lot. I assumed it was because so many of our friends were starting their families and seemed to do strange things. Like George and Kimberly. They decided not to pick a name for their child until the moment he popped out of Kimberly's womb. They were convinced that the baby would indicate what his or her name was to be. It seemed like an interesting approach to choosing a name until George called early one morning announcing the birth of Shark, their eight-pound baby boy.

Tom and I wondered what the poor infant had done to make George and Kimberly think of Shark? "What could they be thinking of?" we giggled and joked. Then we spent hours talking about names we liked even though we would never have a child.

Several years of a happy marriage and enough distance from my sister and uncle caused me to bury and numb most of the painful memories and emotions of my past, enough so that, as Tom and I observed how happy our friends with children seemed to be, I would go home and wonder if we wouldn't make good parents too. Even when those memories of Wendy and Rollie did surface, warning me of what life would be like with a troubled child, I refused to pay attention.

Gradually, Tom and I spoke more and more about the possibility of having a family. "Just for the purpose of discussion," I would emphasize.

But by our eighth anniversary, Tom and I came to the conclusion that we very much wanted to have a child of our own.

Tom said he'd been secretly praying all those years for us to finally plan for children. Why had I suddenly felt uneasy when he said this? And why had the saying, "Man plans while God laughs," passed through my mind?

But we did make a plan. And it was the perfect plan. We would wait six more months so I could complete my degree. Then we'd start our family.

Tom and I were almost giddy with our decision but wanted to keep it to ourselves until I was actually pregnant. We thought it would be fun to surprise friends and family, since it would be the last thing anyone would expect.

For the first time in my life, I let my mind wander with daydreams and fantasies of children and a family of my own. It was such a strange sensation after all those years of being vocal and militant about not wanting to have children. How many years had it been? Since high school? I had never told people that the reason was because of Wendy and Uncle Rollie and the fear of giving birth to a child with a mind and soul as troubled as theirs. Instead, I had proclaimed to the world and anyone who would listen that I'd done enough babysitting to see how boring and unfulfilling parenting could be. I had said I wanted a career that didn't include babies. And all through those years I had managed to convince myself that these truly were the reasons.

So, it was a strange sensation to be suddenly thinking about having a child of my own. I was elated, excited, and terribly confused. Who was this woman who kept track of each day of the month, hoping for a missed period, a sure sign of pregnancy? It was me, Katy Welborn McAndrews. I even found myself offering prayers of gratitude to God, thanking Him that Tom's prayers had been answered, thanking Him for such joy and hope.

But then the missed period never happened, and after a year of trying to become pregnant, Tom and I began to wonder why. We weren't worried, though. Lots of people our age took longer to conceive. We were still hopeful – until that fall when I was about to turn thirty-five.

"Katy, I have something to tell you," Tom said while we were on a walk through our neighborhood.

I made fun of his serious tone of voice before he spoke again.

"I felt a lump on your left breast last night," he said with great concern.

I laughed at Tom for being so serious and reminded him that I'd always had little lumps in my breasts, fibrocystic breast disease. They were harmless.

But Tom said the lump he'd felt was not little, and he wondered why I hadn't noticed it too.

I told him he was worrying over nothing. I told him this despite the knot of fear that abruptly burned inside my stomach.

We didn't talk about the lump for the rest of our walk, but the instant we returned home, I told Tom I was tired and wanted to take a shower before going to bed. I felt numb and wanted to be alone. I must have known what I would find.

I turned on the water and slowly undressed in front of the mirror without looking at myself. I didn't want to see my breasts; I didn't want to touch them. I was so very afraid that I would find the lump Tom had felt. My heart raced, and my mind seemed in a fog as I slowly stepped into the warm shower.

I stood under the pulsating water, allowing it to beat against my face for several minutes before I reached for the soap and forced my lathered hands to slip across my left breast. And then I felt it, a lump as big and hard as a grape. Why hadn't I noticed it before? How long had it been there?

A few days later, one week before my thirty-fifth birthday, I sat in my doctor's office and heard the words I never, ever thought I'd hear. I had breast cancer.

"Katy?" Tom's voice drew me back into the present. He tied the string on the front of his pajama bottoms, walked to my side of the bed, and blew out a weary sigh. "I've done a lot of thinking and praying this past week. I know you don't like to hear me say that I've been praying. But I have. You know I believe in prayer."

"Don't, Tom. Please." I could tell by the tone of his voice that he was going to say we should stop trying to have our own children. Just because of what Dr. Chang had said. Even though I'd been free of my cancer for three years.

"No, listen Katy," Tom continued. "You were right all along when we first met."

"Please don't," I softly begged.

"I really think life without children could be interesting. We can afford to travel all over the world, take ski trips every year. We'll be free to do anything we want, whenever we want."

I didn't say anything right away. I just rested my head on Tom's chest as he quietly sat beside me on the edge of our bed.

Several minutes went by before I carefully but haltingly told Tom that I'd been praying too. And then I sat up and looked into his eyes. "I'm going to go the hospital tomorrow, and I'm going to get copies of all my medical records."

"Why?"

"Tonight, while I sat in the kids' room, I prayed, Tom. I really did."

I knew Tom was shocked to hear that I'd been praying. I'd stopped believing prayer was useful long ago when the world seemed to be crumbling all around my family. If God hadn't responded to my desperate pleas then, why would He respond at any other time in my life? When Tom and I dated at Northwestern, we had occasionally attended the campus Presbyterian church together, but I'd made it clear to him that I didn't believe in prayer, and I didn't want him to ever propose that we pray together for any kind of divine intervention when we faced problems. It wasn't that I didn't believe in God. I just knew from experience that God did not believe in me and did not want to hear from me. Tom realized that any personal relationship I'd had with God had ended long before I met him. So, I understood why Tom had a look of stunned disbelief when I told him I'd prayed in the kids' room that night.

"Tom, it seemed as if God and I were having a quiet conversation. Not with words - just quiet, peaceful thoughts. And then, as I was praying, it occurred to me how little I know about my cancer."

Tom didn't say anything. I'm sure he was still shocked.

"I don't understand why Dr. Stone and Dr. Chang think pregnancy's too risky."

"Katy, stop. You know we've been told why," Tom said, as if I'd forgotten.

"I just don't think Dr. Chang should be the person deciding our future. So, I want to look over my medical records and do some research at the library about my cancer. Maybe it will help us understand; then we can decide for ourselves."

There was a long pause before Tom spoke. "How long do you think it will take for the hospital to give you the records?"

I knew by the sound of his voice that Tom had a tiny bit of hope.

CHAPTER

THREE

I didn't know why Gram's ethereal visits hadn't troubled me just a little bit. After all, I had been hearing a voice no one else could hear. I'd watched the spirit of my grandmother walk around Tom's and my home, sit in our chairs, and remove and replace framed pictures from our walls. She'd even made knocking noises on a door that had been transformed into a table. Why was I not shocked, or at least slightly distressed? Why was I so accepting, even accommodating each time Cornelia Colburn Welborn made a social call?

Oddly, after each of her visits, I went about the tasks of each day as though nothing unusual or amazing had occurred, and at night I fell asleep effortlessly, never lying in bed awake and unsettled, never contemplating the bizarre nature of Gram's visits, never wondering if she might appear again. It was almost as if she had never visited. Almost. Though not quite, for uncertain moods and cloudy images vaguely reminiscent of my childhood hovered softly above my consciousness, wooing me to sit with them for a while, to ponder and reflect upon them like one does when trying to remember a dream.

But I didn't sit with them. Not until the Saturday, a week after Gram's visit to the kids' room. I was on my way to a baby shower for a friend of mine. The early afternoon sun blinked on and off my windshield as I drove under majestic pine trees lining the streets in the better part of Westwood. Large Monterey-style houses with perfectly manicured lawns and opulent flowerbeds of purple and pink hydrangea aroused an odd mixture of emotions within me. I felt a serene and peaceful familiarity in this neighborhood of beautiful, stately homes and manicured yards, yet swirling within the calm churned a slow but forceful swell of dread and foreboding. I lingered a little too long at a stop sign in order to quiet the growing agitation within me.

Then I noticed a home ahead and across the intersection. It was a one-story Spanish hacienda that sat at the top of a wide, sloping front yard of dying grass. Patches of green grass here and there made it apparent that the sprinklers were still being used but not nearly often enough. It was also obvious that the house itself had not undergone the same modern renovations and face-lifts that the other neighborhood homes had clearly endured over the last ten to twenty years.

The hacienda looked tired and out of place, almost embarrassed to be seen in the same pampered neighborhood. A leafless bougainvillea with thick, woody branches clung to the front wall of the two-car garage while drawing attention to a sagging roof of mossy and cracked tiles. Awkwardly framing the entire length and width of the expansive front yard was a low-cut, water-deprived hedge with noncompliant branches bursting through the shrubbery's once carefully sheared formation. Each shooting limb resembled arms and legs reaching out in desperation, attempting to escape, begging for help.

I became aware of a large flowerbed at the top of the driveway, lining the entire frontage of the house beneath the windows. It was conspicuously absent of any living flowers with the exception of a single row of yellowed and withered gardenia bushes. Miraculously, some of these half dead bushes had produced a profusion of brilliantly white gardenia flowers. If there were twenty of the scattered, newly blossomed gardenia flowers, there were three times as many dead, brown and shriveled buds attached to the same sun-damaged branches and leaves.

Without restraint, a light breeze carried the pungent and distinctive fragrance of gardenia through my open car window. I took a deep breath, expecting to enjoy its sweet perfume; instead, a bitter and sour aroma pummeled my senses, and at once, a wave of foreboding rose up my throat. Instantly, I felt desperate to escape. But from what? And why?

At once, I fixed my eyes on the invitation I held in my right hand and purposefully noted the address on the blue and yellow card. I spoke it out loud as if to scare off the anxiety within. Frantically, I looked farther up the street for addresses on mailboxes and driveways only to realize that the home of the baby shower sat one house ahead of me, directly across the street from the house with the dying grass and gardenia bushes.

I pulled the car to the curb and turned off the motor. I needed to take a moment to calm down, so I sat in the driver's seat and looked upward. I watched the branches of the fir trees sway with a light breeze, but vague, unwelcome thoughts of my Uncle Rollie clanged sharply out of tune through the prickly pine needles like cheap, metallic chimes hanging from a balcony roof.

"Dear God, why?" I silently and earnestly prayed, beseeching Him respectfully and with my whole being.

Sitting in the hot car was not helping me at all. So, I straightened my back and shoulders, opened the car door, firmly planted my feet on the asphalt street, and marched to the passenger side of my car.

As I opened the door and leaned into the front seat, I heard her voice.

"Isn't this a pretty neighborhood?" Gram joyfully proclaimed just steps behind me.

"Um-hum!" I said with a sudden jolt that caused the gift box to plummet to the floor of the car.

I quickly glanced over my shoulder to be sure it was Gram who'd spoken to me and not a rapist. It didn't occur to me that Gram would ever visit me outside my home, but there she was, dressed in a pale blue suit, looking as if she were going to church. Gram was standing under the only sliver of shade our side of the street offered, and I was struck by how remarkable it was that the midday sun shone all around Gram, but not one ray of sunlight rested on her. "I can't tolerate the sun on my skin. Makes my freckles come out," she used to say on hot, sunny days.

I turned my attention back to the fallen baby gift and saw that its large, yellow bow no longer stood crisp and bold against the top of the box. The fall to the floor had smooshed the pretty ribbon and dented a corner of the box. With a sigh of forlorn, I reached for the gift.

"Katy, do you see that charming house across the street?" Gram asked. "Doesn't it remind you of my darling little house in South Pasadena?"

I turned to look at the same neglected house I'd noted just moments ago.

"No," I said unflinchingly.

"No what? No, you don't see the house across the street or no, it doesn't remind you of my house in Pasadena?"

"No, it doesn't remind me of anything," I answered.

"Well, it most certainly does!" Gram argued with more than a hint of indignation. "Look again, Miss Katy girl!"

Because I knew Gram would not easily accept any other answer, I reconsidered and turned my attention once again to the "charming house across the street."

"Maybe it does," I said with unease.

But I couldn't deny the fact that Gram's Spanish bungalow was slightly reminiscent of the home across the street. Both homes, like the more authentic, Spanish style homes, had the same signature living room window, tall and wide, reaching from floor to ceiling, rounded and arched at the top. And each of the other more conventionally shaped windows at both Gram's house and this one were accentuated and framed with green shutters. Though I remembered Gram's shutters as being a darker green, not as weathered and worn down.

"Oh," twittered my grandmother, "don't you want to go up there and knock on that magnificent front door?"

"Definitely not!" I instinctively knew I had to answer with such resolve. My old and living grandmother would have done just that, walked up to the door and knocked, confident the resident of the home would be delighted to discuss the beauty and similarity of their grand entryways, which was why I was not so sure I could trust the new apparitional facsimile of my grandmother.

Nevertheless, I understood why Gram thought so highly of the grand, heavy wooden door across the street. It was as imposing and regal as my grandmother's former front door and, like their signature windows, also measured to be almost as wide as they were tall, boldly and generously arched and rounded at the top. Unique to both doors was a six-inch by six-inch porthole, cut squarely in the center and protected by four iron bars that crisscrossed over the opening.

Long ago, when I was much younger, I needed Gram's assurance that the door's "secret peep window," as she called it, wouldn't allow easy access for robbers and boogeymen.

"Oh my." Gram would gasp. "Not only is it safe, but," – and then, whispering as if to signify that I was about to hear some very confidential information – "this little window is camouflaged so we can spy on whoever is standing on the front porch."

To prove her point, my grandmother would launch into her "top secret" technique for opening the "camouflaged" window. Gingerly, without a sound, she'd slide the iron bolt from its locked position and, ever so delicately, pull open the porthole's dollhouse-like door just a sliver. Pausing for a second or two, Gram would raise her chin and tilt her head to steal a quick peak. If she decided she didn't like the imaginary person she was pretending stood on the other side of the door, Gram would quickly shove the bolt back into its locked position, turn to me, and explain, "Well, Katy dear, we can close our secret peeping window like that and never let him in."

I appreciated Gram's confidence, but more than once I challenged her sense of secrecy and security regarding the secret peep window by pointing out that the person standing on the other side might notice the movement and light coming from the window opening and closing.

I tried to warn Gram of the consequences. "And, Gram, that person will know we are spying on him and get mad and grab us through the opening!"

Gram did not seem any less confident in the sanctuary of the hidden window. Instead, she countered my concerns with impressive and convincing details that included the words "invisible, opaque, and transparent," and I'd once again, but only temporarily, become a believer in the security and safety of our secret peeping window.

"I suppose the landscaping is a little different from mine," Gram added with her eyes fixed on me.

"Yes, it is," I said uncomfortably. I was preoccupied with trying to find my car keys, which had dropped into my cavernous purse.

"But then, I had a much more creative landscaper." Gram giggled.

I looked at my grandmother long and hard, trying to understand why she seemed determined to mention her landscaper.

Gram continued to chuckle at her little joke. But I refused to join her in her frivolity for the very reason that I never, ever considered Gram's landscaper or his landscaping a laughing matter.

The landscaper she was referring to happened to be my Uncle Rollie, and "creative" was definitely not the word anyone other than

Gram would have chosen to describe his botanical efforts. Lunatic, crazy, mad – those were closer to the truth, for it was during those periods of time when Rollie became more and more unhinged, slipping into his own private world, that he made solitary pilgrimages to Gram's front yard "to create," he would say with the air of an inspired, insane genius.

There on Gram's once beautifully maintained, lush and green Bermuda lawn, among her fragrant gardenias, pink and red azaleas, and weathered olive trees, my uncle would pace up and down, back and forth, huffing and puffing. He would cross his arms tightly against his chest one minute, then suddenly flail his hands and arms skyward the next. As he paced and flailed, paced and flailed, Rollie argued aloud with the sky above, with the tree across the street, even with the car driving by or the bird watching from the safety of the telephone wire and with no one but himself. But then, as if receiving a cosmic answer from the heavens above, Rollie would abruptly drop his arms, run to the garage, return with a rusty, old shovel, and recklessly dig a hole for yet another one of his ugly and unsettling shrubs.

This ritual began when I was in grade school, and by the time I was in high school, my uncle had succeeded in planting hundreds of shrubs in Gram's front yard, not in organized rows lining the boundaries of her property or neatly planted and pruned within the borders of her flowerbed, but everywhere and every which way. Over time, Uncle Rollie's bizarre, miniature jungle devoured every inch of Gram's once lovely, rolling, green lawn, allowing only scattered clumps of weeds and overgrown blades of grass to sprout between his disturbing shrubs.

Even as a young child, my instincts warned me that my grandmother's front yard was abnormal, but as the years passed and Rollie's horrid jungle grew, I decided that it wasn't just odd and unusual, it was depraved. For it became clear to me that my uncle and his army of shrubs not only intended to suck the life and beauty from Gram's front yard, they were resolute in sucking the life and beauty from my grandmother.

Once when I was in elementary school, I daringly asked Gram if she liked the way her front yard looked. I didn't want my question to cause her discomfort or embarrassment, which I was certain she must have felt every time she saw a neighbor walk by. I sincerely wanted to know why she allowed Uncle Rollie to make her front yard look as if it had been invaded by a riot of dreadful, unsightly vegetation. Didn't she worry what her neighbors must think?

"Well, to tell you the truth, Katy, I don't like it one little bit!" said Gram. "Do you?"

I shook my head hard, signaling a speechless but exuberant, definite, "No!" I was momentarily stunned but greatly relieved to know that Gram, too, was not fond of Rollie's garden.

"Gram, I have a great idea. Why don't you and I pull all those ugly plants out today?" I asked so fervently that my voice cracked as it rose in pitch. My face instantly flushed a bright red with high hopes that we, Gram and I, would do just that. Together we'd dig and pull every one of those shrubs out of the ground and dump them in her trashcans, and then the garbage truck would carry them off to never-never land before Rollie returned.

Foolishly, I imagined that my grandmother and I were at war, and my uncle's plants were our enemies. And for one short instant, I was certain that my simple question would also incite Gram to ban Uncle Rollie from any further gardening anywhere in her yard, in her neighbors' yards, even on the rooftops!

"Oh," Gram sighed heavily. "I did pull out a few little trees the first time your uncle planted some. But I waited until he was on one of his trips." Gram didn't know that I'd already figured out what 'one of his trips' really meant.

"I didn't think he'd notice," Gram continued, "but noooo, would you believe it? The very instant he returned home, Rollie realized those plants of his were missing. Oh, my, Katy dear, he was so troubled I decided it was easier to let him have his way. If it makes your uncle happy to see all those preposterous shrubs in the front yard, well, it makes me happy too."

Gram must have seen me staring at her in disbelief. She giggled and added, "They're really quite funny, just a little comical, aren't they, Katy?"

I silently answered, "No, Gram, they're not funny."

Now, almost thirty years later, I still couldn't bring myself to laugh at the memory.

"Who is the baby shower for?" Gram asked, waiting patiently inside her tiny wisp of shade.

"Janet Burns." If I sounded distracted, it was because I continued to search for my car keys.

"Well, Janet must be a very close friend of yours to invite you to her baby shower."

I jiggled my shoulder bag. The clanging sound of my keys echoed from the never-ending depths of the bag. "We had fun working on a church project together," I answered. "We're good friends, but I wouldn't call us very close friends."

My fingers blindly fumbled deep within the purse. "Eureka!" I pulled my keys from the bag and held them up for Gram to see.

She didn't seem to be awed by such an impressive feat. Instead she looked puzzled. "Let me get this straight. Janet is just a good friend, not a very close friend."

I was now holding the baby present in one hand, the car keys in the other, and clutching the shoulder bag precariously between my rib cage and arm. Simultaneously, I balanced my uneven body weight on my left foot, and with very little grace but a sufficient amount of confidence, I shoved my available leg and foot backward and successfully closed the car door.

Gram ignored one more of my amazing feats. She was working something out in her mind, and I knew exactly what it was.

"Gram, Janet and I don't sit and share our innermost thoughts, if that's what you're getting at. We mostly see each other when our mutual friends get together. So, I guess we're not really close, close friends."

"Um hummmm." Gram sounded as if she were interrogating someone - like me. "Then I suppose more of your mutually not really close, close friends will be at Janet's shower."

I chose to ignore my grandmother's sarcasm, because I knew where she was going with her little cross-examination about close friends. I stepped from the curb onto the sidewalk, paused to drop the keys back into the shoulder bag, placed the shoulder bag over my shoulder, and held the baby present with both hands. The once beautiful bow sat lifelessly on top of the cheerful, yellow and white wrapping paper.

"Look at this sad thing," I said trying to change the subject.

"Awwwww," Gram said feigning sympathy. She stepped out of the shade and began to stroll beside me along the sidewalk.

"So, who do you share your innermost thoughts with these days?" she probed.

Incredulous! I cocked my head towards Gram. I wanted to say, "Enough already." But I stopped myself.

"Just Tom," I said, then added, "and before Tom, you when you were – " I was about to say 'here,' but she was here. I was about to ask Gram if she happened to be an angel, but she cut me off.

"Oh, Katy, you are such an enigma." She sighed.

I hadn't been called an enigma in a long, long time. Often during my teenage years, she had said, "You are such an enigma, Miss Katy girl. No one is ever invited inside your sweet head, are they? You need to share your feelings with your friends; that's what friends are for. You'd be so surprised to learn that your friends have the same worries and fears as you." Gram didn't say this often, just when I seemed spiritually paralyzed.

I didn't try to enlighten Gram on howthen I knew she was greatly mistaken. My friends could never have the same feelings I had, and they would never understand what made me sad and afraid. Mental illness wasn't weaving its insidious fingers through their relatives' lives, paralyzing their entire family, and draining any happiness each day tried to offer. I knew too well how cruel friends would be if I told them of the helplessness, if I 'shared' with my friends how I intuitively saw what no one else could see: the germs of Uncle Rollie's disease slowly destroying another member of my family, someone I loved very much. Gram was so mistaken thinking that friends were for sharing one's fears and worries.

I had learned this lesson well the year I entered ninth grade, the same year my parents began taking Wendy to see a child psychiatrist. Up until then, I had watched as my once adorable, sweet-natured sister became increasingly angry and incorrigible, hating the world and everyone in it. It was frightening to see how Wendy was becoming a stranger to the rest of us with no apparent or obvious reason.

At the start of my freshman year of high school, I was tormented with the realization that Wendy needed to see a psychiatrist. Back in the 1960s, children never saw psychiatrists. Never. Unless they were really, really mentally ill. More than anything, I was terrified the psychiatrist would tell my parents what I alone had suspected over the years - that the germs of Uncle Rollie's unnamed disease had infected my sweet sister.

I desperately needed a close friend to assure me that Wendy wasn't like Rollie and never would be, that my sister would be okay all her life. I prayed every night, but God didn't seem to be listening. I prayed that Wendy didn't have Rollie's disease, but I begged God to cure her if she did. Instead, I watched my sister become angrier and more distant, more hateful.

The worry became unbearable at times, so I suppose it was inevitable, even predictable, that a day would come when my guard would be down, leaving me vulnerable. And that day did come. Only halfway through the ninth grade, I broke down and confided in a close friend, the one I called my best friend.

We were at her house after school, working on homework together, when I did what Gram had encouraged me to do: I shared my innermost feelings, and I told this good and close friend about Uncle Rollie and how worried I was for Wendy. Worst of all, I told this very close friend that Wendy was seeing a psychiatrist.

At first, this ally of mine listened to my pain with what appeared to be genuine sympathy, but as my story unfolded, I noted how her eyes widened with shock and how her neck and back stiffened and straightened with each word I spoke. When I finished, when my tears stopped, my friend gracelessly offered a few wooden words of encouragement and even seemed sincerely committed to her promise to not tell anyone anything I'd revealed to her about my sister.

A few days later, as I walked down the school hallways, I began to notice how girls I knew, even girls I didn't know, cupped their hands around their mouths and whispered in each other's ears. A few even dared to call out as I walked by, "Hey, Katy, how's Wendy doing these days?" "Hey, Katy, is your sister hanging out with your uncle today?"

I felt sickened and betrayed. The pain of having others make fun of something so terrifying was agonizing and unbearable, but having others ridicule and mock my sister, lump her together with Rollie, pierced my whole being. I made an oath promising God and myself forevermore until the end of time to keep all my emotions locked and buried deep inside where no one could hurt me or my sister or my family ever again.

But Gram didn't have to worry. Even though I never exchanged intimate details of my life with other women, I never lacked in friends. I was being honest when I told her I did not feel intimately close to anyone who would be at the baby shower.

"You needn't worry, Grandmother," I said as we continued to meander, following the path of the sidewalk. "I have more than enough friends."

"Well, that's nice, Katherine," Gram said condescendingly. "And I'm looking forward to seeing some of them at the party."

I stopped short of a raised crack in the sidewalk. "You can't come to the baby shower!" I spoke much too loudly which caused me to quickly look around making sure no one else heard me. As I did so, I spotted my friend Nita waving from her car parked across the street.

"You don't mind, do you?" There was a hint of hurt in Gram's voice.

I haltingly waved back to Nita. "But Gram, what if someone sees you?" I suddenly felt very anxious.

"No one will have the slightest idea I'm there." Gram smiled sweetly.

I lifted my sunglasses from my eyes and stared sideways at Gram while keeping an eye on Nita, who was now crossing the street to join me. It was one thing to have Gram visit at home when no one else was around, but having her present with lots of other people was not a good idea.

"I promise," Gram whined, and then she lifted her right arm and waved to Nita.

"Gram!" I quickly reached for her arm to push it down to her side, but the only thing I pushed down was air. This motion must have given the impression of a low, slightly awkward wave, because Nita, who was watching me while crossing the wide street, abruptly stopped right in the middle, looked down at her skirt and quickly tugged at it.

"Oops, is my slip showing?" she called out.

"No! No!" I called back. I looked at Gram with a tilt of my head as if to say, "See why you can't come with me?" But Gram ignored me and waved at Nita again. With a reflex action similar to the first one, I grabbed in the air for her arm only to produce the same klutzy wave to Nita, but this time it was more sudden and pronounced.

Poor Nita instantly bent her knees, hunched her shoulders, and with both hands raised to protect her eyes, she looked skyward. "What?" she squealed. She was still in the middle of the street, ducking as if preparing for a bomb. "Is something falling?"

"Seeeee?" Gram smiled benignly. "She doesn't know I'm here."

"Hah," I quickly countered. "Nita, you need to get out of the street. I was just waving away some flies."

Nita looked real hard at me as she slowly straightened her back, squared her shoulders and straightened her posture; then she deliberately smoothed out her skirt, all the while keeping a sharp eye on me.

"Your friend's a little jumpy," Gram whispered. "How did you say her name?"

"Nita," I whispered back. I watched Nita look to her right and then to her left before continuing to cross the rest of the street.

"A-nita?" Gram queried.

"Don't you just love this neighborhood?" Nita asked as she stepped from the street to the sidewalk where Gram and I stood.

"No, Nita," I whispered to Gram, misjudging the timing of my response to Gram.

"No? Are you crazy?" Nita asked with dismay, throwing her arms out and twirling a complete twirl.

"Lo-lita?" my grandmother persisted, not the least bit worried about the position she was putting me in.

"No, Ni-ta," I said, sounding edgy and impatient.

"Ok, ok. Jeeesh," Nita said. She looked bewildered and I knew exactly why.

I rolled my eyes at Gram and then looked over at Nita and said, "Uhhh. I'm sorry Nita, I do love this neighborhood."

"I should hope so. What's not to love?" Nita huffed as she looked at the gift in my hands and attempted to fluff up the yellow bow.

"It fell off the car seat while I was driving," I told her.

"Nice job." Nita offered a droll grimace, which made me think she had already forgiven my strange behavior.

"Over here, girls," a woman's voice called to us from ahead. Gram, Nita, and I looked up at the impressive front entry belonging to the house above us and saw Janet Burns, eight months pregnant, waving.

Our trio, Nita, Gram, and me, waved back in unison and walked up the escalating brick path. At the same time, I did my best to disregard Gram, who continued you-hooo-ing and fluttering the fingers of her eternal waving hand.

Thankfully, the two perfectly and expensively coiffed women waiting at the top of the path were oblivious to Gram's antics. But I felt a stab of apprehension as we reached the top step of the magnificent terrace.

"Ahh'mm so glad y'all could come," greeted the woman standing beside Janet. She spoke with such a thick southern accent it was difficult to entirely understand all she was saying. "Ahh'mm Peaches Madigan."

I recognized Peaches's name from the shower invitation and knew she was Janet's childhood friend who had recently moved here from Georgia.

Nita and I introduced ourselves to Peaches, who grandiosely rewarded each of us with kisses on our cheeks.

"Mmm-wah! Mmm-wah!" was the sound of Peaches kissing Nita once on her left cheek, once on her right, followed by slightly bigger "Mmmm-wahs" on both my cheeks.

"Why, thank you," I stammered, stunned by the enormity of Peaches's kisses, "for, for having us."

"Well, Ahh jus' know y'all are goin' to have a mawww-velous time!" Peaches spoke each word as if she were breathlessly overjoyed.

As Janet briefly greeted us with short hugs and quick pats on the back, Peaches looked at the presents Nita and I were holding.

"Oh, maaah." Peaches sighed with sugar and spice in her voice. "What a sad look'n bow."

She began to delicately fluff my collapsed bow. She, too, felt a need to resuscitate it.

"Maaah, what a sad look'n bow," Gram mimicked with a very poor imitation of a Georgian accent.

"Please, don't do that." I meant it for Gram's ears only. I rather enjoyed Peaches's twangs and drawls.

"Oh, dear. Ahh'mm so sorry." Poor Peaches looked puzzled and a little offended. She quite dramatically withdrew her hand from my floppy ribbon and acted like she didn't know what to do with her hand anymore.

Nita, her mouth agape, turned with a slow, exaggerated motion, distorting the look on her face as if to say, "Are you crazy?"

I stared back at Nita with a blank look, swallowed hard and then returned my gaze to Peaches. A long and uncomfortable moment of silence hung in the air; I did not know what to say. It wasn't going to help if I told Peaches I was talking to my rude grandmother.

Finally, Nita started to fake a laugh. "Katy, behave yourself. Poor Peaches doesn't know you well enough to understand your odd sense of humor." Nita added another forced laugh as she fluffed the yellow bow and dismissively added, "Katy was teasing."

And with that, Nita began toying with the same droopy bow. She looked at Peaches with the same look I'd seen on pet owners when encouraging fearful strangers to go ahead and pet their angry, snarly looking dogs after they'd already been bitten. Nita was letting Peaches know it was now safe to touch my wimpy bow, even to fluff it up a little bit.

Gram jumped in, "Oh, here, let me help them with that." And simultaneously with Peaches, she reached for my bow.

I gasped! It was just instinct that caused me to involuntarily gasp as if it was my last breath – not a quiet, feminine kind of gasp but more like a rush of wind bursting through a tunnel.

Completely startled, Peaches withdrew her delicate hand from the bow so quickly it slapped Nita's nose and forehead on the uptake.

"Katy, stop it," Nita pretended she couldn't stop laughing. Then she reached for Peaches's arm and acted as if it was the only thing keeping her from falling down from the hilarity of my little surprise prank.

For a long second, Peaches looked completely befuddled, but when Nita continued to feign choking with laughter, Peaches's nervous giggle grew with childlike delight, as if finally understanding the little joke I had played on them.

I was so grateful that Janet stepped toward us and indicated she wanted to introduce two more guests to Peaches.

"Ahh can tell we awhr just goin' to have to get to know y'all better," Peaches twittered and hurriedly guided Nita and me up the rest of the porch to the entrance of the foyer.

I looked to see if Gram was coming, but of course she wasn't. She was standing beside Janet, nodding her head as the women around her chatted. I was a nervous wreck and was honestly thinking of an exit plan when Bonnie, a friend of Nita's and mine, walked up to us.

"Here," Bonnie said reaching for our gifts. "Let me take these for you. I'm supposed to be sure all the presents are placed on that table over there." She pointed toward a large, circular table covered with a blue and pink tablecloth and piled high with an array of beautifully wrapped baby gifts.

"Bonnie," Nita paused and looked knowingly at Peaches who was still with us. "Better not say anything about Katy's floppy bow. She's very touchy about it."

Nita's sarcasm was not lost on Peaches. She thoroughly enjoyed the newly formed camaraderie and began hooting – I mean really hooting with laughter. Nita, not so much.

"It fell on the car floor," I explained, grateful to hand the gift over to Bonnie.

Bonnie paid little attention to Peaches, Nita or me. Something else seemed to be on her mind. She took our gifts to the table and quickly returned. "You two have got to come inside and take a look at this house. Peaches has decorated it so beautifully!"

Peaches obviously appreciated the compliment and, with feigned humility, smiled at us. "Y'all just go on in and take a tiny tour if y'all want." Her southern drawl made everything Peaches said sound like a question, not a statement.

"Oh, I'd love to take a tooer," Gram said with a jingly voice and then marched through the foyer ahead of us.

I made up my mind that I needed to calm down and completely ignore Cornelia Carlton Welborn.

Bonnie led us through the rest of the spacious, marble foyer to the archway leading to the living room. Nita and I stared at the grand room before us. Bonnie was right. Peaches's house was stunning, impeccably decorated, the kind of place one sees in House Beautiful. The living room was large and airy with light flowing through the cathedral windows lining the far wall. Three ample couches, richly upholstered in fabrics of floral pinks and yellows, surrounded a massive stone fireplace that was framed by a hand-carved mantle. Large crystal vases of fresh cut flowers appeared everywhere.

"Did you know it would be such a big party?" Nita asked.

"No," I said.

There were sixty to seventy women huddled together in various cozy areas of the living room. Some of the women looked vaguely familiar, but most of them I'd never met before.

I scanned the room, hoping to find Gram, but before I could locate her, Nita motioned for us to walk to the far corner of the room where Janet stood. She was leaning against a very majestic, very black baby grand piano while several women fluttered around her.

"Oh," Janet moaned as Nita and I joined the group. She was holding her enlarged belly. "I will be so glad to have this baby and have my body back to myself."

"That's exactly the way I felt," announced a woman whose nametag read Roberta. "By the time I was eight months pregnant, I didn't worry about labor, I actually looked forward to it." She nodded at everyone in the circle. "Am I right?"

Everyone laughed with Roberta.

A recognizable voice giggled. "You are so right."

I turned to look across the piano. Gram was sitting on the bench. I chose to remain calm.

"Though labor is nothing to look forward to," Gram continued as if everyone in the group could hear her. Clearly no one could, except lucky me. Several of the ladies interrupted with increasingly dreadful labor stories of their own.

"I couldn't have made it if I hadn't kept up with my aerobics," Roberta told the group.

"In my day women were advised not to exercise while they were pregnant," Gram countered.

"Breath in, breathe out" became my silent mantra.

"Let me tell you, Janet," Roberta continued. "Keep up those Kegel exercises. They're a big help before and after labor."

"Kegel?" Gram asked. "Katy, have you ever heard of Kegel exercises?"

"Yes," I answered without thinking.

I then realized everyone else thought I was agreeing with Roberta - that Janet should keep up her Kegels. I nodded my head to show I was in accord with them.

"Well, what in the world is a Kegel?" Gram asked.

"Breathe in, breathe out," I repeated over and over in my head.

"My doctor had me doing Kegels twenty-four hours after delivery," one of the other women said with utter vexation.

"I wish someone here would please explain what a Kegel is," Gram said intolerantly.

I breathed in my silent mantra.

"Twenty-four hours after a twenty-six-hour labor, and I'm supposed to practice my Kegels, as if I can even feel the muscles around my vagina!" This woman rolled her eyes with contrived agony, then added, "I told my Mr. Doctor he should do the Kegels."

"Oooooo." Gram's face scrunched up and exposed her mortification. "I think I know what a Kegel is."

"Good!" I said aloud and a little too ardently. What happened to my mantra? It was working so well.

Promptly everyone in our little group looked at me expectantly. Was I supposed to share my own gruesome birthing story? I stared above everyone's heads, shifted my stance, and cleared my throat. More silence.

"And," Roberta paused. "How many children do you have?"

I cleared my throat and said, "I don't have any."

"Oh." She paused as if confused. "Are you planning on having any, or are you one of those women who's decided to be carefree all her life?"

A few women twittered politely, and I lightly twittered along with them until it became apparent that Roberta was awaiting my answer.

"No, no, my husband and I are still thinking about having children," I replied with the line Tom uses whenever anyone asks this question.

Tom will say, "We're still thinking about having children," as if two people in their late thirties still have time to think about it. I cringe knowing how ridiculous this must sound to everyone who hears us, but we can't exactly answer with, "Actually, cancer has forced us to wait," or "The doctors tell us we shouldn't have children of our own."

Obviously, Roberta thought my response to her question was absurd, because all she said was, "Oh," and with raised eyebrows she turned to Janet and asked, "Did you hear Nancy decided not to breast-feed her baby?"

"Noooo," sounded the gaggle of alarmed mothers.

"Just the other day, I read how formula-fed children tend to be less intelligent," one of the women said with great authority.

"And less healthy," chimed another.

"Can you imagine why anyone would choose to deprive her baby of mommy's milk," a large breasted woman standing to my right addressed only me.

"You could give her a reason," Gram tried to provoke me. "Ask her if she's heard of breast cancer."

I slowly shook my head for both Gram and the woman.

At the same moment, a tray of hors d'oeuvres was being offered to our little gathering of militant breast-feeding, Kegel-minded moms.

Several moms "oooo'd" while others "ahhhh'd" at the elegant selection of crackers and petite toasts topped with sardines, glutinous cream cheeses, and tips of asparagus. Nothing looked appealing to me, but I determined I'd feel less vulnerable holding something in my hands, even if I wasn't going to eat it.

"It all looks so good," I lied to Roberta, who had reached for the hors d'oeuvres at the exact moment I did.

"I wish someone would save me from myself." Roberta sighed as if in pain while helping herself to three cheesy crackers.

I gave a polite laugh and took a cracker with the least amount of goo.

"I'm just a little curious." Roberta paused to munch on one of her crackers. "Why are you still thinking about whether to have children?"

Roberta's air of self-importance reminded me of many of the girls I knew in high school, asking direct questions under the guise of innocence. Maybe Roberta knew I'd been told not to get pregnant. Janet might have told her. Oh, forget it! Why would my name ever come up for discussion between my "not close, close friend" Janet and Roberta, someone who'd never met me until this very day?

"What I mean to say is, you can't have a whole lot more time to just be thinking about having children, can you?" Roberta seemed to be poking around for something.

Gram's voice huffed from the piano bench. "Good Godfrey, this woman needs someone to save her from more than the hors d'oeuvres."

"You're right," I said.

"I hope you don't mind if I give you some advice." Roberta's voice did make it sound as if she knew a whole lot about everything.

"Don't pay attention to her," Gram urged. "But take some of the asparagus before the woman takes the tray away."

"I don't want it," I said to Gram and then quickly pointed to the asparagus for Roberta's sake. "The asparagus. It makes me gag."

Roberta looked at me for a moment, looked at the asparagus and decided it had to be the asparagus I was rejecting and not her advice. She continued. "A dear, dear friend of mine waited and waited to become pregnant. She's around your age, maybe a little younger." Roberta sighed a long sigh, then put her head down and looked despairingly at the last cracker and cheese in her hand.

"Good grief!" Gram barged into the moment Roberta was feeling. "I can't tell if that woman is feeling glum over her dear, dear friend or over having just one cracker and cheese left to eat."

I continued to ignore Gram but did feel a little awkward waiting for Roberta to continue. Maybe she expected me to say something, but I was feeling a little insulted that she'd decided someone I'd never met was 'maybe a little younger' than me.

"Now, it's too late," Roberta suddenly divulged.

"Too late," I repeated after her.

Roberta's demeanor suddenly turned perky, and she began to nibble on her last hors d'oeuvre.

"Is your friend okay?" I asked. "I mean, she adopted or something, didn't she?"

76

Roberta put her hand on my shoulder. "Women's bodies were meant to bear children early in life, not late in life," she warned with a trace of doom in her voice.

"Katy," said Gram, "tell this woman to mind her own business."

I was reminded of how spirited and steadfast Gram had been when she was alive and how distraught but feisty she had become when I first revealed the hurt I felt from the high school Robertas. "Tell them to mind their own business! Fight back, Katy!" Gram had lovingly ordered me. But I never did. I was not a fighter and avoided confrontation whenever it came my way. I hadn't known any witty lines or cutting remarks that could stop the Robertas from prying in hurtful ways. I guess I still didn't.

"You better not wait any longer," Roberta repeated.

"Tell her, Katy!" Gram commanded.

"No," I said to both Roberta and Gram. "I'd better not."

Peaches Madigan bustled up to our group. "Ladies," she said, "I hope y'all don't mind, but I'm going to steal Janet away so she can sit and open her shower gifts. I recommend y'all find a comfortable seat toooo."

As everyone dispersed and found places to sit, I moved to the piano bench and sat beside Gram. The buzz of women's chatter grew distant, and I began to feel separated from the others, almost invisible like Gram.

"I always wanted a baby grand," Gram sighed.

"You did?" I asked.

"Oh, yes. They are so graceful looking, don't you think?"

"Well, yes, but I always thought you loved your upright piano. At least until –"

"If I'd had a baby grand, I wouldn't have put it in the music room where I kept the upright," said Gram.

"I don't think a baby grand would have fit inside Grandpa's music room," I said as I recalled the little room next to the kitchen in the back of Gram's house.

When I was a young girl, I thought Grandpa's music room was wonderful and magical. Its worn down, wood floor made friendly creaking noises whenever I stepped on it, and the four knotty pine walls welcomed me with an orangey warm, almost misty glow. Grandpa's cello leaned gracefully against an empty wood chair in the far corner of the room, and his metal music stand stood dutifully in front, still embracing the sheet music to Pachelbel's Canon in D, the last piece Gram ever heard Grandpa play.

After my grandfather died, Gram refused to store the cello in its case or remove the music from the stand. All because she believed with her whole heart that my grandfather would one day return to his corner of the room and play for her. I believed he would too.

The modest oak piano with worn, cloudy white keys stood against the wall to the right of the entryway, looking as if it were napping, waiting to be stirred awake. One afternoon while I lazily toyed with the keys of the upright, I heard a sweet melody resonate in Grandpa's corner, and I thought I saw a shadowy outline of him sitting in his chair.

When I ran to the kitchen to tell Gram, she smiled knowingly and said I'd simply heard gentle breezes skip across the cello's strings, and I'd merely seen dancing sunlight cast a shadowy image of Grandpa.

Sometimes, while I lingered in the music room, those same beams of light would shoot through the window, stretching their fingerlike rays to the pictures on the wall, pictures of Grandpa sitting in the front row of the Los Angeles Philharmonic Orchestra and of Gram in long flowing gowns, bowing gracefully from a stage. And if the yellow pages of sheet music spilled from the top of the upright, I pretended their fluttering was the sound of applause coming from within the metal picture frames, not the ruffling pages falling to the floor.

Now I silently ran my hand along the ivory keys of Peaches's pristine, probably-never-been-played baby grand piano and remembered the times Gram and I sat at her overly-played oak upright, with its worn-out keys.

"I loved hearing you play," I said to Gram, focusing my attention on the women in Peaches's living room.

Janet held a blue and white blanket for everyone to see.

"It's too bad you never really learned," Gram said, shaking her head. "One minute you were begging me for lessons, and then just when you were beginning to show a hidden talent, you decided you didn't want to play anymore. And you never did. Such a funny thing." Gram sighed heavily, a little too dramatically.

I loved those lessons with Gram, sitting beside her on the oak bench as she patiently showed me how to match the notes on the sheets of music with certain keys on the piano. Gram said I was very good, a natural musician, and I beamed with pride and happiness whenever she praised my musicality. Secretly, I imagined someday being a musician like my grandparents.

But then everything changed. Rollie returned from one of his "trips," and I had the nightmare for the first time. I could never go near Gram's piano again.

"Katy, y'all look so lonely over thar. Would you like to help me put theeese in the back bedroom?" Peaches stood before me with an armful of opened baby gifts.

I focused on her for a moment as the room once again filled with the sounds of laughter and chattering women, and I realized that Janet had opened all her gifts. Everyone began to stand and move to the dining room.

"Oh, of course, Peaches. I'd be happy to help." I stood and took the packages from Peaches but first glanced behind me at the piano bench. It was empty.

"Just go on through the foyer and turn left at the hallway. Y'all can put theeese on the bed in the second bedroom," Peaches directed.

I carefully weaved through the crowd of women then turned into the hallway. I would have walked past the first room if I hadn't breathed in that undeniable scent, the sweet, indescribable smell of a baby. I paused in front of the half-closed door and looked inside. A few feet away, stood a white crib with soft yellow and pink bedding.

"Shhhh." Gram was beside the crib, motioning me to come closer. "Reminds me of the one Wendy had," Gram whispered.

I remained at the doorway, not certain I should go inside, not certain I wanted to.

"I suppose it does," I whispered, recalling the big crib with the rounded headboard. It had been mine until the day my mother and new baby sister came home from the hospital. I was three and felt very grown up knowing my sister would sleep in my room with me.

But that first night, when I was awakened every hour by Wendy's screams, I knew this arrangement wouldn't work, and I let everyone in the house know it. "Get her out of here!" I screamed at the top of my lungs. For some reason, my parents looked upon that moment in our family history as something humorous and cute. But then, they've never heard me silently screaming the same words ever since: Get her out of here! Get her out of my life!

"Come over and look." Gram motioned.

The temptation was too great, so I gently pushed the door with my shoulder and tiptoed in to stand beside Gram, who was quietly humming "Brahm's Lullaby."

"Such a pretty infant." I sighed as I looked at the sleeping child.

"As beautiful as your sister was," Gram said.

Actually, Wendy was more beautiful. It would have been an understatement to say that my baby sister, with her strawberry blond hair and big dimples, was the most adorable baby ever born. Her presence caused everyone from relatives to strangers to dote on her endlessly, even to the exclusion of my older brother and myself. I don't remember feeling hostile or jealous about the endless attention Wendy received. I, too, couldn't help but want to play with her and watch all the cute faces she could make.

I looked down at the sleeping baby. I wanted to brush her cheek, but I still held the shower gifts. "I'd better take these to the other room," I said.

I quietly tiptoed to the hallway. Gram gave a little wave of her hand. "Aren't you coming?" I whispered.

"No, no, you go on ahead."

"Oh, Katy," I heard Peaches's hushed voice behind me. "Not in that room. The baby's sleeping in there. You follow me." Peaches scooted down the hall carrying her own armload of packages.

"Oh, how pretty," I said as we entered the most beautiful little girl's bedroom.

"Isn't it sweet?" Peaches chirped.

I looked around and admired the pink and white striped wallpaper and the miniature sofa chair covered with a yellow and pink floral pattern. Everything in this house had pink and yellow flowers.

"I wanted a bed just like this when I was a girl," I said as I walked to the four-poster princess bed with frilly, white curtains overhead and zillions of stuffed animals resting against heart shaped pillows.

"Oh, Sarah jus' loves it. It's her first big girl bed, and she picked it out herself." Peaches had already placed her gifts on the bed and began to fidget with a puffy, pink ribbon that held two curtains to one of the bedposts. "We thought it would help her adjust to havin' a new baby sister and it really ..."

The sound of Peaches's voice grew distant as I thought about my own first big-girl bed. A few weeks before my sister was born, I had been told that I was too big for sleeping in a crib and was big enough to have a real bed. I was just three, but I knew it was a momentous event when my father pushed the crib to the wall across from the window, then brought in pieces of an old, queen-size bed that had been stored in Gram's garage. I had been mesmerized watching him carefully fit the pieces together. And when he finished, I could not believe that this bed with a mattress as big as an ocean and a headboard looking very much like the crown of a majestic and noble matriarch was mine. A bed fit for a queen.

It didn't remain just mine. Three years later, Wendy's crib was moved to the garage, and my sister took possession of half my queen bed. "You'll have more space for your toys," my parents told me.

They had been right. There had been more room for our playthings, but it hadn't been worth waking up night after night in sheets soaked with my sister's urine. Wendy didn't wet the bed because she wasn't toilet trained or couldn't walk to the bathroom. She just didn't want to be bothered. So, while she slept, I would get up to change the sheets, to clean up her messes, so I could go back to sleep.

As I stood in Peaches's daughter's room, I stared at the blissfully adorned princess bed and wondered why I was still cleaning up Wendy's never-ending messes. But then while Peaches chatted on, I realized the answer was simple. I had continued, and always would continue, to clean up my sister's messes. So I could sleep. So I could sleep.

"...and she just loves all the Disney songs." Peaches pointed to a shelf under a quaint picture window. It was neatly filled with colorful books and music tapes.

"I used to like them too," I said, remembering the many records Gram had given Wendy and me when we still shared a bedroom. My favorite was Cinderella. Wendy's was Toyland.

Toyland. It was the only song Wendy ever wanted to play on our red and white record player, and she threw raging tantrums if I attempted to play anything other than Toyland. I would do almost anything to avoid her wrath, so I always waited until she was busy in another part of the house before I dared to play a different record.

One such day, I'd put on the Cinderella record, and just as Cinderella's fairy godmother began singing, "Bibidi-bobidi-boo," Wendy had stormed into our room. She furiously ripped the vinyl disk off the player and threw it to the floor. I ran for my mother, but by the time she came to see what was wrong, Wendy had smashed every one of our records. Every record except Toyland. It was spinning on the record player, and Wendy, sitting cross-legged among the strewn and broken records, sang along as if nothing had happened. "Toyland, Toyland, beautiful girl and boy land..." Wendy's sweet voice filled the room as she innocently looked at my mother and me, inviting us to join in.

"Of course," cooed Peaches, "no little girl wants to sleep in the dark. And nothing else would do but a Little Mermaid nightlight."

Wendy and I had used a nightlight. My mother said it would help me to be less afraid of the dark, to see that it was not the voices of unknown things or creatures that woke me up but only the sound of my sister as she talked in her sleep.

The nightlight helped for a time, but eventually it, too, became something that caused unrest and anxiety. Many nights, I awakened to find my sister sitting on the floor close to the nightlight. Her hands and fingers moved about the glowing bulb, creating giant, hideous shadows that fiendishly danced along the walls and ceiling. And all the while Wendy sang in a sweetly hushed voice, "Toyland, Toyland. Beautiful girl and boy land..."

I would silently watch from my side of our bed as fear and dread stirred deep within, warning me of something I had no control over.

"It's a beautiful room, Peaches," I said with a slight shudder to help break the memory of my past. "I bet she sleeps well in here."

"Oh, mawh, Sarah jus' loves it. Though she wishes we would let her baby sister sleep with her," Peaches said, guiding me out of the room.

"I think it's nice for sisters to have their own rooms," I said quietly.

CHAPTER

FOUR

It was early October, and I'd not seen Gram since the baby shower at Peaches Madigan's house. Almost three weeks had passed, but the fragile memories nudged back into existence by each of Gram's visits drifted softly in and out of my consciousness like the autumn leaves that listlessly floated from the branches of their detached, emotionless tree trunks. And with each whispering breeze, I'd wonder if Gram would return or if, like the falling leaves, I'd been dismissed, left to float aimlessly and alone with the unbearable disquiet once tightly contained and hidden. How cruel of her to unearth and expose such pain without returning it to the place where it had been secreted and entombed so long ago.

These thoughts clouded my mind one rainy fall evening as I sat alone and tired in the main room of UCLA's Medical Library. The table in front of me was scattered with medical journals and the medical records I'd received from the hospital earlier that day.

I'd spent several hours researching the individual attributes of breast cancer that pertained to my specific cancer. I'd hunted down current and available studies involving thirtysomething women who had varying stages of breast cancer and who, intentionally or unintentionally, had become pregnant. I wanted to know what the odds of survival were for both mother and baby. What were the odds of me, Katy Welborn McAndrews, becoming pregnant and surviving long enough to watch my own child grown into adulthood? I desperately needed to understand why breast cancer allowed some women to survive and become pregnant and cancer free for the rest of their lives and some women not.

The endless pages of notes I'd written and the small pile of studies I'd prudently copied from the library's nickel-per-page Xerox machine only left me confused and emotionally depleted. Nothing I'd read told me what I desperately wanted to hear; nothing said, "It's okay, Katy, your cancer won't come back. You and Tom can get pregnant now."

Wearily I sat up and stared through a lofty, rectangular window offering an ample view of the library courtyard. The glistening October rain rushed past towering outside lights that lined the quad's leaf-strewn sidewalks. I watched as sporadic bursts of wind erupted with fierce emotion, then promptly settled down with a peaceful resolve, only to rupture once again with impatient passion. A young fir tree desperately pushed its branches against the window as if pleading to come inside, and with each new gust of wind, its unyielding pine needles screeched along the beveled glass, causing discordant cries to resonate within the sanctity of the library.

"What a nice, old room," Gram's sweet, nonthreatening voice whispered from across the table.

Without thinking, I slowly looked around as if seeing the library for the first time. It was a typical college library, nothing architecturally spectacular about it from what I could tell: high ceiling, tall wooden bookshelves, faded worn-down wood flooring, and the ubiquitous echo of a closed book or the careful footsteps trailing from the front desk to a library table. I should have laughed at Gram dressed in a yellow plastic rain hat and matching plastic raincoat reminiscent of the seasonal attire she'd worn on rainy days so many years ago.

"But not as quaint as our little library in South Pasadena. Not as picturesque," Gram added.

"Hmmm," was all I would offer.

"Is it still there?" Gram asked.

"I think so." I wasn't positive that the little library was still there, on the same street in the same spot, but I definitely did not want to pursue this topic.

Since Gram's death, I rarely drove to South Pasadena, but on those occasions when I needed to, I went out of my way to not drive along Hidden Oak Avenue where the library had resided since the 1930s. Unlike Gram, I did not have fond memories of the two-story structure with its mixture of early Urban American architecture and Gothic design.

It's too bad because I truly loved Lily Street, Gram's charming tree-lined cul-de-sac. The problem was that "Charming Lily," aptly named by Gram, ran perfectly perpendicular into Hidden Oak Avenue and straight to the library's entrance. I would hold my breath whenever our car entered Hidden Oak Avenue and not inhale or exhale again until we'd turned onto Lily Street with the library to our backs. I'm not sure what I believed would happen if I allowed a trace of the library's contaminated air to enter my lungs, but I knew this – I didn't want to find out.

"Oh, Katy, I wonder if those magnificent sphinxes are still there," Gram said with a misty, romantic tone in her voice.

How was it that Gram saw beauty and art when looking at the chiseled statues standing sentry at the top step of the library when all I saw were identical evil and pitiless creatures – two hideous beings whose bodies, from their thick, muscular necks down to their sharply filed claws, had been molded into violent, other-worldly animals. Their faces, alive with distinct human features, were tightly framed by densely gnarled manes and oozed with ominous, portentous leers. And though they appeared to be immobile, with their long, front legs standing stiff and straight, anchored by firm, unyielding backbones that sloped at eighty-degree angles down to their posteriors, I detected a restlessness, a cunningly subtle twitching and flexing of their overly developed haunches. I knew the two dreadful creatures were primed to lunge at and devour any and all unsuspecting prey at lightning speed.

The sphinxes, Gram once told me, stood guard, flanking the library's imposing glass-and-metal door to instill a sense of protection and safety for all who passed between them. Not for me. Instead, those creatures ignited the exact same fear that halted my breathing whenever Uncle Rollie entered a room, the same fear that kept me awake when Wendy made her ghoulish shadow puppets. This very fear convinced me that hidden within the impenetrable, stone facades of Gram's magnificent sphinxes swirled an ancient evil I was powerless to expose or reveal.

But then, there was that one day, I was only seven years old, when I recklessly blurted out my earnest understanding of the sphinxes. Gram and I were on a short walk to the ice cream store, an adventure I always welcomed. But as we approached the end of Lily Street with the library looming straight across Hidden Oak, I felt the steely eyes of those demons aimed directly at us. I heard their fiery breath inhaling and exhaling through flared nostrils. Each step we took, which brought us closer to the snarling beings, pounded and reverberated inside my head until I couldn't stand it another second.

I suddenly yanked Gram's hand, pulling her in the opposite direction of the library and its sphinxes. Gram's irate protests made me know she was not happy, but when I frantically cried, "Hurry, Gram, so the sphinxes won't take me away from you," she stopped dead in her tracks.

I don't think Gram actually laughed, but for a brief instant, a look of amusement skipped across her face. A car waiting at the stop sign tooted loud enough to let us know it hoped we'd soon make a decision about crossing or not crossing the street, so Gram allowed me to finish dragging her to safety.

Standing on the curb of Lily and Hidden Oak, Gram took a long, deliberate look at the beasts and then looked down at me. "You know," Gram said softly, "I used to be afraid of the sphinxes."

"Really?" I said incredulously.

"Then I discovered a secret about them," Gram whispered. She bent her knees to be on my level, but her eyes were fixed on the two figures whose piercing eyes were locked on ours.

"What secret?" I asked with dismay.

Gram put her finger to her lips. She didn't want the sphinxes to hear. "The secret that makes them weak and you strong, much stronger than they could ever be."

"Can you tell me?" I quietly but desperately breathed into her ear.

"I can," she whispered back, "but you must always, always remember it, even when you are much older, or you will give the power back to the sphinxes, and you will find yourself hiding and running from them all your life."

When I promised Gram I would never forget the secret, she took my hand and coaxed me across the street, sweet-talking me all the way up the library's steps. She stopped directly in front of the monsters. "Do you see how evil their eyes look right now?"

I nodded and gulped.

"Whenever you sense that they are trying to make you afraid, you must walk up to them and look right into their faces and straight into their eyes. Like this." Gram then kneeled down on one knee and pushed her face to the nose of one of the hideous creatures. "And then you tell him, 'I am not afraid. I have a loving protector greater than you, greater than all the evil in the world!'" Gram turned to look at me. "You know who your protector is, don't you?"

"Yes," I barely heard my own voice answer.

"Who?" asked Gram.

"God," I whispered carefully.

Gram stood tall, as if a victory had just been won, and to each of the sphinxes, she gave a deliberate, triumphant nod.

"Now," Gram said as she stretched out both arms, "they can't hurt me. They know I am not afraid, and I can't be harmed."

I was stunned by this act of bravery. "I could never do that."

"Katy," Gram softly spoke. "Is God in you?"

"Yes." That's what I'd been told over and over again at church and by Gram, but I didn't really understand what it meant. I only knew I was supposed to understand it.

"Well then," Gram took me by the shoulders, pushed my stiff body in front of the creature on the right, and urged me to repeat after her, "I am not afraid. God loves me, and He is my protector."

I wanted to join in with Gram. I even tried forming the words with my lips, but no amount of air would come up my throat to force the words out of my mouth. I suppose Gram thought my soundless attempt was good enough, because she quickly pulled me to the monster on the left and encouraged me to repeat the same words along with her. All I could do was stare impotently at the fiery eyes that stared back at me, daring me to tell them how unafraid I was because God was within me.

"There!" Gram said. "Next time, you can tell them all by yourself."

I silently vowed that there would never be a next time, because I wasn't entirely convinced that God, my protector, was stronger than Gram's two "magnificent sphinxes."

Now remembering those sphinxes, I shuffled a few papers in front of me. "I never liked them, you know." Without looking at Gram, I quietly added, "They still scare me."

"Oh, Katy, what an enigma you are." Gram sighed heavily.

I had never wanted to be an enigma to Gram or to anyone else. Had there been no Uncle Rollie in my life, no mental illness in my family, I might have grown up lighthearted and untroubled. But I couldn't afford to be like other children who were spontaneous and carefree. I had to be on constant guard to prevent the germs of Rollie's disease, the same evil germs the sphinxes possessed, from contaminating the people I loved.

"It's a mystery why you never outgrew your fear of those harmless, lifeless sculptures," Gram continued and clucked with her tongue twice.

It was a mystery to Gram, because I had not told her everything I knew about the sphinxes. But I should have. I should have told her the moment I realized it wasn't just me they were after.

A week after Gram had shared her secret of the sphinxes and had made me confront them, my sister developed a severe ear infection and urgently needed to see the pediatrician. My mother knew I'd be happier visiting Gram for a few hours than sitting for what would seem to be eternity to a seven-year-old in a doctor's waiting room. But Gram's phone had been busy all morning, so gambling on Gram being home, my mother drove the three of us in Dee Dee, Wendy's name for our 1949 burgundy DeSoto, to Gram's house on Lily Street. I sat in the front seat holding Wendy in my lap with my arms wrapped snuggly around her waist to prevent her from sliding onto the slippery plastic seats.

"Look Katy," my mother said as she carefully edged our hulking car along Gram's narrow driveway. Up ahead, to the left of the one-car garage and under the shade of an overgrown pepper tree, sat Gram's car.

"Does that mean Gram is home?" I asked as Wendy began thrashing around, trying to free herself from my locked arms.

"I think so," my mother said. She pulled on the emergency handbrake, removed the keys from the ignition and got out of the car.

By the time my mother walked around the car to lift Wendy from my lap, I began to doubt Gram was actually home.

"She might have walked to the store," I said as I held onto the car handle and reached for my mother's hand.

"I doubt it," she replied and then hurried us up the steps to Gram's front door.

I rang the doorbell, and we waited for Gram to open the door, but she didn't. My mother knocked five times, paused, and knocked five more.

If my mother hadn't been distracted by Wendy's feverish crying, she might have noticed, as I did, how the living room drapes opened ever so slightly in the middle, just enough for someone to peek out at us. But before I was able to formulate a plausible reason for the moving drapes, the front door abruptly opened.

Gram, seemingly surprised to see us on her porch, instantly threw her hands to her cheeks and kept them there while bobbing her head back and forth and going on and on about what a happy, happy surprise it was to see us and how happy, happy she was that we were there.

But even a seven-year-old could tell that my grandmother was only acting as if she were happy, happy.

Gram had always been a terrible secret-keeper and an even worse actress or pretender of anything. My dad once told me that Gram grew up during the birth of the first silent movies and the invention of the "talkies." He said Gram was a believer, hook, line and sinker, of every artificial display of emotion, every grand and effusive gesture, and every over-the-top facial expression ever presented on screen. Worse yet, Gram assumed that by imitating the same embellished techniques of the silent film stars, she could camouflage any secret she'd been made privy to and any promise or surprise she vowed to keep from being disclosed. For the life of her, Gram could not understand how everyone seemed to know when she was acting.

So, on that morning as Gram feigned such joyous happiness over our unexpected visit, I knew my mother had sensed that something was amiss, because she interrupted Gram's histrionics by saying, "Mother, you look so tired today. I think maybe Katy should come to Wendy's doctor after all."

But Gram wouldn't hear of it. "No, no, no," she said. And she instantly morphed into her real self, genuine and sincere, when she added, "It would make my heart so happy if Katy and I could have another one of our wonderful adventures today!"

My mother looked at me, and I nodded with the hope that she no longer thought Gram looked too tired. She gave me an understanding smile and then thanked Gram, quickly telling her the name of Wendy's doctor. She even offered to write down the doctor's phone number and address if Gram would let her borrow a pen from inside.

Gram's body stiffened. "Never mind, dear. Katy and I won't need that," Gram said stealing an almost indiscernible glance over her shoulders.

My mother hugged both Gram and me and scurried to the car with Wendy. Wendy's whimpering had steadily expanded into a painful wail, and with each bounce on my mother's hip, the pitch and volume grew ever higher.

Our old Dee Dee must have felt Wendy's pain, because the instant the ignition was turned on, Dee Dee's engine passionately rattled and roared high above Wendy's tearful cries. While my mother eased the car down the driveway, she called out to Gram with a last-minute thought. She apologized that she didn't know how long they'd be at the doctor's, but she'd call Gram to let her know if there were any complications.

Instantly, Gram stood on her tiptoes as if it might help her voice rise above the blended cacophony coming from Wendy and Dee Dee. "Don't forget, I can't have Katy more than a few hours. And she won't be able to sleep here tonight."

I know my mother heard not one word of Gram's proclamation, because she was looking out the rear window, totally absorbed in maneuvering the car down the skinny driveway, careful to not roll over one of my uncle's cherished plants.

Nevertheless, Gram twice more called out, "I can only have Katy a few hours, dear." It was as if she was trying to make this decree very, very clear – to someone other than my mother.

With a nervous sigh and a quick kiss on top of my head, Gram grabbed my hand and shot into the house with such force, I thought I'd been launched into air. Nervous chatter passed through her lips in rapid fire ("Must be hungry...make a tuna sandwich...plan adventure... surely Wendy's doctor would see her right away...") as she dragged me through the foyer, skirting the living room and dining room, and headed straight to the kitchen.

Then, pushing a little too hard on my shoulders, Gram sat me in one of her modern chrome chairs with the shimmering turquoise plastic seats. "You sit here while I make a sandwich for you," she said as she scooted me much too close to the matching, sparkly and always gleaming, turquoise Formica kitchen table.

I suggested to Gram that she let me be her "Smooshing Chef" who smooshed the tuna in the bowl before she added her secret ingredients. In Gram's kitchen, for as long as I could remember, I'd been her Egg Beating Chef, her Cookie Dough Squeezing Chef, even her Butter Smearing Chef. But that particular day, Gram insisted that she didn't need a second chef and instead of smooshing, she needed me to remain at the table and tell her about my week at school.

I wanted to tell Gram that chefs could smoosh tuna and talk about school all at the same time. Instead, I prattled away, updating Gram on anything that entered my head – though I became somewhat distracted, even flustered, by the speed with which Gram pulled white bread from her bread box, slapped a messy dollop of yellowish mayonnaise on a piece of bread and a messy blob of tuna on the other, then slapped the two pieces together, cut the newly formed sandwich in half, poured a glass of milk, and brought both sandwich and drink to the table. It was an amazing feat, and I was about to tell her so, but she cut me short.

"Katy, I have to check on something in the back of the house, but I'll be right back."

I was certain Gram would enjoy having my company in the back of the house, so I left my chair to follow her. But at the sound of the chair's chrome legs against the linoleum floor, Gram turned around and shrilly scolded me, saying I must not leave the kitchen. She waited until I returned to my chair and then disappeared.

I sat alone, not wanting to eat a sandwich that hadn't been smooshed by the Smooshing Chef. The lump in my throat prevented me from taking a sip of milk that hadn't been poured by the Spilling Chef. I'd never before been scolded by my grandmother – not like that.

Gram wasn't gone long, and when she returned, she pulled a chair right next to mine, put her arm around my shoulders, and kissed the top of my head. "Forgive me, Katy," Gram asked with pain in her voice.

I do not know what possessed me to say, "Father, forgive them for they know not what they do." But I'd just recently memorized that verse in Sunday school, and as it popped out, it instantly struck my funny bone the same way it instantly struck Gram's. We sat side by side, giggling like two silly schoolgirls, and I felt the lump in my throat dissolve.

Feeling much better, I began to tell Gram my plans for Halloween, which, I reminded her, was just a few days away. I knew I couldn't tell Gram that my father would be driving my brother and sister and me to Gram's house on Halloween night. He'd said it was a secret, a surprise for Gram since she lived alone and so few children lived in her neighborhood, so there was no way I would let this secret surprise slip from my lips. Besides, I was a much better secret keeper than my grandmother. But I did tell her I wanted to be a hobo for trick-or-treating.

"A hobo? My goodness! Why did you choose a hobo?" Gram asked.

"Because they're nicer people than ghosts and skeletons," I answered. To me, hobos were carefree, emotionally unencumbered spirits who wouldn't hurt a flea and didn't want to scare people on Halloween night.

"Oh, I see." Gram was mulling this over for a moment when the slamming of one of the bedroom doors broke our silence.

"Must be the wind," Gram said. She jolted from her chair. "Katy, let me just be sure the wind didn't blow something other than the back door. Will you promise to stay right here?"

I promised, and Gram left in a hurry.

I pushed the sandwich and milk an arm's length away and stared past the doorway between the kitchen and dining room. The lavishly framed painting that hung above the dining room buffet table was mostly visible from where I sat, and I found myself drawn into it. A strikingly beautiful ballerina stood tiptoe on her left foot and, seemingly without effort, held her right foot high in the air. Her right arm flowed gracefully above her head, the other elegantly extended from her side. I wondered how it was possible to look as tranquil as this ballerina did when every muscle in her body was being tightly stretched in every direction. Was it that she did not feel pain, or did she truly hurt but could look peaceful despite it?

My spell with the painting was soon broken when Gram walked into the dining room. She paused in the archway to discern what I was staring at.

"I think she is the most magnificent ballerina in the world. The artist must have thought so too," Gram said as she came to stand beside me so she'd have the same visual perspective I had.

"Was it the wind, Gram?" I asked.

"Was what? Oh, yes," Gram said. "It was the wind, and nothing was broken."

"Oh," I said.

"So! What do you suppose a hobo wears?" Gram asked, bringing us back to our discussion before the wind had interrupted us.

"A raincoat," I answered authoritatively. "A dirty one," I added.

"A dirty one?"

"Uh huh."

"And what else?" Gram asked, now completely engaged in our conversation.

When I told Gram that I wasn't entirely sure, since I'd never met a real live hobo, she raised her hands in the air and said, "Katy! Let's have our adventure at the library today!"

"Why?" I gulped uneasily, for the image of the library sphinxes immediately came to mind. We'd have to walk past them before entering the library.

"We can be archaeologists digging for ancient books with pictures of very old hobos," Gram said with renewed enthusiasm. "It will help us decide what else you need for your hobo costume."

I actually liked her idea of finding pictures of hobos – but the sphinxes – and then I remembered: I knew Gram's secret of the sphinxes. "Well, okay," I said, feeling somewhat empowered by this realization.

Suddenly, Gram was reaching for her purse, her keys and her glasses. She was in such a hurry to get us out the door that she didn't notice my untouched tuna fish sandwich and my full glass of milk. I was grateful for that and the fact that Gram stopped being in such a hurry once we reached the sidewalk.

Gram happily chatted away about hobos and Halloween and candy, but as each of our steps brought us closer and closer to the library, I became increasingly aware of my racing heartbeat. Over and over, I silently told myself that I knew the secret of the sphinxes and was ready to face them to show them I wasn't afraid anymore.

By the time we reached the first library step, a surge of cockiness had burst through any remaining anxiety, and I boastfully, even sanctimoniously, told Gram to watch me. Then I skipped up the steps to those sneering creatures. I fully intended to shout, "You ugly monsters don't scare me," but before I could let out the words, my right foot stumbled on the last step, and I skidded with my body flat on the ground and both arms stretched out before the gnarled feet of one of the sphinxes.

I looked up into his mocking face and cried, but it was not the burning pain on the palms of my hands that caused me to cry; it was the realization that the sphinxes had caused my feet to trip, the realization that I wasn't stronger than they, and I did have reason to fear them.

Gram rushed to my side and kissed the tears on my cheeks, brushed off my scraped hands and knees, helped me to my feet, and quietly guided me past the sneering sphinxes. I could feel their victorious gaze on our backs.

With Gram's arm around my shoulders, we walked through the marble floored foyer and past the large checkout desk. I tried to stifle my whimpers as we walked past the endless aisles of grown-up books.

We were headed to the stairway that descended into the bowels of the library where all the children's books were kept, and I remember wondering why the children's section was kept in the basement. Grown-ups didn't get scared in dark underground places, so why couldn't the grown-ups have their books down there?

Gram and I reached the bottom of the stairs and walked toward the desk with a metal plaque that said "Children's Head Librarian." The woman behind the desk didn't look like a librarian to me. She had long, thick, graying brown hair that draped below her shoulders, forming a straggly v-shape. She smiled at me, but it was a forced smile that made me think she didn't like children and really didn't like me.

With a brisk tone, the officious librarian instructed Gram to follow her. She stopped suddenly and pointed down an aisle of bookcases that seemed to form a dark tunnel. "You will find books on Halloween, costumes, and related subjects in the bottom rows of the shelves on the left. Though I doubt you will find anything specifically related to, ah, hobos. Good luck." And then she left us with the sound of her rubbery, black shoes making squishing noises as she returned to her desk.

I followed Gram through the row of books, running my index finger along their spines.

Gram reached the end of the aisle and bent down to view the books on the bottom shelf. "Oh, look here, Katy." She pulled at my arm, coaxing me to kneel down with her. "Lots of books about Halloween. We need to go through them and see if there are any pictures of hobos." Then Gram pulled several books out and shoved them into my arms.

I sat on the cold linoleum floor and began turning pages.

"Katy, you keep looking through these books while I go upstairs to the adult section to look for more hobo books. I won't be long."

Obediently, I scanned the pages of the books in front of me. The clicking of Gram's shoes grew fainter.

I probably wouldn't have noticed the oversized, orange and black book at the end of the shelf if a beam of sunlight hadn't flickered on and off its cover. Like a siren, the finger of light lured me to the book, telling me to come closer. Instead, as if to break its spell, I looked upward and followed the beam's path to the opening of a small rectangular window. Placed where the ceiling and the wall joined together, this basement window provided only a partial view of the outside entrance to the library exactly where the sphinxes stood guard.

I watched for a moment as torso-less, headless people walked by the torso-less, headless sphinx. Each time someone passed by, the sunlight flickered in my eyes as it had flickered on the book covers.

I followed the beam's path back to the orange and black book. As if hypnotized, I slowly pulled it from the shelf. The outline of a man wearing a dirty, beige trench coat and a brown hat became clearer as my eyes adjusted to the dimly lighted room. The man's face was covered in soot and he held a dirty bag in one of his hands. Hobo! I immediately thought I had struck gold!

I looked closer to make out the title as the light from above continued to dance with a strobe-like effect. I slowly moved my index finger under the words in the title, and I quietly mouthed, The...Boogeyman...Is... In...Your...Closet.

"Huh!" I gasped. Boogeymen and closets did not sit well with me.

Suddenly, the beam of sun disappeared. I looked up and saw through the window that someone was leaning against the sphinx and blocking my light. All I could see were the boots and black jeans. My heart thundered inside my chest. Those boots, the ones with the pointy toes and the silver chain around the left ankle – I knew them.

I slowly bent down and cranked my head hoping to get a full view of the person outside but managed only to see up to his waist. I could tell he was wearing a raincoat like the one Gram had hanging in her hall closet, Grandpa's old coat, the one I planned on borrowing for Halloween, just like the one on the cover of the book. My hands suddenly released the book, and it slammed to the floor. I looked down but instantly returned my eyes to the window.

At that moment, a pair of black pumps shuffled past the window and stopped at the foot of the sphinx right in front of the person with the boots. Those pumps – no, they couldn't be Gram's. She was upstairs. Lots of women wore shoes like that.

I crouched lower, my cheek touching the floor, but I still couldn't see the heads belonging to those feet. The window was sealed shut, and all I could hear were muffled voices. But did one of them really say, "Go home. I will call her"? And when the booted person lunged forward and the woman's feet stumbled off balance, did someone say, "Don't bring her home"? Didn't I see a cigarette drop to the ground and get mashed by one of the boots before both black boots stormed away?

It all seemed like a bad dream as I watched the black pumps pause, walk around the sphinx and then slowly limp up the steps to the adult section. Was it my imagination, or did I really see the haunches of that demonic creature lift slightly as if to follow her?

I shook myself away from the memory, pulling one of the medical journals closer to me. "I always thought they were after us," I said.

"Us?" Gram quizzed.

"They were after you, too," I said seriously.

"Oh, Katy," Gram groaned.

"Well." Feeling a little embarrassed, I shuffled some of my note pages together.

"Anything interesting?"

"What?"

"The doctors' notes and all those medical books with the big words," Gram said, pointing to everything on the table.

"Yes."

It had taken the hospital three weeks to get everything copied for me – the lab reports, the hospital records, and the doctors' summaries – but there they were. I'd gotten a phone call from the records department at five o'clock that afternoon saying they would mail the information the next day, but I hadn't wanted to wait. I had driven to the hospital, picked up the packet, and then hurried over to the Westwood Library to sift through what seemed to be hundreds of pages.

Hours later, my hands finally stopped shaking, and after several read-throughs, certain words like carcinoma, stage II, incompletely excised, and infiltrating didn't explode as stridently inside my head. I'd been at the library for three hours and was stunned by how much I had learned.

"There's so much here, Gram. Things about my cancer I never knew."

None of my doctors ever told me that I had something called negative estrogen receptors, which the medical journals and articles explained was less desirable than having positive estrogen receptors. The lab reports described my first tumor as being undifferentiated, meaning the cancer had become messy by spreading and not staying in a neat little ball. Not a good sign, or so said the journals. My age, thirty-five at the onset of the cancer, and the size of the tumor, over two centimeters, also weighed heavily against me.

But the most disturbing thing I learned while sitting in the library was what I found in a bulletin published a few months earlier by the American Medical Association. It strongly recommended that all breast cancer patients have adjuvant therapy, meaning radiation, chemo, or hormonal treatments. The studies showed a much greater recurrence rate and an earlier death rate among women who'd had no adjuvant therapy. I'd had nothing. No adjuvant therapy.

I wanted to know how all of this related to my getting pregnant, but I found very little information to help me.

For every report claiming former breast cancer patients posed no threat to themselves by becoming pregnant, there were an equal number of studies saying the opposite – that there was great risk involved.

"Look at all these articles," I said.

Gram tilted her head to look at the pages I pushed in front of her. "Hmmmm," was all she said. She didn't seem too impressed.

"I've learned more about my cancer on my own in one day than I learned from my oncologists in the past three years!" I was surprised to hear anger pushing its way through my quivering voice. The feeling of anger was frightening to me. Wendy had demonstrated time and again how frightening it could be.

I swallowed hard, forcing the putrid mix of old and new anger – or was it fear? – down my throat so I could control the sound of my voice. "I can't believe none of my doctors provided information, specific information about me, about my specific cancer."

"Did you ever ask to be informed with specifics?" Gram sighed as if annoyed with me.

"Well, I, I never knew what to ask," I said quietly.

"Maybe you didn't want to know the specifics of your cancer. Maybe you thought it was easier to keep them hidden from yourself, hidden behind a closet door."

"Maybe," I said softly as I pulled the pages closer to me.

I felt a little foolish. Why had I waited three years to do what I was now doing?

"I didn't know there were factors making my cancer different from anyone else's," I said defensively.

Gram didn't respond.

"I assumed breast cancer was breast cancer, obviously different from brain or lung cancer. I had breast cancer, the same kind every other breast cancer patient had with no variations."

"And?" Gram said.

"And the doctors took it away."

"No questions asked," Gram sighed. "Nothing more to think about."

"Maybe I was too scared to think about it. Maybe I didn't want to think about it anymore," I added without looking at Gram.

"But you haven't."

"I haven't what?"

"You haven't stopped thinking about the cancer or stopped worrying about it, have you?"

"No."

In that brief moment, I realized that Gram was right. There wasn't a day when I didn't think about my cancer. How could I not? The mastectomy scars dared me to look every time I undressed, and even though I quickly covered them to hide the long, red railroad track scars, the numbness in my arms and chest gave a constant tingling reminder of what had been taken from me.

"Sort of like the boogeyman hiding in your closet, isn't it?" Gram whispered, leaning her head closer to mine.

"Like what?" What a bizarre grandmother mine was.

"You know, boogeymen and hobos."

I looked at Gram, not sure what she was getting at.

"Oh, Katy. I was just suggesting that maybe your past fear of knowing anything more about your cancer is a little bit like the child who won't look inside a closet where he's certain there's a boogeyman."

"How's that?" I said, now feeling insulted by Gram's analogy.

"Well, a child doesn't stop worrying about what's inside the closet, does he? If he'd open the door, he'd see that what's inside is not so scary."

Out of nowhere, with no connection that I could come up with, Gram asked, "Have you prayed, Katy?"

I stared at the pages in my hands, thought for a moment, and said, "Yes, but it doesn't help."

"How do you want it to help?" Gram asked

"I want my prayers to give me answers! They should give me peace. They should take away my cancer. Forever!" There was the anger in my voice again.

Gram's silence was wrapped in a smile of warmth and kindness that said she understood. She pointed to a Ladies' Home Journal someone had left at the end of the table. "Oh, is it Halloween already?"

I looked at the magazine cover. On it was a picture of a young child, maybe seven years old. An oversized hat covered his eyebrows, and he wore a dirty adult-size raincoat with the sleeves rolled up to his elbows. The child's toothy smile matched the smiling, freshly carved pumpkin he held in his hands.

"Reminds me of you."

"Why? I never dressed up as a hobo," I said.

"You didn't?"

"No."

"I distinctly remember you telling me one year you were going to be a hobo."

"I changed my mind." How could Gram have forgotten?

"Oh..." Gram tilted her head as if trying to recall.

In fact, I had changed my mind that day inside the children's library as I stood under the window, frozen with fear and worry. My seven-year-old mind had wrestled frantically with thoughts of what I'd seen or not seen. Those couldn't have been Uncle Rollie's black boots.

He was supposed to be on one of his trips. Hadn't my mother told me that? Yes. She'd said Uncle Rollie wasn't well and needed to take a long vacation. And Gram. She would have told Mom if Uncle Rollie was back from his vacation. Wouldn't she?

I had felt numb emotionally and physically that day as I walked to the table by the librarian's desk. I carried no books to the table – no hobo books, no Halloween books. Instead, I sat with my hands clasped tightly on the table and my eyes focused at the entrance as if willing Gram to come down the stairs and rescue me. And as I sat, I silently chanted over and over again, "Please, God, tell me that wasn't my Gram outside. Please, God, tell me that wasn't my Gram outside."

Within a few short moments, my desperate pleas were interrupted by a slow, rattling sound pushing through the heating vents. I turned to stare at the rusty vents high above the bookcases behind me. Even though I couldn't see anything, I was certain I felt a distinct presence swoop down from between the books, through the aisles, and then across the back of my neck. Suddenly gasping in a warm, musty odor, I knew it was the spirits of the two sphinxes that had taken their seats beside me.

I sat frozen in my seat, unable to move and aware that every muscle in my body was locked in fear. I sat this way for what seemed to be a long time until Gram finally appeared at the top of the stairs.

Slowly, the dark presence of those sphinxes withdrew to the bookshelves, but I felt certain they were looming around the corners watching us, watching my grandmother limp across the room to the table where I sat statue-like in fear.

Gram looked nervous and upset as she pulled the heavy, library chair closer to me.

"Why are you limping?" I asked. My voice sounded as if it had come from someone else's body.

"Oh, silly me. I slipped on a step," she told me. And then she sat down in the sphinxes' chair.

"Outside?" I asked.

"Oh," Gram looked on edge. "Actually, yes, but I'm just fine. How about you, Katy? Couldn't you find a hobo book while I was gone?" Gram asked.

"No," I lied.

"Well, mmmm, wait here."

I watched her hobble down the aisle and then hobble back with the very same book I'd left on the floor.

"Look at this!" Gram whispered with excitement. "Doesn't this look like a hobo?" She nervously flipped through the pages of the book while pointing out pictures of hobo-esque beings and making suggestions for my costume. I was too numb to tell Gram I was not going to be a hobo after all.

"By the way," Gram said without looking at me. "I used the library's pay phone to call your mother at the doctor's office. They're almost done, so she's going to pick you up here. Isn't that nice? We'll just keep looking for hobos until she arrives."

I didn't tell my mother what I'd seen that day through the library window. I was certain she would think I was imagining it. I only prayed that I had.

As Gram now flipped through the pages of the Ladies' Home Journal, she said, "Well, I always loved Halloween. The carved pumpkins and children knocking at my door were such a treat for an old lady."

"I'm surprised to hear you say that."

"Why?" Gram seemed genuinely shocked.

"Well, I remember one Halloween night when you weren't so happy to see your three grandchildren at your door."

"What? Oh, Katy, I was just caught by surprise. I didn't know it was you."

But Gram really had been caught by surprise that Halloween night of 1957. My parents had piled my brother Sam, my sister, and me into the family Ford and had driven us to Gram's house. As my father parked the car, he noted how Gram's porch light was off and her house dark inside.

"I don't think she's home," I said from the back seat.

"She's home." My father smiled as he reached over the seat to open the back door. My mother lifted my sister, who was dressed as a ghost, into my brother's arms.

"Aren't you coming?" I asked as a light chill ran down my back.

"No, you go ahead," my father whispered. "Gram will know who you are if we go with you. Ring her doorbell and see if you can scare her with your costumes."

My father didn't realize that I didn't like Halloween anymore and didn't want to scare anyone. If I'd wanted to scare people, why would I have dressed as a ballerina all in pink – pink tutu, pink tights, pink slippers and pink leotard?

I reluctantly followed my brother and little sister to Gram's front porch. Halfway there, I turned to look down the street. In the distance, I saw the sphinxes with their eyes on fire. And when I saw them blow their cloud of evil toward Gram's house, I knew it was the same evil that had descended from the bookshelves and surrounded Gram and me in the children's library.

This realization caused me to gasp and stumble on the top porch step just as Sam rang the doorbell. No answer.

My knee hurt, and I saw that my pink tights were torn. I reached for Wendy's hand. "Let's go," I said.

Instead of turning to leave, Sam pounded on the door yelling, "Trick or treat!"

 The door opened slightly, and Gram peered out at us.

"It's much too late for treats," Gram's voice weakly reprimanded.

"Trick or treat, pardner!" yelled my eight-year-old brother, who was dressed as a cowboy bandit, red scarf pulled over his nose.

"Go home, children. I have no candy." Gram sounded nervous and edgy.

My father had been right. Gram didn't realize that her own grandchildren were standing right in front of her.

I was certain I was the only one who saw the living room curtain open a crack.

"Trick or treat," squealed my three-year-old sister as she broke away from my hand and pushed Gram's door.

"Children, you must leave my door now!" Gram said shrilly, and she reached down to gently guide Wendy away.

"Gram, it's us," Sam whined. "Sam and Wendy and Katy."

"Who? Oh, dear," cried Gram.

We heard her fumble with something before she came onto the porch, closing the door behind her. The crack in the curtain opened a little more.

"Why, well, I didn't recognize you, did I? My, my, what a surprise!" I could tell by the sound of Gram's voice that it was not a good or happy surprise.

"Aren't you going to offer three hungry trick-or-treaters and their mom and dad some milk and cookies?" my father asked from behind us. He and my mother stepped up to the porch.

Gram's eyes darted from my parents to the curtains. "Oh, dear, this is such a surprise," her voice warbled. "I, um, I really am sorry, but I can't, well, I can't ask you to come in. I, I um, have no lights."

My dad stared at Gram. "Mother?" he questioned.

"It wouldn't be a good idea for the children or you to come inside right now," Gram said and tilted her head in the direction of the window.

Suddenly, the curtain closed shut. I knew my dad had seen it too, because he turned to my mother. "Gram's probably right," he said. "Why don't you children go to the car with Mommy, and I'll stay a minute with Gram to help her with her lights."

Inside the car, my mother tried to make happy conversation with the three of us, but I kept watching the porch and could tell by Dad and Gram's body language that they were not discussing electricity. Dad kept shaking his head, and it looked like Gram was crying. Then suddenly, my father turned and walked back to the car.

"Is Gram going to be okay?" I asked when he was behind the steering wheel.

"Yes, she just needs some help," my father said quietly as he looked at my mother in secret code.

"Aren't you going to help her with her lights before we go?" my brother asked. We were driving away from Gram's dark house.

"She doesn't want help right now. I'll have to wait until she does."

Two high school girls giggled from a library table nearby. "You weren't alone that night, were you?" I asked Gram.

"No." Gram paused in thought and then offered, "Rollie was with me."

"Did Mom and Dad know?"

"No, not until you all came to my house to trick or treat."

"But why?"

"Oh, I knew your father would be angry with me."

"Why with you?"

"Well, I had signed Rollie out of the mental hospital. Again."

Gram paused for a moment. "You see, it was only two months earlier when I called your parents for help."

"What kind of help?"

"Your uncle was not himself. He was angry because I hadn't served his dinner on the good china."

"That's why you called Mom and Dad?"

"No, Rollie was throwing the china at the walls, breaking everything. He had begun to throw lamps onto the floor, and I was afraid he would hurt himself – and me."

116

"Gram." I gasped with profound sadness.

"By the time your parents, two policemen, and two mental health medics arrived, Rollie had calmed down and seemed quite normal."

"He seemed normal?" I asked in disbelief.

"Yes, it was strange, but the moment Rollie saw the police at the door, he welcomed them inside and said he was happy they were there. He told them I was the one who had made the mess."

"They couldn't possibly have believed him! Couldn't they tell he was acting, that he was sick?"

"The truth is Rollie was in such complete control, he was so lucid and polite, I'm afraid he was very convincing. On the other hand, it was I who appeared unstable. My hands shook and my voice quivered, I was agitated and upset. I'm sure I didn't make any sense. Maybe the police and doctors began to wonder if I had been the one who was disturbed."

"So what happened?"

"The doctors sat down and asked Rollie a lot of questions. The police did the same. They were all there quite a long time. Maybe an hour. And the whole time Rollie appeared calm and intelligent. Very pleasant."

"Couldn't Dad do anything?"

"Oh, he tried, but eventually the police said they could do nothing, since Rollie appeared fine to them and because they had no proof of who really caused all the damage in my house. It was Rollie's word against mine."

"So, they left you alone with Rollie?" I was shocked.

"Just about. Actually, the doctors were packing up their written reports and the police were leaving when Rollie started to pace the floor. Back and forth, back and forth."

"And?" I sensed that even now Gram wanted to protect her son.

"Well," she continued, "one of the policemen started to watch Rollie. He didn't say anything. He just watched with a frozen look on his face. Pretty soon he nudged his partner and nodded at the floor where Rollie kept pacing."

"What was the matter?"

"Your uncle had been barefoot the whole night."

"Why was that so strange?"

"It wasn't really, except Rollie didn't seem to be aware of the blood streaming from the bottom of both his feet. He was walking on the broken light bulbs and china with each step he took. And he didn't feel a thing."

I stared at Gram as I took in this information.

"Everyone in the room – your parents, the two doctors, and the two police – watched in silence as each of Rollie's steps crunched with the sound of the broken glass beneath his feet."

"What did they do?"

"The doctors quietly pulled out a restraining jacket and asked Rollie to come with them."

"This happened just two months before that Halloween night?"

"Yes. Maybe a little less."

"But Gram, why would you pull Rollie out of the hospital so soon?"

"Well –" She sighed. "He seemed so much better each time I visited him. And he was so unhappy in the hospital. It broke my heart when he'd cry, begging me to get him out."

"But why would the hospital let Rollie leave when he was so sick?"

"He really was better, Katy."

"How could he be better so soon?"

"With his medication, he was quite relaxed and normal. They couldn't refuse me. I was his mother, his guardian. And I assured them that Rollie would take the medication and see his doctor regularly. So, the doctors released Rollie."

"Dad didn't know any of this?"

"Not until Halloween night when you children surprised me at the door."

"Was he angry?"

"Yes, but he was understanding. Your father said I should call him if I needed help."

It was only three weeks later when Gram's call for help came. I knew because I'd been home from school with a bad cold. I'd awakened from a nap and had gotten up to ask my mother for some soup, when I heard hushed voices coming from the living room. I stood quietly in the entry hall across from the coat stand. The oval mirror above the stand allowed me to see Gram and Mom's reflections without being seen myself. Gram sat stiffly on the green couch. Mom sat across from her in the big cream-colored chair.

"So, how is everything at home?" I heard my mother ask.

"Oh, fine," Gram said with some hesitancy.

"And Rollie? He's fine?"

"Yes." Gram fidgeted with the handkerchief in her lap. Then she cleared her throat. "He's made a new friend."

"That's nice," my mother said with caution in her voice.

"Uhm, yes." Gram continued to fidget. "Rollie talks to him quite a lot actually."

"Really? Is he a nice person?" my mother asked.

"I don't think so. Rollie yells at him a lot." Gram looked out the window to avoid my mother's stare.

"He yells at him?"

Gram nodded.

"Well, what does Rollie talk about with this friend?"

"I don't know for sure except Rollie is always shouting for his friend to shut up."

My mother blew out a long puff of air. "What's the friend's name, Mother?"

"Oh, I don't know," Gram said, still staring out the window. "I've never met him."

Looking grave, my mother probed further. "Does Rollie talk to this person on the phone?"

"No, no, just around the house," Gram answered.

"Well, Mother, are you in the same room when Rollie talks to his friend?"

"Yes, usually, but I still don't see anyone."

"You mean no one is there, but Rollie is talking as if someone is there."

"Yes, but I can't tell Rollie that, because he gets very angry if I say I don't see his friend."

There was a long moment of silence.

"Mother, has Rollie stopped taking his medication?"

"Well, he says he feels much better without it," Gram said defensively.

"Does his doctor know this?"

"Rollie really doesn't think he needs to see his doctor anymore."

My mother was quiet for another long moment, and then she asked, "Would you like some help?"

I watched as Gram put her hands to her face and cried.

I slid my medical records and note pages into a folder and asked, "How long did Rollie stay in the hospital that time?"

"Almost two years," Gram answered.

I thought this over for a moment. "Did you know I was afraid to spend the night with you after that Halloween?"

"Yes. I felt so badly about it. We always had so much fun together." Gram looked down. "I shouldn't have been so secretive about Rollie."

"But then you sent me the suitcase," I smiled.

"The one with the ballerina. It reminded me of you the year you decided not be a hobo," Gram smiled.

The instant Gram said this I realized she had not forgotten how I was dressed that Halloween so many years ago.

I had received the ballerina suitcase the following spring. I'd come home from school and was sitting at the kitchen table, eating a cookie, when my mother handed me a large box wrapped in pretty pink paper. She said Gram had dropped it off.

It wasn't my birthday or Christmas. Why was Gram sending me a gift? I slowly opened the box and looked inside. My breath was taken away as I lifted the tissue paper and saw the round, bright red, patent leather suitcase. It was the most beautiful gift I'd ever received. On the front was a dainty ballerina made of a fuzzy, not quite velvety, pink material. She appeared to be twirling on her tiptoes as she held her hands high above her head. This was no ordinary suitcase, for it had a zipper that had to be pulled a full three hundred and fifty-five degrees in order for it to open.

"Gram thought you'd like to use this to carry your pajamas in when you spend the night with her," my mother said as I rubbed my hand on the fuzzy ballerina.

I looked at my mother. "I can't spend the night at Gram's house. Uncle Rollie might be there." I put the case into the gift box and pushed it to her.

"No, Katy, Uncle Rollie is living at a hospital now. He will be there a long time, and he won't be able to leave until he's much better."

"He could take a bus to her house," I argued.

"No, his doctors won't let him."

This was fairly convincing information to me. I trusted doctors, policemen, and teachers almost as much as I trusted God. So, if my mother said the doctors wouldn't let Rollie out of the hospital, then it had to be almost true, about three hundred and fifty-five degrees almost true.

With reluctant relief and guarded excitement, I packed my ballerina suitcase several times over the years and spent many weekends with my sweet grandmother.

The library lights flashed on and off, announcing it was closing in ten minutes. I began to gather my belongings.

"Didn't we have fun when you spent the night?" Gram asked.

"Yes," I said and smiled.

"You were so funny the way you would beg me to stay up all night, even though you could barely keep your own eyes open." Gram laughed.

Ever since the ballerina suitcase, Gram and I had shared an unspoken agreement: the slightest mention of my uncle was forbidden. Which was why I never told Gram why I pleaded with her to stay up and watch one more movie with me. I am certain she knew that I hated sleeping in her guest room, the one with Rollie's belongings in it: Rollie's bed, his dresser, his clothes, and his closet. Our code of silence didn't allow me to tell Gram that the closet door waited for her to turn the lights off and leave Rollie's room before it would silently inch open wider and wider, taunting me to peek inside. And when it creaked in the darkness, mocking me and goading me to glance in its direction, I squeezed my eyes shut all night long, fearing it wasn't Rollie's clothes standing inside the closet but the real boogeyman, my uncle.

Together, Gram and I walked through the library turnstile and out into the cool autumn evening. The rain had stopped, and a light fog was beginning to roll in.

"So, why didn't you tell me about the closet door?" Gram asked.

"Rollie's?"

"No, the boogeyman's," Gram said sarcastically. She was standing

123

beside me, wrapping her ethereal arm around mine.

"I was afraid to tell you."

Gram thought this over for a moment as we stood at the top of the steps. The fog seemed to slowly gather around our legs.

"No matter, you've finally started to look inside."

"What?" I asked, wondering what Gram meant.

She tapped the folder of notes and medical records I held in my arms. "Maybe you're ready to look the boogeyman in the eyes and tell him you're not afraid anymore."

I glanced at the folder. A light breeze lifted its cover to the first pages of notes, where I'd written the words Breast Cancer.

Gram looked to both sides of the library steps. "Too bad there aren't any beautiful sphinxes here." She sighed.

"I always thought it strange the way you thought of them as beautiful," I said. "Like –"

"Like angels on a mission," said Gram.

I stared at her in disbelief.

"And I always thought it strange –" Gram smiled at me – "the way you thought the sphinxes were –"

"Terrifying. Like –"

"Like your sister and uncle?" Gram asked.

"Yes." I sighed wearily.

CHAPTER

FIVE

It was a sunny but chilly November afternoon when I found myself alone in South Pasadena not too far from Gram's old house. My car needed a tune-up, and the closest Subaru dealer was in South Pasadena. So, while the mechanics tuned up my car, I walked a few blocks away to Darleen's Diner and ordered breakfast.

After reading the entire newspaper and finishing my eggs and toast, I used the diner's pay phone to call the mechanic about my car. The mechanic said he had found a problem with "the rings," and he needed another three hours to fix the problem.

Three hours? I had waited two hours already. The thought of waiting another three hours seemed agonizing. When I asked if the ring problem could wait a week or two, the mechanic said he couldn't predict when the rings would completely blow out. I could drive the car for another thousand miles and the rings would be fine, or I could drive out of the lot that day and the car might break down on the freeway.

It was all he needed to say. I instantly envisioned my car stalled on the shoulder of the fast lane of the Pasadena Freeway while blasts of wind created by speeding trucks rocked my car back and forth. Or worse yet, some unscrupulous person could pull up behind me to rob and murder such a vulnerable and defenseless woman.

"Go ahead and fix the rings," I told the mechanic. Better to wait the three hours in South Pasadena than end up another tragic statistic of the Los Angeles freeways.

I hung up the pay phone, looked out the window of the diner, and wondered what I was going to do for the next three hours. It wasn't as if I didn't know this town. It was where Gram had lived, and it was a few miles from where I'd grown up. But there wasn't a whole lot to do in South Pasadena if one needed to idle away three hours.

I stepped outside into the warm sunshine and began walking up Main Street. From the looks of things, Gram's sleepy little town had not changed since the day she died. I strolled past the same shops Gram had always shopped at: Frank's Shoe Repair, Mike's Grocers, Betty's Women's Apparel, Mr. Fix-it, Ethel's Flower Shoppe. There were a few other stores with names not identifying the owner, like Pet's Delight, where Gram used to have her dog groomed, and Heavenly Desserts, the ice cream shop where Gram and I had always stopped for a cone.

Eventually, I came to the end of Main Street, where the Rialto Theater stood. I looked at my watch, calculated that it had taken me a whole fifteen minutes to walk the distance of Main Street, and knew that if I continued to wander up and down it for the next two hours and forty-five minutes, I'd begin to look a little suspicious, not just to the Main Street merchants but also to the local police.

The only other option was for me to walk three blocks east and end up at the library. Gram's library. The library with those heinous sphinxes that, more than likely, continued to stand sentry at its entrance. Ever since Gram's death, I had imagined the stony beasts lying in wait for me to appear without Gram by my side. No. I was not up to facing them alone and telling them they didn't scare me. Not on this particular day just forty-eight hours after my phone call to Dr. Chang.

A week earlier, Gram and I had sat in the Westwood Public Library with the piles of research I'd gathered on breast cancer. Since then, I'd reread all of the articles, especially the ones reporting the effects of pregnancy on recurring breast cancer. I chose to discount the studies warning women with histories of breast cancer not to become pregnant; instead, I built up hope from the case studies where pregnancies following the treatment of breast cancer had not adversely affected the outcome or recurrence of the cancer.

And then there was an astonishing article daring to suggest that pregnancy actually protected a woman against breast cancer because of the increase of a certain kind of hormone that did not bind well to the breast. If this were true, why hadn't Dr. Chang recommended that I get pregnant immediately? And stay pregnant? Maybe he didn't know about this finding. Maybe he would rethink his recommendation once he read the article. That's why I had called him two days prior.

127

Dr. Chang had been pleasant enough when I spoke to him on the phone, and he listened quietly with no interruptions as I summarized the results of the study.

When I finished, he was silent for a moment longer and then spoke in a cold, clinical, authoritative voice. "Katy, pregnancy acts as a protective factor only when it occurs early in a woman's childbearing life, before age twenty. At your age, thirty-eight, a first pregnancy and a history of a malignant breast cancer will only increase the risk of recurrence."

"But –"

"No buts, Katy. That study does not relate to your situation. Hormones did not cause your cancer. If I knew the source of your cancer, I would know what we were dealing with, and then we might be able to consider a pregnancy."

Why did he use the words "we might be able to consider a pregnancy?" Shouldn't the decision to become pregnant be my decision? Shouldn't the we making this decision be Tom and me? Not Dr. Chang and Tom and me?

When my cancer had first been found, I went along with Dr. Stone and Dr. Chang's advice – modified radical mastectomy – even after I'd pleaded for them to consider a new procedure that Tom and I had read about called a lumpectomy. And didn't I go along nice and easy a year later when a lump in my right breast appeared? "A second mastectomy is imperative," they'd said.

Suddenly, as I listened to Dr. Chang on the phone, a surge of militancy welled up inside of me, and I was about to tell him that I wasn't convinced he was right.

But then he quietly added, "Katy, wouldn't it be better to have no children than to have children with no mother?"

I leaned against the weathered brick wall of the Rialto Theater, took a deep breath and looked up Main Street once more. I kept hearing those words again and again. Wouldn't it be better to have no children than to have children with no mother? Why did Dr. Chang have to say that? For the past two days, those words had taunted me the way a bad song plays in your head and will not go away. No, I didn't feel strong enough to face the sphinxes at the entrance to Gram's library. They'd know how vulnerable I felt.

An older gentleman in a loose-fitting red jacket and black trousers walked out the theater door and placed a tent-like billboard a few feet in front of me. "PENNY SERENADE - 1:00 and 3:00" it read.

Penny Serenade? It couldn't be the same Penny Serenade that Gram and I had watched on late night television. Not the same Penny Serenade that had caused Gram and me to sob uncontrollably into bunches of Kleenex as we watched Irene Dunne and Cary Grant fall apart over the death of their adopted daughter. I stepped closer to see the poster on the billboard and, sure enough, there they were - Cary Grant and Irene Dunne, cheek to cheek, eyes gazing upward.

My watch read twelve thirty – a half-hour before the movie would start. "Is it too early to go inside?" I asked the gentleman who'd carried out the billboard.

"Noooo," he said merrily. "Go in now and you can have any seat you want. Never know when the crowds will start showing up." He gave a slight wink and chuckled as he motioned me over to the door.

129

I smiled and handed him a dollar fifty.

"Want any popcorn?" he asked, stepping up to the concession case.

I looked at the giant popper and watched popcorn explode every which way and then fall into a fluffy white mound at the bottom of the glass case. The distinct aroma of popcorn and melted butter wafted in my direction.

"No, thank you. I just ate at the diner."

The poor man already had a red and white striped cardboard container in his hand and had begun scooping up some of the popcorn. He stopped in midair and looked at me with hurt in his eyes.

"Well, maybe just a little box."

He perked up and immediately busied himself filling the carton with popcorn then adding butter to the top.

I glanced around the lobby. Nothing had changed since the years when Gram and I had come here for the newest motion pictures. The carpet, now worn to its threads, had the same purplish red tint to it, and I could tell the dark tan walls had not been washed or painted in decades.

"Eighty-five cents," sang the old man.

As we completed our transaction, two women who appeared to be well into their seventies arrived at the ticket booth.

"Here come the crowds," he said. With a lilt in his step, the old man walked over to his new customers.

I walked toward the entrance of the theater and was not surprised to see the same wood framed seats with the worn maroon cushions. Straight ahead, the big screen hid behind heavy, reddish-purple curtains. The row of braided tassels that ran the length of the curtain's hem, once thick and shiny-gold, no longer made the curtains appear regal and stately. Instead, due to clusters of missing tassels, the curtain's hem appeared to be smiling a long, almost toothless, not so regal smile. I looked up to the ceiling. Yes, they were there: specks of twinkling stars that had smiled down at Gram and me when the lights dimmed.

Feeling comforted by the memory, I walked partway down the aisle and took a first seat on my right. The springs from the inside of the dry, leathery cushion were doing their best to push through, but I didn't bother changing seats. I could tell it would be the same wherever I sat, so I leaned back and took a bite of my popcorn.

Then, as I leaned to my left in order to avoid one of the more prominent springs, I noticed a little old lady shuffle past me. She wore a flowery blue and green dress and daintily carried a white and green purse over her arm. As she looked from side to side trying to figure out which seat to take, I saw that she was wearing round earrings speckled with a kind of silver and blue glitter.

Just as I began to think this old woman's attire looked vaguely familiar, she turned around and said, "Oh, there you are!"

I was startled and was about to look behind me, thinking she must be talking to someone else, but then I realized that, of course, she was talking to me. This was my grandmother, wearing a favorite cotton dress.

"Did we have plans to meet here?" I don't know why I asked this, because none of Gram's other visits had been pre-scheduled and entered into an appointment book.

"Nooo," she said as she stood before me. "I didn't know we'd be going to the movies until a moment ago. Just like you." Gram motioned

131

with her left hand as she asked, "Could you move over, sweetie? You know how I like to have the aisle seat."

Vaguely aware of moving over, I watched Gram plunk down in her seat and clutch her purse close to her chest as if she were worried someone would snatch it from her.

"Gram, why would you worry about someone stealing your purse?"

"Well, why wouldn't I?" She motioned with her head toward the aisle as if the answer were obvious.

A man in his seventies walked down the aisle and sat three rows in front of us. He was followed by two middle-aged women, who sat together across the aisle from Gram and me.

"Because of them?" I giggled. "But how in the world could they take your purse if you're an angel?"

It was presumptuous of me to say this, since I'd not yet been able to even ask Gram if she were an angel. But I'd become increasingly convinced and comfortable with the idea that my grandmother was an angel sent to watch over me. I'd even searched the Bible for some kind of proof that angels were real, not figments of a crazy person's imagination. I'd memorized Psalm 91:11 and repeated it often: "For He will order His angels to protect you."

"Angel?" Gram stared at me with amused surprise.

Why did she say 'angel' with a questioning tone in her voice? Was Gram implying she was not an angel? And if she wasn't an angel, was I talking to the air like Uncle Rollie?

Before I could reply, Gram blurted out "Oh, cat's liver!"

"What?" I asked with surprise.

"Oh, I really hoped they would be showing An Affair to Remember today. I guess that's next week's feature."

"What?" I repeated, trying to remember what I'd wanted to ask her.

"An Affair to Remember. You know it's my favorite Cary Grant movie," Gram said.

Gram and I had watched all the old movies together. Many times while I was in junior high and high school, she'd call me up in the middle of the week to tell me the TV Guide listed one of our favorites, such as William Powell and Myrna Loy playing in The Thin Man on Channel Nine's Saturday Night Movie of the Week.

"I thought Notorious was your favorite Cary Grant movie," I said.

"Oh." She paused in thought. "That's right. An Affair to Remember is my favorite Deborah Kerr movie," Gram twittered while fiddling with her purse some more.

"Are you looking for your glasses?" I asked. I was fairly sure angels didn't need to wear glasses, but then neither would a figment of my imagination.

"Of course not," Gram said, casting me an insulting glance. "I'm looking for a Kleenex."

"Do you have a cold?" Real angels probably didn't need Kleenex either.

Gram looked up from her purse and furrowed her brow. "I want to be prepared for when the sad parts begin. You know I cry harder at this picture than any other."

I opened my mouth to say something just as the lights of the theater began to dim.

"Shhh," Gram said excitedly as she patted my hand. "The movie's about to start, and I don't want to miss a thing."

Gram was a fine one to shhh me. She was never able to sit and watch a movie without commenting on every little thing. "Did you know Merle Oberon was married four times?" she would ask as Lawrence Oliver held a dying Merle Oberon in his arms. I was willing to bet that Gram's movie-watching habits weren't going to be any different now.

Together we watched the opening scene of Penny Serenade as Irene Dunne placed a record on an old Victrola.

"Your grandfather and I had one of those," Gram said referring to the Victrola.

"I know," I whispered.

"You Were Meant for Me" began to play.

"Shhh, shhh," Gram motioned again with her hand.

"You were meant for me," the Victrola serenaded.

"I was meant for you," Gram crooned along.

I was comforted to see that the two ladies across the aisle paid no attention to Gram, nor did the old man three rows ahead of us turn to look our way with annoyance.

Soon the music and Gram's singing faded into the next scene where Cary Grant's faithful friend Applejack appeared.

"Wasn't Edgar Buchanan a marvelous actor?" Gram whispered.

"Who?"

"Applejack!" she said, as if I should have known the name of the actor playing Applejack.

"Oh," I said.

"I used to think your Uncle Rollie and Edgar Buchanan looked alike." Gram sighed.

I couldn't believe my ears. Edgar Buchanan was a middle-aged man, short and chubby, with a kindly air about him. And Uncle Rollie, well...

"After Rollie was released from Camarillo State Mental Hospital, that is," Gram added.

"Maybe," I said, trying to remember what my uncle looked like after he'd been proclaimed mentally healthy by the psychiatrists at that hospital.

Uncle Rollie's outward appearance had changed quite a lot since Halloween – the Halloween before he was taken to Camarillo State Hospital. I had hoped he would remain there forever, but he hadn't, and when he was released, he was allowed to take up residence once again in his old bedroom at Gram's house.

I remembered the first time I saw him after his release. I didn't recognize him. He wasn't wearing the same black jeans and the pointy black boots. Instead, he wore an old, brown tweed coat and a pair of brown wool trousers that had been my grandfather's. Rollie had gained a lot of weight, and his hair, no longer greased back, had taken on a reddish-brown hue; the fire in it was gone.

He didn't walk with the same contemptuous stride either. Instead, he plodded along from side to side as if he was tired, as if he could barely get his legs to move. His cheeks were fuller and blotchy, his teeth had yellowed quite a bit, and the insolent look on his face was gone. No longer did a cigarette dangle from the side of his mouth; no longer did Uncle Rollie nod his head and squint his eyes in an intimidating manner.

His eyelids drooped slightly, and the brown pupils that used to stare through me were clouded. It was as if Uncle Rollie had metamorphosed into another being, another soul, someone harmless and weak.

My mother tried to convince me that Uncle Rollie was different now that he took medicine to keep him healthy.

"What if he forgets to take his medicine?" I asked her.

"He won't forget, because he wants to stay healthy," she told me.

Well, Uncle Rollie's changed appearance and demeanor may have fooled everyone in my family, but it didn't fool me. I knew it was only a facade. Rollie's darkness had not been exorcized, it lay hidden deeper within him, waiting for the right moment to surface again.

I considered Applejack on the big screen a little longer.

"See how much they look alike?" Gram pushed me to agree with her.

"At least Uncle Rollie and Edgar Buchanan were both short and chubby," I whispered to appease Gram.

"I think Rollie stayed in the hospital too long," Gram said softly. "He never was the same after that visit."

The voice coming from the movie's Victrola overlapped with Gram's words. "It might seem you're near to me, dear to me. No, it's just a memory."

I said nothing as Irene Dunne, sitting at a picnic table, read her fortune from a fortune cookie. "You will get your wish - a baby," she read.

Suddenly, I looked at Gram and recalled how on her first angelic visit with me, she'd said she had come to help me remember something. Maybe this was why we were sitting together in a theater on a weekday afternoon. Had she wanted me to remember the fortune in Irene Dunne's hand and see it as a sign for me? Was this Gram's way of telling me that I would get my wish – a baby?

Gram looked at me with tears in her eyes. "It's so sad." She dabbed her eyes with her bent finger. "She's going to find out she'll never be able to have children of her own. Remember?"

I felt as if my lungs had been punctured and all the air was slowly escaping as the voice of Irene Dunn lamented, "The thing I really wanted, I'm never going to have."

But not long after that, Gram motioned toward the screen. Applejack and Irene were sitting at a table. "We ought to have a kid around," Applejack told her. He meant Irene and Cary ought to have a kid, but because Applejack was part of their family, he included himself as part of the "we."

"I'm talking about adopting one," Applejack continued. "Can get some pretty good ones that way," he added.

Gram bent her head towards me as if to say, "Are you listening?"

Ahh, this was the reason I was watching Penny Serenade with my dead grandmother. Well, maybe she didn't know that Tom and I had discussed the possibility of adoption many times, but we had decided it was too uncertain, too risky.

"People in those days didn't have to worry about the same kinds of problems with adoptions you have to worry about these days," I whispered into Gram's ear.

"Oh?" she whispered from the side of her mouth without looking at me.

"Today a lot of pregnant women take drugs and drink all through their pregnancies and then put their babies up for adoption. Women didn't do those things in the old days, so a person didn't have to worry about mental retardation and all sorts of physical and psychological problems with adoptive children." My whispering had turned up in volume, and I realized I sounded a little hysterical.

"Interesting," Gram said, keeping her eyes on the screen.

Why did it feel as if I was arguing with Gram? She hadn't suggested that Tom and I adopt. She was just happy that Cary Grant and Irene Dunne were adopting a child.

I collected myself and focused my attention back on Cary and Irene as they sat at a table across from the woman who ran the adoption agency. Her name was Miss Oliver, and she looked like an old battle-ax. She wore a black dress, her jet-black hair was pulled tightly into a bun on the top of her head, and the pince-nez that sat on the bridge of her nose appeared to squeeze the color out of her face. Miss Oliver seemed all together unsympathetic toward Irene and Cary, leading the audience to believe that she would never consider them as adoptive parents until a few scenes later when Miss Oliver placed a baby into the arms of Irene Dunne.

Tears welled up in my eyes, and I looked at Gram. She was slowly shaking her head as a stream of tears rolled down her cheeks.

A new record and a new scene appeared on screen. Baby Trina had grown into a little girl.

"This is one of my favorite scenes." Gram sighed.

I watched as a young Trina helped Applejack prepare a surprise birthday party for Irene Dunne.

"Your sister and Uncle Rollie were close like that for a while." Gram smiled over at me.

"Wendy and Rollie were close like what?" I asked.

"Like Trina and her Uncle Applejack," Gram answered.

I looked at the screen and back at Gram. "Wendy and Rollie were never..." but my voice trailed off as I recalled the first family dinner Rollie had attended after his release from Camarillo Hospital.

Wendy had been only six years old, but she was cuter than ever with her freckled nose and long red hair tied into two pigtails. She still had that horrifying temper, but when she wasn't angry, she was charming, a gregarious child who befriended anyone who came her way.

I used to watch with a kind of detached interest each time Wendy paused along the sidewalk to chat with an old man waiting at the bus stop or when she left her seat at the local malt shop for a short discussion with the young couple at the counter. She always walked away with a token – a piece of bubble gum, a nickel, something her newest victim had in a pocket or a purse. It was almost like a game to her – I'll charm you and then I'll con you – as if she calculated what little prize she could get for her time. But it seemed harmless enough; she was just a little girl. I didn't see how she could get hurt by it, that is, until Uncle Rollie came back into our lives.

That first family dinner when Gram and Rollie arrived at the front door, Wendy ran up to Rollie, took his hand and dragged him to the backyard so he could push her on the swing. I watched from the kitchen window as she sang, "Toyland, Toyland, beautiful girl and boy land," while she and the swing swayed up and down. Rollie, wearing

Grandpa's tweed coat and trousers, stood to the side of the swing gazing numbly into air. I could tell he was listening to my sister, and I worried that Wendy thought she could con something out of this uncle of ours.

I shuddered, trying to shake off the memory of those family dinners, while on the screen ahead of me, I heard little Trina tell her parents and Applejack about wanting to sing in the school choir.

"I remember your church choir." Gram smiled.

"Mmm," I said faintly.

Then I recalled another family dinner that same year, when my mother had asked Gram if she would drive Sam and me to our choir practice the next day. Gram had said she was happy to do the favor and wondered if we minded having Uncle Rollie come along, since he'd never heard us sing. In a flash, I had darted a look at my mother that said, Don't let him come! But she ignored me.

The next day after school, I found myself sitting beside Sam in the back seat of Gram's car. Rollie, wearing one of Grandpa's long sleeve shirts and a pair of Grandpa's beige cotton pants, sat stiffly in the front seat beside Gram. I wondered what had happened to all of Rollie's old clothes. Why was he always wearing Grandpa's things?

As I pondered over this, Sam kept talking away to Uncle Rollie. He was always doing that, talking to Rollie as if he were a normal person. I didn't worry when Sam talked to Rollie, because it seemed Sam's motivation was different from Wendy's. I knew Sam didn't want anything from Rollie except to make him feel accepted.

"I threw a curve ball at Tommy Hutchinson at lunch time today and struck him out," Sam told Rollie from the back seat of Gram's car.

140

"Very good." Rollie responded with no enthusiasm and only a sideways glance in Sam's direction.

"You ever hit a guy with a hard ball?" Sam asked.

"Uh, no," Rollie answered.

"Well, I did, just the other day. Didn't mean to, but Joe Whiting leaned into home plate too far and got hit by my fastball. Right on the noggin."

"Mm." Rollie pondered for a second. "High fast ball."

"Yeah." Sam chuckled. "It wasn't my best one."

Rollie looked back at Sam and sort of smiled.

"It hurt him too." Sam shook his head.

"Mmm," Rollie murmured.

The two of them kept talking like that until we drove into the church parking lot. The second Gram stopped the car, I jumped out and joined the other children who were already gathered in the chapel. As I took my place in the first row of the choir pews, right next to Betty Edwards and Tina Brown, I saw Sam direct Gram and Rollie to the front seats, then take his place in the choir, two rows behind me.

There were about thirty children in the choir, ranging in age from eight to twelve, and while there were a few good singers, like Sam, who sometimes sang a solo, we usually sounded pretty bad. Mr. Dew, our choir director, said that we mumbled our words and sang out of sync. Which was why he spent a lot of time during rehearsals making us say the words to each hymn without singing them. "Walking through the song," he called it.

The day that Gram and Rollie watched us was no different than any other practice day.

"Everyone," Mr. Dew said to the chattering group of children, "let's slowly walk through the first two stanzas of 'In the Garden.' Page two hundred and fifty-nine."

We all began speaking. "I come to the gar-den a-lone, while the dew is still on the ros-es..."

"No, no," Mr. Dew called out. "You must enunciate! Like this: While the-dew is still on-the ros-es."

My two friends and I giggled at the image of our Mr. Dew as the dew on the roses. It helped us to walk through the same two lines ten more times before Mr. Dew allowed us to move on to the next two stanzas, walking through them, of course.

As we began to carefully speak the words, "And the voice I hear," a single voice, deep and robust, arose from the congregational pews, singing, "And-the voice I hear, fall-ing on-my ear..."

Everyone, including Mr. Dew, stopped to look. There beside Gram stood my uncle with his chest puffed out and one hand holding a hymnal. His other hand swayed in the air.

"The son of God dis-clo-ses," Rollie's voice echoed from the walls of the church.

Children started to giggle and poke each other, and Mr. Dew, mouth wide open, squinted his eyes trying to see if he knew the chubby male who had interrupted choir practice.

Gram patted Rollie's arm, trying to get him to stop, but Rollie paid her no attention. He took a deep breath, and I could tell he intended to continue with the hymn.

I was prepared to die at that very moment and might have done so if I hadn't heard a second voice join Uncle Rollie's to sing the refrain of "In the Garden."

"And he walks with me, and he talks with me," sang Rollie and the voice that definitely was coming from a pew behind me.

I looked over my shoulder two rows and saw Sam with his head held high, throwing his voice out in unison with my uncle's.

"...and he tells me I am his own," they sang together.

By then, I was too shocked to bother dying and only wondered what could possibly happen next. That's when my brother jabbed his friends, David and Mitch. They must have thought it was a game, because both boys stood up and joined in with Sam and Rollie to finish the refrain, "And the joy we share as we tar-ry there, none oth-er has ev-er known."

This memory of my brother was almost too much for me to recall. I tried to focus harder on the movie.

"You know," Gram said. "Watching you and Sam at choir practice is what gave Rollie a renewed interest in singing and playing the piano."

I tried not to pay attention to Gram.

"Remember Rollie's Mini Concert?" Gram asked.

"No!" I snapped. I desperately did not want to remember.

"Oh, Katy, how could you forget," she pushed.

"I remember it," I said coldly, as the thought of Rollie's Mini Concert brought on a familiar wave of nausea.

A month after the infamous choir practice that Gram and Rollie had attended, an invitation with my grandmother's handwriting had arrived in the mail. It formally invited the whole family to her house for "a tea and special performance by Roland Carlyle Welborn," who would be performing original vocal and instrumental compositions.

My mother had soon discovered that Gram hadn't invited just our immediate family members but all her neighbors and friends and anyone she knew, including the grocer, her cleaning lady, and her hairdresser. The invitation said the dress for the evening was formal, black tie optional.

I tried every excuse I could think of not to attend the event, but my parents accepted none of them, and I found myself two weeks later on a Sunday afternoon crowded into Gram's living room with people I knew and didn't know, everyone dressed in suits and elegant dresses, all of whom had come to the special event as a favor to Gram. A woman in a black and white maid's outfit served finger sandwiches, while a gentleman in a black suit served tea and coffee. Gram flitted around the room, nervously chatting with everyone.

"Nellie, what will Roland be playing for us today?" I heard one woman ask my grandmother.

"He hasn't told me a thing. In fact, Roland wouldn't let me come near the music room these last two weeks. He said he wants me to be as surprised as everyone else."

"Isn't that sweet," the other woman patted Gram on the hand and moved on.

I hadn't been at the gathering long before Uncle Rollie peeked around the corner of the dining room and motioned to Sam. Something was up, and I prayed that Sam wasn't going to sing along with Rollie like he'd done at choir practice.

A few minutes later, Gram dangled a tiny bell in her hand and nervously tried to get everyone's attention. "Today's concert will be held here in the living room. So please find a comfortable seat, as it is about to begin."

Once the room quieted down and everyone was seated, Gram scampered to the dining room entrance and delicately called, "Roland, I think we are ready."

Moments later, a heavy rolling sound came from the music room. It gradually became louder and seemed to be approaching the living room. Just as everyone leaned in the direction of the dining area, trying to see what was making all the noise, Sam's back appeared. He was pulling hard on something large and heavy, covered by several white bed sheets. Seconds later, Rollie appeared wearing Grandpa's old tuxedo. He was pushing the other end of the rolling object.

It didn't take a genius to figure out that Gram's upright piano was under the sheets. The big question was, why had Rollie covered it up? Everyone watched quietly as Rollie and my brother centered the piano in front of the group.

Then Sam took two steps forward. "Ladies and gentlemen," he began, "my uncle has worked very hard these last few weeks on a special surprise for his mother, Cornelia Welborn, and he would like to present it to her now."

I watched as brows on foreheads furrowed and heads tilted slightly in Gram's direction. Gram blushed at the attention, and I could tell that she was uncomfortable.

Rollie remained stiff and silent, but the moment Sam stepped back to his end of the piano, Rollie raised both hands high into the air, paused for a second, and then threw them onto the sheets. Sam did the same, and together they whisked the sheets away, revealing what had once been Gram's beautiful, oak upright piano.

Gasps of horror from family members filled the room, and Gram put her hand to her mouth to stifle an uncontrolled groan. Her beautiful piano was no longer stained in a rich, reddish brown. It had been painted pure white, and it looked utterly atrocious. Uneven streaks of paint ran every which way. Even the foot pedals had been painted.

"Mother, for you," Rollie said as he swept his right hand down and bowed in her direction.

"Oh...oh, my," Gram stumbled. "This...this is such a...a...surprise, dear." Then she stood up, walked over to Rollie, and gave him a timid hug.

The guests who didn't know Gram very well, like the grocer and the hairdresser, the ones who didn't know that the upright had been a wedding gift to Gram from Grandpa, were the ones who politely clapped their hands to acknowledge Rollie's wonderful surprise. I suppose it's the reason she gathered herself together and turned to the audience.

With her face flushed and drops of perspiration building on her forehead, she spoke. "I don't know how many times over the years I complained about how dark the music room seemed. Well." Gram breathed out. "Well." She paused again. "Well, won't this help to lighten it up a bit?" Gram gave a slight giggle before going back to her seat.

Sam looked at Rollie, reached into his pocket, and pulled out a crumpled piece of paper.

"Tonight, Roland Carlyle Welborn has planned a second surprise. For his niece, Wendy Eugenia Welborn, he has composed his own original adaptation of the musical Babes in Toyland, which he has titled Wendy in Toyland."

Wendy squealed and clasped her hands together with utter excitement. People in the room made approving sounds of ooooos and ahhhhhs, and I...I felt as if something had punched me hard in the stomach. I was paralyzed as I watched Sam look at Rollie, nod his head, and then take a seat next to Gram.

Suddenly, Rollie flung the tails of Grandpa's worn tuxedo into the air and plopped onto the piano bench. His hands slowly, dramatically landed on the black and white keys, and he began to play a variation on the theme from Wendy's favorite song, a variation that sounded like a morbid hymn.

Wendy didn't look too happy at first, and I knew the reason why. Her song had been bastardized.

But then, as my sister's face grew red with frustration, Rollie began sadly warbling out the words, "Toyland! Toyland! Wendy's girl and boy land, while you dwell within it, you are ever happy then."

The red left Wendy's face. She rose from her seat and began swaying to Rollie's slow, melodic trills.

"Childhood's joy land, mystic merry Wendy land," he continued.

People in the audience smiled kindly with more ooos and ahhhs as Wendy joined Rollie at the piano. Together my sister and uncle sang, "Once you pass its borders you can never return again."

In the darkness of the Rialto Theater, I heard Gram whisper, "Wasn't it sweet of Rollie to compose a special rendition of Toyland for Wendy?"

"Not really," I said under my breath.

"Oh, I know it wasn't very good, but I was happy to see Rollie develop a special relationship with your sister."

Maybe Gram wouldn't have been so happy about Wendy and Rollie's relationship if I'd told her about the dream I had the night of Rollie's concert. Nightmares were not something new to me, but increasingly horrific nightmares had started a year earlier, about the time my family moved into our new home five miles from Gram's.

It had been in my new bedroom and my new bed where I had dreamt of tidal waves swallowing me and of ferocious gargoyle-like beasts in pursuit with open mouths. Most of those nightmares could be comforted away by my mother's soothing voice. But the one I'd had the night of Rollie's concert could never be hushed away. It would return when I least expected it with the power to dismantle what little peace I had left in my soul.

The dream would always begin happily as an eerie melody lured me down a tree-lined street to a house resembling Gram's. There were many little shrubs like the ones Rollie had planted in Gram's yard, except they were all brown and dead. I noticed that in the middle of the yard, lying on the ground, was a very big, very white cow, and as I looked closer, I could tell that he was sick. His sagging white skin heaved in and out, outlining every bone in his rib cage, and he painfully moaned the eerie melody coming from the house. I wanted to give him some food from my pocket, but as I approached him with my hand held out, he began to metamorphose into a huge white snake.

I would start to run, but the eerie music would be joined by a little girl's voice that sounded faintly familiar, so I would walk up the steps to the front door. I'd hesitate only a moment to look back at the snake. He had grown thicker and longer and was beginning to surround the entire outside of the house as if to strangle it.

The little girl's voice became clearer to me; it was Wendy's. Then the curtain from the living room window moved. I noticed the front door was open, but it was too dark for me to see anything, so I stepped inside the house.

The moment I walked through the doorway, I knew I was inside Gram's living room. The music began to play louder and seemed to be coming from a back room, but as I tried to follow it, Wendy's voice sobbed the words, "Toyland, Toyland —" Suddenly she stopped and cried out, "Katy. Katy!"

I would panic and run into a hallway, trying to follow her voice. The music grew louder, and then I heard Wendy's voice again, this time begging me, "Katy, save me...save me." I'd be crying as I dashed into an empty room. It was Gram's bedroom, but all her furniture was gone. The music was coming from another room. It was coming from a pounding, threatening, thundering piano.

I'd run down the long hall and throw open a door. There, in a white tuxedo standing at the white piano beating both hands on its keys, was Uncle Rollie. He would laugh pitilessly and, with an evil look on his face, he would sing over and over again, "Once you pass its borders, you can never return again!"

I didn't want to go inside, but Wendy's voice called to me again, this time with pain like I'd never heard before. I looked at the door behind Rollie and knew it was his closet door. It was open just enough for me to hear Wendy's tormented voice coming from inside. I didn't want to look, but before I could turn my head, Rollie threw open the door and revealed my sister writhing on the floor. All of Wendy's skin had been torn from her body. She had no face, no eyes, and as she lifted up her red, bloody arms, reaching out to me, I'd let out a horrifying, blood curdling scream. And then I would wake up.

Music from Penny Serenade lifted me from the memory of my nightmare.

"This is so sad," Gram whimpered. She was handing me a tissue, and I realized that tears were streaming down my cheeks.

I stared at the screen as Miss Oliver opened a letter from Irene Dunne telling of a mysterious illness that took the life of Trina. Miss Oliver and Gram cried over the loss of the child. I cried, too, but not for Trina. My tears were for the sister I'd lost a long time ago.

Gram patted my hand. "Remember, dear. It turns out happy."

She was right. It did turn out happy for Irene Dunne and Cary Grant. They survived the loss of Trina and adopted a new baby boy.

The end credits began flashing on the screen.

"Oh, what a wonderful story!" Gram sighed. "Aren't you glad we saw it?"

"I don't know. I'm not sure I like watching sad movies anymore."

"It wasn't so sad," Gram said.

"They lost their little girl."

"But everything turned out happily ever after."

"Yes. Isn't it too bad that everything turns out happily ever after only in the movies," I mumbled.

"In real life, too," Gram said.

I wanted to ask Gram if she thought everything in real life had turned out happily ever after for my sister and uncle. I wanted to know if she thought everything in my life – the threat of recurring cancer, the hope of having a child – would turn out happily ever after. But the lights to the theater turned on, and when I looked at Gram's empty seat, I knew I'd have to ask her another time.

CHAPTER

SIX

"Katy, don't water that tree or it will grow some more." It was my neighbor, Heddy. She was calling from her sewing room window, the window facing our front yard, the one where her sewing machine and table rested. It was where Heddy sat, day and night, so she wouldn't miss all the important things that took place in our quiet, boring cul-de-sac. Important things, like noticing how the mailman arrived an hour later than usual or how Bennett Miller, the neighbor whose house sat between Heddy's and mine, swept out his garage on Sunday.

It was impossible to go out the front door without Heddy calling to me, which wouldn't have been so bad, except she then hurried out her door and over to our house to offer endless monologues on things I should be doing, things other neighbors should be doing, things her own grown-up children should be doing, ingredients that should have been included in the latest recipe she ate at her church circle meeting, and all the minutia that had taken place on our street over the last thirty-five years.

When Tom and I first moved to our house, I was slightly concerned at having Heddy for a neighbor. I'd never been so watched, so observed in my whole life. Feeling hopelessly trapped, I quickly developed hostage-like behaviors and worked out elaborate strategies for escaping the house without being caught by Heddy. It was futile, though, and eventually I surrendered, deciding that in the long run, it would be much easier to lend her my ear for a while each day. I didn't even mind it anymore.

"Why wouldn't you want that tree to grow?"

"Gram!" I looked behind me and found my grandmother sitting on one of the three brick steps leading to our front porch. Then I heard Heddy's front door slam shut, and I knew she was on her way over. Frantically I looked from Gram to Heddy's yard and back to Gram.

"Don't worry. She can't see me."

"Are you sure? Heddy sees everything." I looked across the yard. Heddy was storming across her lawn.

"So, why don't you want the tree to grow?" Gram demanded.

"I do, but Heddy thinks it's too big for the spot it's in. She's probably right."

Heddy marched closer and closer as if on an important mission.

Gram cocked her head around the porch to get a better look at Heddy. Panic thickened in my throat.

"Well, won't she think the driveway is going to grow too much too?" asked Gram pointing to the hose I was carrying in my hands. In my nervousness, I'd stopped paying attention to the plants I was watering and was giving the driveway a good soaking. Heddy would probably have something to say about that.

Heddy unlatched the catch and opened the gate to the white picket fence, not waiting for an invitation to enter the front yard. She never did. "Back Andy! Back!" Heddy barked at my brown and charcoal colored Airedale, who had slowly sauntered up to her with his wagging tail.

Andy had been with Tom and me for ten years and was an important part of our lives. And due to Andy's tail-wagging insistence, Tom and I never skipped taking a long, leisurely walk each evening. But within the last year, Andy had started to show signs of his age. He was walking slower, sleeping more, and having a harder time getting up, so it upset me whenever Heddy yelled at him as if he were an unruly, disobedient mongrel.

"Come here, Andy," I softly commanded, reaching for his collar with my free hand to keep him from sniffing in the vicinity of Heddy's crotch.

"You know what I've told you to do to stop him from being so rude," Heddy reprimanded me.

"What's that?" Gram asked from the steps.

Without thinking I looked behind me in Gram's direction and answered, "She thinks I should kick Andy hard in the throat with my knee every time he sniffs there."

Heddy looked over by the steps to see who I was talking to. "Kick him once and he'll never sniff there again." Then Heddy stomped over to my oak tree.

"Good grief! He'd never breath again, either," Gram huffed.

"Heddy, you know I'm never going to kick Andy in the throat." I bent down to give Andy a hug around his neck and to kiss the top of his head. He gratefully licked my cheek before sauntering over to sit beside Gram.

"I say, tell your neighbor to take a bath before coming over here," said Gram. "Maybe dogs wouldn't find her privates so interesting."

Andy was now lying beside Gram, looking somewhat redeemed, as if he'd heard Gram, as if he knew she was there. As if he could see her.

"I can't tell her to take a bath," I blurted under duress.

"Andy's going to have a bath?" Heddy asked, standing under the elm tree.

"Um, yes." I walked over to the faucet and turned off the hose.

"Well, that's not going to stop him," said Heddy. She was examining a large, Y-shaped branch on the tree and then pointed at it. "Next big wind and this one will blow off. Then you'll have real trouble. It falls on the Bakers' roof and they'll sue."

"Do you think?" I looked upward, trying to figure out which way the branch would fall if a big enough wind came along. "It looks pretty sturdy to me, Heddy."

"That tree never should have been planted there in the first place. It's what I told Mrs. Thomas thirty years ago, but she didn't listen."

"Katy, tell this woman to go home and badger someone else," Gram called out. "Does anyone live in that house with her?"

"Olive and Cora," I said. Olive and Cora were Heddy's sister and aunt, both old maids.

Olive was a tall, sixty-seven-year-old woman, and I'd say she was fairly attractive for her age if it weren't for the inordinate amount of gray and white nose hairs protruding from each nostril. You'd have thought that with all the opinions Heddy had, she'd have one about Olive's nose and nag her into trimming the hair.

Olive probably wouldn't have paid attention anyway, because she wasn't the kind of person to care about her appearance. She spent most of her days working on their yard and vegetable garden, which was a pretty sizeable one. A couple times a week, she'd appear at my front door with a few ears of corn or some broccoli, whatever the produce of the month seemed to be. It was fresh and excellent, and I would have appreciated the gesture even more were it not always accompanied by Olive's pontifications on the most recent topics she'd read in her Encyclopedia Britannica.

"We thought you and Tom would enjoy some fresh cauliflower tonight," Olive would say to me.

"Thank you, Olive."

"Bet you don't know how many Crusades there were," Olive would then egg me on.

"Crusades?" I would ask, remembering that she had been reading the "C" encyclopedia. I would quickly try to calculate how much time this topic would take.

"Eight of them. Did you know...?"

And Olive was off and running on this subject for the next twenty minutes unless my telephone rang. It was not always a sure thing that the sound of the phone would rescue me either, since Olive was hard of hearing. Even if I didn't lift my finger and point in the direction of the phone, she wouldn't necessarily understand and would just keep on talking.

Once I was so desperate to end one of Olive's encyclopedic lessons, I pretended the phone was ringing. I figured that if she was hard of hearing, she wouldn't know the difference. So, I said something like, "Oops, there's my phone."

But Olive held her hand to her ear, furrowed her brow – which caused the nose hairs to scrunch up around her nostrils – and then shook her head. "Can't be yours," she said.

And then there was Cora. Of the three, she was the least loquacious and demanding of my time. Cora had raised Heddy and Olive when they were children and had lived with them ever since, even when Heddy was married. Cora must have thought of them as teenagers, because she was always saying things like, "I keep telling the kids to go on a vacation and not worry about my heart."

The first couple of times Cora mentioned the kids, I didn't know who she was talking about, but I eventually realized she was talking about Heddy and Olive, who, in case she hadn't noticed, had become senior citizens.

Cora and I had something in common, though. We both wore size ten shoes. She was the only other woman I knew who had feet that big. Except Princess Di, but she didn't count, because I didn't know her personally. Cora was kind of funny about this, too. Once when I'd mentioned I was off to buy some black dress shoes, she asked what size I needed. Usually when someone asked me this, I would tell them a size eight or nine, but I figured this eighty-four-year-old woman would not think less of me if I told her the truth.

"Size ten," I told her.

"Size ten!" Cora shrieked. "You don't need shoes. You need boxes!"

I laughed so hard I almost spit my teeth out. I thought it was a pretty quick response for someone her age, but then she confided in me that she, too, had size ten feet.

"Bunions," Cora had whispered to explain her matching deformity, as if we were two peas in a pod.

Now whenever Cora saw me, she would end our conversations with the promise: "When I'm gone, I'm going to leave you all my shoes. They're real comfortable, too." She usually paused for a moment before she whispered with the left half of her lips, "Don't tell Heddy or Olive I told you." And then she would give me a little wink.

"What about Olive and Cora?" Heddy inquired while moving from under the shade of the elm tree to the flowerbed near the front porch.

"Olive and Cora?" I asked.

"You said Olive and Cora twice!" Heddy sounded irritated. "What do you want to know about them?" She began studying the flowers, and I knew she was looking to see if I had cleaned out the dead leaves.

"Oh, um." I made a face at Gram. "Are they home right now?"

"Cora's in bed. Olive's in the garden. Could you use another artichoke?"

"Well, I still have one left over from Saturday's batch."

"Better throw that one out."

"I thought you hated artichokes," Gram called out to me.

"I still do," I said.

"You still do what?" Heddy asked with some irritation.

"Ah, I still do," I stuttered. "I still do have an artichoke."

"Well, you should have eaten it when it was fresh. I'll have Olive bring you a fresh one."

"No, really," I pleaded. I worried that Olive might have started the "D" encyclopedia.

"Say," Heddy interrupted. "Did you see that the young couple the next street over had another baby?"

"I saw the pink windsock hanging from their porch. It said, It's a girl." I smiled thinking it was a nice way for new parents to announce their baby's arrival.

"Wasn't it just a month ago the couple across the street from them had a baby boy?" Heddy asked. She was bending over one of my gardenia bushes, Gram's and my favorite flower in the whole world, the whole universe.

Gram used to have an entire wall of gardenias planted outside her dining room window, and in the spring, the sweet fragrance of the gardenias could just about knock a person over. When they were in full bloom, it looked like a silky ribbon wrapped around the base of her house. That's when Gram would snip a few of the creamy-white flowers and place them in a delicate, cut glass candy dish, and within minutes, her entire house would be filled with the pungent aroma of those two or three gardenias. Now that I had my own gardenia bushes, I did the same thing with the exact same candy dish.

Heddy began plucking away the dead and dried up flowers I'd left on the branches. She's always telling me that I should be doing this or else the bushes won't have room for the new buds. I figure there's no need for me to do it, since she does it for me.

"I think they did have a baby boy." I smiled thinking how nice it must be for the two mothers to have each other nearby with babies so close in age. I didn't know them, but when Andy and I would go on walks around the neighborhood, I'd see the two women, both in their late twenties, with their young children sitting on their front lawns. We'd exchange hellos, but that's about all. They belonged to an exclusive club. Without a baby in your arms, you couldn't be admitted.

"Katy, you and Tom have to work harder, or all the babies around here are going to be grown before you have one." Heddy crunched the dead flowers with her hands and dropped them into a pile next to the steps. Then she sat down. Right beside Gram, practically on top of Gram's lap.

Stunned, I looked at Gram as she lifted both shoulders and made a funny face. I giggled.

"I'm serious, Katy. You've been talking about wanting children ever since you moved here." Heddy rubbed her hands on her housedress to wipe away the remaining fragments of dead flowers. "You're not getting any younger, you know."

Gram slowly turned her head in an exaggerated motion to look directly into Heddy's face. She clearly could not believe what she was hearing.

I'd had my second mastectomy a month after Tom and I moved into our house, thirteen and a half months after the first one, but I hadn't wanted Heddy to know about the cancer, so I had told her I was recovering from shoulder surgery. I hoped it would explain why I couldn't move my right arm very well.

During one of my first conversations with Heddy, she had asked if Tom and I planned on having children. I'd said that we did. I'd felt it was okay to say this since the doctors had told us to wait three years, and we only had twenty-two and a half more months left, less than two years. Back then I'd been so hopeful about still starting a family, and I hadn't let it occur to me that Dr. Chang would change his opinion.

Every couple of months, Heddy would inquire about the progress Tom and I were making, but I would brush off her questions with light-handed comments that tended to end the discussion.

"I guess I am getting older. But Heddy, we're working on it," I said, even though we really weren't.

"You know —" Heddy paused and put her index finger to her lips as if she was thinking something through. "Charlene and her husband had a boy the first time, and they really wanted their next child to be a girl. So, you know what Charlene did?"

I shook my head. "No."

"Well, she found out about these special techniques and positions you use when you make love. Certain techniques if you want a boy and certain other ones if you want a girl. I thought they were crazy, but they got their little girl."

Charlene was Heddy's daughter, and I was pretty sure she wouldn't appreciate having this information broadcast by her mother. But then, there was a lot I knew about Charlene that I didn't think she would like me to know. I was always a little uncomfortable about Heddy giving me such personal details about anyone, but I'd never known how to stop her.

I nodded at Heddy, not sure where this line of thinking was leading her.

"I think I'll ask Charlene for those babymaking techniques and write them down for you and Tom."

Gram, whose mouth was now wide open with her head tilted to one side, continued to stare into Heddy's face.

"Oh, I don't –" I started to say.

"You don't have a preference, do you?" asked Heddy.

"Hmm?" I grimaced.

"About it being a boy or a girl. You might as well use both techniques. Better chance of getting pregnant."

"Good Godfrey," twittered Gram. "Am I hearing right?"

"Well, um, Heddy. I don't think you should ask Charlene. But thanks anyway." I swallowed.

"It's no problem. Charlene will be happy to help out. She's a nurse, you know, so she gets all this secret inside information from the doctors in the hospital."

"Heddy, I ah –"

"I'll bet you and Tom aren't using the right lovemaking position. Probably using the same one over and over, huh? You know what they say: variety is the spice of life."

"Good Godfrey!" squealed my grandmother. "I do believe your neighbor is senile." Gram said senile the way she used to when she was alive: sin-nile, with the accent on the second syllable.

How did I get trapped into this conversation? I could think of nothing more revolting than to have Heddy advising Tom and me on lovemaking positions. Immediately, I imagined her telling us, "First you have to lie like this, Katy, and, Tom, you will have to move like that." I could even hear her asking for updates on which of Charlene's secret techniques we'd tried. No, if I didn't stop Heddy right here and now, she'd be back the next day with the Charlene Specials. Or sooner!

There was only one thing for me to say. "Heddy, that's not really our problem."

"You never know," Heddy chimed.

"Well," I paused rethinking what I needed to say. "You see, Heddy, I've had breast cancer, and...and Tom and I are waiting for the go-ahead from my doctors. They think we should wait a little longer, that's all." No need to tell her what Dr. Chang really thought.

I was not embarrassed about having had breast cancer. The reason I hadn't told Heddy sooner was the same reason I didn't tell anyone anymore. People acted strangely when they heard you were sick or had a disease like cancer. After my first mastectomy, I looked terribly lopsided in the chest, so there were close friends Tom and I had to tell, only because it seemed impossible not to tell them.

One of those friends was Mallory, a woman I'd known since college. She and her husband were visiting Los Angeles a month after my surgery, and I hadn't started wearing a prosthesis. While the four of us sat at a restaurant, I told Mallory and her husband about my cancer and mastectomy. I gave them the facts without tears or sadness in my voice.

"Well, Katy," Mallory had said, "you almost seem happy about the whole thing."

Mallory had never written or called since that day. But her husband had. Just once. He phoned Tom at his office to say that Mallory felt uncomfortable keeping in touch with me, but she wanted me to know she loved me. She hoped I understood.

Well, okay. Whatever that meant.

Then there were the friends who, after hearing about my cancer, felt compelled to tell Tom and me about the people they had known who'd died the previous year or week of breast cancer. "Oh, yeah, didn't that actress with the blond hair die of breast cancer?" someone asked us. "She was young, too."

But the most disturbing reaction had come from a friend in my PhD program, a feminist. She said she was very, very angry with Tom, and she blamed him entirely for my cancer. How had she come up with such an idea?

So, Tom and I learned. We decided to tell no one else about my cancer, even after I'd had the second mastectomy. But I didn't seem to have any other choice that day in my front yard with my neighbor Heddy anxious to give Tom and me pointers on babymaking positions. I suppose I wasn't really surprised to see how uncomfortable she suddenly became when she heard the words "breast cancer."

"Oh," Heddy said abruptly. She bolted to an upright position and nervously dusted off her skirt with both hands, as if it was dirty.

"What's she doing?" Gram asked. "Wiping off cancer cooties?"

"I don't have my cancer anymore," I quickly added, trying to make Heddy more at ease. "I'm perfectly healthy. Tom and I just have to wait a bit longer before starting our family."

"Katy, why in the world are you trying to make her feel more comfortable?" Gram scolded me from the front step. "You're the one who was sick."

"Well, when you do start, let me know, and I'll talk to Charlene about those secret positions." Hastily, Heddy walked right past me and was at the end of our driveway before she turned around to add a final thought. "It can't hurt to try them when you get the go-ahead."

"Depends on which position," Gram chided.

I watched Heddy march to her yard as quickly as she had marched to mine minutes before. But this time, the cadence of her step seemed more frantic, almost as if she were running away from something, as if she were being followed.

"She's afraid your cancer is going to jump on her," Gram mocked.

"Don't be ridiculous," I said looking back at Heddy.

"She's just like you," Gram sighed.

"What?" I was certain I'd misheard Gram.

"You've always been afraid Rollie's illness is going to jump on you."

I shot a look at Gram but didn't say anything. Instead, I began winding up the hose to put it away. The slamming of Heddy's front door broke the silence.

"Bet you don't get a fresh artichoke today," Gram twittered.

I laughed and sat on the steps beside my grandmother.

"Your friend is frightened by the mere thought of illness and death," Gram puffed.

"Well, I don't mean to defend Heddy, but death does seem to be a scary prospect," I said with a touch of sarcasm. Maybe it wasn't so intimidating from Gram's side of the fence, but it didn't look real inviting from this side.

"Oh, cat's liver!" Gram groused.

Gram always used to say this. The whole saying was, "Oh, cat's liver on the goat's behind," but Gram never said, "on the goat's behind," because my mother would reprimand her. Once in a while Gram would accidentally blurt out, "Oh, cat's liver!" and then quickly cover her mouth. "Ooops," Gram would whisper into my ear. "Your mother doesn't like me to say that, does she?"

"No, no," I would tease loud enough for my mother to hear. "It's 'on the goat's behind' she doesn't like you to say."

"Death is nothing to be afraid of," Gram continued. "Once the soul has learned what it came here for, the body is no longer needed."

I paused, suddenly feeling numb. Was this why Gram kept visiting me? Was she here to prepare me for death? "Am I going to die of cancer, Gram?"

"Hmm," she said as if the thought hadn't occurred to her and she needed time to think about it. "Only you can know," she answered.

"How can I?"

"Because you're the one who created it in the first place."

"What?" It sounded so cruel, so cold. Why would I create my cancer? "Why would you say this to me?"

"Because it's true, sweetie. You needed it. You created it. So, how can I know if you'll decide you need it again?"

"No one wants or needs to have cancer, and I can tell you this: I never wanted or needed mine."

"Katy, dear, are you aware that you always refer to it as your cancer, as if it's still in your possession and you're holding onto it. Sounds to me like you have your cancer safely hidden somewhere just in case."

167

"Just in case what?"

"Just in case," she echoed back.

"Why would I want my – it?"

Then suddenly I remembered the times in high school when I did want a terrible disease to invade my body to make the girls who taunted me about Wendy and Rollie feel unbearably remorse for being so cruel to me. At night, I would lie awake fantasizing about having an illness so fatal that those girls would sit at my bedside begging my forgiveness. I wanted them to sob helplessly at my funeral and to wear the guilt of their cruelty upon their souls for the rest of their lives. But I was so young then; those naive thoughts of illness and death couldn't possibly have been the seeds to my cancer years later. I hadn't even known what cancer was.

Gram stood and walked over to my gardenia bush.

Thinking she had not heard my question, I asked her again, "Why would I want something as horrifying as cancer to enter my life?"

"Well, for one thing, your cancer excused you from coping with the fears you have carried inside since you were very young." Gram bent over the gardenia bush and extended her hand to gently touch one of its delicate, snowy-white flowers. "And if the things you fear most start to resurface, and they will, Katy," – Gram made a slow, deliberate turn of her head and stared straight into my eyes – "well, you could bring out your cancer once more in order to avoid facing those fears again."

I assumed Gram was referring to my fear about the mental illnesses from which both Rollie and Wendy suffered. "Well, guess what, Gram," I said haltingly. "Nothing, not even the distraction of my breast cancer, has ever given me a moment's rest from the pain and torment of Rollie and Wendy's mental illnesses." I swallowed hard to force the lump of emotion back down my throat. "So, that can't possibly be why I would hold onto my cancer, just to keep me from facing that cruel horror." I was shocked to feel tears streaming down my cheeks.

Gram continued to look at me but with a loving, peaceful, angelic stare. "Well, then maybe you had it and are still holding onto it to help you learn something else about life." She turned her gaze back to the gardenia bush.

I thought this over for a second and was about to tell Gram that I'd learned quite a lot from my cancer. I'd learned to be afraid of it returning, afraid of living my life without children. I'd learned to be afraid of dying.

Gram said, "Some people feel they've learned what they came here for and just need a way for their souls to move on."

"By dying?"

"Physically dying is how souls move on," Gram said matter-of-factly.

I'd had enough of this conversation. It made me uneasy. People didn't choose to get sick, and even if they did, how could they – how could I – know how to create something like cancer? Gram made it sound as if I had gone to the library and pulled out a how-to book, Five Steps to Creating Your Own Special Cancer.

And what about Wendy and Rollie? Was Gram ready to tell me they had created their illnesses? And what were they supposed to learn from such troubled lives? What was anyone to learn from mental illness? And if even if they had created their sickness as a way to help their souls move on, why hadn't they moved on long ago? Why hadn't they died before causing so much pain in my life?

I wanted to shout these questions at Gram, but I realized I'd be shouting at the wind – at nothing, like Uncle Rollie. With a quiet, sincerely resigned voice, I asked, "Gram, am I mentally ill too?"

"Good heavens, why would you ask such a thing?" Gram replied with great alarm in her voice.

"Maybe because I am a thirty-eight-year-old woman who keeps talking to her grandmother who died eleven years ago," I answered somberly. "Because I have an uncle who talks to lots of people who do not exist. Because my sister suffers from some form of mental illness. Because my genetics come from the same gene pool as theirs."

"Oh," Gram murmured sympathetically. "No, Katy, you are not crazy."

"I'm not?" I was certain I'd heard wrong.

"You are not struggling with mental illness," Gram said quietly.

"But I'm talking to you, my dead grandmother, aren't I?" Tears were running down my cheeks.

"That's because I am real," Gram said ever so kindly.

I stared at her with a look of confusion and gratitude.

"I am your guardian angel," she added matter-of-factly.

I was stunned into silence.

"Yes, I am." Gram smiled.

I smiled, too, inside and out.

"Gram, were you an angel when you were alive?"

"Oh, no, no, no," Gram said. "Human beings cannot be angels."

170

"So, then after you died you went to Heaven and then you became an angel?" I asked, trying hard to understand the dynamics of becoming an angel.

"Oh, no, no, no," Gram repeated. "That's not how it is."

"Well, how is it?" I asked.

"It's simple. God creates His angels with their own individual personalities and spirits and purposes that are distinctly different and never in harmony with a human body."

"But you have a human body," I argued as I pointed at her.

"Sometimes angels are allowed to take on the appearance of a human body. And I have to tell you, rarely are angels female."

"But you're a female."

"Well, that's because you wouldn't accept me, your own guardian angel, until I appeared as your grandmother."

"Does that mean you're not Cornelia Carlton Welborn?"

"To you, I look and sound like her. To you, I am Gram."

I watched as Gram lowered her nose into the snowy, white, perfectly formed gardenia flower, the one she still held in her hand. Slowly she drank in a long breath of air.

"Do you have a sense of smell?" I asked.

"Oh, yes. But it is the essence of the gardenia that I take in. It is absorbed through the essence of who I am."

Moments before, the essence of my grandmother had spoken of the strangest things – like my need to hold onto my cancer just in case and needing a way to move on. Couldn't she just tell me whether my cancer would return or tell me if I should become pregnant?

I looked at the ground by my feet and fixed my eyes on the crumbled, dead flowers Heddy had left by the steps.

"Gram," I paused to let out a deep breath, "I don't want my cancer back." I listened to the sound of those words. It was as if someone else had spoken them. Quickly but carefully, I corrected myself. "I don't want the cancer or any cancer back. I want to have a child with Tom. I want to enjoy a happy, healthy life and grow old with him. Gram, I'm not ready to die, to move on."

When there was no answer, I looked up expecting to see

Gram still standing beside the gardenia bush. But it wasn't my grandmother or my guardian angel that I was staring at. It was the black silhouette of Heddy sitting by her window, peering out at me. A slight breeze blew across the driveway and caused the pile of dead flowers to scatter around my feet. I took in a deep breath. The essence of Gram and her gardenia flower had moved on.

CHAPTER

SEVEN

During the years when Tom and I lived in Evanston as students at Northwestern and then as newlyweds, we had attended Northwestern's football games at Dycke Stadium. Year after year, our teams had been terrible, the crowds had been small, and the few loyal fans in attendance had never worked up much of a roar, there being so little to roar about.

It was funny, though, despite the Wildcats' inability to lift themselves from the bottom of the Big Ten standings, each fall the stores in our little college town would plaster big purple and white banners in their display windows proclaiming "Rose Bowl in '76" or whatever the current year was. Tom believed that Northwestern had given us only an illusion of what college football was really like and thought it was important to experience the real thing.

That's why, on a chilly afternoon last November, Tom and I had sat about twenty rows above the thirty-yard line at the Los Angeles Coliseum. The USC Trojans were running off the field as their mascot, a white stallion known as Traveler, came galloping on. Everyone in the stands rose from their seats and began waving arms to the beat of the "Trojan Fight Song."

"Want something to drink?" Tom asked me as he stood up.

"Mmm. Maybe a hot chocolate," I said.

"Ok. I'll be right back," he said and then edged himself in front of me and into the crowded aisle.

"Is it halftime already?" the voice next to me asked.

"Yes," I answered and looked to my left. Gram was sitting beside me in Tom's seat.

"Hmm," she said. "Football wasn't my favorite sport. Never could get into it."

"I know." I lifted my coat collar up around my neck.

"But baseball." Gram sighed. "Now there's a great sport."

I smiled and thought back to summer afternoons and evenings when she would come to my parents' house and watch with my father and brother as the Dodgers battled out another game on our small black-and-white television set. It was the late 1950s, and summers seemed unusually hot then. We didn't have air conditioning, so Gram and Dad would each sip on a cold bottle of Hamm's, "The Beer Refreshing," while Sam sipped on a bottle of Hire's, what Gram called "The Root Beer Refreshing." Every now and then, Gram's voice would ring out. "You dummies!" she'd scream, overpowering Sam and Dad's sudden shouts of "No!"

My mother and I would run to the family room to see what was wrong. We usually found Gram standing up, waving a handmade paper fan toward her face. Completely and utterly exasperated, she would throw her hands in the air and turn to Sam and Dad. "Can you believe your eyes? How could he miss such an easy fly ball?"

I looked around my section of the Coliseum, hoping my neighbors would not think I was talking to myself as I said, "As I recall, Grandmother, baseball was only your second favorite sport."

"Oh, dear." She giggled. "I suppose I also embarrassed you with my enthusiasm for the roller derby."

I would have never said that Gram had embarrassed me as we watched the Los Angeles Thunderbirds on late night television but only because no one else was around to see my petite, ladylike grandmother turn into a veritable wild woman. The nights that Gram and I sat watching the roller derby in her cozy little family room were not exactly the quiet, dignified evenings one imagines a grandmother and her granddaughter spending together, especially when the grandmother had been trained in all of the cultural arts.

Every couple of weekends, I'd pack up my red suitcase with the velvety ballerina, knowing that Gram and I would be staying up into the wee hours of the night lounging in our nighties, eating cheese puffs, drinking root beer ("rut beer" as Gram called it) and cheering on the televised L.A. Thunderbirds as men and women alike got thrown over rails, hit in the gut, kicked, dragged around by the hair, and, in my mind, just about beaten to death.

Being a roller derby devotee, Gram knew the name of each skater, including members of the opposing teams. Throughout each game, Gram would jump off the couch, screeching and yelling at the referee, jabbing at my arm, asking if I'd seen the terrible injustice leveled at one of her beloved Thunderbirds. Of course, the opposing team's players were monsters compared to our angelic Thunderbirds, who only punched and kicked and beat up their opponents out of self-defense.

"Oooo, good for you, Ralph!" she'd shout to a Thunderbird skater. "Number twenty-eight deserved that kick to the stomach." Or "Watch out, Punky! Thirty-two is right behind you! Oh, no! Did you see that, Katy? Thirty-two just tripped Punky. Oh, oh! What did he do that for? Did you see it? He jumped on Punky's back while he was on the ground! I can't believe it!" And then, "Look! Look! Big Red is moving in on thirty-two. Kill him, Big Red!" she'd scream at the television set.

After each of Gram's tirades, she'd take a deep breath, smile sweetly at me, and sit back down on the couch, saying, "I suppose you think your grandmother is crazy."

The thought had occasionally passed through my mind, but I had come to accept, even look forward to, her brief spells of bizarre behavior as momentary escapes from decades of demure, ladylike comportment and maybe an escape from the daily realities of Uncle Rollie.

I never told Gram that deep down I despised the violence of the game, mainly because everyone else in our family enjoyed making fun of this pastime of hers. I could see how upset she became each time someone suggested that all roller derbies were fixed, that the skaters were really actors on wheels.

It wasn't just for Gram's sake that I feigned interest in the absurd form of competition. It was the pure excitement and drama that Gram created while watching her "actors on wheels" that made me want to be just as devoted to the Thunderbirds and to cheer them on right along with her.

Gram pointed to the football field. "What in the world are those girls in the drill team doing down there?"

I looked at the field and saw the USC drill team and band marching around in a scattered formation.

"I think they're going to form the letters U-S-C," I answered.

"Hmm," Gram said as she tilted her head and squinted her eyes, trying to make out the letters. "Remember the time we went to Olympic Stadium?"

Because I had never told Gram about my aversion for the roller derby, she had assumed that I held it in the same esteem as she did. My deception caught up with me when I was ten. It was a Friday evening, and I had just placed my red suitcase by the door to Rollie's bedroom when Gram proudly placed in my hands two tickets to Olympic Stadium. I didn't understand at first. Were we going to the circus?

"No," Gram told me. "Our Thunderbirds are in town. They're playing at Olympic Stadium tomorrow night, and you and I are going! Isn't this exciting?"

A little too exciting, I thought.

It had scared me to death. The night of the roller derby, we'd gone to dinner at a coffee shop close to the stadium, and because we couldn't find parking nearby, we'd had to leave the car on a dark, deserted corner. Both Gram and I had felt jittery and out of place as we walked from the car to the arena, which was located near the western fringe of downtown Los Angeles adjacent to tenements, flophouses, and abandoned buildings.

I had never been in such a neighborhood, and I was certain that Gram hadn't either. Beer and wine bottles lay in the gutters, old couches and rusty lawn chairs sat in front of boarded-up windows, and shabbily dressed street people milled around in every doorway watching Gram and me, inspecting our every move. We held on to each other as we quickly shuffled toward Olympic Stadium. With each tentative step we took, I felt our hearts racing at the same frantic pace.

Our collective nervousness and quickened steps caused Gram to trip on the raised sidewalk. One second she was standing right beside me, and the next she was down on the ground. Gram let out a gasp and a weak moan, and I instantly thought my grandmother had suffered a heart attack. Gram quickly collected herself as I helped pull her to her feet, but her knees were bleeding and her nylons were torn. Gram said I wasn't to worry; she was fine and could still make it to the stadium.

Gram and I both wore dresses to the event, as if we were going to church or a concert. There had been lots of other women and young children in the stands at Olympic Stadium but none of them in Sunday dresses with bows in their hair. Many of the fans looked as if they hadn't bathed or seen clean clothes in a year. It took my breath away to hear some of the women spew forth strings of ear-tickling profanity, the likes of which I'd never heard before, their eruptions exposing missing front teeth or mouths void of any teeth at all. Most of the men, young and old, wore sleeveless tee shirts designed, I was certain, to show off arms and shoulders plastered with tattoos of snakes and naked women. I watched as they greeted each other with a quick fist to the arm and stomach or a friendly chokehold before admiring the engravings on one another's bodies.

Down on the football field, the band moved into formation to the beat of its drums. "I really don't think your torn stockings and bloody knees were enough for us to blend in with the roller derby crowd," I said.

"Oh, I felt comfortable enough," Gram lied.

"Well, you didn't cheer for the Thunderbirds very loudly that night, not the way you did when we watched from your home," I said to Gram.

Gram giggled. "I was too worried about the walk we still had to make back to the car."

"I'm glad we never went again." I said.

"Oh, I did."

"Really?" I asked with amazement.

"It was during your uncle's Roller Derby Phase, when he decided to become a Thunderbird."

I'd never heard Gram refer to periods of Uncle Rollie's life in such a way.

"When was this?" I asked, not sure I needed or wanted to know.

"Oh, sometime after his Mini Concert Phase."

I was fairly certain this Mini Concert Phase was around the time of Rollie's Toyland performance, but I wasn't going to ask. "How much after?"

"Well, let's see." Gram looked up to the sky for a moment. "After his release from the Camarillo Mental Hospital, he was allowed to live with me for six months."

"I remember, but I thought he lived with you longer than that."

"Oh, no. It was a condition of his release. Rollie's doctor said Rollie needed to live in familiar surroundings for the first six months to help him make the transition outside the hospital, which is why he came to stay with me. But at the end of the six months he had to move into his own apartment." Gram paused. "All his rent and living expenses were covered by the state's mental health department, you know."

"Is that when he decided to join the roller derby – when he moved into the apartment?"

"No. He was still in his Composing Phase."

"Oh." Once again, I did not encourage an explanation, but I knew it was coming anyway.

"His doctor felt it would be healthy for Rollie to have something to do while he lived in the apartment. Rollie said he wanted to compose music, so I let him move my upright to his apartment. It went better with his decor," Gram twittered. "And, of course, all your grandfather's clothes went with Rollie. He wouldn't wear anything else, you know?"

"I remember, though I never understood why," I said.

Gram shook her head.

"So, when did he decide to become a Thunderbird?" I was beginning to wonder if I'd ever find out.

"Let's see, I think Rollie lived in the apartment about a year. Did you know he was allowed to visit with me one day a week?"

"Yes. Every Wednesday."

"Well, anyway, he'd lived in the apartment almost a year when Rollie's doctor insisted that he join a club or organization to help him interact with other people. The doctor didn't think Rollie's work as a composer was getting him out enough." Gram stopped as if this was all the explanation needed.

"And?" I prodded her on.

"So, Rollie told his doctor he wanted to roller skate, to try out for the Thunderbirds."

"Didn't his doctor think that was an odd choice?"

"No, he only said that Rollie would have to show proof that he practiced his skating every day by giving the doctor each day's ticket stub from the roller rink. After twelve months, Rollie was to attend the tryouts for the Thunderbirds. So, it wasn't even a year after you and I went to the roller derby when Rollie and I went to watch the Thunderbirds. Rollie wanted to study their skating style before trying out."

"Did he actually try out?"

"Good heavens, no. He lost interest in the whole idea a few weeks after he began. He didn't want the doctor to know, so he went to the roller rink every day, bought his ticket, and returned to his apartment, never putting on a skate."

"Did you know what he was doing?"

"Not right away," Gram said. "The doctor found out, but not until many months later."

"What did he do?"

"He threatened to have Rollie put back in the hospital unless he became involved in a group activity. So, I called my old friend Thora Hinkelmier."

"Thora Hinkelmier?"

"Thora used to head up fund-raising for the Los Angeles Master Chorale. She was very dear and used her influence to get Roland a singing position. Remember?"

"Was this Rollie's Master Chorale Phase?" I asked, thinking back to the evenings when my parents had forced Sam, Wendy, and me to attend Master Chorale concerts. We had sat for hours listening to what I then considered the most depressing music ever conceived, things like Mahler's Das Klagende Lied, or Mozart's Choral Mass, or Bach's choral cantadas.

I had tried to tune out the music while I studied the members of the choir, their faces, their clothing, even the way their mouths moved as they sang. I tried to determine if all the singers on stage were as sick as my uncle. Did they also come from mental hospitals and insist on wearing their dead relatives' clothes? Usually, I concluded it was only my uncle, standing in the last row of the men's tenor section, wearing Grandpa's old black suit, who was mentally unstable.

Then I would wonder if the other choir members had a sense of Rollie's illness. Couldn't they tell during their weekday practices? How could they not? And if they did have an inkling of his mental instability, why did they allow him to sing in their group?

"I can't remember how long Rollie stayed with the Master Chorale," I said to Gram.

"Oh, quite a while. I think almost two years. He had to attend practices every Monday, Wednesday, and Friday, and except for Wednesdays, he took the bus all by himself to each of the practices. His doctor let me drive Rollie on Wednesdays, since it was his day to be with me."

"Didn't Rollie spend Wednesday nights with you too?"

"Yes," Gram paused. "He wasn't supposed to, you know, but Rollie hated going back to his lonely apartment, and I loved fixing a good dinner for him. It was nice for both of us. So, he'd stay the night, and I'd take him home on Thursday. I didn't think it would do any harm."

"Mmm," I said. I knew that my mother and father had suspected that Gram and Rollie were doing this but could never get Gram to admit it. What my parents didn't comprehend was that Gram and Rollie's Wednesday nights had slowly evolved into Wednesday through Friday night visits.

"I shouldn't have allowed it." Gram sighed. "Rollie began skipping Monday practices, and sometimes he'd also skip his Wednesday practice. He wanted to stay at my house and work in my front yard – those shrubs of his, you know. He was always thinking the yard needed more." Gram paused for a moment. "And then by the end of his second year with the Chorale, he'd stopped going to the practices altogether, and he refused to sleep at his own apartment."

"Did you tell his doctor?"

"I didn't have to. The director of the Master Chorale called the doctor, wondering why Rollie had stopped attending rehearsals. He said he couldn't reach Rollie at his apartment and wondered if the doctor had a new phone number for him."

"I bet the doctor was surprised," I said.

"I was afraid he would have Rollie committed to the hospital again. But he was patient and told me we needed to start over again. He insisted that Rollie come to his office every Monday, Wednesday, and Friday. He wanted to try something new."

"Something new?"

"He wanted Rollie to buy a newspaper every morning, take it back to his apartment and look in the Classified Section for jobs that Rollie thought were interesting. He was to circle those ads, then bring them to each of his therapy sessions. Rollie and the doctor talked about the jobs and tried to determine if they were positions Rollie could handle."

"Did he really expect Rollie to get a job?" I asked.

"Not right away. He and Rollie did this for a year before Rollie became more realistic about the kinds of things he could do."

"But he never found a real job through the newspaper, did he?"

"Oh, yes. Don't you remember the short time he had the dishwasher position?"

I thought back to the spring of my sophomore year in high school and vaguely remembered the evening that Gram and Rollie had come to our house while my family was eating dinner. Gram apologized for interrupting, but Rollie had an important announcement to make.

Then Rollie mumbled something about getting a job, and my parents made a big deal about it, saying they thought it was wonderful.

But I don't remember hearing anything more about it after that. "How long was he a dishwasher?" I asked.

"Oh, maybe a week." Gram sighed.

"A week? He had the job for only a week? What happened?"

"I believe customers at the restaurant complained about dried food on the sides of plates and lipstick around the rims of water glasses." Gram paused before adding, "There might have been a few other complaints about spinach stuck to the silverware."

"How picky of those people," I said with a little too much sarcasm.

Gram raised her eyebrows. "Yes, well, Roland really didn't like dishwashing. He told his doctor that he preferred doing something where he could work outdoors."

The music from the USC Marching Band started to get on my nerves as I realized where Gram was heading with all her stories about Rollie and his Roller Derby Phase and Composing Phase. I no longer wanted to hear about the phases of my uncle's life anymore.

"Look, Gram," I said, pointing to the football field. "The drill team is spelling out the word T-r-o-j-a-n-s."

Gram looked at the field for a moment, then turned to me. "It wasn't until the next fall when Rollie got the gas station job."

"I wonder how many girls it takes to form all those letters," I said, hoping to divert Gram from her train of thought. "What do you think? Looks like maybe twenty girls just to form the T in Trojans."

Gram squinted her eyes. "Twenty-eight," she said, and I thought I had succeeded in changing the subject until she tapped my knee and said, "I had seen a Help Wanted sign in Mr. Osaka's window. You remember Mr. Osaka, don't you?"

"Yes," I faintly answered. I knew I'd lost the battle. Gram was going to summon up a period of time that was too painful to recall.

"You remember, I'd been a loyal customer of his for many, many years. His gas station was only three blocks from your parents' house, and I always had him fill my gas tank before I drove back home. When I inquired about the job opening, Mr. Osaka was kind enough to offer it to Rollie."

"Mm," was all I could utter.

"Rollie's doctor really wanted him to find a job on his own, not through his mother, but he decided it might work out as long as Rollie only washed windows, which was all Mr. Osaka wanted him to do."

Gram paused, waiting for me to say something.

I remained quiet as a familiar sickness filled my stomach.

Gram went on. "Those were the days when you had full service at a gas station. Imagine! It took two men, one to fill the gas tank and check under the hood and one to wash the windows and white walls. Remember?"

"Yes," I said with my eyes closed.

"Rollie liked the job with Mr. Osaka..."

Gram's voice and the cacophony of the USC marching band faded away as I began to recall September of 1967, my junior year in high school. Sam was a senior and had just bought his first car, a 1955 brown and white, two-door DeSoto. It was hideous and old, but Sam was extremely proud of it and insisted on driving the whole three blocks from our house to the school parking lot each day. My friend Nancy Snyder and I felt so cool on the mornings when Sam and his friend Ed let us ride with them. My sister was always invited to come along, but she never did. She was a freshman at our high school, and by then she refused to have anything to do with us or anyone else who showed signs of being well adjusted.

Rollie had begun working around the corner at Mr. Osaka's gas station, a place where all the high school lowlifes and outcasts, better known as "the hoods," hung out after school.

Gram interrupted the long-ago memory. "It was so good of Sam to stop by and say hello to Rollie each afternoon."

Did Gram know this was the very reason I never rode home with Sam and Ed? Sam didn't seem to mind having his friends know that Mr. Osaka's window washer, the odd man with the slow shuffle and the twitch on his left cheek, was our uncle, but I did.

"Rollie appreciated Sam's kindness," Gram whispered, as if anyone in the stands might hear her.

I knew that Sam hadn't dropped by the corner gas station each afternoon just to say hello to Rollie. My brother's daily appearances and friendly overtures with Mr. Osaka's helper sent a clear message to the hoods who hovered by the bathrooms and pay phone: Rollie was not to be bothered by them. So, they left Rollie alone not because they were afraid of Sam but because Sam was one of those guys whom everyone liked and respected. Even the hoods wouldn't cross him.

"Oh, dear." Gram sighed heavily, continuing to look toward the football field. "I'm sure Rollie never would have behaved the way he did if..."

My friend Nancy had had a crush on Sam. Lots of girls had, but I still wondered why I had let her talk me into asking Sam and Ed to drive us to her house one Friday after school. Sam didn't mind doing us the favor, and I knew Ed didn't mind having us along, because he had a crush on Nancy. I mentioned that we were in a big hurry and asked if Sam could drop Nancy and me off before going anywhere else.

"No problem," said Sam, and then he drove right into the station. "This will just take a second," he added as his car radio began to play,

"There is a house..."

"...in New Orleans," sang Ed and Nancy.

Sam steered up to the gas pumps right behind a green Cadillac.

"They call the ri-sing sun." Ed and Nancy continued singing, even though Sam had turned off the engine and the radio had gone dead. They didn't care; they just kept singing the song acapella.

My brother opened his car door and waved to Mr. Osaka, who was pumping gas into the Cadillac. "Hi, Mr. Osaka," Sam called out.

Mr. Osaka waved.

"Rollie here today?" Sam asked.

Mr. Osaka motioned his head to the front of the Cadillac. Rollie was furiously rubbing the passenger side of the car's windshield.

"Hey, Rollie!" Sam called out.

Rollie obviously didn't hear Sam. He kept rubbing away at the window.

My brother nodded to Mr. Osaka and said, "Just need some air in the tires." Sam must have decided to talk to Rollie after he finished cleaning the Cadillac's window.

Mr. Osaka nodded to Sam.

"It's been the ruin of many a poor boy..." crooned Ed and Nancy.

When Sam bent down to remove the air cap from his front left tire, I noticed the woman in the driver's seat of the Cadillac. She was pointing at her windshield and calling out to Rollie. I didn't hear what she said, but whatever it was, I could tell Rollie didn't like it.

All of a sudden, Rollie's whole body flinched and his face turned red with anger.

"...Thank God I know I'm one," sang out Ed and Nancy.

"It's clean!" my uncle shouted, veins nearly popping from his neck.

I froze in my seat and prayed that my friends hadn't heard Rollie's outburst.

But they had. Both Ed and Nancy stopped singing and turned their attention to the car ahead of us.

"It's still filthy!" squealed the woman from inside the Cadillac.

Rollie's body wound itself up like a corkscrew. "You bitch! You bitch!" he screamed.

Mr. Osaka dropped the gas nozzle. Sam stood up from his kneeling position, releasing the air hose with a hiss. And from behind me I heard the hoods, with their cigarettes dangling from their lips, laughing and calling Rollie names. Sam didn't have time to stop them, because Rollie had already charged the passenger door of the Cadillac and flung it open.

Rollie reached inside and grabbed the woman's arm. "I'll wash your filthy eyes out!" Rollie shouted at the poor frightened woman.

Everything seemed to happen at once. Mr. Osaka ran to the woman's door and began pulling her from Rollie's grasp. At the same time, Sam ran to pull Rollie out of the car. Ed jumped from the DeSoto and tried to help Sam hold onto Rollie.

All I remember hearing afterward was the soothing sound of my brother's voice saying over and over again, "Calm down, Rollie. It's okay. It's okay."

But things were never okay after that. Not in our house, anyway, for it was just a week later that my sister decided to consume a variety of red, yellow, and green pills before walking into her English class. In her hands, she held her homework assignment, a poem, which she began to recite out loud to the room full of students. "Peace of life, you hold nothing for me. I'll let you go before I destroy thee." And then she dropped to the floor unconscious, unaware of the turmoil and confusion she had created.

At the end of the class period when the halls filled with students on their way to lunch, I was given the news of my sister. "Didn't you hear?" a girl I didn't know very well asked me with excitement and forced sympathy. I remember feeling the sickness swell upward to my throat as a million eyes watched to see what I would do, where I would go. And then I felt Sam's hand on my shoulder.

Sam took my books and led me to the school office, telling me softly, "Don't worry. Wendy's going to be okay."

But I knew that Sam was wrong. Our sister was never going to be okay. She never had been okay. From the day she had entered kindergarten, she had been labeled a behavior problem. Her teachers had all said she was a sweet child but talked in class and did whatever she liked no matter what punishments were doled out.

I could still see Wendy as a little girl, sitting at the kitchen table with Mom night after night going over spelling words and not being able to hold Wendy's attention for long. Mom would talk about her needing to pay attention in the classroom, and Wendy, who sincerely wanted to be good, would plead her case, saying, "I want to be quiet, Mommy, and I tell myself not to talk, but then something makes me do it." My sister couldn't help herself. Not even then.

Many of my friends had sisters Wendy's age, and Wendy played with most of them until the fourth grade. But by then, her poor grades and incorrigible behavior were so pronounced that she began rejecting stable friends and started hanging around with other troubled children.

It took a few more years before Wendy perfected the art of lying. It finally got to the point where she truly believed she had not skipped school; her teachers just hadn't seen her. And she hadn't really stolen her girlfriend's heart-shaped locket; someone else had put it in Wendy's drawer. And she hadn't really run away from home; it had slipped her mind to tell my parents she was staying overnight at a friend's house.

There had always been teachers, principals, therapists, and school counselors who believed Wendy's lies and thought she was the product of unloving parents. But she wasn't. I know. I saw the love, the concern, the patience and involvement my mother and father provided. Why couldn't those doctors and counselors see what I saw? Wendy was a victim of the same illness my Uncle Rollie had.

Wendy began private therapy when I was in the ninth grade. Sam and I and my mother and father attended family counseling sessions where Wendy said over and over, "I hate you all. I hate living in the same house with you!" The problem was, Wendy hated living with everyone, even the girls at the summer camp she'd begged my parents to send her to.

That summer, our family forfeited our vacation at the shore for Wendy's sake. Mom and Dad thought it might be good for her to spend the summer away from home. But they were wrong. Wendy hated everything and everyone at the camp. Within two weeks, she was kicked out after she was found smoking pot and sleeping with a male counselor.

Four years of therapy never helped, even though Wendy's therapist said it did. Any form of parental guidance and authority created increasingly worse outbursts, and all overtures of love and understanding were rejected. It got to the point where Wendy's emotional outbursts, her screams full of anger, hate, and vitriol, were a regular part of our lives, leaving everyone in my family drained, confused, and scared.

So, it wasn't as if my parents and Sam and I hadn't seen it coming, Wendy's first attempt at suicide. There hadn't been anything any of us could do to stop it.

Sam and I visited Wendy in the psychiatric ward of the community hospital the day after she'd passed out at school. It was eerie, for I'd never seen my sister look so peaceful. She didn't respond to anything Sam or I said to her. She just lay still with the most serene smile, as if she were completely untroubled.

It was baffling that her doctors, psychiatric professionals, believed Wendy when she said she hadn't meant to kill herself; she was only trying to knock out a bad headache and didn't realize the colored pills she'd gotten from a person she'd never met before weren't aspirin.

A month later, Wendy returned home. The doctors told my parents that Wendy was not mentally ill. She was just going through the typical teenage rebellion stage. She'd made a mistake with the pills and probably wouldn't do it again. The doctors were agreed and confident in their diagnosis and prognosis.

Gram pointed toward the football field. "Oh, Katy, look at the colorful uniforms those young men have on."

The USC football players were running onto the field as the band and drill team formed a human tunnel for them to pass through.

"Gold and red are such a nice combination. Aren't those the same colors your high school football team had?" Gram asked.

"No, ours were blue and white," I answered.

"Oh, I must have been thinking of your basketball players."

"No, they wore blue and white too."

"Hmm." Gram thought for a moment. "Well, I could be wrong. I never went to those games."

I watched the band and drill team march off the field and began to wonder what was taking Tom so long.

"You went to all the high school games, didn't you?" Gram asked.

"Yes."

"And Sam," she added.

"Yes."

"Even Wendy went to some of your school games, didn't she?" Gram asked.

I didn't respond, but it didn't keep me from remembering those months after Wendy returned home from the hospital. About the same time, Uncle Rollie had been transferred to a halfway house closer to Gram. Both Wendy and Rollie seemed to go about life as if nothing had happened, as if nothing had changed. I guessed that for them, nothing had changed. Rollie continued to wear Grandpa's old clothes, stay with Gram on Wednesdays, and attend family gatherings. Wendy went back to school, skipping most of her classes and causing horrible scenes at home if anyone questioned her behavior. Only the people who loved Wendy and Rollie had changed.

Especially Gram. She appeared nervous and more cautious about the information she shared with the family, as if afraid she might say the wrong thing. I noticed how her face looked older with the lines around the eyes and mouth more pronounced. Her smile wasn't as generous and her laughter was less infectious. At family gatherings, Gram seemed to have lost her sense of humor, her spontaneity. More and more, she became a passive spectator instead of the active participant she had always been before.

Sam changed too. Others might not have noticed, since he remained a star runner on the varsity track team, he worked on our school paper, and his grades never slipped. But I could tell my brother was different. He didn't tease me as often, and every night after dinner, he'd take long, long walks by himself. Sometimes he'd ask me to join him, and when I did, we'd talk about unimportant things.

Once, though, after we'd walked in silence, Sam told me he was responsible for Wendy's suicide attempt. There was such pain in his voice, and I was petrified that he would think such a thing. I should have let him talk some more. Instead, I stopped him from continuing by shouting out that he was the best brother in the world to me and to Wendy.

But Sam shrugged as if to say I didn't understand. He didn't speak for the rest of our walk, nor did he ever bring it up again.

I saw changes in my mother and father, too. I could see the tension in their faces. They still kissed and hugged each other when Dad came home from work. They still went out with friends and hosted all the family gatherings. But my parents were different. Something in the air caused them to move differently, laugh differently.

And me, I became increasingly obsessed with neatness. Everything in my room – my clothes closet, my drawers, even the pages in my school notebook – had to be in an exact order. Too many times on my way to school or to a friend's house, I felt the urgent need to run home and check to be sure the oven hadn't been left on or the faucets left dripping. At school, whenever I heard a siren in the distance, I was certain it was heading for my house, and I would be anxious until the end of the day when I could go home.

A constant and relentless disquiet sat inside my stomach, clouding my every thought and emotion with an uneasiness that at any minute something terrible was about to happen. This apprehension never subsided. Instead, I felt as if it was growing round and hard like a tumor, like an invisible, cancerous tumor.

"Look!" Gram said to me. "The game is starting again."

I watched for a moment as players from USC and their opponents, the Washington Huskies, filed along the forty-yard line for the kickoff. The ball sailed high in the air, and players began colliding with each other.

"Gram," I asked, "do you ever wonder what our lives would have been like if Wendy and Rollie had been healthy?"

"Not really."

"I do."

"And when you wonder about this, do you also wonder if you still would have gotten breast cancer?" Gram asked.

"Katy?" a voice much different from Gram's called to me.

I looked to my right and saw Tom standing with a Coke in one hand and a cup of hot chocolate in the other.

"Are you okay?" Tom asked as he handed me the hot chocolate. I looked to my left. Gram was no longer there. Tom edged past me and eased into his seat.

"Yes. I was wondering what it would have been like if Northwestern had been a better team."

CHAPTER

EIGHT

M y insomnia had returned. It was three in the morning, and I was wide awake and tired. Extremely tired. Insomnia was not something new to me. Ever since high school, I had experienced bouts of sleeplessness when I would lie awake for four or five nights in a row. How many nights had it been this time? Three? No, four.

At least with this episode, I knew why I couldn't sleep. It was because of Dr. Davis. I'd met with him five days earlier and had been feeling anxious ever since.

Dr. Davis and my previous oncologist, Dr. Chang, were good friends, Dr. Davis said, and often sought each other's medical opinion. When I had said that I had great respect for Dr. Chang but wanted a second opinion, Dr. Davis had said it was 'prudent and practical' of me, if only to ease my mind. So, he scheduled a battery of tests over the next eight weeks.

Why? The doctor had in his hands all the results from the tests I'd taken for Dr. Chang eleven months earlier. Everything was fine. No cancer. Nothing. Three years of being cancer free. Wasn't that enough? All I wanted was for him to look at the results and say, "What's the problem? Go ahead and start a family." But Dr. Davis said he wouldn't be able to tell me anything until after the new tests were completed and he'd had time to evaluate my whole situation. "Every case is different, you know," he'd said. Yes, I knew.

I hadn't planned on Dr. Davis knowing Dr. Chang. They'd probably talk, which meant that Dr. Davis would be less objective in looking at my case and end up telling me the same thing Dr. Chang had told me.

Well, so what if Dr. Davis reached the same conclusion? I could still decide to get pregnant. It was my own body, my own life, wasn't it? A few days earlier, I'd read about three women who'd had breast cancer and whose doctors said they should not get pregnant. Each of those women went ahead and had healthy babies, and not one of them had the cancer return. I knew every cancer was different, but those three women took a chance, and now they all had babies and their health.

These thoughts had played over and over again in my head during the last five days and four nights, and I knew it was no use trying to sleep when I could not relax my mind. I quietly slipped out of bed, put on Tom's black terrycloth robe, and went into the kitchen to fix a cup of warm milk.

I poured the milk into a saucepan and slowly stirred. The sound of the spoon against the metal caused every nerve to rise to the surface of my skin, tight and prickly. I rubbed the back of my neck, trying to knead away the knot of tension and fear, but I knew it would not go away.

So, I poured the steaming milk into a cup and slowly shuffled into the living room in front of the wall-to-wall bookshelf. I wanted something to read to make my eyes tired. I stared at the titles until I spied the row of photo albums, all thirteen of them. They were lined up side-by-side on a bottom shelf. Twelve of the albums held memories of each year of our marriage. I was always comforted knowing they were there for me whenever I felt like looking back in time to remember who Tom and I had been, to remember the things we once found important, to see how much we had changed. But on this particular night, I reached for the last picture book. It was Gram's.

Hundreds of times over the years, Gram had said, "I don't suppose you'd like to look through my old memory book."

I'd always answer with an enthusiastic, "Yes." And then I'd follow Gram into her bedroom and watch as she carefully opened her top dresser drawer and removed a layer of tissue paper.

With great reverence, Gram would lift out a large, black leather album with the initials C.C.C. embedded in the center. Gram never failed to point to the initials and say that they had been filled with a delicate gold inlay, but time and handling had made them dull imprints.

Always impressed by this, I would gently rub my fingers over each C.C.C. before Gram opened to the inside of the photo album.

With the turn of each page, I felt I had entered the most fascinating and romantic world imaginable, a world where women wore dresses down to their ankles and men wore high-topped shoes. These people, all friends and relatives of Gram's, smiled at me from horse drawn buggies and rowboats docked by grassy shores of a distant era. I would stare back, wishing I had lived then, wishing I were one of those people. Life would have been happier, I was certain.

I could hear the padding of Andy's feet on the hardwood floor, and I knew he was coming to keep me company. He always did. I watched him slowly enter the living room and look at me with sleepy eyes, asking to sit on the couch. So, I put the milk and memory book on the coffee table and bent down to lift his hind legs, since he could no longer climb up by himself. Then I snuggled next to Andy's warm body and put Gram's memory book on my lap.

I opened the book to the last page, knowing I would find a picture of Gram and Grandpa Welborn standing together, arm in arm. It had been taken the year I was born, the year Grandpa Welborn died, and, Gram would always tell me, the year her spirit went away.

As a young girl, I had often asked Gram if she thought she would marry again. She'd always let out a dreamy sigh and tell me that Grandpa was the only man she could ever love. Then she would ask if I knew how, while still in high school, Grandpa would show his undying affection for her.

I'd heard the same story many times over, but I loved hearing Gram tell it, so I'd shake my head saying no. Immediately, Gram would take her hands and, with great exaggeration, draw an imaginary heart from the top of her chest to the bottom.

"Grandpa would do this every day when I arrived in class," Gram would tell me.

"What class was that?" I'd ask, thinking that somehow the class subject had some significance.

"Oh, I don't remember," Gram would reply, wrinkling her forehead and pursing her lips as she tried to remember.

"Did the other students ever see him do that?" I'd press.

"I don't know," she'd say, still meditating on the previous question.

"I bet you would have been embarrassed if they had."

"Of course not," Gram would say, as if hearing an absurd thought.

I didn't want to hurt Gram's feelings, so I'd always tell her how romantic I thought it was for Grandpa to show his affection in such a grand, symbolic manner. I knew it was what Gram wanted to hear, so I never told her that I would have been embarrassed if a boyfriend of mine had drawn giant hearts on his chest whenever I entered a room.

Since then I'd come to understand how Gram felt. When I had been a student at Northwestern, I'd taken a class in sign language. Tom asked me to teach him the sign for heart, which happened to be the exact same gesture Grandpa had made on his chest, except in sign language, the gesture was done over the small area of the heart, not the whole chest.

Tom could never master the technique of the sign, so he modified it by tapping one of his index fingers over the left corner of his chest above his heart. He called this his secret code for letting me know he loved me.

I loved that Tom still used his secret code. We could be anywhere – at a party, out to dinner with friends – and if I caught his eye from across a room or a table, Tom would put his finger to his heart and tap it three times. I was supposed to return the gesture, but sometimes it seemed too conspicuous, so I smiled back, thinking this would suffice.

But Tom would fix his eyes on me with an exaggerated tilt of his head and keep tapping away until I tapped my own heart three times. It made me smile inside and out whenever he did this.

Someday, I thought, if my own granddaughter was interested, I'd share this story with her, and should she ask if I'd been embarrassed if someone had seen Tom using his secret code, like Gram I'd say, "Of course, not!" Of course, not? I might never have a child of my own, so there was a great possibility that there would be no granddaughter to whom I could tell this story.

"I always loved that picture of your grandfather and me."

I looked up from the picture book. Gram was sitting across from me in the oak craftsman chair with the sloping back.

"It was the last picture taken of us together," Gram added.

"I know." I sighed, hesitating. "Gram?"

"Yes, sweetie."

"Were you ever asked out by other men after Grandpa died?"

Up until I was in high school, I'd wanted Gram to remarry so she wouldn't be lonely and so I could have a grandfather. I had known it could be risky, since the grandmother of one of my friends had remarried four times, and each new grandfather had seemed creepier than the previous one. But I had been fairly certain that Gram would never pick a creepy grandfather for me.

"Oh, dear, yes." Gram giggled. "Do you remember Arthur Erpelding?"

"No."

"Yes, you do. The man who lived on the corner of my street. You know, the one who would come over and offer to take care of the weeds in the front yard."

"Oh, yeah." I hadn't thought of Mr. Erpelding in a hundred years, but, yes, I did remember him. He was the large, balding man who sported a white goatee and spoke with a thick Norwegian accent. He had been tall and meaty, but he hadn't had the bulging stomach most older men had. What had impressed me the most about Mr. Erpelding was his impeccable attire. He always wore a suit when he knocked on Gram's door, a sure sign that he was interested in my grandmother.

On the few occasions when I answered Gram's door to Mr. Erpelding, he'd smile politely and, with a slight bow, offer his hand to me saying, "How do you do. I am Mr. Arthur Erpelding." His "do" always sounded like "to," and he couldn't pronounce the "th" in his own name, so what I always heard was, "How to you to? I'm Artur Erpel-ting."

Once, after Mr. Erpelding had introduced himself, I told him I liked his suit.

He smiled, straightened his neck and said, "Tis is a new zuit. Unce a yur I buy new zuit."

I just knew that even though he was a little hard to understand, Mr. Erpelding would make a perfect grandfather. I envisioned him arriving at family gatherings behind the oversized steering wheel of Gram's turquoise Impala with Gram sitting beside him. Never in my fantasy was Uncle Rollie in the car. I saw my new grandfather resting in the big stuffy chair in our living room, where he would regale us with a joke or two. Later, he would sit beside Gram at the dinner table, occasionally patting her hand and whispering in her ear.

It wasn't to be, though. Gram had always been polite each time she joined me at her front door to greet Mr. Erpelding, but I could tell by the tone of her voice and the way she stood in her doorway that

Cornelia Carlton Colburn Welborn would not be inviting Mr. Arthur Erpelding inside. She always rejected his offers to help prune the front yard shrubs, saying that her son, Roland, would soon be returning from "his trip" and would take care of the yard.

Why did Gram have to go and mention Uncle Rollie, I would wonder. There was no need for this future grandfather of mine to know about Rollie until after Gram became Mrs. Arthur Erpelding.

"Well, did you go out with Mr. Erpelding?" I asked Gram.

"Yes, I did. But only because he kept pestering me and pestering me. After too many invitations, it became embarrassing, so I agreed to attend a dinner at his church."

"A date with old Mr. Erpelding," I said, more to myself than to Gram.

"I suppose you could call it a date, but that's not what he called it."

"What did he call it?"

"An appointment."

"A what?"

"I'd never heard of such a thing either, but the day I agreed to go to the dinner with him, Mr. Erpelding told me I should pick him up at seven for our appointment."

"He asked you out and wanted you to drive?"

"I didn't mind. I knew Mr. Erpelding had poor eyesight and couldn't drive. I assumed that was the reason he wanted me to go out with him in the first place, you know, to provide him with transportation."

"Hmm," was all I said.

"But I found out differently."

"What do you mean?"

"Oh, dear, I don't know if I should I tell you this." Gram paused for a second. "Oh, well, I suppose you're old enough." She paused once more and then continued. "When Mr. Erpelding and I arrived at his church, a lot of friendly old Norwegians were there talking in a hor-d-hor sort of way. You know how Norwegians talk. Everything has a singsong beat and sounds like hor-d-hor, hor-d-hor. Everyone was nice, but I have to admit I had the hardest time understanding what anyone was saying. And the food they served! Nothing but hard bread topped with cream cheese and raw fish! Well, I can tell you, I didn't eat a thing the whole night. Of course, I didn't mind, since I'd been watching my weight." Gram stopped as if she'd finished her story.

"So, was this your whole date with Mr. Erpelding?"

"No, there was more." Gram started to giggle. "You see, one of the couples at the dinner was scheduled to show slides of their recent trip to Scandinavia."

"Oh. That's nice," I said.

"I thought so, too. At least until people started to get ready for the slide show, moving chairs around and turning off the lights. Then the real entertainment happened."

"What do you mean?"

"Well, when it became apparent that there weren't enough chairs for everyone, because two chairs were needed to hold the projector, Arthur Erpelding motioned for me to come sit on his lap. I shook my head no, but everyone in the room laughed and shouted, "Go on. Go on." So, I thought, why not go over to him and sit for a second. Just for a laugh, you see."

"Cute, Gram," I said.

"Cute! Hah! When I sat down on Mr. Arthur Erpelding's lap I found myself sitting on theeee biggest and theeee hardest cucumber of my life!"

"What!" I shrieked with laughter. "Cucumber?"

Gram nodded her head indignantly and repeated, "Cucumber."

"Gram, do you mean he...?" I wanted to be sure I understood her correctly.

"Exactly!" Gram said, squaring up her shoulders.

"Gram, I am shocked!" I truly was shocked.

"You? What about me? Can you imagine how shocked I was? That man knew what he was doing, and I was in a terribly uncomfortable position with everyone watching me. Of course, they didn't know what I was sitting on."

"I should hope not," I said.

"It wasn't easy, but I remained quite calm, and as naturally as I could, I stood up and said, `Arthur Erpelding, I'm afraid this appointment is over. I assume you can find another appointment to take you home tonight.' And then I quietly left."

"Did you ever talk to him again?"

"Oh, yes. You would know, because he would drop by for a visit sometimes while you were staying with me. Of course, I never let him inside. I was polite, but I always made it very clear that there would be no more appointments."

"How long did he keep coming by?" I asked.

"Oh, he knocked on my door about once a month for the next fifteen years."

"Poor Mr. Erpelding." I sighed, thinking that he must have felt something for Gram. "Whatever happened to him?"

"Last I heard, he'd ended up in a retirement home and was such a hit with the women that he was named King Arthur."

"I can't imagine why." I giggled.

"Cucumbers." Gram nodded with authority and then added, "Anyway, that's what I call my cucumber story."

"Your cucumber story?"

"Yes, but please don't ask your mother about it, because I never told her. I was too embarrassed."

"Are there any other cucumber stories I should know about, Grandmother?" I taunted.

"Oh, cat's liver, Katherine. I should hope not."

"Well, there had to be other men who were vying for your attention," I said.

"I wouldn't really know. I wasn't a flirty kind of woman. Not like other widows who I'd see throwing themselves at any man with trousers."

"I remember a few times when you were flirty," I said slyly.

"I beg your pardon," Gram said with indignation.

"What about the summer before you died?"

"Oh, Katy, please. I was senile by then, and I can't be held responsible for my actions."

Tom and I had married the previous year and moved to Illinois. I had missed Gram terribly, so the next summer we drove to Los Angeles for a visit. The day we arrived, I made Tom stop at

Gram's house even before going on to my parents'.

When Gram greeted us at the door, I immediately sensed that something about her was a little off. She was thrilled to see Tom and me, but somehow, she seemed different, sort of girlish. I tried to put a finger on it as Gram escorted us into her family room but was quickly distracted when I looked out the window to her large backyard. The grass and flowering bushes were overgrown, and weeds had sprouted everywhere.

In all the years that Rollie planted his miniature shrubs in the front yard, not once had he ventured out to the backyard, and not once had he acknowledged that Gram had hired a gardener for her backyard.

"Did you let your gardener go?" I asked as Tom and I sat beside Gram on the couch.

It was odd the way she giggled like a little girl and then asked, "Which one? My front yard gardener or my backyard gardener?"

"Your backyard gardener," I told her.

Gram clasped her hands together with excitement and said she had found a new one, "A darling, young boy in the neighborhood." She looked extremely perplexed as she added, "Though he doesn't always show up, because he has problems with his back. He told me this the other day when I paid him."

It was obvious the "darling young boy" was taking advantage of my grandmother, and because Tom could tell I was upset about it, he offered to mow her lawn before we left for my parents' house.

"Oh," Gram twittered like a flirting teenager, a tone I'd never heard from her before. "It would be sooo nice of you, Tommy. But I'll only let you cut my grass if you'll let me fix you something nice and cold to drink."

Tom said she had a deal. Then he went outside and got Gram's old push mower from the garage.

I remained in the house with Gram, thinking we could visit for a while, but she was nervous about Tom working outside in the hundred-degree heat and insisted on fixing him something to drink right away. "I want to make him something special," she said.

She rushed to the kitchen, reached inside the freezer, and pulled out a quart of ice cream, then carried it to the turquoise table and began scooping mounds of vanilla ice cream into a tall glass of root beer.

I tried to tell Gram that just root beer would be better for Tom, but she didn't seem to hear me as she hummed the tune of "He Walks With Me." Minutes later, she danced out to her back porch.

"Tommm-eee! Oh, Tommm-eee?" my grandmother called. The frothy glass of root beer and ice cream glistened as Gram held it high in the air for Tom to see.

Tom was in the back part of the yard pushing hard at the mower. At first, he didn't hear Gram, but after a second round of "Oh, Tommm-eee?" I saw my husband look up from his mowing. He squinted, put his hand above his eyes, looked in the direction of the porch, and squinted some more. I could tell he wasn't sure he was seeing correctly.

Gram waved at him, and he waved back. When Gram began her "Oh, Tommm-eee" again, he moved away from the mower and hesitantly walked toward Gram and me.

I worried that he would reject Gram's offering, so I gave him a pleading look, beseeching him to accept Gram's innocent gift. I even added three taps to my heart.

My wonderful husband slowly walked to the porch, weakly tapped his heart not quite three times, and then smiled at Gram. "Thank you, Gram," he said before taking the sticky glass from her hands. "Just what I needed."

He took a sip, wiped the foam and ice cream from his lips and handed the glass back to Gram.

"No, no, dear, you need your strength. Drink up, now." Gram shoved the glass back into Tom's hand.

Tom looked over Gram's shoulders at me, and then opened his eyes wide as if silently pleading, "Help me."

But I tilted my head and wrinkled my brow pleadingly. What could I do?

Tom took a deep breath and gulped down the drink – the whole thing, melted ice cream and all.

While Gram couldn't have looked prouder as Tom handed her the empty glass, I thought my husband looked awfully hot and sweaty and maybe a little grumpy, so I told Gram I would stay outside for a while and help with some of the edging.

Gram said that was a wonderful idea and skipped back into the house singing.

I couldn't figure it out. What was going on with Gram? She'd never behaved like this before, like a ding-a-ling teenage girl. I worried about this as I picked up Gram's old sheers and began trimming the hedge by the side of the yard.

I wasn't outside more than ten minutes before I heard from a distance, "Tommm-eeeee, oh, Tommm-eee." I looked at the back door and saw Gram waving another glass of vanilla ice cream and root beer. I frantically looked at Tom.

He paused for the longest moment, looked at Gram, slowly turned his head to look at me, and then looked back at Gram.

"Oh, gee, Gram. I couldn't. Thank you, though," he called out.

"Nonsense!" Gram called back. "I've made this especially for you. You wouldn't want to hurt my feelings, would you?"

"Well," Tom stalled for a moment to glare at me before adding, "It sure does look good."

I watched with utter dismay as Tom sauntered up to the porch, took the glass from Gram and gulped down the whole mushy drink.

"There," Gram sighed. "Wasn't that just what you needed to quench your thirst?"

"Just right," he said stifling a burp with what I thought was a hint of agony. "I don't think I'll need anything more to drink the rest of the day. Maybe just some water later on."

"Alright," Gram twittered and sang as she turned her back to us and retreated into the house as if on a mission.

Tom marched over to me and kissed my sweaty cheek. "Is she okay?" he asked.

"Well, I –" I started to say something about never seeing Gram like this before, but I was interrupted by the sound of Gram's voice.

"Tommm-eee, oh, Tommm-eee!"

I looked over Tom's shoulder – his back was facing the porch where Gram stood. "How did she do that so quickly?" I said incredulously.

Tom didn't need to turn his head to know what was waiting for him. He stared hard into my eyes, "No, Katy! No, no, no!"

I'd hoped that the heat was the reason for Gram's behavior and that she'd get back to normal when the weather got better. But she didn't. After Tom and I returned to Chicago, I called Gram every week to see how she was doing. She didn't remember I'd moved away and asked me again and again when I'd be coming to spend the night.

As bad as Gram seemed, I wasn't prepared for the drastic change in her a few months later when Tom and I flew home for Christmas. She had lost a lot of weight, and her beautiful brown eyes no longer twinkled with warmth and love. They had turned dark and distant. Several times, she called me by Mom's name, but then she'd catch herself and say she was just tired. She continually asked where we were or where we were going, even though I had told her moments before.

It was a tradition for my mother, Gram, and me to attend at least one Christmas program for the holidays. So, two days after Tom and I arrived in Los Angeles, my mother, thinking Gram would enjoy the Christmas extravaganza at the Crystal Cathedral with live animals, professional dancers, and singers, bought tickets for the three of us. We didn't plan on the weather being so cold and drizzly that December evening when we went to the Cathedral, and we certainly didn't expect to see a line of at least two hundred people waiting outside in the damp air.

The elderly woman in line ahead of us explained that the previous show had just finished, and we all were in for a long wait before the doors would open for our scheduled program. She'd no sooner told us this when one of the Cathedral ushers, a man in his mid-seventies, unlocked and opened one of the massive glass doors to make an announcement to the waiting crowd. He said it was still too early to let everyone in, but because of the weather, he and his fellow ushers were going to invite those who were handicapped or frail to come inside at that time.

I recall rolling my eyes, thinking that it would be at least another fifteen minutes of waiting, but I was wrong, for the elderly usher walked directly over to Gram and invited the three of us to follow him.

A wave of shock traveled through every nerve in my body. Why had he chosen to let us in before everyone else? Gram wasn't handicapped, and she wasn't anymore frail than half of the other people waiting outside. Was she?

Before I had time to think any further, I saw Gram link her arm with the usher's and gracefully, almost regally, walk past the waiting crowd into the Cathedral and down the red-carpeted aisle. My mother and I wordlessly watched Gram smile upward at the usher as sweetly as a blushing girl. With our tickets in hand, the gracious old gentleman led us to the front of the sanctuary, located our row, and then gingerly held Gram's arms, guiding her into her seat.

I was settling into my own seat when Gram waved her finger at the usher. "I'll bet you'd like to chase me up those stairs," she twittered. She was referring to the steps leading to the massive concert stage.

I immediately shot a look of surprise at my mother, who was seated on the other side of Gram.

The unsuspecting usher looked quite flabbergasted. "Well, I better not," he said smiling. "I have to worry about my old ticker!"

But Gram would not be cast aside. She winked at him and fluttered her eyelashes. "I'll bet you would if my slip was showing below my knees."

I don't know who was more embarrassed, the well-mannered usher or me. I stared long and hard at my mother and silently mouthed, "Mommmmm," as if she could do anything.

Gram's ill-equipped escort weakly smiled at her and then stammered, "Oh, I better not. I might get in trouble."

To which Gram giggled, "I'd let you catch me too."

I slumped deep into my seat, allowing only my eyes to show over the collar of my coat. What had happened to my straitlaced, even prudish grandmother?

Even after the bemused usher had left us and the lights had dimmed, even after the joyous sounds of Christmas filled the Crystal Cathedral, I found myself unable to enjoy the evening. My grandmother, my best friend, my roller derby partner, my Thinking Chair confidant had slipped away from me, and she didn't even know it.

"Gram?" I asked.

"Yes, sweetie?"

"Did you ever sense you were becoming senile?"

"When I first started having memory lapses, I suspected senility was settling in."

"Did you ever tell anyone?"

"Noooooo." She winced. "I didn't want anyone to know."

My parents hadn't told me until after Gram died. More than once, the police had called saying Gram had been found alone in her car, parked on a dark street, unable to tell them where she lived or how she had gotten so far from home.

"But didn't it scare you when the memory lapses happened?"

"Terribly. But as my memory became more and more foggy, I felt as if I were living outside of my own body. I knew I was dying, and I wasn't even bothered."

"How strange," I said.

"No stranger than the time you sensed you were dying."

I was pretty sure Gram was referring to the time after I'd been in the hospital for three weeks. An infection had set in after my first mastectomy. Unable to digest food, my weight had gone down to eighty-three pounds, and no one knew how to stop me from throwing up. I remember being pushed to an x-ray room in a wheelchair, and when it paused in front of a long, sliding glass window, I saw my reflection. There were dark circles under my eyes. My cheeks were hollow, bones protruded from my hospital gown, and I looked like someone who'd been in a concentration camp. Oddly enough, I wasn't scared. I saw this person who was supposed to be me, and I knew she was dying. It was just an observation.

"But I didn't die," I said.

"No, you didn't."

"Was I?"

"Were you what?"

"Dying."

"Yes, I believe you were," Gram said solemnly.

I swallowed hard. "Why didn't I die?

"Why do you think?" Gram asked.

I stroked Andy's head for a moment. "Because I loved living?" I said, not certain this was the right answer.

"Oh, not really. You've always been too afraid of living fully and enjoying all the things life has put before you." Gram spoke softly, looking me in the eyes as if looking right through me.

Andy began to change positions on the couch, and I leaned over to help him maneuver his hips. "Gram?" I said, looking up.

But she wasn't there.

Why was it that she never warned me of her departures, always leaving a thought or a question hanging in the air? You're too afraid of living fully?

I knew Gram was partially right. I was afraid of a lot of things: afraid Dr. Davis, like Dr. Chang, would caution me to not have children; afraid Tom and I would remain forever childless; afraid that if I did get pregnant, the cancer would return and my children would end up without a mother. I was afraid of passing on to my children the seeds of Wendy and Rollie's disease. And like most nights, I was definitely afraid of fully enjoying sleep, because sleep might drag me once again into the chilling nightmare where Uncle Rollie and his grotesque white piano amplified the screams of my helpless, little sister.

CHAPTER

NINE

A week later, I sat in the waiting area of the hospital's X-ray department. Dr. Davis had scheduled a liver scan for three o'clock, and it was already three twenty-five. I wouldn't have minded the wait, but I'd been required to drink two gallons of water two hours earlier and was not allowed to use the bathroom until after the test. I'd already gone to the nurses' station to let the R.N. know I was feeling uncomfortable, but all she offered was a sympathetic, "Oh, I'm sorry, honey. It will only be a few more minutes." When I returned to my seat, I tried to think of something, anything, to take my mind off the building pressure in my bladder.

I sat down and looked around the room with its 1960s décor. But it was too depressing, so I began to stare at the extremely overweight gentleman seated across from me on the orange, plastic couch. He kept breathing in and out with a series of short pants followed by a massive burst of air, and all the while, little grunts vibrated within his throat. I noted how limply his arms stuck out at the sides. Too much flesh between the bones, I deduced. I watched as beads of sweat dripped from his forehead to his chin. He looked as uncomfortable as I was feeling, and I wondered if he, too, was sitting on a full bladder, waiting to have a liver scan.

Then I began to have absurd thoughts. I started to estimate how much water a man his size would have had to consume to fill his bladder – certainly a lot more than I had needed to fill mine.

When the obese man looked in my direction, I lowered my head just enough so that I could continue to monitor his behavior. I silently prayed to myself. "Please, Mr. Fat Man. Please do not have an accident. There are no life preservers in this room, and the Coast Guard would never make it here in time." It was a little joke just for me, a way of humoring myself in such an uncomfortable situation.

"Katy, how can you think such things?" Gram was sitting across from me, right beside Mr. Fat Man.

"What are you doing here?" I asked.

Immediately, Gram shook her head and rolled her eyes in the direction of Mr. Fat Man.

"What?" asked Mr. Fat Man with a groan.

"Oh, um," I paused, staring icily at Gram. "I asked why you were here, but really, you don't have to tell me. I, ah, I know it's none of my business." This was truly a sincere apology.

"I have bladder issues," he said gravely as his right index finger pointed at his lower stomach.

I looked at Gram, who was also pointing at the fat man's lower stomach.

"You, too?" he asked me.

Gram chortled while she covered her mouth and shook her head, "Ask our friend if he can hold on." Gram spit out an unladylike laugh. She took a deep breath and completed her thought, "Ask him if he can hold on while you think about it." She could barely spit out the words.

Instantly, Gram's juvenile joke hit me as the funniest thing I'd ever heard, and it caused me to blurt out the most unrefined guffaw I'd ever heard. I don't know why Gram's joke struck me as so funny, but I began to laugh so hard I had to stand up and pace the floor with my knees pressed together. I held my stomach, as if that was going to keep me from leaking.

"I'm so sorry, I," but more laughter involuntarily erupted from my mouth. "I..."

Gram was mimicking the stunned look on Mr. Fat Man's face, which made me helpless to complete my apology.

"Stop it!" I pleaded while looking at Gram.

"Stop what?" asked Mr. Fat Man. He looked to his left and then his right but saw no one. The now affronted look on his face caused me to sober up.

"Oh! I was just telling myself to stop laughing."

I didn't blame him for staring at me with contempt.

"I wasn't laughing at you," I said sincerely, for it truly was my grandmother who had caused all the hilarity.

But it was apparent that I had not appeased Mr. Fat Man at all.

"You see, I, too, am having bladder problems because I have to keep holding water until I take a liver scan." I smiled at the poor man, but he remained stoically silent before me. "It's kind of a funny situation to be in, isn't it?" I asked him meekly.

"I don't see why you think this is so funny," he said indignantly. "You obviously didn't drink as much water as I did, not enough to get good test results anyway. You wouldn't be able to laugh and be dry at the same time if you had," he sneered.

Why did he have to go and say that? Gram and I burst into unstoppable laughter again.

"Well! You'll probably have to take the test again," he warned with hurt in his voice.

"Please forgive me," I begged as I gulped down more laughter. "I was only laughing at a memory of my grandmother."

"Did she have bladder problems?"

"I beg your pardon!" Gram rose from her seat. She wasn't laughing anymore.

"There was a time when we thought she did."

"What in the world! I've never heard such a thing!" Gram fell back into her seat.

"I wasn't laughing at you," I lied to Mr. Fat Man. "I was remembering a family gathering at my grandmother's house." I could tell I was not very convincing, but I'd started the story, so I decided to finish it.

"My grandmother had just served dessert to everyone when she excused herself to go to the ladies' room. After a while, we all began to notice she had been in there an awfully long time."

Grandma scowled. "Katy, I forbid you to tell this story!"

"Yep, first sign of bladder problems." The fat man nodded with authority.

"Oh, for cat's liver!" my grandmother shrieked.

"There was just the one bathroom," I said, "so after a while, a line started to form as everyone waited for my grandmother to finish. It got a little embarrassing, too, because we could hear through the door that she was definitely still going. It seemed unbelievable that such a petite lady could hold so much inside her."

"You can't control that kind of thing," the fat man interjected with genuine sympathy and understanding.

"Oh, shut him up," Gram snapped.

I ignored her and continued.

"Well, she was controlling it. You see, my grandmother had been playing a trick on us. She had filled a douche bag with water and was letting it slowly trickle into the toilet, and the whole time she was in the bathroom, she was laughing at our muffled jokes."

"Well, then, it was wrong of her to make all of you wait so long," judged the fat man. "You all could have gotten sick."

"No sense of humor," my grandmother cried as she threw her hands into the air.

"Sitting here reminded of my grandmother's little prank, because I'm holding so much water right now. I was just laughing at the memory," I said to the fat man.

"Oh," was all he said.

"There! You wasted a perfectly good story on him," Gram said. "One you should never share with the public."

The glass window to the nurses' area opened and a voice called out, Harvey Paddle."

"Did she say Hardy Puddle?" Gram asked.

Once again Gram and I burst into irrepressible laughter, while Mr. Fat Man, better known as Mr. Hardy Puddle, stormed through the door to the X-ray room, shooting an angry glance my way.

"No puddle here," howled Gram as she peered into his now empty seat.

"Oh," I groaned with pain. "Please Gram, don't make me laugh any more. I'm really afraid I'll lose control."

"You worry about it a lot, don't you sweetie?" Gram had suddenly become very serious.

"I worry about what?"

"Losing control of your life," Gram said, as if this were a logical thought and not the most ludicrous jump I'd ever heard.

"My life? Gram, I was referring to my bladder."

"I know, dear, but it's really the same thing, isn't it?"

"Excuse me? My bladder and my life?" I said incredulously.

"I wonder when you first worried about losing control?"

"About ten minutes ago when I was told to hold ten glasses of water inside of me for a while longer."

"No, no. I mean when do you suppose you were first afraid that you'd lost control of your life?"

Okay, I thought. I'll play this game of Gram's, but only because she had me in a vulnerable position.

"Well," I sighed, patronizing her. "Maybe the day my doctor told me I had cancer, when he said the cancer had spread. I didn't have control of anything anymore."

"No, I don't think that was the first time," Gram argued patronizingly.

"It's not?" I asked. "Well, Gram, when was the first time?" Obviously, she knew the answer she was looking for.

"Oh, you know," she pushed.

"Katherine McAndrews," called the same nurse who had taken Mr. Puddle into the examining room.

I bolted from my seat, grateful to finally have been called. Gram did not follow me into the X-ray room, where, wrapped a paper dressing gown, I had to lie perfectly still on a cold metal gurney. And she wasn't there as heavy machinery hovered above my stomach and chest, threatening to find signs of a cancer I didn't want. I was left alone to ponder over her parting words. Last week she had said that I was afraid of life, and now she was implying that I was afraid I would lose control of it.

The more I thought about this, the more I realized that Gram was a fine one to be accusing me of being afraid of losing control.

What about the week before my father and mother were to be married? I'd heard the story a hundred times before: how Gram had hoped my father would marry Margie Kilfeather, the daughter of a friend of hers and a girl Dad had dated a couple of times when he was in high school. But then World War II broke out and Dad joined the Navy. He met my mother in San Francisco; they fell in love and became engaged.

Gram had pretended to be happy about the whole thing, because no date for the wedding had been set, but in truth, she hoped my parents would wait until the war was over in order to give Dad time to fall out of love with my mother.

When Gram and Grandpa got a call from Dad telling them his ship had just docked in Los Angeles and my mom would be arriving in three days, Gram panicked. My parents were going to be married as soon as my mother arrived from San Francisco, which was to be any day. Gram didn't like having lost control of this situation, so she decided to take charge. Without informing my dad, she sent a telegram to my mother telling her not to come to Los Angeles because there would be no wedding.

There was a terrible scene when Gram and Grandpa and Uncle Rollie met Dad at his ship and told him what Gram had done. My father picked up his bags and told Gram he was going to San Francisco to get married whether Gram liked it or not. It was hard enough on Dad to hear his mother cry, telling him he was hurting her beyond repair. But I was told that the worst part for him was watching Rollie, who was only eight at the time, cling to Gram as he screamed out his haunting promise, "Don't worry, Mommy, I'll never leave you. I'll never hurt you like my big brother!"

The X-ray technician had stopped moving the machinery and was looking intently at the screen.

"Everything ok?" I asked.

"Just relax and hold still," he said without looking at me.

I closed my eyes and began to think about the question Gram had asked me. When was the first time I felt I'd lost control of my life?

Maybe it was with Doug Bradford.

Doug had been a junior, a year ahead of me, and from a different high school. I had liked the idea of dating someone who knew nothing about Wendy and Rollie, and besides, Doug wasn't just someone. He was good looking and very cool. Too cool, actually.

Doug had asked me out the week after a friend introduced us, and I'd assumed it meant we'd go to a movie. So did my parents. But after Doug picked me up in his open-air Jeepster, he drove straight to a secluded hilltop. We talked, and I think he kissed me once. I enjoyed being with him and was thrilled that he wanted to take me out again.

But the next Saturday night when Doug picked me up and headed to the same hilltop, I began to wonder if he had ever heard of ice cream shops or movie theaters. At sixteen, I was neither sophisticated nor assertive, so when Doug started to make his moves with busy hands and moist lips, I panicked. All I could think of was how I could stop Doug without having him think I was a prude.

I can only believe I did what any other creative teenager would have done. I told Doug I really couldn't get into kissing him so soon.

"So soon?" he asked.

"So soon after the death of my boyfriend." I sighed.

"Are you kidding me?" Doug asked sympathetically.

"No." I closed my eyes while vying for time. "He died of a brain tumor last summer."

This was not a prepared or voluntary response to Doug's romantic overtures or his sudden surprise. It was simply the most available explanation I could think of at that moment.

In my defense, I had not told a complete lie. There had been a boy who'd gone to my school and who actually had died of a brain tumor the year before. I hadn't known him very well, but my brother Sam had. Once, I'd fantasized about how romantic my life would be if I'd been this guy's girlfriend. What delicious tragedy would fill the halls at school as I walked through them? I could see the other students smiling at me with a kind of reverence. There goes Katy Welborn. She's so brave. My fantasies back then were heavily influenced by Doctor Kildare, which happened to be my favorite television program.

To this day, I don't know what possessed me to make up such a grand lie, but it worked. Doug's hands stopped everything they were doing, or trying to do, and he suddenly became interested in the details of my tragic past. How long had my dead boyfriend and I dated, the gullible Doug wanted to know. And how long had my boyfriend been sick? Wasn't it hard for me to get over? Doug's questions made me feel so uneasy that I finally told him I needed to go home, because it was too difficult to keep talking about.

Doug didn't ask me out again, which was just as well, because he was too much of a Romeo for me to handle. Besides, I didn't want to answer any more questions about my dead boyfriend.

It was about a year and a half later when Sam, who had just started at Stanford as a freshman, had written home from Palo Alto saying he had a great roommate whose name was Doug Bradford. He didn't say anything else about this roommate. Nothing about where he was from or if I'd known him. It had to be million-to-one odds that Sam's roommate was the very same Doug Bradford with whom I'd shared my tragic past.

Still, I lived in fear for the next three months until Thanksgiving when Sam came home. I'd almost convinced myself that God wouldn't play such a horrible trick on me. But I was wrong.

Sam came home that Thanksgiving, bringing with him the one and only Doug Bradford. Both my brother and my one-time date acted innocent when introductions were made to the family, but I knew my brother and his college roommate had something planned for me.

I didn't have to wait long to find out what it was. With the dinner dishes cleared and all my uncles and aunts, cousins and close family friends sitting at the table waiting for pumpkin pie and coffee to be served, my mother made her annual Thanksgiving request. She wanted each person to name one thing he or she was thankful for.

Sam had forever hated this tradition and habitually groaned his unhappiness at having to come up with something. And each year when it was his turn, he'd say something stupid like, "I'm thankful Katy brushed her teeth today." My mother would stare at him until he'd say something a little more thoughtful like, "I'm thankful for good tasting toothpaste."

But this particular Thanksgiving, after my mother made her annual request, Sam stood up and asked to be first. Everyone smiled affectionately at him, thinking how mature he'd become after one semester in college. I, instead, said a silent and desperate prayer.

Sam said, "I'm thankful that my good friend Doug is here with us today."

"So are we," a few relatives chimed in.

227

My hands were clenched on my lap, and I knew there was no stopping my brother.

"He might not be here next year if the doctors don't find out what's wrong with him."

"Oh," everyone at the table said with genuine surprise and worry.

"Yes," Sam said, putting his arm around Doug's shoulders. "Doug's been having terrible headaches, and his doctors think it might be a brain tumor."

"Oh, no." Gram sighed as she sat beside me at the table. She loved Doctor Kildare as much as I did.

"Noooo," said everyone else.

"Yes." Doug slowly nodded his head at everyone. "I don't know how long I have to live." He rested his eyes on Gram.

"How could this happen to such a nice boy?" she whispered in my ear.

If only she'd known what was going on! She would have helped me out! I was being humiliated, and I couldn't stop it from happening.

"That's why Sam suggested I come to see Katy," Doug continued, now tilting his head in a sorrowful manner.

"Hmmmmm?" everyone at the table hummed together as they turned their attention to me.

"We thought that since Katy's had firsthand experience in helping terminally ill boyfriends, especially ones with brain tumors, she could comfort Doug during his trying time," said Sam with a theatrical plea toward me.

Sam started laughing, not in a mean-spirited way. He was laughing as if begging me to laugh along with him.

Instead, I began to laugh and cry at the same time. My hands flew to my open mouth and I looked around the table at the faces of my relatives, each of their stares revealing worried concern about my sanity.

Completely and utterly humiliated, I left the table and ran to my room.

Sam came after me and tried to coax me back to the table.

I screamed at him to leave me alone.

But Sam kept pleading with a gentleness that said he was repentant and sorry. "Katy, it was just a joke. That's all. I misunderstood and thought you'd think it was funny too. I'm really sorry."

I could tell that Sam was sorry, but I was too hurt and embarrassed to hear the depth of his pain. I cried, "I hate you, Sam! I thought you were my friend. A friend wouldn't have humiliated me!"

I didn't mean what I'd said, and I certainly didn't understand where those words were coming from. But I'll never forget the look on Sam's face. It was filled with such hurt and pain that I was suddenly afraid that my uncontrolled emotions and words had irreparably hurt my brother, someone I loved so deeply.

"That was the moment, wasn't it?" I whispered inside my head. That was when I decided I would never lose control of anything ever again – not my words or my thoughts, not my actions or emotions, not anything in my life.

A voice broke into my thoughts. "I know you're uncomfortable. Are you doing okay?"

My eyes bolted open and I saw the technician looking at me. The scanning machine was hovering over my upper abdomen.

"Yes," I answered.

"Well, hang in there a little longer," he said.

I closed my eyes and thought of how different life at home had seemed to be after that Thanksgiving, after Sam had returned to Stanford. Wendy had become more volatile and unpredictable. I began to come straight home after school, turning down invitations to friends' houses. I quit my membership in the French club and the drill team. Too much activity, too many friends, too much fun – those things would make me sloppy and off guard, causing me to lose my grip, my control over the important things in life.

The sound of the scanning machine slowed, and I suddenly realized that I had never stopped being afraid of losing control.

"Okay. That's it for now," said the technician.

"When will I know the results?" I asked, rubbing my eyes.

"Your doctor won't have them until after Thanksgiving."

"But Thanksgiving is six days away," I said with alarm.

"I'm sorry; I'm just a lowly technician. I have no control over when patients get their results."

"It's really ten days, you know, because the Friday after Thanksgiving is a holiday, and my doctor won't be in on Saturday or Sunday." I was hoping the technician might think of a way to get the results to my doctor sooner.

"Just relax and enjoy the holiday."

Tom and I would be spending Thanksgiving in Minneapolis. How was I going to relax and enjoy my holiday when my fate lay hidden in a lab report somewhere in Los Angeles, a fate and a report over which I had no control?

CHAPTER

TEN

Tom was one of those people who hated flying. Not me. Sitting in an airplane and flying high above the ground made me feel peaceful and hopeful about life, about the world in general. I actually looked forward to being able to stare out an airplane window, to daydream the time away without any guilt. So, why, on this particular flight back to Los Angeles, wasn't I able to shake the sadness inside me? It wasn't because Tom had to go on to New York without me for a few days. I didn't mind flying alone. Then why did I feel like crying? It had to be Thanksgiving Day.

The Thanksgiving holiday was Tom's favorite time to go home to Minnesota. It was the only time of the year when his relatives from all over the Midwest got together, including Tom's favorite cousins, the ones he grew up with, the ones with so many children. We had not attended his family Thanksgiving in five years, mainly because Tom's work schedule had seemed to get in the way. We'd visited several summers and once in the spring but never when all the relatives were together. So, Tom was determined that we not miss the next turkey dinner in Minnesota. And we didn't.

I liked the Midwest and was happy to be riding with Tom and his parents along a tree-lined, winding road that followed Minnehaha Creek through the southwestern corner of Minneapolis. We were on our way to the suburb of Edina, to the home of Kevin and Shelley, Tom's brother and sister-in-law, for Thanksgiving dinner. The gray November sky billowed with storm clouds and the wind blew the last remaining leaves from the trees. A few snowflakes danced in the air and I found myself wishing for a major snowstorm.

Kevin and Shelley's home was one of those huge, rambling old houses with three stories and a basement as big as the whole upper level. It was surprising how crowded the house felt once all the relatives arrived. There were so many children running around, some of whom I'd held in my arms as babies a few years earlier. The rest were children whom I'd received birth announcements for but had never met. No child at the gathering was over eight years old.

During the early part of the day I hung around the living room with the adults and listened to their stories while nibbling on too many nuts and chips. After an hour or so, I became restless and decided to walk around. I aimlessly wandered from room to room until I ended up in the basement, where all the children seemed to be.

There was so much activity down there, so much energy, and it was fun to watch. Two young girls were playing ping-pong, and several smaller children scooted around the stairwell on small cars and trucks. A group of four boys – I guessed they were five or six years old – were playing floor hockey in their socks and paid no attention to the occasional basketball rolling between their goals. This was where I wanted to be for the moment, so I quietly seated myself on an old sofa right behind three other boys who were playing a Nintendo game. I knew each boy by name, but I was a complete stranger to them.

They were fairly intent upon their game until Jonathan, who was obviously the leader of this trio, stopped to look at me. He squinted his eyes in my direction and then pointed at his younger cousin, Preston. "Are you his mother?" Jonathan asked me.

"No." I smiled. "Your Aunt Nancy is Preston's mother."

"Oh," Jonathan replied. As he let this information soak in, he kept both eyes locked on me.

I assumed he knew Aunt Nancy. She lived in Minnesota, and Jonathan had met her at many gatherings. Maybe he hadn't made the connection between Preston and Aunt Nancy before. I waited for Jonathan to return to his game, since I'd answered his question.

Instead, he squinted his eyes a little tighter and pointed to my nephew Mark. "Are you his mother?"

"No. Your Aunt Shelley is Mark's mother," I said, trying not to laugh. How could he not know to whom these cousins belonged?

"Oh," he said with a growing air of suspicion. Jonathan's eyes would not leave mine. He was obviously confused, and my answers were not helping him.

Jonathan put both hands to his hips and tilted his head. "Whose mother are you?" he demanded.

His words hit me hard, like a bolt of lightning right to my heart. But it was a wonderful and logical question for a five-year-old to ask.

"I'm nobody's mother," I said.

Nobody's mother echoed softly in my head.

"Mmm," Jonathan said, pursing his lips and tightening the squint of one eye. Then with a cock of his head, Jonathan shot back at me, "Well, why are you here?"

He was no dummy, this child. He'd obviously decided that adults were admitted to this yearly gathering only if they flashed a child in front of them like some kind of I.D. In his mind, I was attending the party illegally, and he was ready to bounce me out of there.

"I'm married to your father's cousin. Do you remember meeting Uncle Tom?"

"No."

"Well, Uncle Tom is the tall man with blond hair. He grew up with your father."

Jonathan remained silent, still looking suspicious of my credentials.

"Uncle Tom and I don't have any children." I paused. "Not yet. But we'd like to have a child," I added, hoping I'd be more acceptable to him.

"Mmmm." Jonathan nodded slowly and looked down at the floor. I guessed he was considering whether this last bit of information would suffice. Then, without another word, he had turned away to play the Nintendo game.

The airplane bounced around for a moment, and I tightened my seat belt. Why couldn't I get those words out of my head? Whose mother are you? I'm nobody's mother. Whose mother are you? I'm nobody's mother. They developed their own cadence and rhythm in my head and sent waves of nausea down through my throat to the pit of my stomach. Would people be asking me this question the rest of my life? Would the answer always be the same? I'm nobody's mother.

I looked away from the airplane window and realized that this would be a long trip home if I didn't do something to stop the throbbing of those words. So, I pulled down the tray table and took a notepad and pen from my bag. The photo of Emily and me slipped from the pages of the pad. I'd placed it there to remind me of my promise to write her a letter as soon as I got home. But now was as good a time as any. I thought for a moment and then began to write.

Dear Emily,

It was so nice to meet you and to play
with you on Thanksgiving Day. It made me
feel so good when you asked me to go on a walk
with you and your mother. The best part of
Thanksgiving Day was making a new friend.
You.

I am sending this picture of our dog Andy.
He is sitting on the front porch where he can
see all the cars and people go by. I think he
looks a little bit like your dog, Camille.

I hope you will come to California and stay

at our house someday soon, but in the meantime,

I know that Uncle Tom and I will be back in Minnesota,

and I will get to see you again then.

I couldn't think of anything else to say, so I dropped my pen and stared out the window again. As I looked out at a wall of gray clouds, I made a mental note to remember to pull a picture of Andy from the picture book and send it with the letter. Maybe I could think of more interesting things to say to Emily once I got home.

"Why don't I remember who little Emily is?" a voice casually asked me.

I turned my attention from the window to see that the gentleman who had started the flight in the aisle seat next to me was gone. He must have gone to the restroom without my noticing it. Instead, Gram was comfortably settled in his seat, seat belt locked across her waist and all.

"Because you never met her," I said as I folded the unfinished letter and began to slip it into an envelope. "Emily's the daughter of Tom's cousin, Brad. I think you met him at our wedding, but Emily wasn't born yet."

I looked toward the front of the plane and saw my former seatmate standing by the rest room waiting his turn.

"She looks so much like you, she could be your daughter," Gram said as she pointed to the Polaroid picture of Emily and me. Tom had taken the picture as Emily and I were saying goodbye on Thanksgiving night.

After Jonathan's basement cross-examination, I had decided to walk upstairs to join the adults, but Emily had intercepted me and shyly asked if I'd be her partner in ping-pong against two boy cousins. She'd said no one else wanted to be her partner, so what could I do?

My little six-year-old niece-in-law and I made a pretty good team against her seven- and eight-year-old relatives. We lost two close matches and were about to begin a third when we were called to dinner.

Emily took my hand and led me up the stairs to the dining room. Everyone hovered around the table, checking to see where their name card was placed, and I pretended not to see Emily take hers and exchange it with the name card next to mine.

After the whole family was seated, we all joined hands to give thanks. There I was, holding Tom's hand on my left and Emily's hand on my right. As my brother-in-law gave the blessing, I opened my eyes slightly and looked across the table. Jonathan was staring intently at me. I smiled, but he promptly bowed his head and closed his eyes. His innocent words had quietly filled my head again: Whose mother are you?

"Gram," I said, "did you know I called some adoption agencies last week?"

"Nooo," Gram said, but I could tell by the tone of her 'nooo' and the way she avoided looking at me that she did know.

"Well, I did. Just before Tom and I flew to Minnesota," I said, turning over the picture of Emily and me.

"What a good idea." Gram smiled.

Why was it such a good idea? Did Gram know the results of my tests? The hospital technician said I might get the results the Monday after Thanksgiving. Twenty-four hours away. Was adoption going to be Tom's and my only choice, because Dr. Davis would tell us not to have our own child?

All at once I felt nauseous. "Why did you say that?"

"Say what?"

"Why did you say it's a good idea?" I pressed.

"I don't know. It's not a bad idea to check out all your alternatives while you wait to hear from your doctor."

"Gram, do you know something I don't know?"

"Oh, cat's liver, Katy. I know so many things you don't think you know, but you do, and I don't know many more things you may or may not know. But there are just as many things I don't know that you don't know." She took a long breath and continued. "So, what is it you think I know that you don't know and you want me to help you know even though you probably already know?"

I held up my hand to stop her. Gram wasn't going to tell me about the test results. This I knew. "I told you that I called some adoption agencies just before Thanksgiving."

"And I said what a good idea," countered my guardian angel.

"Well, probably not such a good idea," I said. "The first adoption counselor I called told me that her agency would need to receive medical records of both Tom and me before they could start the adoption process."

"Interesting," Gram said.

"When I explained that I'd had breast cancer, she said they couldn't even consider me as an adoptive parent. She said she was sorry, but the chances were too great that I'd die before the child was grown up."

"What in the world!" Gram gasped.

"That wasn't the worst part. When I told her I'd not had the cancer for three years and was basically cured, she said, "You never know for sure, do you?""

"Good Godfrey! She didn't really say that, did she?" Gram asked.

I tried to slip the picture of Emily and me between the pages of the note pad, but the photo fell to the floor. I unbuckled my seat belt and bent down to retrieve it.

"I called other agencies," I said reaching under the seat in front of me. "But they all said basically the same thing. My having had cancer and Tom's and my age make us unlikely candidates for adopting a child. Can you believe that?" I asked, stretching my arm and neck and head farther under the seat in front of me.

"No, I can't," Gram said.

I caught a corner of the picture between my two middle fingers and started to pull myself up.

"So, is that it? Are you giving up on adoption?" Gram asked.

My hand bumped against the bottom of the seat and the picture slipped from my fingers.

"No." I sighed with the side of my head pressing against the seat in front and my arm stretching as far as it could reach. "I think I'll keep trying for a while."

"Can I help you?" asked a voice much deeper than Gram's.

My fingers grabbed a hold of the picture, and I carefully pulled myself up to see that the gentleman had returned from the restroom and was easing himself into his seat. Gram was gone.

"Oh, thank you. I just dropped this," I said holding the photo out for him to see.

He leaned back his seat while looking at the picture of Emily and me.

"How nice," he smiled. "Are you her mother?"

"No," I said. "I'm nobody's mother."

ELEVEN

Forgotten Cookies...where was that recipe? Gram and I had made them so often that I almost knew it by heart: egg whites, chocolate chips, and sugar. Those were the only ingredients, I was pretty certain. Simple. Beat the egg whites, but how many? Add the sugar until everything peaked. How much sugar? Then add the chips. The only thing left was to put drops of the dough onto a cookie sheet. But was it supposed to be greased or ungreased? Well, hmmm. That card had to be in the recipe box.

"Two eggs," said Gram matter-of-factly.

I looked up from the assortment of recipe cards I'd scattered on top of the kitchen table and was relieved to see my grandmother sitting in the chair across from me.

"I thought so," I said, not sure I really would have remembered how many eggs without Gram's help.

"You forgot the cream of tartar," she added.

"Oh, thanks." I'd never have remembered that on my own.

Andy was lying by my side with his head resting on my right foot. He'd always had a thing about my feet. He either had to sit on them or sleep on them. When I was home those months recuperating from cancer surgery, I spent a lot of time resting on the couch or the bed but never without Andy right beside me with his head draped over my feet. And when I'd open my eyes, there were his big, brown eyes connected to mine.

I think he knows I'm okay now, but he still insists on sitting or lying on one of my feet, even if I'm standing. And it's no use moving a foot. He'll just scoot his derriere right back onto it.

Andy must have sensed Gram's presence across the table, because he lifted his heavy head and sniffed in her direction.

"One cup chips," she continued. "And two-thirds of a cup of sugar."

"Thanks Gram." I smiled at her but continued to search through the box.

"Why don't you get a piece of paper and write it down as I tell you?" Gram suggested.

"I can't. It wouldn't be the same if I didn't use the piece of paper you wrote the recipe on. Do you remember?"

"Let me think. It was the year you were teaching at the little church school in the mountains."

"Yes." I smiled as the memory of that fall swept over me.

It was the fall after I'd graduated from college. Tom and I had broken off our engagement the month before graduation, so I had returned to California and found a teaching position at a small Episcopal school built in 1918 at the foot of the San Gabriel Mountains. The founding fathers had chosen the location well, building a modest, California mission style church and adjoining school under a stand of towering, spectacular evergreens obscuring any clue that the suburban sprawl of Los Angeles was just an hour away.

Each morning, I hiked up the hill from my apartment to the school's ivy-covered gray stone walls and into my classroom, which had once served as sleeping quarters for seven cloistered Episcopal nuns. The room was long and narrow, with three stained glass windows along one wall. My thirteen sixth graders with their desks and books, our three gerbils, and two rabbits squeezed comfortably into this chamber room.

I still remembered the names of each of my students, but it was Larry who first came to mind when I thought back on those days. He had been the class troublemaker, not a terrible one, and it had been he who would knock on my apartment door each morning to escort me the five blocks to school.

I had rented a one-bedroom apartment located behind the volunteer fire department. My paychecks from the teaching position were so small I couldn't afford a telephone. I had no car and no television. But I didn't need much. I had the old queen bed from home, my Thinking Chair, an old sofa borrowed from a neighbor's garage, and a clock radio.

"Your Forgotten Cookies made Christmas very special for the kids and me," I said to Gram.

"I think you were just being nice to an old lady by making me think I was needed," she said.

Not true. I really had needed Gram's help. I'd promised my students a Christmas party and wanted to make Gram's Forgotten Cookies as

243

a special treat – the same cookies she made for me each Christmas. My only problem had been that my tiny kitchenette was missing the necessary utensils and equipment for making the cookies. I couldn't afford to buy them.

So, the evening before the Christmas party, Gram drove to my apartment with paper bags that she had filled with her own weathered spatulas and greasy cookie sheets, measuring cups and spoons, all the ingredients needed to make her famous recipe, and most important of all, the yellowed and stained recipe card for Gram's Forgotten Cookies. We spent the night together preparing the cookies and talking and wrapping the presents I'd made for each student and singing and talking some more.

By the time we went to bed, it was obvious that Gram was more than a little tired; she was utterly worn out, completely depleted. I recall feeling a twinge of concern over how exhausting our evening had been for her, so I was grateful that our plan for the next morning was to let Gram sleep in while I borrowed her car to transport the presents, the decorations, and the party food to school. She would be able to relax and nap, even read her movie magazines until I returned in the afternoon.

Gram's instructions for her Forgotten Cookies required me to turn off the already preheated oven, place the cookie sheets with the large dollops of Forgotten Cookie dough in the oven, and leave them there overnight. So, of course, the next morning, when I loaded everything for the party into the back seat of Gram's car, I remembered everything - everything except the Forgotten Cookies. They were still in the oven and definitely forgotten.

I didn't discover this until twelve noon when the party was about to begin. I made my students sit and watch me pull each item, one by one, from Gram's brown paper bags. With great fanfare, I slowly revealed the red napkins, then the green paper plates, and by the time I pulled out the white paper cups, the kids were clapping and cheering. But when I reached for the two cartons of punch and saw just the bag of pretzels remaining, panic blazed through my entire nervous system. I suddenly realized I had completely ignored the note I'd taped to my apartment door, a note to remind me not to forget the Forgotten Cookies, the ones still sitting inside my oven.

There I was, thirteen sets of excited eyes locked on me, all waiting in anticipation for their teacher to pull from the bag the special surprise: the famous Cornelia Carlton Colburn Forgotten Cookies.

Two weeks before the party, I'd fabricated a story about the Forgotten Cookies and the woman who had invented them. I had told my thirteen trusting students that the recipe was a secret that not even kings and queens from as far away as Albania and Afghanistan could procure from Cornelia, even though they'd offered their jewels, their crowns, even their kingdoms. My students were even more intrigued and believing when I'd said that just two people in the whole world knew this secret recipe.

"Who are those two people?" the children had asked.

"Cornelia Carlton Colburn —" I paused to add to the drama.

"And," my anxious students called out in unison.

"Aaaaand," I teased. "And her beloved granddaughter."

"Where did they keep the recipe?" they wanted to know.

"Safe inside their memories," I answered.

"So, how come you know the recipe?" Larry, my not-so- troublesome troublemaker, taunted me.

I smiled slyly.

"Oooooo," the kids said simultaneously.

"Are you the granddaughter?" asked one of my students.

"Or are you Cornelia?" taunted Larry.

I answered them with a roll of my eyes and a one-sided smile. For the next two weeks, there had been endless questions and interrogations about my knowledge and relationship to the now famous Cornelia.

So, on the day of the party when I looked into the bag that was missing the Forgotten Cookies, the kids all giggled thinking I was teasing them as I gasped in terror. They shrieked with laughter when I said I was sorry, but I'd forgotten the Forgotten Cookies.

All the while my mind raced, trying to find a way to get those cookies into the classroom. I couldn't dash to the apartment and leave the kids alone in the classroom. I couldn't send a child running the five blocks to my apartment; I'd need a parent's permission slip. And I couldn't use the pay telephone in the office to call Gram; my apartment didn't have a phone.

"I was looking at an angel of mercy when I saw you standing at the classroom door," I said to Gram, who was still sitting across from me at the kitchen table.

"I knew you would forget to pull those cookies out of the oven," Gram said as she leaned her head down to look at Andy under the table. "I fretted the whole night as I slept in your apartment."

Gram had later told me that she had woken up two hours after I'd left for school and, sure enough, had found my cookies forgotten and still in the oven. So, being Gram, she had wasted no time getting dressed, wrapping the cookies in waxed paper, and walking her seventy-nine-year old body all the way uphill to the school.

By the time Gram had appeared at the classroom door, she was out of breath. Sweat had beaded around her upper lip and forehead, but she was smiling and singing, "Yoo-whoooo!"

It only took me a second to compose myself and make an announcement. "Students, I'd like you to meet Cornelia Carlton Colburn."

My students were wonderful. They cheered and applauded as Gram stood in the doorway, holding the large platter of Forgotten Cookies, but it was Larry who went up to Gram and escorted her to his chair as if she were royalty. He even bowed to her, with one hand behind his back and one sweeping the floor, before he took the plate of cookies and carried them high above his head. The other students clapped and hummed to the beat of "Pomp and Circumstance" while Larry marched up and down the narrow desk aisle.

Every child in that room had been convinced that Gram and I had planned the surprise visit from the one and only Cornelia of Forgotten Cookie fame. I had seen no reason to make them think differently.

It still tugged at my heart when I remembered how tired Gram looked as she sat in Larry's chair. I could tell she didn't really feel like staying, but she did. She was even coaxed into singing a solo of "O Holy Night" that no one snickered at, even though her voice warbled with each note the way old ladies' voices tend to do. I had been proud to be the granddaughter of Cornelia Carlton Colburn and proud to be the teacher of those thirteen extraordinary sixth graders.

"Katy," Gram said, "what was that oath you had the children recite before you gave them your little Christmas present?"

I had to think a moment to remember the little pledge I'd written on my blackboard.

"Oh, it was something like 'I, student of Cornelia Carlton Colburn's granddaughter, promise to honor the secret of the sacred Forgotten Cookie Recipe and to share it only with those who prove themselves to be worthy.'"

"Well, I have to say, Katy, I was astonished that those children were so excited over such unusual gifts." Gram gave a light chuckle as she said this.

I was as surprised as Gram. I'd taken thirteen index cards and made them look weathered, slightly yellowed, and lightly burnt along the edges in the hopes of making them appear as if they were a hundred years old. Then in my own amateur version of Old English cursive, I'd written, Secret Recipe for Cornelia Carlton Colburn's Forgotten Cookies at the top of each card. The recipe and directions were written underneath the title. These were the Christmas gifts Gram and I had wrapped the night before in red and green cellophane tied with sparkly gold ribbon.

"They couldn't wait to be the next one to say the oath and receive that recipe card." Gram chuckled again. "I wonder if any of them kept it."

Andy slowly lifted himself up and sauntered over to Gram. Did he actually rest his head on Gram's foot?

"I felt so alone after you'd gone home that night," I added.

"I know, sweetie." Gram smiled.

I had wanted Gram to stay with me one more night, but she had said she was tired and needed to be in her own bed. I knew now that the sadness I'd felt as I watched her drive away was because I'd seen the first signs of Gram's spark beginning to fade. When I had gone to bed that night, I had found the envelope sitting on my pillow. Inside, in Gram's handwriting, was her own original copy of the recipe for Forgotten Cookies. At the bottom of the card she'd written, "Never ever forget that I love you. Love, C.C.C."

Gram hit both hands noiselessly on the table. "So, would you like me to help you with your Forgotten Cookies?"

"Yes, please," I said, still pondering over why Gram's recipe wasn't in my recipe box. I distinctly remembered putting it in the F section. Oh, well, I'd look for it later. I pushed the scattered cards into a neater pile and got up from the table.

"Are you making these for a special occasion?"

"The family Christmas party." I smiled. "Like you used to do."

"Good thing I brought those each year. You didn't like anything else I made for the dinner."

I looked at Gram with a guilty smile.

Every Christmas, Gram had prepared the same vegetable dish: a combination of squash, melted cheese, shredded coconut, baby marshmallows and almonds. I absolutely hated it and would try to pass the dish to the next person before Gram noticed I hadn't taken any, but I was never successful.

"Katy, don't you want some of my squash?" she would ask.

I couldn't tell her it made me gag, which it did, so I'd always put a splotch of her squash onto my plate.

By the end of dinner, when Gram spied the squash untouched and hidden under a half-eaten roll, she'd say with hurt in her voice, "Katy, you haven't touched your squash."

I would lie and say I was saving the best for last, but Gram would stare at my plate until I slipped some squash onto my fork.

Gram looked down lovingly at Andy. "Roland used to love my vegetable dish, you know."

"I remember," I said as I bent down to get a cookie sheet from the bottom cupboard.

How could I forget? Every year Rollie had made the biggest deal out of it. He'd say over and over again how Gram's squash was the best thing at the table. Family members would echo the same compliment, which would be the end of it. Except for one Christmas, the one three months after the gas station incident.

Rollie had really outdone himself that Christmas. All the hot food was still being passed around the table when Rollie started mumbling, sort of under his breath. Something about Mother's special dish and the trouble with people and how you couldn't trust anyone anymore and no appreciation of talents like Mother's and thieves within one's own family.

At first, no one but Sam and Gram and I heard Rollie. We were the closest to him with Sam on Rollie's right, Gram on his left, and me sitting next to Gram. But then Rollie's voice increased in volume and speed, and he spit out something about ungrateful relatives and recording special moments and knowing all about his record.

Little by little, the other family members quieted down and turned their attention toward Rollie.

Gram patted Rollie's arm and nervously told him, "Dear, your dinner's getting cold."

Without warning, Rollie stood up and shouted, "Applause!" He looked intense and agitated.

Gram, flustered and scared, whispered, "Roland, please sit down." But he didn't.

"Applause! Applause is in order for my mother, who has generously shared her great culinary gifts with us on this special occasion!"

No one moved. I saw blood rush from the faces of relatives as a quiet panic filled the air.

Then, suddenly, my brother bellowed out, "Hear, hear, Rollie!" Sam rose to his feet and clapped his hands with great gusto.

Everyone stared at my brother with mouths open and eyes wide with shock. I knew each person was trying to figure out who the crazy one was.

"Here's to Gram's great culinary gifts!" my seventeen-year-old brother sang out.

There was another excruciating moment of silence. But then, miraculously and one by one, everyone caught on and began standing and clapping with cheers and laughter, telling Rollie how right he was.

At first, Rollie shot suspicious looks at each person, but when Sam patted him on the back and gave him a warm and genuine nod of approval, Rollie's whole body had relaxed, and he had begun to laugh and nod his head with exaggerated joy and self-importance.

As I pulled the cookie sheet out, it banged against the cupboard door.

Gram sighed. "I don't suppose Rollie will be at this year's Christmas dinner."

Still bent down, I looked behind me to answer Gram. She was standing at the doorway between the kitchen and the dining room, but her back was turned to me.

Holding the cookie sheet, I stood up and tenderly said, "Gram," but she didn't wait for my answer. None was needed. She strolled into the dining room, humming a vaguely familiar melody. It wasn't quite a hymn but something like one. Andy lifted his heavy body and hobbled after her.

I put the cookie sheet on the counter and tried to conjure up the words to her humming. It was almost haunting.

"Where is your Christmas tree?" Gram called from the living room.

"We haven't gotten it yet," I called back.

I heard Andy's feet padding on the hardwood floors.

"Do you always wait this long to get a tree?" she asked as she and Andy entered the family room.

"No, not usually. Most years Tom and Andy and I get one on my birthday."

It was our own little tradition. We would load Andy into the back seat of the Subaru and drive to the railroad yards south of downtown Los Angeles near skid row. It was an odd mix of Christmas and commerce, of cultures and characters, with the blended scent of burritos and ponderosa pines – made you know for certain that you were in the third world, the real Los Angeles. With hundreds of other people, we'd wander along the endless line of boxcars and survey the fresh, beautiful pine trees from Idaho, Oregon, and Northern Nevada as they were unloaded from trains.

Occasionally, Tom, Andy, and I would stop near a cluster of people and watch as the auctioneer standing inside the boxcar lifted a tree, shook it out, and paraded it in front of the crowd. The staccato echo of his voice extolling the merits of each individual tree would mingle with the sound of piped-in Christmas carols: "Who will give me thirty for this fine Douglas fir?"

"Peace on earth and mercy mild," came a reply through the speakers above.

"Now come on, folks. This tree is a beauty!"

"God and sinners reconciled..."

"Fifteen dollars, do I hear twenty? Yes, just one little limb missing, yes sir."

"Hark the herald angels sing..."

"Twenty dollars going once, going twice. Sold to the man in the Raiders cap!"

"Glory to the newborn king."

Gram folded her arms and looked dismayed. "Your birthday was four days ago, and Christmas is three days away."

"I know." I walked to the pantry and reached inside to get the chocolate chips and sugar. "Andy hasn't been feeling well."

"His hips?" Gram asked.

"Yes." I looked toward the sofa, where Gram was now seated. Andy was lying on the floor beside her. "They seem to be giving him lots of pain these last few months. And then, just this week, there were times when he couldn't stand up."

Andy had been in the most pain on my birthday, but the veterinarian had assured me that it was only his arthritis. He thought that once the rain stopped and the air became less damp, Andy would be walking better with less pain. I felt relieved, but it had been obvious that Andy wouldn't be able to wander along the train cars with us on the night of my birthday. I asked Tom to let us wait a day or two.

"Maybe you should go without him this year," Gram said.

"No. He's walking better today." I looked at Andy. "You can make it tonight, can't you Andy?"

He looked at me and wagged his tail.

"Yeah, you wouldn't want us to go without you, would you?"

Andy made a quiet guttural sound, the one he used to talk back.

"See?" I said to Gram.

"I guess it isn't too late to be getting your tree," she said. "Come to think of it, after your grandfather died and Rollie no longer lived with me, I often waited this long to get my Christmas tree."

"I remember. You used to tell me it was because you could get a better price," I said.

"Did I tell you that?"

"Uh huh."

"Well, perhaps I thought you didn't want to know the real reason." Gram sighed.

I looked at Gram. "Oh yeah? What was the real reason?"

"You might remember that during those years when your uncle was hospitalized or living in one of those government homes, he was allowed to stay with me at Christmastime for a few days before and after Christmas." Gram paused and fixed her eyes on me. "His doctor and I thought it was good for Rollie to spend time with his family, you know."

Yes, I knew this was the reason Rollie had attended most of our family Christmas gatherings. I could see why Gram had thought it was a good idea. She was Rollie's mother, so who could have blamed her? But I couldn't figure out why Rollie's doctor had thought it was such a good idea. He probably wouldn't have thought so if he'd observed Rollie the way I had on Christmas Day of 1967, three months after the gas station incident.

Gram and Rollie had arrived at our house in Gram's powder blue 1962 Chevy with Gram in the driver's seat, her gloved hands fixed upon the big round steering wheel. I had watched from the living room window as she steered the car ever so carefully into our circular driveway. Until that moment, I'd held out hope that my uncle wouldn't be in the car, but there he was beside her in the passenger seat, staring out the car window, looking anxious and much too old to be driven around by his mother.

As Gram's car rolled to a stop, everyone except me dashed out the front door to welcome Gram and Rollie and help them unload their gifts from the car. I watched from inside, wishing so badly that my uncle had not come, and as I watched, I could see tension build in Uncle Rollie's face.

He responded to each of his relatives' hugs and kisses with a stiff, "Merry Christmas." Then he'd looked toward the living room window as if one last hug was missing, as if that hug was waiting for him inside behind the curtains.

I darted behind the curtain, knowing he had seen me, and then quickly peeked out again as Gram's voice shrilly commanded her son, "Roland, don't forget to close the back door, and be sure the window is up."

Rollie's whole body had stiffened. His jaw had jutted out, his teeth had clenched, and he had spoken slowly and deliberately. "I was about to do that, Mother."

Gram shook me out of the memory. "It made our family complete," she said, watching me collect the cookie ingredients.

"What did?" I asked as I looked inside the pantry and began to shuffle through the seasonings.

"Having your uncle there to celebrate the holiday with us."

"Um," I said, not wanting to disagree with Gram, "do I have to have cream of tartar for this recipe? I don't seem to have any."

Gram gasped. "Oh my, yes."

"It's just such an odd ingredient, and the recipe just needs a quarter teaspoon," I whined on purpose, hoping that Gram would concur that her Forgotten Cookies could still taste amazing without the cream of tartar.

"My Forgotten Cookies would not be as deliciously unique without all its ingredients." Gram paused and tilted her head to emphasize her point. "Sort of like families who gather together without all their magnificently different family members present, my cookies are not as deliciously unique nor as harmoniously complete."

I stared wide-eyed at Gram to convey to her that the overly obvious analogy had gone right over my head. She smiled back sweetly.

"Well, hm." I cleared my throat and returned my attention to the pantry to search a little harder for the cream of tartar. A random thought involuntarily floated from my mouth. "Gram, when Uncle Rollie came home for his holiday visits with you, did he like going out to look for your Christmas trees?"

"Oh, yes," Gram said. Then she paused to think. "Well, until that year."

"What year?"

"The year he made the speech about my squash dish."

"Oh," was all I said, wishing I'd not asked the question.

"I suppose I shouldn't have made your uncle come with me, but I had hoped that his getting outside, being around other people, and hearing the Christmas music would do Rollie some good."

"Didn't Rollie want to go with you?" I still couldn't find the cream of tartar and wasn't feeling like going to the store to get it.

"No, he didn't want to leave the house."

"Why?" I asked, wondering if anyone would really notice a difference in taste if I left the cream of tartar out just this one time.

"Oh." Gram frowned. "The minute I brought Rollie home from the hospital, he decided there was something wrong about the house."

I looked around the panty door and stared hard at Gram. "Really?"

"Yes," she said. "As soon as he put down his suitcase, he started to open every closet door and cupboard."

"Why?"

"He felt something was missing."

"What did he think was missing?"

"I don't think he really knew at the time; he just had it in his head that something was missing. Something of his."

"Was something of his missing?"

"Of course not. But he was making me nervous, running around the house and checking under and behind furniture, and he wouldn't let me close all those doors after he'd opened them. I finally talked him into coming with me to the tree lot, but only after I promised to leave all the cupboard and closet doors open."

"Hmm." I began to think that maybe people would taste a difference in the cookies without the cream of tartar. "Did you get a tree?"

"Well, no." Gram sighed. "Something happened."

"Something happened?" I felt slightly alarmed.

"Oh, Katy, you don't want to hear about this."

"Okay," I said in agreement. I really didn't want to hear any more about what had happened.

"Well, as I drove to the Christmas tree lot, your uncle started talking," Gram continued as if she misunderstood my okay to mean okay, go ahead, keep telling me something I don't want to know about.

"But not to me," Gram added.

I let out a hard, long breath of air, knowing that Gram was not going to stop her story.

"What do you mean 'not to you'?" I asked with the sound of defeat in my voice.

"Rollie rambled on and on nonstop, making no sense at all. But then when I pulled into the parking lot and he saw all the green trees and pretty lights, he stopped talking to himself and seemed fine."

"That's good," I said half-heartedly.

"Mm. It was the same Christmas tree lot Rollie and I had gone to for years. Mr. and Mrs. Foley, the owners, always remembered our names and always were helpful in finding the right tree for us. That day when Mrs. Foley saw my car, she came over to wish us a Merry Christmas. She was such a nice person."

Gram paused. "We wandered through the trees with Mrs. Foley, and every once in a while, she pointed at one she thought we would like. Rollie was more picky than usual, but he was fine – that is until Mrs. Foley made us stop to listen to the Christmas music playing over the loud speakers. It sounded so beautiful."

Gram started to hum the same curiously familiar tune, the one she had been humming in the dining room moments ago. "I didn't have time to tell Mrs. Foley that the music was beautiful, because Rollie suddenly became very angry," she said.

"Really?" I looked at Gram again.

"Oh my, yes. He wanted to know where Mrs. Foley had gotten the record. When she said she really didn't know, Rollie accused her of stealing it from him."

"Gram," I whispered with complete dread.

"Poor Mrs. Foley looked so startled, but she calmly told Rollie that the record had belonged to her and her husband for many years."

"Did Rollie calm down?" I asked.

259

"No." Gram shook her head. "He screamed at her and told her she was lying, but I really don't think your uncle would have chased her through the rows of Christmas trees if she hadn't told him he was out of his mind."

"What? Rollie chased her?" I couldn't believe what I was hearing. "Did he hurt her?"

"No. Mr. Foley and two of his helpers heard his wife screaming, and they were able to catch Rollie and stop him."

I gently stepped away from the pantry and moved into the family room. My hand covered my mouth as I silently wondered why I'd never been told about this incident.

"Rollie was so frightened," Gram said softly.

"Rollie was frightened? What about Mrs. –"

"Katy," Gram interrupted, "you've never understood, have you?"

I tilted my head not sure what I was supposed to understand. "Your poor uncle had a horrible illness, and it frightened him. Did you know that he lived in fear every day of his adult life, afraid of when a new episode would occur, afraid one had already occurred without him realizing it? His life was a living nightmare, and he had no control over it."

It had never occurred to me that Uncle Rollie knew that he was mentally ill. Did he know he had schizophrenia? Was this possible? I'd always assumed that people like Uncle Rollie, mentally ill people, saw themselves as healthy and everyone else as crazy.

I sat down on the ottoman across from Gram. "I'm sorry, Gram. I didn't know how he felt. I didn't understand."

"Oh, don't, sweetie. I could never understand his illness myself. In those days, people thought schizophrenia was the result of one's upbringing, their childhood, bad parenting. I spent so much time feeling guilty, trying to figure out what I had done to my own son to make him so sick, and I knew my friends and anyone else who knew about Rollie wondered the same thing. Sometimes I was more concerned with how his illness affected me than how it affected him."

Gram paused and looked around the family room. "You know, your uncle was very self-conscious about not living a normal life. He was embarrassed that he didn't have a job and his mother drove him everywhere. He was especially embarrassed because you knew how sick he was."

"Oh, Gram." I sighed.

"He knew you were frightened of him."

"Well, I was." Maybe with good reason, I failed to add, given the Mrs. Foley episode.

"He thought you hated him."

"I didn't hate him, Gram," I said softly.

"Maybe you hated his being your uncle."

I didn't respond. I did hate having Rollie as my uncle. Why couldn't he have been someone else's relative?

"Gram, did Mr. Foley call the police?"

"No. He was about to, but I begged him to let me take Rollie home. He agreed only after I promised I'd never come back to his tree lot."

"Did you call Rollie's doctor?"

"Not right away."

"But why, Gram?"

"I knew Rollie would calm down once we got home and he took his medication."

"Did he calm down?"

"Yes, but before the drugs had a chance to take effect, he started checking behind the doors and furniture again."

"What was he looking for?" Figuring the worst of Gram's story was over, I got up and walked to the kitchen where all the ingredients for the cookies sat. Except the cream of tartar.

"A record," she said from the sofa.

"A record?" The dread inside me grew.

"Mmm."

"When did he decide a record was missing?"

"At the Christmas tree lot." Gram sighed while she slowly shook her head. "Somehow, Rollie decided that Mrs. Foley had been playing his record and accused Mrs. Foley of stealing it and bringing it to the tree lot to play over the speakers. Of course, I tried to reason with Rollie, to make him realize that Mrs. Foley couldn't possibly have stolen his record, because she didn't know where we lived."

"Did he finally realize that she didn't steal his record?"

"Well, yes, but –" Gram cleared her throat as if she was hesitant to continue.

"But?" I prodded her as I opened the canister of sugar.

"But he still thought one of his records had been stolen."

"Well, who did he think had taken it? You?" I reached for the measuring cup.

"No, someone who'd slept in his bedroom." Gram looked up at me. "Just three-fourths of a cup."

"What?" I shrieked.

Obviously startled, Gram shrieked back, "Just three-fourths of a cup!"

"No." I put the measuring cup and wooden spoon on the counter. "Rollie thought someone who'd slept in his room had stolen his record?"

"Oh, hmmm." Gram composed herself. "Yes."

"Gra-aaam, I slept in his room. Lots of times!" I squealed.

"I know, dear."

"Did Rollie know?"

"Yes, I believe so." Gram put her hand to her mouth as if she needed to think for a moment, and then she mumbled, "I told him."

"What?" I squealed again.

"Katherine, please stop startling me like that. If I weren't your guardian angel, I could have a heart attack."

"You weren't ever supposed to tell Rollie that I stayed in his bedroom. Remember? You made that promise when I was seven."

"I know, I know. But I didn't know what else to do under the circumstances. You see, Rollie could tell that his bed sheets had been changed since the last time he'd been home. He was right. You'd spent the night with me the week before, and after you left, I made his bed up again. He'd never noticed this before, but for some reason, he did notice it on this particular visit. He became so upset that he started throwing everything out of his closet and pulling furniture into the center of the bedroom."

I stared at Gram.

"I was so frightened. I had to think of something to calm him down."

"So, you told him I'd slept there," I said with an air of disbelief.

"You were his niece. He loved you."

"He loved me?" The thought seemed absurd.

"Yes. Rollie loved each of you children. Very much. You were his family."

"He never said anything. I, I never heard him say anything like that."

"He never felt he had a right to love you or to be loved by you."

I let this sink in for a moment. "Well, okay, but –" I sighed. "Did Rollie calm down after you told him who had been in his room?"

"Yes, for a day or two."

"Well, I guess maybe it was a good thing you told him if that made him calm down," I said quietly. I picked up the measuring cup and decided to measure the chocolate chips instead of the sugar.

"Not really," Gram mumbled.

A chill ran down my spine. "Not really?" I looked at her as chips flowed from the bag into the measuring cup and onto the counter.

"No, not really," Gram said, sneaking a sideways glance at me and then looking away.

I waited for her to continue.

"Well, you see, Rollie had somehow come to the conclusion that you were the one who had stolen one of his records."

"What?" I banged the measuring cup on the counter. Chips jumped out and bounced all over the floor, jolting Andy and Gram from their relaxed positions.

"Do you mind? You are scaring both of us to death!" Gram scolded. In a huff, she walked over to the cabinet where Tom and I kept our tape deck and audio disc player. She kept fanning her face as if to keep herself from fainting, but I wasn't worried. As far as I knew, angels didn't faint.

"Rollie thought I'd stolen his records?" I wanted to be clear about this new information.

"Just one," Gram corrected me.

"Oh, just one." I pulled myself together. "When did he decide this?"

"Well, not right away, not that night."

"What a relief" I said sarcastically. "When?"

"I'm not sure," Gram said, a bit distracted. She was reading the labels on the record jackets and tapping her finger on one of them. "Oh, my, I haven't heard this in a hundred years."

I squinted to see which record she was talking about but couldn't quite make it out.

"Do you mind if we play this while we make the cookies?" Gram asked.

"While we make the cookies?" I repeated, wondering how she was being any help at all. I walked to the cabinet and looked to where she was pointing. A beautiful sadness swept through me.

"I haven't heard it in a long time either." I sighed. I reached for the record jacket and smiled. "Sam gave this to me, you know," I said almost whispering.

"I know. Wasn't it the same Christmas?"

"What same Christmas?"

"The same Christmas when Rollie made that laborious speech." Gram paused. "The same Christmas Rollie decided you had stolen this record from his room." She pointed at the record in my hand.

"This very record?" I asked with shock.

"Mmm," Gram nodded.

"Well, when did he decide this?" I moved closer to the turntable and lifted the cover.

"I'm not certain of the exact moment, but I think it was Christmas night while the family opened gifts." Gram smiled serenely and then added, "Rollie loved that tradition, you know."

"What tradition?" I removed the record from its jacket, carefully placed it on the turntable pin, and pushed the on button. The needle hit the record, and beautiful but scratchy music started to come through the speakers above where we were standing.

"The family gift giving, the way we all sat in a circle and watched each other open presents one by one."

This was news to me, because Rollie had never looked like he was enjoying himself during the family gift giving. Who could blame him? Anyone would have been a little uncomfortable if they'd been Rollie on Christmas Day. It was a known fact throughout my family that Gram would purchase gifts for herself, things like a purse or a slip, maybe a pair of gloves or a frying pan. Then she'd wrap them and attach tags saying, "To Mother, With Much Love, Rollie." She'd do the same thing with the pants and socks and shirts she bought as presents for Rollie, except she'd write "Love, Mother."

We all knew that Gram and Uncle Rollie opened gifts at her house on Christmas Eve. Then, before coming to our house for Christmas Day, Gram would rewrap the gifts and bring them to our house. Then she and Rollie would open the very same gifts in front of the whole family.

The funniest thing about all this was the way Gram tried with all her might to act totally surprised at finding that there was a gift for her from Rollie. She'd gingerly put on her glasses, the ones attached to the beaded chain around her neck, and then read aloud with feigned emotion, "From Rollie." She'd pause, smile sweetly at him, and then with a look of wonderment, Gram would carefully unwrap the gift. Once she saw what was in the box, she'd sigh and say, "Oh, Roland! What a wonderful surprise! This is just what I wanted. How did you ever guess?" Gram reminded me of the old silent film starlets who fluttered their eyelashes and mouthed gooey words of affection.

I could tell that Rollie wasn't comfortable about the whole thing, because he never smiled or looked at Gram. He sat stiffly and held his hands clamped together between his knees. Eventually, he would mumble, "I'm glad you like it, Mother," and then kiss her cheek.

"Isn't this just wonderful?" Gram would ask the whole family as she held the gift up high for all to see.

By then, Rollie always looked as if he was going to crawl out of his skin. "It's someone else's turn to open a gift, Mother," he would say with a fake, frozen smile.

It wasn't as if Rollie and Gram didn't have other presents to open. They did. Lots. They got gifts from everyone else. So, I had never understood why Gram put on that charade.

I was now ashamed to remember how juvenile and heartless I had been each time Rollie stiffly told Gram that he was happy she liked the gift he'd given her. Back then, I would have looked over at Sam or Wendy and snickered. Wendy would snicker back, but not Sam. He had always given me a severe look to make me stop mocking Uncle Rollie. And I would have, but only because I hadn't wanted Sam to think badly of me.

I remembered one Christmas gathering when Sam had scolded me, saying, "Rollie couldn't very well tell Gram in front of the whole family, 'Of course it's the perfect gift, Mother. You bought it yourself.'"

I had told Sam that he was right, though I'm not sure I had felt any shame about mocking my uncle. I should have.

The music coming from the turntable was cheerful. It had been such a long time since I'd listened to La Boheme. The scratchiness of the record only mildly interfered with Rodolfo and Marcello. Or was it Rodolfo and Schaunard? I looked at Gram. Her eyes were closed as she moved her head to the rhythm of the music.

"It's Rodolfo and Marcello," she said.

"Thank you," I said, thinking it must be wonderful to be able to read other people's minds.

As the mood of the opera became more festive and joyous, Gram moved both hands in the air as if conducting an imaginary orchestra. "I was so impressed that my granddaughter appreciated opera," Gram said with her eyes still closed. She began dancing around the family room in a careful but lighthearted two-step.

"Were you?"

"Oh, yes," she said and continued to hum to the quartet's raucous banter.

I thought back to my junior year in high school and Bobby Monelli, for it was Bobby whom I had hoped to impress, not my grandmother. In my mind, and the mind of every other girl at school, Bobby was the most breathtaking male specimen to walk the earth. And he was in my English class. But so was our teacher, Miss Jumper, whom every boy, including Bobby Monelli, had a crush on. It was so obvious. Like the day when Miss Jumper was discussing a passage from Oedipus Rex. Bobby had raised his hand and let it be known that he had seen the opera Oedipus Rex performed in Edinburgh, Scotland, by the Hamburg Company. Miss Jumper had found this bit of information interesting and had asked Bobby if he'd enjoyed the performance.

"Very much," he told her. "Actually, I've become something of an opera fanatic."

"Ohhh," Miss Jumper said and then moved on with the lesson.

Well, Miss Jumper may not have found it too important, but I certainly did. Bobby Monelli, an opera fanatic! That day, right after school, I dashed to the public library and seized the first librarian to cross my path. I asked her for information, anything, on opera music. Within minutes she handed me a book with the storylines of the most well-known operas. I still remember the title: *A Treasury of the Great Operas* by Artur Holde. I was satisfied with this until the librarian told me I could also check out, one at a time, recordings of any of the operas they had available. Well, this was too good to be true, more than I had hoped for. All I needed was to listen to each of the records, get a few

269

opera facts under my belt, and then accidentally bump into Bobby on the way to English class. He'd help me pick up my books, notice the one on opera, and ask me about it. I'd shyly say I lived for opera and Bobby would suddenly realize he'd met the girl of his dreams. It was such a good plan.

For the next three weeks, after my homework was completed, I'd go into the living room and carefully place one of the library records on the turntable. Every once in a while, Sam would stroll into the room and sit in the chair across from me. It wouldn't take long before we were both throwing out our arms and raising our voices along with the singers on the record. I can still see Sam getting up from the floor to dance with me to Carmen's famous "Seguidilla." I'd end up falling to the floor rolling with laughter as Sam, sofa pillow stuffed under his shirt, mimicked the voices of Aida and Ramdames from Aida, or Violetta and Alfredo from La Traviata.

I was listening to La Boheme the day that Becky called, a day I shall never forget. I'd finished my homework and was listening to Rodolfo and his friends bantering between themselves. So far, La Boheme wasn't a terribly thrilling opera, at least not compared to Carmen. But then Mimi's voice sang through the stereo speakers, "Mi chiamano Mimi," and I was hooked. Could anything be more romantic? Mi chiamano Katy, I sang to Bobby Monelli in my daydream. But then Sam yelled from the hallway, "Becky's on the phone for you. She says it's very, very important!"

I got up as Rodolfo's friends began calling out to Rodolfo.

"Did you hear?" Becky screamed in my ear.

"What?" I asked her with excitement.

"Bobby Monelli has moved to New York with his father! That's why he wasn't in class today."

"He's moved?" I asked, certain I had heard wrong.

"Forever!"

Becky was the only person who knew why opera had become so important to me, so she was the only person who could possibly understand the tragic nature of her words. I hung up the phone and wandered into the living room as Mimi and Rodolfo began professing their love for each other. "Amor! Amor! Amor!"

I didn't notice Sam sitting in the stuffed chair as I slumped onto the couch, tears running down my cheeks.

"What's the matter with you?" He laughed.

I couldn't possibly tell Sam about Bobby, so I pointed to the stereo. "It's so sad. She dies in the end, you know." And I had sobbed.

Gram sighed. "Anna had such a beautiful voice."

"Anna?" I asked.

"Anna Moffo." Gram was still swaying to the music as Anna Moffo's Mimi filled my family room. "I think this is the finest recording of La Boheme. I wonder what made Sam get you such an unusual Christmas gift?"

Sam had told me a few days after Christmas that when he saw me crying over a "stupid opera," he decided I should have my own copy and stop borrowing the scratchy ones from the library. He'd gone to the local record shop and asked the storeowner to special order the best recording of La Boheme. It had arrived a few days before Christmas.

"Si, mi chiamano Mimi," sang out my grandmother along with Anna Moffo.

I looked at Gram and began dancing and singing along with her. Gram and I laughed as we danced around Andy and the coffee table. Suddenly she stopped in mid-air. "Now I remember!"

"What?" I stopped dancing too, but the music played on.

"I remember when Rollie decided you'd stolen his record."

Out of breath, I plopped onto the couch. "When?"

"When you opened Sam's Christmas gift."

I thought back to that long-ago Christmas night. It had been my turn to open a gift. I had read Sam's card aloud to everyone and ripped off the wrapping paper. I must have looked as foolish as Gram when she acted totally surprised over Rollie's gifts, but I really was surprised. No, I was flabbergasted. I read out loud, "In Living Stereo, Puccini's La Boheme with Anna Moffo, Richard Tucker and Robert Merrill." On the jacket cover was a beautiful watercolor painting of Mimi and Rodolfo standing beside Cafe Momus.

"Sam! How did you find this? It's just too wonderful! Amor! Amor! Amor!" I sang out to my brother, and in true operatic style, I lifted my arms toward him.

The whole family had roared with laughter, everyone but Uncle Rollie. He had glowered my way as everyone merrily applauded Sam's surprising gift. But I hadn't thought much of Rollie's odd fixed stare, because he had never really understood anything the family found funny.

Now I saw it in a different light. "Gram, how could Rollie think I'd stolen his record? He was there when I read the card from Sam. He heard me thank Sam for it. Why didn't he think Sam had stolen it?"

"I don't know. He just decided you'd taken it from his room, wrapped it up yourself, and then made out a card saying, "From Sam.""

"Well, I wonder how he thought of something as crazy as that," I said sarcastically.

"Now, Katy, it was a difficult Christmas for me. After you opened the La Boheme record, Roland wouldn't let me be. He kept whispering that he wanted his record back before the end of the night. I tried to hush him, but he wouldn't let up"

"I never heard him," I said. "I didn't notice."

"No, but your father did, and he finally asked Rollie what he was so upset about. Rollie said that 'his mother' would call later to explain what had happened."

"What did Dad say?"

"He told Rollie that he would wait for my call. It seemed to calm Rollie down a little."

"Did you really call Dad?"

"No. When the party was over, your father helped carry Rollie's and my gifts to the car. When we started to say our goodbyes, Rollie yelled at him, 'Aren't you forgetting my record? The one your daughter stole from me?'"

Gram stopped and looked at me. I knew I had a look of horror on my face. She was not smiling as she continued. "Well, I know your father was trying to figure out a way to send us home without a scene. He could tell that Rollie needed help again. He told Rollie to go home with me and he would find the record and drive it over within the hour."

"But—"

"Your father waited for us to leave, and then he called Rollie's doctor and the hospital. Your father and mother met them at my house that night and Rollie was taken away. Again."

"I never knew this," I said "Dad never told me. You never told me."

A scratch in the record interrupted us with Mimi's voice repeating, "Addio-Addio-Addio-Addio!" I got up from the couch and moved the needle.

"You'd better clean up those chocolate chips before someone steps on them," Gram said pointing to the kitchen. "The sugar, too."

The music continued playing, but it sounded sad, and I knew that Mimi did not have long to live. As I went to the laundry room to get the broom and dustpan, I wasn't sure if the sadness I was feeling was for Mimi or for Uncle Rollie.

"My, you have quite a lot of cards here," Gram chirped from the couch. A basket on the coffee table held all the different Christmas cards we'd received from friends and family. She began to look through them as I swept the floor.

"Oh, isn't this cute!"

"What is?" I asked, since I couldn't see what she was talking about.

"This card. It says, 'From Don, Julia and the girls.' They're very sweet looking. Now, what kind are they?" Gram asked.

"Labrador retrievers," I answered.

"They don't have children?"

"No. They've decided not to have them."

"Well, then, the dogs are almost like a real family, aren't they?"

"Mmmm." I began to clean the counter with a sponge.

"My, my, look at this one. 'From Larry and Carol and Schnizoldoodle'? Good Godfrey! What kind of a name is that for a child?" Gram asked.

I knew the card Gram held didn't have a photograph with it, so Gram wouldn't know Schnizoldoodle was a dog. "That's the name of Larry and Carol's schnauzer."

"No children?" Gram asked.

"They don't want them."

"Well, for pity sakes! Don't you and Tom have any friends who want children?"

I smiled. Tom and I had plenty of friends with children, and their cards were also in the basket. The truth was, Christmas greetings from friends like Larry and Carol or Don and Julia made me nervous. I loved them dearly, but I didn't want Tom and me to end up like them, having our Christmas pictures taken with our pets until we were a hundred years old. But the way things were going...

I reorganized the chocolate chips, sugar, and eggs and felt ready to try again with the Forgotten Cookies.

The last words of Rodolfo sadly cried out, "Mimi... Mimi!"

And then it hit me.

"Gram, this is the same music Mrs. Foley had you and Rollie listen to in the tree lot, isn't it?"

I looked into the family room. Gram was not on the couch, and I instantly knew that she had left me to make the Forgotten Cookies alone.

She had never asked me about the results of my liver scan and bone scan. She must have known I'd met with Dr. Davis the week before, and both tests looked good. "Clean" is what he'd said. Just two more tests to go: the chest X-ray and the brain scan. I knew they'd be clean too.

The family room looked empty without Gram dancing around, and I was sad that she hadn't stayed long enough to hear my news. I'd wanted to tell her how hopeful I was feeling and how certain I was that Dr. Davis would soon be telling me to hurry up and get pregnant.

I went to turn off the stereo and put the record away, but as I reached for the jacket, I noticed something familiar. Gram's recipe card was sitting on top of the jacket right under the words, "In Living Stereo." I picked it up and knew it was the exact same one she'd left on my pillow almost seventeen years ago, except something new had been added below the list of ingredients. In Gram's handwriting, it said, "A family without children is like a recipe without all its ingredients."

Andy looked at me, and I smiled. "Want to go to the store with me, Andy? We need some cream of tartar."

TWELVE

I had just gotten off the phone with Wendy and was feeling shaken. Upset with myself, I began to wonder why every time I heard her voice, each muscle in my body tightened and contracted in preparation for the inevitable emotional blow, the one Wendy would level at me before our conversation came to an end. It was a useless contemplation, for I knew there was no protecting myself from her words, which acted like a rusty knife cutting into my stomach, then twisting, turning, and opening the scars of old, deep wounds.

Our conversation on that rainy afternoon in February hadn't been any different than the others in our past.

"Hi," Wendy had said with a familiar tone of emotional instability and calculated shrewdness.

"What's up?" I asked with a deliberate, unapproachable tone in my voice. I had learned long ago how an innocent "hello" to Wendy made me vulnerable.

"Nothing," Wendy said defensively.

I imagined her sitting in a dark, filthy apartment, empty wine bottles strewn here and there. Wendy would be smoking a cigarette, an overflowing ashtray somewhere nearby, a glass of cheap wine within reach.

"I just called to talk to –" She paused and let out a breath of air emphasizing the hurt I'd inflicted upon her by my guarded question, which insinuated that she'd called for something other than friendly talk.

Wendy never called just to talk, but she desperately wanted me to believe it was her sole purpose in calling. She wanted to believe we were like other sisters who are able to laugh and talk about life without upsetting and offending each other.

But we weren't like other sisters. I knew that after a few preliminary niceties, Wendy would begin one of her painful stories of how she'd lost her job – a job she'd never held – or how an unscrupulous landlord had kicked her out of her most recent apartment, leaving her once again living on the streets of Los Angeles, or how her latest lover had left her and taken everything, or how some mysterious person had stolen her purse with all her cash. Those things actually happened to Wendy on a regular basis, but they weren't the real reasons she called. It was because she had run out of money for her drug and alcohol addictions. This was the only reason Wendy picked up the phone "just to talk" with me.

"I just called to see how you are." Wendy sniffled heavily, and I knew she had successfully forced real tears to flow from her eyes.

How many times had her tears flooded my own heart and caused me to believe that she really wanted to change and that I could help her? And how long after I set her up in a new apartment, helped her find a job, paid for a new round of therapy, and provided her with money to help get her started had it taken for me to figure out that all I'd really done was buy my sister's next high?

"I'm kind of busy, Wendy," I said, hoping to stop her before she initiated a few cheerful and lighthearted queries about Tom and me, queries which functioned only as calculated preludes to her pleas for help. I had to stop her before she began spinning each syllable and sentence into the same intricate web that would trap me into feeling desperately sorry for her, reminding me that I loved her.

"I need your help," Wendy said.

There it was. I need your help was all she had to say, and she knew it.

I didn't respond. I lowered myself into my desk chair and waited for her next, all too familiar line.

"You're the only one I can go to."

I knew that, once again, Wendy had run out of all her other options. I was her phone call of last resort. There was no one left to bail her out of trouble. Even my parents, who had repeatedly plumbed the depths of their souls, not to mention their savings, had stopped rescuing Wendy in a final effort to preserve their own sanity.

I remained silent, hoping she would understand that I would not be moved this time.

"Sam would help me if –"

"Stop it," I hissed into the phone. I lowered my head as the wound inside my heart, the one that would never heal, seared with pain and agony.

"Sam would help me," Wendy said again as if she enjoyed the sound of those words and the pain they caused me.

She was right, though. Ever since her freshmen year in high school, Sam had rescued Wendy no matter what she had done, no matter what kind of trouble she was in, no matter how terribly she had treated him in the past.

Sam was the one who had seen Wendy leave the high school gymnasium during one of the Friday night dances. He was the one who had followed her to the parking lot and watched as she allowed three boys in leather jackets to lead her into their orange colored van. It was Sam who had charged the van, threatening to kill every one of those boys as he dragged out a drunken, screaming Wendy.

And when Wendy had finally received her high school certificate, wasn't it Sam who talked a friend's parents into hiring Wendy as the receptionist for their travel agency? And wasn't it Sam who had used his own tuition money to pay the three hundred dollars the owners accused Wendy of stealing?

When Sam was still living in Palo Alto, working as a newspaper reporter at the Palo Alto Star News, he had been the one Wendy had called from the police station in South Pasadena. She had been arrested for drunk driving and wanted Sam to rescue her. And he had. He had dropped everything he was doing, even missed a deadline for a story he was writing and drove the six hundred miles to bail Wendy out.

And when Wendy ran out of friends in Los Angeles, when no one would provide her with a room, when no one else would hire her, it was Sam who had allowed Wendy to move into his one-bedroom apartment. Sam, who barely eked out a living himself as a junior reporter, somehow had managed to pay for a month of drug rehabilitation for Wendy.

Three weeks after her release, Wendy had returned to Sam's apartment, high from the cocaine a fellow rehab patient had given to her, but Sam hadn't give up. He continued trying to help Wendy.

But then Sam's help stopped. Not because he refused to take Wendy's calls anymore like everyone else. And not because he decided he couldn't stand the torment Wendy caused him.

"If Sam hadn't –" Wendy said to me over the phone.

"Stop it!" I interrupted in order to prevent Wendy from saying what my ears refused to hear. Not because I didn't accept the fact Sam had died ten years ago at the hands of a drunken driver. I couldn't tolerate being reminded. As long as I kept remembering Sam while he was alive, I didn't have to acknowledge that he was dead.

"Katy, please. You're my...my best friend."

I could hear the thickness building in her voice. Wendy sniffled again as if she were valiantly holding back the tears. "You're my best friend," she repeated.

"Wendy, I'm your sister, not your best friend," I said without the sympathy she'd hoped for.

"You are my best friend!" she screamed at me. "I don't care what you say! Don't worry that I am..."

I held the phone away from my ear, because my head and heart couldn't take it. Andy, who had been sleeping by the doorway, lifted his eyelids and looked to the left and then to the right trying to figure out where the noise was coming from.

Wendy's screaming stopped. I brought the phone back to my ear. "Wendy –" I was about to say that best friends know how to help each other, and I had never known how to help her, but she didn't give me the chance.

"Forget it! If you don't think you're my best friend, then forget it!"

"Wendy," I repeated, feeling a surge of anger building inside me.

"I know I'm not the best friend you've ever had but you are my best friend, and don't you ever try to tell me you're not!" And then she hung up.

Why hadn't I kept quiet when she'd said I was her best friend? I had only ended up giving her the opening she needed, the one that would bring to the surface the same horrible guilt that had tormented me most of my life, reminding me that I must have been the reason for my sister's emotional instability, how everything I'd ever said and done to her was a direct cause of her irrational behavior and her unhappy existence.

I slumped in my chair and stared down at Andy, who had painfully dragged himself over to my feet and flopped his head down on them. Such a good old boy, always there to comfort me.

"You're feeling guilty again," the voice behind me said, causing my left hand to jerk the phone off the hook.

"A little." I attempted to put the receiver back in place.

"Did I scare you? I thought you saw me sitting here while you were speaking with Wendy."

I hadn't noticed Gram while I was talking to Wendy, but there she was in front of my painting easel, looking rather silly as she sat on top of the high-legged stool. Her left leg was crossed over the right, but because she was so short, it didn't drape over the other. It pointed straight ahead, horizontal to the floor as if a string were holding it up.

When I was a girl, I used to tease Gram about this sitting position, but she always said she was quite comfortable with one of her legs sticking straight out.

"It's too bad you and Wendy couldn't talk longer. I think your sister had something she wanted to tell you," Gram said.

She was holding her left arm against her chest allowing her right elbow to rest on top of it and she was strumming her mouth with her fingers and thumb. When Gram was alive, this same pose with the strumming motion had caused her eyes to blink from the impact. I occasionally had tried to tell her it was more effective, better for thinking, if she'd use her index finger and tap lightly on the upper lip. Every once in a while, she gave my tapping technique a try, but she always reverted back to her unique pose with the four-finger strumming.

So, there she was with one leg pointed in my direction and her eyes blinking to the beat of her strumming fingers. I would have laughed out loud, but I was too upset by Wendy's phone call. I was shaking inside. "She always has something to tell me," I said, "and it's always the same thing: she needs my help."

Gram said nothing.

"I'm not her best friend," I quietly said. "Sam was her best friend."

"He loved Wendy very much." Gram clucked her tongue once and then added, "But isn't it a shame that your brother felt so responsible for her pain and unhappiness?"

"I could never figure out why. He was always there for her." I answered.

"The gas station," Gram said matter-of-factly.

"The what?"

"The day at Mr. Osaka's gas station."

"What about it?" I asked.

"That's when Sam began to blame himself for Wendy's troubles."

"He did?"

Gram nodded.

"Why?"

"Well," Gram hesitated, "Wendy was at Mr. Osaka's when the incident occurred."

"I didn't see her there." My mind traveled back to that horrifying day. I had been in the back seat of Sam's car and had never seen Wendy.

"She was by the restrooms with those other boys and girls, the ones who heckled Rollie."

"Wendy was with the hoods," I answered quietly.

"Yes. She was at Mr. Osaka's most days after school, and she was there when your uncle attacked the woman."

"Did Sam know Wendy was there?"

"Yes, and he saw her laugh at Rollie along with those other misguided adolescents."

I turned away from Gram and tried to recall the voices I'd heard shouting cruel words at my uncle. I had never heard Wendy's voice.

"She didn't want her friends to know that Rollie was her uncle." Gram slowly shook her head.

I certainly understood that feeling but – "Gram! She didn't make fun of Rollie too, did she?" I asked desperately hoping she had not.

"Wendy didn't want to, but she felt pressured to at least pretend to be jeering along with her friends or they might figure things out." Gram sighed a long, sad sigh.

"But how does that -" I was confused. "Why did you say that was the day Sam started to feel responsible for Wendy's problems?" I asked.

"After the police took Rollie away, Sam drove you and your friend home."

"I remember. He wanted me to wait for Mom to get home from work and tell her what had happened. He said he was driving to your house so he could take you to see Rollie."

"Yes, but before he drove to my house," Gram said, "he went back to the gas station. Wendy was still there, smoking cigarettes with the same group, still laughing and making fun of what had happened. Sam parked his car and walked right up to them. He screamed at your sister, asking her how she could do that to her own uncle. Wendy screamed for Sam to shut up, but he didn't."

The familiar sickness stirred inside of me, and I didn't want to hear any more of this.

But Gram continued. "Sam pointed his finger at your sister and shouted, 'How can you live with yourself? How can you live with yourself?' Before he walked away, he told her that she didn't deserve to be in your family, that he didn't care if he never saw her again."

Tears streamed down my cheeks. Weren't those pretty much the same things I'd screamed at Sam the Thanksgiving that he and our friend Doug had played their joke on me? No wonder Sam had looked at me the way he had. No wonder Sam had left for Stanford without saying goodbye.

"You see," said Gram, "it was a few days later when Wendy took all those pills right before her Freshman English class. Sam always blamed himself for her suicide attempt."

I stared at Gram while more tears poured from my eyes.

"I'm sorry to tell you this," Gram said.

"Sam never told me." I closed my eyes, and the whole nightmarish moment from so long ago came into focus. "Did Uncle Rollie know Wendy was at Mr. Osaka's?"

"Sadly, yes. When Sam and his friend pulled Rollie from the woman's car, Rollie looked over at Wendy laughing along with the group standing by the bathrooms. And your sister, well, she just looked away."

Gram and I were quiet for a moment. The sound of raindrops hitting the roof filled the void.

Then Gram spoke again. "It's such a shame. Wendy and Rollie had a sweet relationship until that day. But after, Wendy was so ashamed of herself that she didn't know how to apologize to Rollie. So, she never spoke to him again. And poor Rollie, he never mentioned her name after that. It's strange though, over the years, whenever Rollie and I drove by Mr. Osaka's gas station on the way to your parents' home, Rollie would look over by the restrooms where Wendy and the boys in the leather jackets had stood and he'd half sing, half mumble the words, "Boy-and-girl-land...never return again."

Gram looked off into the distance. "I guess you could say that dreadful day at Mr. Osaka's gas station was the end of Wendy and

Rollie's relationship but the beginning of Wendy and Sam's. Sam was convinced that he was the reason for Wendy's suicide attempt. He harbored such guilt he –"

"– became her best friend," I finished Gram's thought.

"Yes, because Wendy desperately needed a best friend," Gram said.

"I can't be like Sam," I said firmly.

Gram said nothing.

"I can't be Wendy's best friend," I said, waiting for a reprimand from Gram.

"She thinks you are," Gram said softly.

Didn't Gram understand? All I'd ever wanted was to be released from the pain of being Wendy's sister. How could I possibly be her best friend?

"Well, I don't know why," I sighed.

"Maybe because of all the happy times you've shared," Gram said.

Happy times? Whatever happy moments we'd shared had been long since buried under years of pain and trauma.

"Don't you remember any of them?" Gram dropped her hand to her lap.

"Not really," I said, not wanting to remember.

"Oh, Katy," Gram whined with disappointment as her right leg continued to point straight at me. "Surely you remember at least one happy time with your sister."

"Not really. Any happy memories of Wendy were crushed by a tidal wave of unhappy memories," I said.

"Humor me with just one happy memory of you and Wendy together," Gram pressed.

It was painful to be pushed once again to a place where I didn't want to go, but I knew nonetheless that Gram was leading me there. "Once," I said, "when Wendy and I were very little, we spent the night at your house. We were pretty upset with you."

"No." Gram perked up. She was only pretending not to know what I was talking about.

"Well, we were, because you made us take a bath together, something we never did at home. We felt we were too old for that."

"Oh, pooh. You were only five and eight years old."

"Yeah, well, the worst part was that you went and invited two of your neighbor women friends to come over and meet us - while we were sitting in the bath water."

"I didn't." Gram giggled.

"Yes, you did. Wendy and I were extremely embarrassed. Humiliated."

"You were too young to be humiliated."

"We had our pride, Grandmother." But I realized that the bath Wendy and I had shared thirty years ago was one of the few moments that Wendy and I could always talk and laugh about without feeling pain or anger.

"You girls were terrible." Gram giggled. "I don't think a family gathering went by when you didn't tell the story and embellish it a little bit more each time. Honestly, it's a wonder your aunts and uncles and cousins didn't believe you when you said I'd brought a movie crew and talent agents to see you."

Gram's voice began to fade away as another pleasant memory of Wendy and me came into focus. We had been in high school – I was a senior – and Dad had grounded me for two weeks, because I had come home two hours late from a day of skiing. I hadn't been upset over the punishment, but Wendy had thrown a major tantrum on my behalf. She had argued with my father, shouting as usual, telling him how unfair he was, and before I knew it, Dad had grounded Wendy, too.

The whole situation was humorous, because I never got in trouble. Ever. And the one time I did, Wendy couldn't keep out of it and got grounded too. It was strange how happy Wendy seemed during those two weeks of shared confinement. She would come into my room, and we would talk and laugh about how she had suddenly become my lawyer and she'd be charging a fee for her future legal services. She seemed proud, as if she'd done me a big favor. I think it was the only grounding that Wendy didn't violate.

And then there was the summer two years later, when I had been home from college. Each morning, Wendy and I took the bus together into the city, where I had a summer job and where, two blocks away, Wendy attended adult vocational school. She'd failed her physical education class the last semester of her senior year and hadn't graduated. Hanging out in the bathrooms to smoke cigarettes had been more important than attending classes. So, that summer, Wendy had to take physical education – not algebra, not English, but physical education – at a special school for high school dropouts.

Originally, I had dreaded having to ride into Los Angeles on a bus with Wendy, but for some reason, those thirty minutes each morning and each evening ended up being a healing time for us. We were quite a contrast as we sat side-by-side on those crowded buses talking to each other, Wendy's carrot-red hair darting carelessly in every direction while my straight blond hair flowed quietly and perfectly into place just below my shoulders.

I don't remember what we talked about. I just remember how we seemed happy together, like normal sisters, almost like friends. Maybe that's why I teased Wendy the way I did whenever the bus was crowded. I would lean back in the seat and slowly extend my arm so it draped around Wendy's back while my hand would latch onto her farthest shoulder, as if I were her boyfriend. This embarrassed her and caused her face to turn bright red, but she laughed and laughed while trying to remove my arm. I benignly smiled, my arm still around her. And I remember watching the change that would wash across Wendy's face. It was almost in slow motion. There, in her laughter, in her embarrassment, was an innocence and joyfulness that I had never before seen in my sister. In those fleeting moments, I had even believed that Wendy would be okay after all.

"Gram, do you have happy memories of Uncle Rollie?" I asked, wondering if there had ever been a time when Rollie had been capable of laughing and having fun the way normal people did. I'd never seen it.

"Oh my, yes! He loved to sing and play the piano, you know."

"Yes," I said. How could I forget?

"Your great-grandmother made sure he did. She gave him singing lessons beginning at age five, and she made him practice twice a day. Those practices were such happy times with Grandma Bertie and Rollie and me singing together."

"Five years old?" I wondered how much a five-year-old would like twice daily music lessons with his mother and grandmother.

"Yes, well, Bertie felt that your uncle needed to be guided in a musical direction at an early age, just like she guided me when I was a little girl. Bertie was a real believer in genes, just like you."

"Me?" I was shocked to be compared to my great grandmother.

"Oh, yes. She was convinced that musical talent ran through our family genes."

Funny Gram should mention genes. It was the same thing Tom and I had been talking about the night before. I didn't know how we got started on the subject, but somehow, we had begun talking about the different relatives we each had. The fat ones, the skinny ones, the tall and short ones, the smart and not so smart ones, and the ugly ones, who we both determined were all on Tom's side. I had thought this was pretty funny until the discussion started to zero in on a new category of relatives, a category that Tom pulled out of his hat.

"What about the mentally unstable relatives?" he asked.

I didn't much like this category, especially when it became apparent that all the mental irregulars were on my side.

Tom began to sound a little smug, a little too superior, as he pried from me never-before-mentioned information about Uncle Rollie and Wendy.

I hadn't felt like talking about them, so I had tried to divert Tom's attention by bringing up other borderline relatives. This wasn't such a good idea, but before I could stop myself, I told Tom about a great-uncle on my mother's side who had suffered from deep depression until he finally committed suicide. I even told him that there was a history of alcoholism on my mother's side – two other great-uncles had died of alcohol related diseases.

At that point in our discussion, Tom's superiority complex reached a higher plateau. He even went so far as to suggest that maybe, with all those faulty genes in my gene pool, not his, maybe we should scratch the whole idea of having our own children. He implied that the odds of having a child who was paranoid schizophrenic or alcoholic were too great.

"Fine!" had been my angry reply, which would have ended our conversation if I hadn't added how all those ugly genes from his side of the family would be reason enough for anyone to become emotionally ill and alcoholic with or without those other "faulty" genes from my side.

"Tom never meant to hurt you," Gram said.

"Apparently, guardian angels can eavesdrop," I said somewhat defensively, since I knew I had been the one to hurt Tom.

"He's just worried, Katy," Gram said.

"I know. He's worried about the genes I'd be supplying our children with."

"No, dear. He only told you that because you already feel that way. Tom is finding it too hard to discuss the thing that really scares him."

"What's that?" I asked.

"He's afraid that Dr. Chang's words of warning might come true."

Dr. Chang's words echoed in my head: Wouldn't it be better to have no children than to have children with no mother?

"Tom would rather have no children if it meant he would be able to spend the rest of his life with you. It's you, Katy, not Tom, who's terrified that Wendy's genes are reason enough not to have children," Gram said as if she were reprimanding me.

"Maybe so, Gram, but anyone who'd grown up with my sister would feel the same way."

"When did you ever decide such a thing?" Gram asked.

I remember the exact moment I'd decided such a thing. It was the day I had come home from school and found my father sitting at his desk in his study. He had never been home before six o'clock, so I knew something was wrong. When I quietly said hello, he just stared out the window as he said hello back. His voice sounded different, far away and tortured, and when I moved closer to him, I saw, for the first and only time in my life, tears streaming down my father's cheeks.

I wanted to go hug him, but all my muscles locked, and I stood still in the middle of the room, frozen and alarmed.

Dad then turned to me, looking years older. He said the high school had called him at work. Wendy had been acting strange in her history class. Her eyes had been dilated, and some red pills had spilled out of her sweater pocket. The school wanted Dad to pick Wendy up.

By then Sam had moved away to Palo Alto. I had felt so alone without him, so alone with the pain, and there was so much of it in our house in those days. I'd witnessed all of Wendy's screaming scenes when she made terrible accusations about my parents and called them vile names, all because they expected her to go to school, to study, to be home on time, to stop drinking and taking drugs. I had been awake the morning the police brought Wendy to our door. They'd found her one block away in the back of a van, smoking pot with one of her tenth-grade boyfriends.

I had been there another time, when Wendy denied stealing the ring my grandfather had given to my mother. It hadn't mattered to my sister that the ring was returned to Mom by a parent who said Wendy had used it to buy drugs from her own daughter. "That mother was lying," Wendy had screamed.

I had watched Wendy verbally tear my parents to shreds without an ounce of remorse. And I had asked myself over and over again, why? They hadn't been terrible people. They hadn't beat their children. They had been loving, supportive parents. Not perfect maybe, but what parent was or could be? Name just one perfect parent.

It hadn't been a sudden decision I came to the day I stood in my father's study. This decision had been growing inside for a long time, like an invisible cancerous tumor whose existence I'd first tried to deny and against which I'd used every mental and emotional weapon to destroy. But the moment I saw my father with tears in his eyes while Wendy, down the hall, slept off the effects of one more ingested drug was the moment I gave in to the tumor of fear. I would never have children. Because of Wendy, I would never have children.

As the years passed and the tumor grew bigger and harder, I had nursed it with a daily oath: "I will never have children." For there was no guarantee that a child of my own would not turn out like Wendy or like Uncle Rollie, and I was not going to risk living through the pain again.

"I couldn't live through the pain again," I said to Gram as she sat on the painting stool.

"Oh, you are such a funny thinker." She laughed.

"What do you mean?" I did not see the humor.

"You have always been so certain that a child of yours would come into the world exactly like your sister or your uncle – a little imperfect."

A little imperfect? How could she say that Wendy and Uncle Rollie were "a little" imperfect?

"No, I suppose you're right," Gram agreed. "It's such a shame Wendy couldn't be a carbon copy of your girlfriends' perfect sisters, no matter how much you wanted it."

"I did want the same kind of sister," I admitted.

"Forgive her, Katy. Forgive her for not being the person you wanted her to be."

"And if I could forgive her, wouldn't it be the same as telling her it's okay to live the way she does?" I asked.

"No. Forgive her, and release her with love. Let her be who she must be without your judgment. And whatever you do, do not make Wendy responsible for your not having a child."

Gram slid off the stool and turned her back on me to look at the unfinished watercolor resting on my easel. "This is quite good," she said, pointing at the painting.

"It's not done." The painting was something I was copying from a picture I'd seen in a magazine. I liked the shape of the woman holding the fire-red and orange clay pot. The lines were simple enough that I thought I could draw something pretty close to it. Anything more complicated and I wouldn't have tried.

"Oh, look at this." Gram reached for the upper right corner of my easel where I'd tacked the small magazine picture. "Your painting looks exactly like this little one." She sounded quite amazed.

"Thank you," I said proudly.

"Now, how did you do that?" Gram asked.

"I just tried to draw the exact same lines and shapes, only I made them bigger."

"Hmmmm," Gram said as she looked at the little picture in the corner and then at my painting on the easel. "But why would you want to make a painting exactly like someone else's?"

"I don't know, I...I feel more secure when I have something to copy from. I'm not very good on my own."

"I'm sure you underestimate your talent. I have to admit, though, this is quite impressive, almost a carbon copy."

I smiled, not too sure she was praising me.

"Did you say it's not finished?" Gram asked.

"I have to work on the woman's hands and arms. They seem to be holding the pot too close to her body."

"Mmmm, yes, I see what you mean. Well, when the painting is completed, whose name will you sign – yours or the artist who painted this little one here?"

"I...I don't know. No one's, I guess."

"Now don't get me wrong, because I certainly am impressed, but I was thinking what a shame it would be if every artist in the world used the same painting method you use."

"What painting method are you referring to?" I asked, feeling slightly defensive.

"The method of copying from someone else's picture because it was easier. I suppose you'd have the same paintings in all the museums and in everyone's living room, wouldn't you?"

Why did it take me so long to figure out what Gram was getting at?

"Wouldn't it be sad if every human being followed the same rules for living, no deviations whatsoever, just because they felt more secure being like everyone else? There wouldn't be any reason to come into this world at all. Nothing for anyone to learn."

Gram was giving me this lecture just because all I ever wanted was a perfectly normal, well-adjusted sister and uncle.

"There wouldn't be any pain," I said stubbornly as I stared at my painting.

Just then the telephone rang. I turned to it but didn't want to pick up the receiver, because I knew it would be Wendy.

"No, you're probably right, there would be no pain." Gram's voice sounded faint as if she'd slipped into the painting.

"Hello," I said into the phone's receiver.

"Katy?" asked a man's voice.

"Yes."

"This is Dr. Davis."

THIRTEEN

Heavy traffic in west Los Angeles was a given no matter what time of day or night one might be driving. And the Monday after Gram critiqued my painting was no exception. I was stuck on the 10 Freeway in gridlocked, rush-hour traffic.

My nine o'clock appointment at the UCLA Medical Center had been scheduled three days earlier, and I could not be late, nor did I want to reschedule the X-rays that Dr. Davis insisted I take a second time. The clock on the dashboard read eight forty-seven. That meant I had exactly thirteen minutes to reach my exit, drive two more blocks to the Center, find a parking spot, and take the elevator to the fifth floor.

I was not feeling optimistic about my situation, but tapping my fingers on the steering wheel and biting my lower lip was definitely not helping me to calm down. I turned on the radio and moved the dial to KABC 790, the morning talk show with Ken and Bob.

"We are talking to Ginny, our first caller on this fine Monday morning," said Bob, the radio host.

"May we call you Miss Ginny from New Guinea?" asked Bob's sidekick, Ken.

The airwaves filled with laughter from Ken and Bob and a high-pitched giggling that could only have been coming from Miss Ginny.

"Well, how are you on this fine Monday morning, Miss Ginny from New Guinea?" asked the overly cheerful Bob.

"EGBOK," said the giggly Ginny.

More laughter erupted from Ken and Bob.

"And a very happy EGBOK to you, too," answered Bob.

"Now, Ginny, can you tell us..."

"EGBOK? What in the world is EGBOK?" requested a voice that did not sound like it came from the radio.

I was about to fiddle with the dial to get a clearer transmission when I glanced at the passenger seat. There she was, my grandmother, my guardian angel, my...figment of my imagination.

"Don't worry," called out Ken and Bob to their radio listening audience. "Because everything is going to be okay!"

"That's EGBOK," I answered Gram while pointing to the radio.

"That's EGBOK?" Gram said looking at the radio with total bewilderment.

"No." I giggled like Miss New Guinea. "The acronym for 'Everything is going to be OK' is EGBOK."

Gram looked at me like I was crazy, then closed her mouth, tilted her head, and tapped her lips with her index finger.

"E in EGBOK stands for 'Everything,'" I began to explain. "And 'Going' is the G in -"

"Oh, stop, stop. I get it now," said Gram. "That is truly the ugliest and most ridiculous word I've ever heard!"

"It is, isn't it?" I agreed with Gram.

I knew that listening to Ken and Bob while holding a conversation with Gram was not going to go well, so I reached for the button again to turn off the radio. I noticed that the lane to my right was moving slightly faster than my lane.

"Did you know that today is Rollie's birthday?" Gram asked.

"No, I didn't," I said looking over my right shoulder to see if I could change lanes.

"He's fifty-five years old," Gram said and heaved a long sigh.

The cars in the right lane would not let me in.

"I didn't know he was that old," I said. L.A. drivers! If you turn on your blinker light, you can be certain that everyone will speed up so you can't possibly move over.

"I don't suppose you'll be celebrating Rollie's birthday with him, will you?" asked Gram.

"No, Gram, I won't," I said softly.

"That's too bad." Gram stared out the passenger window. "Rollie loved his birthday more than anyone."

Gram had always enjoyed making a big deal out of birthdays for everyone in the family, but the parties for Uncle Rollie when he was not 'on one of his trips' seemed desperately overgenerous, with formal invitations sent to every living relative weeks in advance. Gram would set her dining room table with her finest china, silver, and glassware, and she would ask an old friend from the Los Angeles orchestra to come and play the harp or the violin, sometimes the cello, throughout the dinner party.

At one particular birthday celebration for Rollie, Gram had gathered the family into the living room after we'd eaten dinner. The soft strumming of the harpist in the corner of the room calmed the busy energy of everyone settling into their seats.

Gram had been anxious all through dinner about giving Rollie the large white box with the shiny, black satin ribbon and bow. Before she did, she prefaced the offering of the gift by reminding Rollie that he'd complained quite often of his old clothes feeling too tight.

Everyone knew that Rollie's old clothes were really Grandpa's old clothes, the same ones Rollie had been wearing since Grandpa died. It had been Gram's hope that Rollie's complaints were an indication that he would be willing to stop wearing Grandpa's clothes.

But when Rollie untied the fat silk ribbon and lifted the top of the box, he simply stared at the brown tweed sport coat folded inside. It looked almost exactly like Grandpa's tweed coat only much bigger. Rollie slowly shook his head and glared at his birthday gift, giving everyone a pretty good idea of how happy he was to have the new coat.

An air of anxiousness spread through the room until Sam walked over to Rollie, lifted the coat from the box, and held it up for all to see. "That's really boss, Uncle Rollie," he said. "Really boss!"

Everyone exhaled with relief until my grandmother asked Rollie to try on the sport coat for everyone to see.

Rollie's cheeks burned red, and he mumbled, "He will not like this."

"Man! Everyone is going to like this coat!" Sam told Rollie. "Here, try it on."

To my amazement, Rollie allowed Sam to assist him with trying on the new coat. Sam even patted Rollie's shoulders the way a professional tailor would when checking for size and fit, but Rollie continued to shake his head.

"He will not like this. He will not like this," Rollie had repeated over and over.

I knew that Rollie never wore any of the new clothes that were given to him that birthday or any other birthday, because years later, I saw the coat and the other gifts of clothing on a shelf in Gram's garage, each one in its original box, looking as new as the day it had been purchased.

Gram had never given up, though. Rollie once told her that he needed new gardening clothes. He'd always worn Grandpa's white shirts and brown wool slacks to plant the miniature shrubs in Gram's front yard. That birthday, Gram had presented my uncle with a brand-new pair of jeans, a work shirt, heavy-duty work shoes, and a gardening hat. Had Rollie ever put those clothes on? Never. He had continued to wear Grandpa's clothes even though they were threadbare at the seat and elbows and much too tight around Rollie's ever-expanding belly.

I couldn't recall when Gram stopped having those big birthday parties for Rollie, but until that Monday morning sitting in rush hour traffic with Gram, I had never even considered how lonely he must feel, especially on days like this, when he used to have lots of family around to make him feel special.

I knew that my parents would probably see Rollie that night. Ever since Gram had died, they'd taken him out for dinner on his birthday and then, again, a few days before Christmas. Those were the only times they drove into the fringes of South Central Los Angeles, to the halfway house where Rollie currently lived, a dilapidated, fenced-in, two-story bungalow.

Seven other mentally and psychologically-challenged patients lived together in this house, all pretty much like my uncle. They were looked after by an older woman who was paid by the state to care for them and make sure they took their medication and stayed out of trouble. The woman kept everyone busy with daily responsibilities like making beds and helping with dishes. She made sure they all bathed and dressed in clean clothes each day, and she forced them to play games like Sorry or Monopoly so they would not end up watching TV all the time. My mother said that while the residents didn't seem to be thriving, living in the run-down halfway house had to be better than living in a mental hospital.

"It's a lonely way to live." Gram sighed.

Against my will, I imagined Uncle Rollie with my father and mother, slowly walking to a nearby cafeteria, the kind of eatery with lights so bright their fluorescence spills onto the sidewalk. I saw the three of them sitting at a booth with hard, plastic cushions, sharing Rollie's favorite meal of bread-and-onion sandwiches. Finally, I saw Rollie listlessly open presents on the metal tabletop before the three of them walked Rollie back to his halfway house. And for the first time ever, my heart broke a little for my uncle.

A few years ago, my mother had told me that she'd finally figured out a way to get Rollie to wear clothes other than Grandpa's. She would go to thrift shops, buy used shirts, pants, whatever Rollie seemed to need, and then she'd wrap them in a dusty old moving box. On his birthday or at Christmas, she would offer the box to Rollie, telling him she found it mixed in the garage or the attic right beside some of Gram's old belongings. Then Mom would wonder out loud, "Could these have been your father's?"

Rollie would look them over carefully before he told her detailed stories of when and where Grandpa had worn each article of clothing. Mom would finally ask Rollie if he would like to keep the things, and he would instantly say, "Of course! Carlyle wants me to have them. They are my inheritance, you know."

"Well, I suppose your parents will go see Rollie tonight."

"I hope they will," I said in all sincerity.

The lanes of the freeway were beginning to pick up speed, and I began to feel hopeful that I might only be five minutes late to my appointment.

"You don't see Rollie anymore, do you?" Gram asked.

"No," I said, knowing that my refusal to see Rollie still pained her.

I needed to start moving the car over to the slow lane for the hospital exit. I turned on the blinker, hoping some nice driver would let me over.

"How long has it been?" Gram asked matter-of-factly.

"Not since your funeral."

"That's a long time not to see your uncle." Gram sighed.

"Yes."

Gram was right. It had been a long time. Gram had died fifteen months after Tom and I were married, so that would make it over eleven years since I'd seen Rollie. Tom and I had still been living in Chicago, and I had flown back for the funeral service, which was held outdoors right at the gravesite.

It had been early fall in Los Angeles, still very warm, and while everyone gathered around Gram's casket listening to the words of the minister, I studied Rollie as he stood beside my father and my brother. He was wearing Grandpa's brown tweed sport coat, but he'd gained so much weight that the coat would not stretch far enough across Rollie's bulging stomach. Grandpa's gray pants were pulled tightly below Rollie's protruding belly, and the bottoms hung sloppily around his ankles. There were holes at the toes of Grandpa's brown leather shoes; only one of them had laces, and that shoe was tied only halfway up, because the frayed lace had obviously broken. Rollie stood there at Gram's funeral, staring at the ground, his hands clasped in front of him, looking solemn. He didn't say anything. He didn't cry.

I didn't know what I had expected of Rollie that day. His mother, my grandmother, had died, and Rollie was more alone than ever before. So why hadn't I felt any pain for him? Who was going to care for Rollie now? Who was going to care about him? By then I was an adult, but I had still been afraid of my uncle, though more than anything on that particular day, I had been angry with him for being the kind of uncle he'd been to me. For being the kind of son he'd been to Gram.

I was not proud of the fact that I had never gone up to Rollie at Gram's funeral. I had never hugged him. I had never told him I was sorry. But at the time, I hadn't felt that he deserved to hurt, and I certainly hadn't wanted to share my sadness with him. This was the man who had made my sweet grandmother's life a living hell.

I knew that Gram's funeral was the last time I had ever seen Rollie, but I didn't remember the last time I had actually spoken to him. It must have been before my wedding.

Tom's and my wedding. How could I have been so cruel to Gram? Thinking back now, how could I have been so cruel to Rollie? My only excuse was that several weeks before the wedding, Gram had begun to act nervous and distant. Everyone in the family suspected that Rollie was once again living in Gram's home, even though she never admitted it. She kept acting more and more cautious over the phone, saying things like, "I can't talk now. Someone is here and insists on using the phone, but everything is just fine. I'm f-i-n-e." We knew that Gram had somehow gotten Rollie released from the hospital, and we worried that if he stopped taking his medication, it would just be a matter of time before Gram would not be f-i-n-e and she'd be calling my parents for h-e-l-p.

A week before Tom and I were to be married, I had told my mother that I didn't want Rollie to attend the wedding. I had been worried that Rollie might not be so fine at our wedding service and reception. I didn't know why my mother hadn't gotten upset with me and told me how wrong I was to exclude Rollie, but she hadn't. Instead, Mom had called Gram and told her that Rollie was not to come.

What had I been thinking of? How could that have helped Gram? It obviously hadn't. Gram had called the morning of my wedding and told my mother that she would not be able to come. She said she wasn't feeling well, but we all knew that Rollie had forced Gram to make the call. If he couldn't come, neither could she.

Even now, I still didn't know who had gone to Gram's house – probably Sam – but Gram had come to my wedding, sans Rollie, looking nervous and forlorn. There was a photograph of Gram and me taken at the reception, and it showed a sad, tired little old lady standing by my side, tucked under my arm. Her smile was forced, and her brown eyes had a dim, faraway look. Every time I saw this picture, I wondered what she'd had to go home to that night.

It was frustrating how not one car was letting me into the next lane. Tom said that California drivers won't make room for you if they see your blinker on: "They can't stand the thought of one more car ahead of them." Remembering Tom's words, I turned off the blinker

"Gram, can you ever forgive me for not letting Rollie come to my wedding?" I asked.

"Whatever made you think of your wedding?" asked Gram.

"Well, you wondered when I'd last seen him and -"

"Why didn't you want your uncle at your wedding?"

"I guess I've always been so afraid of him and...and so angry with him," I said. "I was afraid he was going to ruin my wedding."

"So, is that what you want me to do? Forgive you for being afraid and angry?"

"No, but maybe –" I paused to consider what I really wanted to say. "Maybe I want you to forgive me for not forgiving Rollie."

"Forgiving Rollie?" Gram looked puzzled.

"Yes, for being the way he was or is." Instantly, I felt uncomfortable by what I'd said.

"Well, my dear, your uncle doesn't need forgiveness for the way he was or the way he is. He couldn't help it and he still can't."

"Gram, I ..." I felt helpless to explain my words.

"Rollie never needed your forgiveness. The only thing he ever needed from you was your unconditional love. But, of course, you can't love your uncle until you stop being angry and afraid of him."

I could not imagine ever being able to feel unconditional love for Rollie.

"It's more for your sake than his." Gram sighed.

"What do you mean?" I asked.

"If you were to release all the fear and all the anger you have toward your uncle, he wouldn't own you anymore, nor would he have so much control over your life."

"Rollie's never owned me," I protested. "And he's never had control over my life."

"Oh my, yes, he has. The fear and anger you harbor towards your uncle has kept you bound to what you think he is, bound to the pain you believe he caused you, and bound to the pain you are afraid he can still cause you."

"Gram, I haven't seen him in at least eleven years! He can't cause me anymore pain."

"Think about it. You're still so afraid, so certain your own child will have Rollie's disease that you still can't make a decision about having children. And you just turned thirty-nine years old."

I had no words with which to answer Gram as I looked in my rearview mirror and attempted to move the car over one more lane.

"I don't know, Gram. I don't think I can ever forget the way Rollie was." I slowly shook my head.

"You don't have to forget. You probably shouldn't forget. Love him anyway."

I looked at Gram and started to tell her that loving Uncle Rollie was impossible, when she spoke again.

"Will you be seeing Dr. Davis today?"

The cars beside me wouldn't let me into the next lane! "No. He said he'd call me with the results tomorrow or the next day after he gets them from this lab."

Immediately, my mind focused on Dr. Davis. He had called the day that Gram sat at my easel and had said he wanted me to take another chest X-ray.

"What was wrong with the first one?" I had asked.

"Nothing's wrong. I just didn't like what I saw."

"Is it –"

"Katy, I've scheduled the chest X-ray for Monday morning at nine o'clock. When the lab sends the results to me, I will study them, and then we'll talk," the doctor said with a tone of finality.

"Look out!" Gram screamed.

I had just eased over into the slow lane, thanks to a kind and generous orange Honda, but Gram's scream caused me to slam on my brakes. I looked every which way for a problem, but I saw no problem except for the nice Honda driver in my rearview mirror, who was not looking very happy.

I looked at Gram and put my foot on the gas pedal. "Are you trying to give me a heart attack?" I asked.

"I'm sorry, dear. I didn't hear your blinker, so I didn't think you were aware that our car was moving into that lane," Gram apologized.

I exhaled long and hard. As I gained speed along with the other cars, I could feel my heart pounding and wasn't sure if it was more from Gram's sudden shriek or if it was because I'd passed the exit for the hospital.

I looked over at Gram with reproach.

"You better keep your eyes on the road," she admonished me.

"You used to think I was a good driver," I countered. "In fact, Grandmother, when you were alive, you were always telling me that I was a very careful driver."

"Oh, you are, Granddaughter, maybe too careful," Gram said.

"Look who's talking," I quickly looked over at Gram only to have her motion for me to look back at the road. "As I recall you got a ticket for being too careful," I teased.

I couldn't have been more than nine years old when Gram had proudly told my family about the nice young policeman who had ticketed her for driving only thirty-five miles an hour on the South Pasadena Freeway. Gram said that the policeman had been so impressed with her careful driving that he had really stopped her just to tell her what a careful driver she was.

"I don't know why you and your parents never believed me," said Gram.

I laughed at her indignation.

"You know..." I paused in thought. "I have this theory about the way people drive."

"Yes?" said Gram warily.

"I think you can tell a lot about how people go through life by watching them drive the freeway."

"That's ridiculous," she said.

"I know it sounds crazy, but I think it would probably hold water if it were tested clinically." I could tell that Gram wasn't buying it. "Take Tom's driving habits. He drives in a way that completely escapes me."

"How's that?"

"Well, for instance, he will be in the fast lane of the freeway, pushing the speed limit just enough to get away with it. And as he's doing this, the signs overhead keep warning that our turnoff is coming up. The first sign will indicate two miles more before our turnoff. Does Tom begin to move over towards the slow lane?"

"Yes?"

"No," I answered. "He stays right there, three or four lanes from the exit lane. That's usually when I point out to him that the turnoff lane is coming up. It's no use, though, because Tom stays in the fast lane. And before you know it, the next sign comes along warning us that the turnoff we want is one mile ahead. Wouldn't you think that Tom would begin to move over a lane or two?"

"I would hope so," Gram said.

"Wrong."

"No?" Gram asked with dismay. I could tell I had her interested in my theory now.

"Then when we see the final sign saying that it's a half-mile before we will miss the whole turnoff, does my husband move over?

"Don't tell me!" Gram huffed.

"Of course not! He waits until the last second to move over, which forces him to dart and dash between cars who don't want to let him in. He never worries that some other driver might not let him over in time. But, get this, he always makes the turnoff!"

"Always?"

"Always!"

"So, how does this relate to your theory," Gram wanted to know.

I was happy she'd asked. "Well, if you think about it, how do you think Tom gets anything done?"

"I don't have a clue," my grandmother said.

"The exact same way he drives on the freeway," I said as if no other explanation was necessary.

"Give me an example," Gram egged me on.

I could tell she liked my little theory. I had her in the palm of my hand.

"Okay." I paused to think of one. "When Tom was working on his doctoral dissertation, he knew that the due date was coming up pretty soon. He'd had the whole thing outlined for over a year, but he kept postponing writing the paper, even though the due date was getting closer and closer. He wasn't being lazy or anything, he was just doing a hundred other things at the same time, like teaching classes, counseling students, writing articles, and even giving a few speeches at other universities. I was certain he wouldn't finish his dissertation in time."

"Did he?"

"Yes! Just like on the freeway! Just before the last second, Tom darted and dashed and somehow completed the whole thing, and his professor loved it!"

"Whew," Gram said with amazement.

"I know. And what about the hundreds of productions Tom has worked on over the years?" I asked.

"Same story?"

"Same story."

Gram shook her head.

"Tom is one of those people who is able to move from the fast lane in life over to the exit lane at the last minute and in time. I've never understood it," I sighed.

We were easing off the freeway and began to head west on Santa Monica Boulevard.

"Does your theory apply to you, too?" Gram asked.

I looked over at her. "Well, I'm always at the place I'm supposed to be way ahead of time." I could tell I was sounding self-righteous.

"I was wondering about your decision to have children," Gram said.

I knew I looked puzzled, but I really had no idea what she was getting at.

"Well, Katy, it seems like this year, you've been darting and dashing around, trying to get to the Baby Exit Lane."

How could Gram be so cruel? What did my stupid little theory have to do with our wanting children?

"Gram, I thought I knew what I was doing when I said I didn't want to have children, that I wanted to pursue a career. And then when Tom and I decided to wait, I really didn't think waiting until I was thirty-four was waiting too long."

"Maybe you should have moved over a lane or two."

I wished I hadn't told Gram my theory. Was it my fault that I had gotten cancer? I never saw a detour sign saying, Warning: Cancer Ahead.

"You need to turn right into that parking lot," Gram calmly directed me.

The sound of the car's blinker lagged behind the beat of my heart. The moment I turned into the parking lot, I spied an open space ahead, as if it had been waiting for me. And then I looked at the clock on the dashboard and saw that it read eight fifty-seven. How could this be?

I looked at Gram. She was smiling serenely at me. I parked and turned off the motor.

"I'm more than a little scared today, Gram," I said in a whisper. "I'm not sure I want to know what today's X-rays will show."

"Katy, look those X-rays in the eye and tell them." Gram took a deep breath then shouted, "EGBOK!"

I laughed. She could always make me laugh, even when I was scared.

"You know you are stronger than anything those X-rays show you." Gram paused and then added, "Just like the beautiful sphinxes."

I opened my door and stepped out of the car. I waited for Gram to get out, too, but she didn't. I looked through the car window. Gram was gone.

There I was at the hospital about to take a chest X-ray because my doctor didn't like what he'd seen the first time, and Gram was gone. Without her beside me, how would I be able to look those X-rays in the eye and tell them I wasn't afraid?

I walked slowly across the parking lot and through the hospital's sliding glass door. "EGBOK," I whispered.

FOURTEEN

I can't get her out of my mind." I mumbled as I sat on the edge of the bed, my hands lying limply on my lap.

"Finish getting dressed, dear. You need to get back to your friend." Gram's voice softly urged me on. She was seated on the overstuffed chair across from the bed in our bedroom.

"She's so sick, Gram." The tears started to stream down my cheeks. "I should be with her."

Two days earlier, my mother had phoned to say, "Wendy's in the hospital. She's very sick."

I had immediately assumed that this call was like so many others I'd received in the past, when my mother would tell me Wendy was in jail or in some hospital detoxification ward, or that she'd once again entered a drug rehabilitation center. But this time it had been different.

My mother had said, "Your sister's six months pregnant and will probably lose the baby."

I continued to listen as my mother explained that Wendy had

complained of severe headaches and double vision during the previous week, and by the time she decided to go the nearby clinic, it was too late. Wendy had collapsed in the doctor's office before he had a chance to discover a blood clot that had traveled to the stem of her brain.

She had been rushed to the hospital, but the clot was lodged so deeply that Wendy now lay in a coma. We were told that the next forty-eight hours were critical. If Wendy didn't wake from the coma by then, she probably never would. And her baby, well, the doctors said that the baby's survival did not look promising, regardless of whether or not Wendy pulled through.

The day my mother had phoned me with this information was the same day Lauren had arrived from Philadelphia. She was my best friend from Northwestern, and she was here for our annual visit.

"Are you wearing this tonight?" Gram asked. She was pointing at the navy-blue linen jacket lying on the bed beside me.

I nodded.

"It's so nice how you can wear anything with a white T-shirt and a pair of jeans."

I could tell by her tone that she didn't mean it. "Uh-huh," I said as I slowly pulled on the jacket. I wanted to be with Wendy, not at a restaurant with Tom and Lauren.

I'd been at the hospital most of the day, sitting beside Wendy whose eyes were open but saw nothing. I had tried several times to tell her that I was sorry for not letting her talk the day she called me at home. I now knew she'd called to tell me she was five and a half months pregnant. I also knew that she probably was happy to be pregnant. I hadn't told

Wendy, as her frozen eyes pierced the dead air of the hospital room, that I was not happy she was pregnant and thought it would be better if the baby didn't survive.

Still sitting in the bedroom chair, Gram said, "It's better for Wendy to be alone and quiet for a while. Her doctors don't want her to go into labor any sooner than she has to. It will give the baby a better chance to survive."

I looked at Gram, wanting to ask her what kind of life a twenty-four-week-old fetus would have, having already suffered from its mother's drug and alcohol abuses. What if Wendy didn't pull out of her coma? Who would take on the challenge of such a premature, sickly infant? Who would want to?

"Besides," Gram continued, "your best friend has come all this way. You need to spend some time with her. It will do you some good."

"I'm afraid I haven't been very good company for Lauren."

"She understands," Gram said.

"I know, but I hate leaving her alone with Andy."

"Why? Andy is a good companion for her while you're with Wendy."

"I don't think so, Gram. Lauren's never liked dogs."

"Why wouldn't she like Andy?"

"I think she was attacked by one when she was an infant or something like that."

"Oh, well, it's true that people who are afraid of animals usually have good reasons for it. Like your Uncle Rollie."

"Like Uncle Rollie?" I asked.

"Did you know that Rollie was afraid of Mamie?" Gram asked.

"Mamie?" I wondered how anyone could be afraid of Gram's big old golden retriever, the one she'd named after President Dwight Eisenhower's wife.

"She was such a sweet, gentle dog," Gram added. "But there were times when Rollie became so frightened of Mamie that he wouldn't let me feed her for days. He wouldn't let her in the house, not even when it rained. Without him knowing it, I'd find ways to slip food to her."

"But why was he so afraid of Mamie?"

"I never really knew why – well, until your mother found the notebook."

"The notebook?"

"The black one." Gram spoke matter-of-factly.

"Gram, I don't know what you're talking about."

"Oh, I suppose you don't, do you. Well, never mind, it's a long story."

I was too emotional over Wendy to beg Gram to tell me about a black notebook. Besides, I had a feeling she was going to tell me about it anyway.

Gram sighed as she motioned me to finish getting dressed. "Rollie was never really a behavior problem until he got into his teens. But then, more and more, he became loud and angry, even threatening. Your grandfather and I couldn't figure out how this had happened. We had raised Rollie the same way we raised your father. But then, I guess between Bertie's pampering and my temper..."

I'd heard about Gram's temper. According to my father, Gram had a dreadful one, which was hard for me to believe, because I had never ever seen Gram get angry. But there was the story about a time when my father was ten years old. The boy who lived next door had trampled over some of his own mother's freshly planted flowers. The same boy had then lied to his mother, saying my father had done it on purpose.

Gram had been in her own backyard hanging laundry on the clothesline when the boy's mother stormed out of her house and over to Gram. After Gram heard what my dad had supposedly done, she called for him to come outside. My father, of course, denied having walked on any flowers, and Gram believed him, but the neighbor kept telling Gram what a terrible mother she was and how it was no wonder Billy was such a liar.

Well, I guessed Gram had had enough, so she turned to Dad who was standing beside her, and she slapped him hard across the face. Twice. Then she turned to the neighbor lady and her son and said, "There! Is that what you wanted to see?" My father never forgave Gram.

"I wasn't always easy to live with – redheads and their tempers, you know." Gram paused for a moment. "Right after I had Rollie, I went through a long and difficult menopause. It made me so moody."

"Hm." I nodded because I had heard that, too. My mother once told me that Gram had suffered for many years with extreme hot flashes, mood swings, painful headaches, and cramps.

"It wasn't easy taking care of a young child and going through menopause at the same time," said Gram. "I suppose that's good enough reason why women should have their children before forty."

Was Gram was directing this at me? She'd once before hinted that thirty-nine was a little old for starting a family, but was she now suggesting that menopause was just around the corner for me? No, it wasn't and, no, I was not going to even consider it up for discussion.

"But what about the notebook, Gram?" I thought maybe she'd forgotten about it.

"Oh, yes, the notebook." Gram closed her eyes as if gathering up the strength to go on. "You won't remember this, because you were just a baby, but about ten months after your grandfather died, Rollie became increasingly angry and threatening."

She paused as if in pain, then slowly continued. "For the first time ever, he physically hurt me. Until then, I had never told your parents about his odd behavior. Then, one night, Rollie struck me and began to throw the china at me. I had no choice. I ran from the house and took a bus to your parents' home."

"Did he follow you?"

"No, but he knew that I'd gone to your parents, so he called them, demanding that I return home. Your father confronted Rollie about what he'd done, but Rollie denied everything and said I was a crazy old lady."

"You didn't go home, did you?"

"No, no. Your parents and I were much too concerned and frightened. It was the first time that this sort of thing had happened with Rollie. Your father insisted that I stay at your house until we could figure out a way to remove Rollie from mine. Your poor mother! As if she didn't have enough to worry about with two little children, your brother not even two and you only ten months old."

"How were you able to get Rollie out of your house?"

"Over the next few days, your mother took me to every doctor and psychiatrist, to every mental hospital and government agency, trying to get help. But everyone said the same thing: they needed more proof that Rollie was a threat. They said it would be Rollie's word against mine as to how I'd gotten the bruises. Laws were different in those days, you know."

"What could you do?"

"Well, your mother decided that the two of us would go back to my house and look through Rollie's belongings. She thought we might find some kind of clue as to what was causing Rollie to behave so irrationally."

"But Rollie was there!"

"Your mother had a plan. She borrowed her neighbor's car, because Rollie would recognize hers, and we parked across the street from my house waiting for Rollie to leave.

"How long did you have to wait?"

"Not long, because I knew his routine. Most mornings, Rollie walked three blocks to the neighborhood market to buy cigarettes and donuts. Then he'd walk to the park to smoke and eat the donuts. He usually didn't come back to the house for at least an hour."

"Weren't you scared?"

"Petrified." Gram nodded. "And sad to be doing such a thing. This was my son." Gram paused again. "Once we got into the house, your mother kept me busy looking out the front window for Rollie while she went into his bedroom. That's where she found it."

"The black notebook?" I guessed.

"Yes."

"What was in it?"

"It was a journal Rollie had been keeping. He had written about some voices that spoke to him."

"Voices?"

Gram nodded. I looked at her with disbelief.

"How many were there?" I asked.

"Just three."

"Did he have names for them?"

"Yes. George, Victor, and Mamie."

"Mamie!" I said with alarm. "He thought your dog, Mamie, spoke to him?"

"Poor Rollie was so tormented," Gram said.

"How long had he been keeping the notebook?

"Well, the first entry was dated the day your grandfather died, so almost a year."

"He began hearing voices the day Grandpa died?" I needed to sit down. "Rollie didn't..." I stammered.

"Good heavens, no, Rollie didn't kill your grandfather. Carlyle died of a heart attack, but somehow Rollie got it into his head that he was the cause of his father's death."

"Did you try to tell him that he wasn't?"

"I would have, but I didn't know Rollie thought this until your mother discovered the notebook."

"But why did Rollie think he caused grandpa's death?"

"Well, Rollie and your grandfather had a terrible argument that morning before Carlyle died. For quite some time, Rollie had been a behavior problem, and he became increasingly disrespectful to your grandfather and me. When he was fifteen, he insisted on calling his father George. He called me some strange name too. I don't remember what. I believe Rollie and Carlyle were arguing about these names just two hours before Grandpa died. Rollie wasn't around when Carlyle collapsed. He'd already gone off to school."

"Were you there when they argued?"

"No. I was at work."

"So how did you know about the argument?"

"Well, taped to the first page of the black notebook, the one your mother found, was a note your grandfather had written to me the morning he died. Carlyle had wanted me to know about the argument he'd had with Rollie, because he'd wanted me to be sure Rollie followed his orders to be home for dinner and not go out with his friends after school. Carlyle often left notes for me, since he worked late on concert nights."

"And you never saw Grandpa's note?"

"No. The day Carlyle died, your father came to my office to take me home. I was so devastated over Carlyle's death, and then there was so much to do, so many people at the house. I never saw the note lying on the kitchen counter."

"Where was Rollie?"

"He was still at school. Your mother was the one who brought Rollie home and told him about his father's death."

"How did Rollie take it?"

"Your mother said that he didn't cry or ask any questions, and when they arrived at the house, he went to the kitchen and got some milk and cookies as if it were any other day after school. I suppose that's when Rollie found the note from Carlyle. Carlyle's notes to me were always left on the kitchen counter. Rollie went to his room and didn't come out for several days, except for Carlyle's funeral." Gram paused. "I now know that Rollie spent all that time alone believing he'd caused his father's death."

"But was the note from Grandpa the only thing in Rollie's black notebook?"

"No. Your grandfather's note had been taped to the first page, but on the lines under it Rollie had written, 'No one must know.'"

"Was that all he wrote?" I asked.

"Yes, but he'd written these same words over and over again, maybe five hundred times, pages and pages with the same words."

There was a long silence. Finally, I said, "Poor Rollie." For the first time ever, I was feeling tremendous sadness for my uncle.

"My son struggled alone with the guilt and pain, because he felt he couldn't tell anyone. It was such a terrifying secret that he kept to himself. Eventually, Rollie's pain and guilt took over his mind, his sanity."

"You said he wrote about voices."

"Yes."

"When did they appear in the notebook?"

"Rollie first wrote about them maybe a month after Carlyle died. At least that was the date shown on the entry."

"What kinds of things did the voices say?"

"At first, it was one voice, George, telling Rollie that someone had seen Carlyle's note, the one he'd written the morning he died. Several pages later, a new voice, Victor's, told Rollie that anyone who knew about Carlyle's note had to be destroyed. But it was the third voice, Mamie's, that ordered Rollie to destroy me. This voice told him that I'd found out about the argument with Carlyle and that I'd tell everyone if he didn't destroy me first."

"I guess that explains why he was so afraid of Mamie. He didn't want her to make him do something like..." My voice trailed off as I tried to sort all this out.

Gram didn't say anything.

"Did the Mamie voice tell Rollie to kill anyone else?"

"Yes."

"Dad?"

"Your parents, Sam, Wendy and you."

I couldn't believe what I was hearing. No one ever told me this. "Would Uncle Rollie really have tried to kill us?"

"I don't think so, but that black notebook was the proof your mother and I needed to show the court Rollie was a serious threat and needed help."

"Then what happened?"

"A day later three policemen drove me to my house."

"What did Rollie do when he saw the police?"

"Nothing. He was very cooperative. I don't think he realized what was happening even as the handcuffs were put on him. But then, when he was led to the ambulance..." Gram stopped.

"Gram?"

"When the ambulance door was opened, it was as if a gust of ice-cold wind had hit him in the face. Rollie suddenly stepped back and looked at me standing on the porch. There was such a look of panic on his face...and then...he quietly stepped inside. It was the first time I had watched my son being taken away. I'd had no idea that there would be so many more in the future."

A long moment of silence sat between us.

"I'm sorry, Gram."

"It was several more years before Rollie was able to tell his therapists about the last day of his father's life. And when he finally did talk about it, well, that's about the time he began wearing Carlyle's clothes."

"But why would he want to wear Grandpa's things?"

"His doctor told me that it was Rollie's way of keeping his father alive; it helped him deal with his guilt. You see, he never stopped believing that he was the cause of Carlyle's heart attack."

I was surprised by all Gram had told me. In the quiet of the bedroom where we sat, I wondered if, had I known these things before, maybe I would have seen Uncle Rollie in a different light. From the open window that faced the backyard I heard the soft mellow voices of Lauren and Tom as they sat by the pool waiting for me.

"How long will Lauren be here?" Gram asked.

"Until Tuesday."

I began to wonder how I would get through the week with Lauren visiting and Wendy in the hospital. Lauren had met Wendy years ago at my wedding, but I'd never told her about Wendy's heartbreaking life, and I did not want Lauren to see Wendy now.

"I wish she hadn't come this year," I said to Gram.

"It must be difficult, but it's not only because of Wendy that you don't want Lauren here."

"Gram," I whispered, fearing Lauren and Tom might be able to hear her.

Gram shook her head and said, "That's what you were thinking last night when you overheard Lauren talking to Tom."

Gram was right. I had overheard Lauren and Tom talking the night before. We'd finished dinner, and they were waiting for me to put on my swimsuit and join them in the Jacuzzi beside the pool. I guess they didn't think I could hear their voices above the sound of the bubbling water, but I could.

Lauren was telling Tom that David, her husband, felt I should not get pregnant. I couldn't believe my ears. How could she say that to Tom? And Lauren of all people! Wasn't she the same friend who had cried real tears at Northwestern when I'd told her I didn't want to have children? Wasn't she the same friend who'd told me that the whole purpose in life was to have a family? Hadn't she said that I would die a sad old woman if I didn't reconsider and have children?

I remember laughing at Lauren and her tears. It had seemed silly for her to take this kind of thing so seriously when we were only sophomores in college.

But then, Lauren had always taken the idea of procreation seriously. She had told me that ever since she could remember, she had known exactly how the rest of her life would be: "I'm going to marry a doctor and have three children." And that's what she did. She had fallen in love with David when he was a medical student, and sure enough, they went and had three beautiful children.

She had even told me that day in our sorority room what the names of her children would be. "Our first child will be a boy, and we'll name him Alexander." Alexander was now ten years old, and Hannah and Michael soon followed, just as she had said they would.

"You were upset with Lauren," Gram said.

"Only because she agreed with Tom that I shouldn't get pregnant," I tried to explain.

"She's your best friend, and she loves you. Lauren's afraid of losing you, her dearest friend."

"But she's not a doctor."

"Her husband's a doctor."

"But Gram, David's never seen me as a patient. He doesn't have all the facts to make an educated opinion about my health." I could hear my voice grow thick with emotion again. I worried that Gram was about to tell me that Tom and Lauren and David were right. I closed my eyes and shook my head as if I could stop her from continuing.

"What about Dr. Davis?" Gram asked. "You said you would listen to his advice."

Tom and I had met with Dr. Davis two days before Wendy went into the hospital, two days before Lauren arrived. Dr. Davis had all my test results in front of him. The liver scan was clean, the bone scan was clean, the brain scan and blood tests were all negative. They all indicated that I didn't have cancer.

"And the mammogram?" I asked.

Dr. Davis had told me that there was a troublesome spot on it, and he had wanted to double check, which is why he'd ordered the chest X-ray. "You don't need to worry," he told us. "The chest X-ray proved my suspicions wrong. Everything's okay."

Tom and I had both breathed a sigh of relief.

"But I have to be perfectly honest with you," Dr. Davis continued. "After looking over your medical history and your unique conditions at the time you had your cancer, I feel in all honesty that I cannot encourage you to become pregnant. It's way too risky. Now I know the decision is entirely up to you, and I will help you in any way I can if you decide to go ahead, but if you were my daughter or wife I would tell you to forget about it. I would tell you to share a new dream and move on."

Gram softly said, "You can't blame Lauren or David for Dr. Davis's medical opinion."

"I know." Tears streamed down my face. "But I'm so frightened that if I listen to them...What if they're wrong?"

"Oh, Katy, haven't you heard a word I've said these last few months? Don't you remember anything?"

I looked at Gram. I didn't know what she was talking about.

"It's like your sphinxes. When are you going to finally decide not to be afraid anymore?" Gram sounded so frustrated. "Katy, haven't you figured out that the power within you, given to you by God, is stronger than any fear, any physical or mental illness?"

The bedroom door opened, and Tom's voice whispered, "Katy, we've got to get going. The hospital just called. Wendy's come out of the coma, and she's asking for you."

I looked at Tom as he reached for both my hands and helped me off the bed. As he led me out of the bedroom, I looked over my shoulder to where Gram was still seated.

"It's like your sphinxes," she repeated, waving goodbye.

CHAPTER

FIFTEEN

I did not know that the wave of Gram's hand was her final goodbye. But I felt her presence in Wendy's hospital room three hours after she'd given birth to a one pound six-ounce baby girl. I was certain that Gram sat with me at Wendy's bedside. I even thought I heard Gram humming by the hospital door and later at the foot of the bed. But it wasn't Gram's voice that finally broke the silence within that darkened room.

"Did you see her yet?" Wendy asked in a pained, barely audible voice.

I looked into Wendy's eyes, stunned to hear her speak. She was lying in the intensive care room with tubes and machinery monitoring every muscle, every gurgle. Premature labor contractions had forced Wendy's doctors to perform an emergency Caesarean an hour after she emerged from her coma. The blood clot remained deeply lodged inside her brain.

"No," I said. "Tom and Mom and Dad went to see her." I decided not to tell Wendy that I didn't want to see the infant who, the doctors had warned, would probably live just a few hours.

"Oh, Katy, you've got to go see her. She's so beautiful," Wendy said dreamily, as if she'd given birth to a healthy, promising life.

"I thought I'd stay here with you for a while," I said.

"Please go see her," Wendy pressed, straining with every word.

"I will, later."

Wendy swallowed hard and closed her eyes as if fighting off pain. "Katy, I had the most wonderful dream."

A nurse walked into the room and began checking Wendy's vital functions.

"Can you tell me your name?" the nurse asked my sister.

Wendy opened her eyes for a second and answered, "Wendy Welborn." Then she closed them again.

"Good," the nurse replied, fiddling with intravenous tubes. "And do you know where you are?" she asked as she lifted each of Wendy's eyelids to be sure the eyeballs had not receded to the back of her head.

"Hospital," Wendy said quietly. Looking at me she added, "She thinks I'm sen-ile."

I smiled, because Wendy had intentionally mispronounced senile, the way Gram had.

"No," the nurse said without humor, "I need to be sure that the blood clot inside your brain doesn't cause you to slip back into another coma before your surgery tomorrow morning." Then she raised Wendy's wrist and checked her pulse before leaving the room.

"I can still hear the music," Wendy said weakly.

"What music?" I asked.

"From my dream," she whispered.

"Oh," I whispered back, hoping Wendy was about to drift to sleep again.

Instead, she began to hum.

"What's that song, Katy?" she asked me.

"I'm not sure," I said with apprehension, for the tune was vaguely, disturbingly familiar.

"It's from my dream and it keeps playing in my head."

"Why don't you let yourself fall asleep?" I begged.

"No, I want to tell you about it." Wendy grimaced and shifted her back slightly. I could tell she was feeling painful muscle contractions from the Caesarean delivery. "I have to tell you about my dream," Wendy added, looking at me in desperation.

"Okay," I whispered.

"There was the sweetest little house, Spanish style. Like Gram's old house. With green shutters on the front windows and a big wooden door."

"Okay," I said. Wendy seemed to be getting stronger with each word.

"And lots of little shrubs in the front yard, like the ones Uncle Rollie planted at Gram's house, except prettier."

"Prettier?" I asked.

"Yes. Each one was beautifully pruned and shaped like a toy car or a toy train, and there were even little girl shrubs shaped like they were dancing – and boys, too. Katy, it was such a happy looking front yard. It looked like a magical toy land."

Wendy pressed her lips together and quietly hummed. "I wish I could remember the song's name." She sighed in agony.

I suddenly knew what she'd been humming. "It's 'Toyland,'" I said icily while dread flooded my whole being.

"No," Wendy narrowed her eyes trying to recapture the words to the song.

But I knew it was "Toyland." Hadn't I had the very same dream?

"I was standing in the street, mesmerized by the shrubs, when I heard the music," Wendy suddenly began again. Her voice was soft and breathy. "It was so joyful and seemed to be calling to me, so I walked into the yard. And then I began to dance with the shrubs until I noticed something long and white moving in slow motion, circling the whole outside of the house."

My heart began beating at a rapid pace. I knew this dream, and I knew what Wendy saw circling Gram's house. "Wendy, was it a white snake?" I could not stop the foreboding sickness from swelling within the pit of my stomach.

"It looked like a snake," Wendy answered with her eyes still closed, "until I moved closer to the house." Wendy paused and sighed heavily. "Oh, Katy, they were beautiful."

"What?"

"All the gardenia bushes. It wasn't a snake surrounding the house. It was hundreds, maybe thousands, of gardenia bushes, all in bloom, all ivory-white and beautiful. They were slowly swaying with a gentle breeze, and I could smell them. Have you ever been able to smell something in a dream?"

"I don't think so," I said.

"I picked one of the gardenias and put it in my hair just as the music grew louder. It was coming from the house, and I wanted to go inside."

"Wendy, please stop," I softly begged my sister. "I don't think you should try to remember anymore."

Wendy ignored my plea and continued to tell me about the dream. She was now totally lucid. "It was beautiful inside, Katy. I wish you could have seen it. The first room was bright and airy, and a wonderful fragrance filled my senses. I was standing in Gram's dining room, except her dining room table wasn't there, just a beautiful vase filled with white gardenia flowers. And then I moved to the next room, and it was filled with even more flowers, the same beautiful, white flowers –"

Wendy breathed in as if inhaling the fragrance of the gardenias and then slowly exhaled. "The music kept playing louder and louder, and as it did, the flowers all started to float in the air, forming a winding path down a long hallway."

"Did you follow it?" I asked.

"Yes. I knew it would take me to where the music was playing."

"What did you find?" I asked.

"A small room – I think it was Uncle Rollie's old room – and when I walked through its door I saw a large, white piano inside. Remember how Rollie had painted Gram's old upright piano?"

"Yes," I said.

"Well, this piano looked like Gram's but much, much prettier. It was bright white, smooth, and shiny as if it had a thick layer of lacquer on it. I'd never seen such a beautiful piano."

I sat frozen in silence.

"You'll never guess who was playing the piano," Wendy's face tensed up niwith pain and her hands tightened into fists.

"Uncle Rollie," I answered without exposing the fear churning inside me.

"No, it was Sam, our Sam, wearing a white tuxedo and singing and playing the song, the same song I heard from outside. He looked so happy as he sang the words. And when he nodded his head at me, I started to sing along."

"Sam was happy?"

Wendy opened her eyes and slowly started to sing, "I come to the garden alone." Her hand lifted from the bed and touched mine before she added, "While the dew is still on the roses."

Tears poured from my eyes as I realized that Wendy was not singing "Toyland." She was softly singing the hymn I'd heard Sam and Rollie sing together long ago at choir practice.

"Then Sam stopped playing the piano," Wendy sighed sadly. "But the music kept going. Isn't that something?"

"Yes," I whispered.

"Sam took my hand, and we walked to the closet door that was behind him. It was open a crack, and he kept motioning for me to come and take a look." Wendy swallowed hard with another pained look on her face. "I heard someone crying inside. It sounded so sad, so familiar. I didn't want to look, but then Sam threw the door wide open."

Believing that I already knew what was behind the door, I pleaded with my sister. "Stop, Wendy. Please stop." I desperately did not want to be reminded of it.

Instead Wendy opened her eyes and stared at the ceiling as she sang the words, "The Son of God discloses."

I jolted from the side of the hospital bed, thinking I could escape before Wendy disclosed what she saw inside the closet. But she had grabbed my wrist and wouldn't let go. I gasped at the strength of her grip. It felt threatening, ominous.

"Gram," Wendy said with a peaceful sigh.

"Gram?" I looked frantically around the room thinking our grandmother, my own guardian angel, had come to rescue me.

"In the closet," Wendy said. "Gram was inside, sitting in a white wicker rocking chair just like yours. And, Katy, guess what was in her arms?" my sister asked, still firmly holding my wrist.

"I don't know, Wendy." I sighed and surrendered with bewilderment.

"My baby. My beautiful, little baby girl dressed in a white linen gown. She looked so tiny and so helpless."

"Was she -" I faltered, because it was too difficult to say "dead," but I was certain that this was what Wendy was about to tell me.

"No, but she was crying a sweet little baby cry. I felt such joy, like I've never felt before, watching Gram rock her back and forth."

I felt my muscles relax.

"And then Gram said the strangest thing. She said she was thinking. I thought it was an odd thing to say, so I asked her what she was thinking about. Gram told me she was thinking of a name for my baby, and I started to cry, because I didn't have a name for her. But then Gram stood up from the rocking chair and put my little girl in my arms.

My baby kept crying until Gram took the gardenia from my hair and placed it in her tiny hand. Then Gram told me to take my baby to you."

"Me?" I breathed in as if my heart had suddenly stopped.

"Yes. Gram said, 'Katy will know what to name her.'"

Wendy looked at me with a soft and gentle smile as her grasp on my wrist loosened. I felt her hand, no longer tight or threatening, slip into my hand.

I remained standing beside her while searching her eyes for something. I didn't know what.

"Do you know the name of my baby?" Wendy asked, childlike.

"No." I tried to stop the tears.

"The music is so beautiful, Katy. I wish you could sing with us." Wendy closed her eyes.

"Us?" I asked.

"Gram and Sam and me." Wendy smiled peacefully.

"I can't," I sobbed as Wendy longingly sang to me.

"...and he-tells me I am his own. And the joy we share as we tarry there, none other has ever known."

There was no indication that night as Wendy told me about her dream that the blood clot inside her brain had begun to swell and travel farther up the brain stem. When I left her bedside, Wendy was softly humming, and I assumed it would be the baby's death I would have to deal with in the morning, not Wendy's.

I was wrong. Three days later, I stood with Tom and my parents at Wendy's gravesite on the same grassy hill where Sam and Gram and Grandpa were buried. I listened as a minister spoke kind words about a young woman he'd never known, a woman none of us had ever really known. And as the minister spoke, my mind drifted, forcing me to remember the little redheaded girl who had been my sister. The little girl whom I had never been able to save from Uncle Rollie's germs, the little girl who had wanted me to be her best friend.

Then I thought of Wendy's little baby lying in an incubator, struggling to stay alive. Tom and I had gone to see her the day Wendy died. She was so tiny. And not beautiful the way Wendy had said. Her skin looked red and tight against her frail little bones. Needles were attached to her arms and feet, and tubes flowed from her throat and chest. Wendy had not named her baby so the tag at the end of the incubator read, "Baby Welborn." That was all.

As the minister asked our small group of mourners to bow our heads and pray for Wendy's soul, I closed my eyes and thought of Wendy's dream. How strange that Gram had appeared in it, telling her that I would know the baby's name.

"Amen," the minister said, ending the graveside service.

After the funeral, Tom and I went to my parents' home for a few hours to quietly share their pain over the loss of another child of theirs. Oddly, none of us spoke about the baby in the incubator, Wendy's baby, the baby who continued to survive despite the doctors' insistence that she could not survive much longer.

Tom and I were quiet as we drove from my parents' home, and it wasn't until Tom turned onto the freeway that I realized I'd been staring at the speedometer. It slowly moved from 35 to 40 miles per hour.

"She's a real fighter," Tom said.

I looked up. Tom was staring straight ahead. I looked back at the speedometer. It moved from forty-five to fifty, then fifty-five miles per hour.

"Who is?" I asked him.

"Wendy's baby."

I said nothing and continued to focus my attention on the speedometer. It didn't move from 55 miles per hour. It just stayed there. I looked up for a moment and noted that Tom kept the car in the slow lane.

"If she lives, she'll need someone to take care of her," Tom said quietly.

I looked back at the speedometer waiting for it to quickly lift itself up to greater numbers. But it didn't. I looked up. Why was my husband still driving in the slow lane at fifty-five miles per hour, as if ready for any turnoff that might come along?

"She'll need a mother and father," Tom spoke again.

I looked out the window ahead of me. "Tom, she's Wendy's child. Who knows what kind of abuses she forced the baby to endure? Do you think Wendy stopped drinking, stopped taking drugs, and who knows what else while she was pregnant?"

"If she lives, she's going to need parents," Tom repeated.

I looked at him. "What if she's brain damaged?"

Tom said nothing.

"She could have any number of physical handicaps, disabilities."

"I don't think so," Tom said.

I looked down at the speedometer. Fifty-five. "What if she grows up to be like Wendy?" I cried.

Tom kept driving at fifty-five miles per hour in the slow lane.

"Or like Uncle Rollie," I said.

"Katy," Tom turned to look at me. "I'm not afraid. I just wish you weren't so afraid."

I turned away from Tom and stared out the window again, not saying anything for several minutes. I watched the green freeway signs swoop overhead and pass us until a sign farther ahead caught my attention: South Pasadena - Next 3 Exits.

I sat frozen for a moment, then looked at the speedometer. Fifty-five miles per hour it read as Tom continued to drive in the slow lane.

"Tom," I spoke with urgency, "would you mind turning off at the next exit?"

He didn't question why I'd asked him such a strange favor. He just slowly eased us off the freeway and followed my directions down the streets of South Pasadena until we reached the sidewalk in front of the old South Pasadena Library. He didn't ask why I wanted him to park down the street and wait for me.

I know he watched as I climbed up the steps to the library entrance, and I know he wondered why I stood so long before each of the stone sphinxes guarding the door. But I'm certain he didn't hear me as I did what Gram had told me to do so many years ago. "I'm not afraid of you anymore!" I shouted with all my might. "I'm not afraid of you anymore!" I sobbed.

I waited for fire to come out of their eyes, for black smoke to spew from their nostrils. Instead, they stood powerless and immobile. I breathed in and then turned my back on those lifeless beings.

When I returned to the car and sat beside Tom, he didn't ask me why I'd taken him to the library. He just turned on the motor. As we drove away, I took one last look at the sphinxes. At that moment, I knew what Gram had meant when she spoke to Wendy in her dream.

"Tom, could we name her Abby Cornelia Welborn McAndrews?" I asked.

Tom was silent for a moment. "Yes. I'd like that," he said quietly.

EPILOGUE

It has been six months since Wendy died. Little Abby remained in her incubator fighting for her life for the next four months. I visited her every day and rocked her in the hospital's wooden rocking chair. I told her stories and sang her songs, stroked her tiny hands and feet and rubbed her forehead. Sometimes Abby and I just rocked back and forth, thinking and rocking and thinking together. I found myself hoping, even willing her to grow strong enough to come home with Tom and me.

And she did. Two months ago. She has learned to smile at the silly sounds Tom makes and to look for our faces when we say, "Peek-a-boo."

In the months before Abby was able to come home with us, I'd decided to finish the painting that Gram had been so curious about the day she sat at my easel. I think she would like it now. The woman in the picture no longer holds a lifeless clay pot to her chest. Instead, she sits beside two other women, one with white hair and the second with red. The arms of all three are raised high, and together they are holding a baby in their hands. Each morning when I enter the kids' room, renamed Abby's Room, to lift little Abby from her crib, I pause to look at my painting hanging on the wall beside the wicker rocking chair, Abby's and my Thinking Chair.

Today, exactly one year after Gram first visited me, I am sitting at the dining room table. Abby is taking an afternoon nap. I am wondering if Gram watched me two weeks ago as I wrapped my La Boheme record in brown wrapping paper and slipped in the note:

Dear Uncle Rollie,

I found this record with some of Gram's old things and thought you would like to have it.

Your niece,

Katy

My parents had told Rollie about Wendy's death and Abby's birth, so as a last-minute decision, I had attached a photograph of Abby and me to my note.

A yellow envelope with the Los Angeles return address arrived in today's mail, and after procrastinating, I finally opened it. Andy is resting his head on my feet as if waiting for me to read the letter aloud.

Dear Katy,

Thank you for sending my father's old record. I never liked that particular opera myself, but he never stopped looking for it. It has arrived at a very good time. Your grandfather and I are presenting a series of lectures to the students here at the university where we reside. The topic of the series is "Operas of the World." This record will be very useful.

Sincerely,

Roland Carlyle Welborn (Your Uncle)

P.S. You are invited to attend any of the lectures. Black tie optional.

P.P.S. The enclosed picture of Nellie, Carlyle, and me was taken on my last birthday, when I turned fifty-six. You might show it to Abby someday.

P.P.P.S. I remember Wendy was the niece who loved music. You were the niece who was afraid of the boogeyman.

P.P.P.P.S. I hope Abby won't be afraid of the boogeyman.

As I look from Rollie's letter to the photograph he sent, I am momentarily puzzled. It shows a rather old-looking Rollie standing in front of a worn-out sofa. His hair is dirty and gray, parted on one side and combed tightly against his head. He is wearing a tired looking tuxedo, one that could not have been my grandfather's, because it fit rather loosely around Rollie's rotund waist. Rollie's arms are raised as if he is embracing someone on each side. But no one else is standing there.

"Or is there?" I wonder out loud. I look down at Andy, whose brown eyes stare back with understanding and wisdom. Maybe Gram and Grandpa are standing beside Uncle Rollie in the picture.

And with this thought, I know that Gram is here with me now, probably guiding me as I reach for a piece of note paper and begin to write.

Dear Uncle Rollie,

Thank you for your invitation to your lecture series. I have always loved opera, but I know so little about it. I would enjoy attending one of your lectures someday.

Thank you also for the picture of you with my grandmother and grandfather. I am going to put it in a frame so Abby and I can look at it often.

Abby will be christened next month, and I am wondering if you would like to attend the service with us. It would make me happy to have you there.

Gram once told me that a family gathering isn't complete without all its members present, sort of like a recipe without all its ingredients.

Your niece,

Katy Welborn McAndrews

P.S. I'm not afraid of the boogeyman anymore.

ABOUT THE AUTHOR

Trish Evans was born in Los Angeles and raised in an eccentric family of journalists, writers and musicians. After graduating from Northwestern University, she became a teacher of deaf and severely hard of hearing children both in Illinois and California. Later, she earned a Master's degree in marriage and family counseling from Loyola Marymount University. She is married and lives in Southern California. Visit her at www. trishevansbooks.com.

CPSIA information can be obtained
at www.ICGtesting.com
Printed in the USA
BVHW032201080120
569047BV00001B/12/P

9 781733 234900